THE WHALE CHASER

# The Whale Chaser

## TONY ARDIZZONE

ACADEMY CHICAGO PUBLISHERS

Copyright © 2010, 2015 by Tony Ardizzone
All rights reserved
Published by Academy Chicago Publishers
An imprint of Chicago Review Press Incorporated
814 North Franklin Street
Chicago, IL 60610
ISBN 978-0-89733-923-0


Cover and interior design: Joan Sommers Design

Printed in the United States of America
5 4 3 2 1

*in memory of Fern Chertkow*

*Hatty told Matty,*
*"Let's don't take no chance.*
*Let's not be L-seven,*
*Come and learn to dance."*

—DOMINGO SAMUDIO, *WOOLY BULLY*

# *Prologue*

SEVERAL YEARS AGO, back during my dark days when I was hauling cannabis for Clarence, before I was hired on as a guide for Chase Whaling and began to draw the threads of my life together, I found myself down-island wandering Victoria's cobbled streets late one mid-September night when I saw a crowd of women and men gathered outside some sort of art gallery. This was the same summer that I sent letters of apology to all the people I'd known back in Chicago, all the people I'd hurt, when I began to piece together the two disconnected halves of my life. My story is about those two halves, my time up here in British Columbia and my earlier life back on the North Side of Chicago. The dark sky above the gallery that night was full of fat, white stars. The crowd outside the gallery spoke in hushed murmurs, as if trying not to call too much attention to itself, genteelly sipping beer from dark-green bottles and white wine from squat plastic cups.

I started to work my way through the crowd, but as I neared the gallery door I grew curious and decided to go inside. I walked past displays of the usual Vancouver Island settings—oil paintings of tender sunsets, rocky beaches splashed with the froth of pounding waves, shore birds gently winging their way over the tops of wind-twisted trees—then through a room of portraits and nudes, the former stern and hip and appearing very knowing and certainly artsy, the latter round and rosy nippled and thickly thighed, with some flattened out in that steamroller style the Cubists made famous. Then I came upon a darkened back room where a woman reclined on a bed of burgundy pillows, entirely naked save for her tattoos. In her hand was a small flashlight and a dull silver speculum, which she was using to allow the gallery's patrons to look into her most private parts. "Performance art," someone said, dismissively shaking his head, pushing his way out of the room and past me.

As I neared the woman I saw that some of her tattoos were actually scars, or maybe they were rough drawings made with henna. I couldn't tell in the dim light. A table lined with candles stood along the far wall, several feet from her mound of pillows. Between the candles were small wicker baskets of potpourri, and in the air was the sweet smell of burning incense. Soon it was my turn to kneel in front of her and look, but instead I hesitated, then let a couple of other people go ahead of me. Finally I leaned toward her and in a low voice asked why she was doing what she was doing.

The expression on her face was distant, flat, as if nothing mattered. Nonetheless her clear, bright eyes met mine. I expected her to say it was because her actions were shocking or personally liberating, or at least something she thought would be fun. This was back when people did the most outrageous things because they were shocking or liberating or because they imagined they would be fun. This was back before disease and fear. Back when you felt that you'd never die and you could push against all the shackles that constrained you. Back when everyone was young, and the world was open and new, before we grew into the adults we are now and felt and understood the true weight of responsibility and consequence for our actions.

But instead she said, "Because I have to, like you know that you have to look."

I understood at once what she meant. It had to do with curiosity, with how people driving down a street or highway can't help but slow down to stare at the scene of a roadside accident. Curiosity was the reason why I'd entered the gallery in the first place and made my way past the more usual sorts of art and into the back room. I knew that the truest things were always kept in the darkness of back rooms. But now that I was beside her I felt differently.

"No," I told her. "I don't have to look."

"Then you must be like me," she said. She shone her flashlight in my eyes. "You must have to show."

She was right because already I was nodding, my eyes wincing against the light, already without thinking my fingers were undoing the second button on my shirt. It was then, at that moment, that I felt there was something I wanted—no, that I needed—to show.

᙮ ᙮ ᙮

If I'm to do that, reveal myself, I'll begin by saying that like my father and my grandfather, I draw my living from the sea.

That's more of an accomplishment than some might think since my early life took shape back on the central prairies, in the heart of the continent, Chicago, *stinking onion creek* in the tongue of its First Nations people. City of big shoulders, as the good Sisters of Christian Charity had us memorize in grammar school, tool maker, stacker of wheat, hog butcher for the world. Or, as Nelson Algren later suggested, city of the red mesh hose and the shoulder bag banging her hip, once the doll of the world, who can't be expected to remember every trick, though he was proud to have slept in her tireless arms.

Decades ago I had to tear myself loose of those arms, arms that threatened to pull me under and strangle me. Much of why I left Chicago was my own doing, consequence of a series of actions I freely and unknowingly pursued. What happened between me and Lucy Sheehan, between me and Marie Santangelo. Some of it, I'm beginning to understand, was not entirely my fault. The fights with my father. The unquestionably wrong war in Vietnam. The shame and silence over what happened to my grandparents two months after Pearl Harbor. And so, one rainy spring night when everything I'd done and hadn't done collided and converged, I made my way up here to Canada, the land of hockey, banana slugs, looneys jingling in your pockets, the clean red maple leaf rippling on the flagpole, snapping sharply in the western wind. Where I would meet Roxanne Parker, Clarence and Harmony, Ignatius George, Emily Fournier, Laurie, Big Ed and Lillian. Now I live a world away from my beginnings, up in B.C., British Columbia, out on the western edge of Vancouver Island on the northern tip of the Esowista Peninsula, in a picturesque fishing and logging village called Tofino, population twelve hundred or so, not counting the black bears and dogs.

ॐ ॐ ॐ

Up here in B.C., I have a lot of time to reflect. There are days, particularly during the off season when the Chase Whaling boats are in dry dock and I'm doing my best to scrounge up other work, when there's nothing to do but listen to myself think. There are days during the high season when I'm out on the magnificent blue-gray waters of Clayoquot Sound, steering against the chop with my crew—a dozen or so tourists eager to lay eyes on a whale—and the past echoes in my ears. I listen to the voices. Like something out of Shakespeare, ghosts from the past rise and swell and splash angrily against one another, then dissolve like a surfacing gray whale's blow into spray and foam and the least bits of light.

Sometimes I talk to the ghosts over the noise of the boat's engine. I invite them to join me, take a seat, go over how things might have turned out differently. Sometimes in winter I walk through town in the persistent rain, reasonably dry inside my gumboots and Smelly Hansen, and the past hovers along the sidewalk beside me, then reaches inside my shirt past my scar and squeezes my heart so firmly that I have to stop and bend at the waist, barely able to breathe. I sip bits of breath as the episode passes and I calm myself. Together, the ghosts and I go over everything that happened, and I think of all the things I might have done, or not done, all the words I should have said and all I should never have given voice to. How, instead of going home or to

Ronny's garage, I should have returned to her house. How a sentence or two might have altered the course of events. Then a swell rocks the boat or someone on the street touches my shoulder and asks me if I'm all right, and as my heart slows I wonder if it's naive to believe that people can control the directions their lives take. Oh, sure, I think, we can change the scenery and select a few of the cosmetic details, opt for the soup over the salad, the blue shirt over the brown, the rutted roads of Tofino over the streets and alleys of Chicago, but as for the grander designs our lives inscribe, aren't we ultimately little more than spectators? Tourists in orange deck suits, out on the blue water, chasing whales?

Events, particularly those that take place when we're young or before we've been born, have a way of overshadowing and stalking our adult days. The past grabs onto our soft parts and doesn't let go, I mutter to the wind and rain. There's simply no escaping it.

🐋 🐋 🐋

When I give voice to thoughts like these in group, the others toss red cards at me. I belong to a support group that meets on Thursday nights in the back room of Queen of All Saints, the Roman Catholic church here in Tofino, and we begin each meeting by passing around an old cedar box full of red and blue squares, each about half the size of a pack of cigarettes, cut from poster board. As we take a handful of cards from the box Big Ed, our group leader, asks us who needs or wants time. The half dozen or so who make up the group—tradesmen and mechanics, fishermen and service workers, most more often than not between jobs or out of work, between maintaining a relationship and divorce, between sobriety and the bottle—pile our cards like poker chips on the old coffee table we sit around, or else we hold our cards in our palms and rhythmically strum their edges, like a chorus of crickets, with our thumbs. Together we share bits and pieces of our life stories. Sometimes Big Ed has to prod us to get the conversation started, but once it's going we talk, listen, sip our mugs of coffee.

Blue cards we toss when someone says something insightful and positive. They're a way of silently expressing encouragement and support, of strongly seconding what's being said without actually interrupting. Yes! a blue card says. Good point! I agree! Right on! Red cards we throw when we find ourselves disagreeing. Red cards are for excuses, false statements. They put the brakes on the conversation. They force the speaker to stop and reconsider, the card tosser to confront and spell out the reservation.

Don't feel that you have to be faithful to chronology, Big Ed tells us. Chronology is only one of the many ways to relate a story. Truth is seldom seamless. Sometimes leaping back and forth between lines of time can get at the truth best. He scratches the top of his bald head, speckled with a mosaic of freckles, with hands leathery as smoked ham hocks. By the tufts of hair on the backs of his hands and on his arms, you can tell that when he had a head of hair it was bright red. You can tell he doesn't suffer fools. If you're ever in a bar fight he's the sort of friend you hope is standing behind you. Feel free to riff about whatever is on your mind, he says, in whatever order seems to make the most sense. This isn't school where the rule is to stay on topic, where A needs to precede B and C.

He listens and nods and scratches his freckled head and asks questions, which nearly always lead us to a deeper discussion of things. Our lives are like the sides of mountains, he maintains, and what we're doing in group is conducting a sort of archeological dig, probing one stratum of story and event before moving on to another. After a while the true nature of our pasts will emerge, and some of our doubt and confusion and anxieties will clear. Open your mouths and talk, he urges us, until you get your narrative right.

Big Ed is very big on getting our narratives right. He says each of us has this tape inside our heads he calls our narrative. Whether we know it or not, this tape plays over and over again inside our minds, 24/7, sort of like the soundtrack to some movie we don't even know we're watching, running in a perpetual, never-ending loop. We get so used to the soundtrack that we forget we constantly hear it. Change it and we change, he says. He tells us the old story about the guy who grew so used to another man banging him on the head that whenever the man grew tired the guy took the wooden club from the other's hand and said, "Here, let me do it while you take a break."

Most of our narratives are warped, Big Ed tells us. They're distorted by falsehoods, misunderstandings, fears. Much of each person's individual narrative was written by others: parents and teachers and neighbors. The core was formed when we were children, Big Ed says, and who's to say that what they told us about ourselves was reliable? How many of their misconceptions have we embraced? For example, one guy in group tells how his father took a claw hammer to him when he was seven and ended up breaking four of his ribs, and the guy remains convinced to this day that he's to blame since that morning he'd let a screen door slam. It was January, the middle of storm season. His mother had abandoned the family a month or so before. The father was lying on the floor, sleeping off a drunk. The boy had just covered him with a blanket. The man can still remember putting on his jacket and cap and trying to slip silently outside. He describes the sudden roar of the wind as it tore the door from his hands. The door banging against the wooden frame, loud as the blast of a shotgun. The pounding rush of the father's steps.

Some of the men in my group go to other meetings, where they work the Twelve Steps. Most of us have problems with depression and anger, drinking and drugs. Nearly all of us had fathers who were summa cum laude graduates of the old school—spare the rod, spoil the child—and who communicated with their worthless progeny through criticism and belittlement, with belts, fists, hammers. That my father took a butcher knife to me puts me near the top of the totem, though talk of totems and boasts regarding the amounts of physical punishment we've received always earns a red card from Big Ed. Abuse is abuse, Big Ed reminds us. Trauma is trauma. No matter the degree.

Each Thursday evening we come in through the side door, by the wheelchair ramp. Whoever arrives there first fires up the coffee pot. I like to wipe down the table and set the chairs so that they're more or less evenly spaced. I like to sort and straighten the books and magazines on the bookshelves. Big Ed always brings the cedar box full of red and blue cards, and lately he's invited another group leader, Lillian, to sit in with us. She's a sweet dumpling of a woman, fond of turquoise jewelry, in her sixties, wise as a crow, with a warm cackle of a laugh and an uncanny ability to cut through our bullshit. Big Ed calls the smokers in from outside and we form our circle and begin.

☙ ☙ ☙

Ignatius George, who prefers prayer and ritual bathing to back-room meetings, and with whom I get together nearly every Saturday night for coffee and a rack or two of pool at the Maquinna Pub, and who knows more about whales than nearly anyone else in Clayoquot Sound and is one of my co-workers at Chase Whaling, tells me there's no sense in talking to the ghosts of the past and trying to relive a life I can't possibly change. "God gives us all we need," he says in his soft, lilting voice, "and his greatest gift to us is the present moment. Our only job is to live well within it. To be grateful and work with what's before us in the here and now. There's no use looking back at things. You're just worrying an old scar, making it bleed again." He rubs his palms together, and when he separates them I half-expect to see them bleeding.

Ignatius is a full-blooded Ahousaht, the son of a man once adopted by his band's chief, who himself was a whale hunter back in the old days when the band hunted whales. He lives in Ahousat, the native village on Flores Island. Given the treatment that the First Nations peoples endured at the hands of the European settlers—or isn't it more accurate to call them invaders?—I figure that when it comes to getting beyond past events Ignatius speaks with some authority. His dark face is lined by years of squinting beneath the sun.

Like me, as an infant Ignatius was sprinkled by the waters of the baptismal font and brought up Roman Catholic. Like me, he was beaten at a tender age by the crucifix and beads. Now he wears a small cedar carving—a native mask—on a leather string over his heart. For years he fished the waters of Clayoquot Sound, making decent money which he periodically drank away in long binges he can no longer remember, revelries that went on for days and sometimes stretched into and beyond a week and inevitably ended with him waking up on some stranger's sofa, flannel-tongued, a flock of woodpeckers drilling holes in his head, the knuckles of one hand cut and bruised from a fight he can't remember, his other hand patting his pockets in search of his wallet and ring of keys while around him in the painful glare of daylight there gathers a knot of someone else's curious children, led by a toddler wearing only a dirty undershirt, the fat wattle of his balls and penis stubbing the air, both arms raised, clambering up onto Ignatius's lap for a hug.

I didn't really know Ignatius then, back in his dark days, and he didn't really know me during my dark days, when I first came up here to Tofino, but like a pair of old warriors we occasionally unbutton our shirts and display our scars, and between racks of 8-ball we tell each other pieces of our stories. We met nearly thirty years ago, a few years before I began my job as a whale guide, or whale chaser, as our boss, Wayne Chester Chase, likes to call us. Back then Wayne told me to learn everything I could from Ignatius. Of all the guides in Clayoquot Sound to take a boat onto water, Ignatius George is the best.

On the subject of scars, I too wear something over my heart, just an inch or so above and slightly to the left of my sternum. A scar in the shape of an inverted V, given me by my father. An A lacking the crossbar, a sort of scarlet letter in progress.

I have no sons, and through the twists my life has taken I've lost my only daughter. My family's long tradition of men who've pulled their livelihoods from the earth's waters ends squarely with me out here on this fragile, wet edge of the northern Pacific.

ↂ ↂ ↂ

When I'm not out on the water, I work in a small storefront office overlooking Tofino's First Street Wharf. The dock marks the literal end of the road, the official western terminus of the Trans-Canada Highway, where in summer tourists and hippies from the mainland gather and gaze at the densely green, cloud-ringed mountains on Meares and the rounder, more distant Catface Range edging the shining blue-gray waters of Clayoquot Sound.

The tourists pose for snapshots at the water's edge, beneath the metal sign marking the end of the highway. A breaching orca tops the sign, which rattles some indecipherable message in Morse-like code whenever there's a stiff wind. The hippies gather near the concrete tables along the shoreline, unyoke their knapsacks, smile, play hackysack, trade jokes.

You can see both groups deciding how close to the dock they should walk, until one group or another ventures onto it, and then everyone saunters to its end, past the shack for Tofino Air and the waiting float planes, to the far corner where they can look down on the idling whale-watching boats and water taxis. The tourists take deep breaths and issue the relieved laughter and sighs of those who've arrived at some long-sought-after destination. They look hopefully out over the Sound for orcas or grays, a flattened hand shading their eyes from the sun. They point down into the water at starfish and crabs. They gaze out at the other islands in the harbor: Vargas, Stubbs, Felice, Meares, Strawberry. They smile and snap photographs. The hippies nudge one another with their elbows, then huddle together in a scrum as someone in the center cups both palms against the wind and lights a little something for all to smoke.

I know the hippies don't think of themselves anymore as such but that's how I think of them, and I mean them no harm or disrespect. It's a better term than punks or slackers or generation this or that. At heart they're all Beats, the offspring of Whitman and the Dadaists and Surrealists, regardless of whatever they call themselves. They come hitchhiking down the highway, bandannaed and blue-jeaned, pierced and ringed, tattooed and scarred, like members of some mighty tribe. Nearly all of them smoke. Several wear their hair in dreads. Most have excellent teeth and endless stories, at least after they drop their poses and attitudes. These are the kids who were given a house key they wore on a strip of leather around their necks and came home each day after school to a blinking answering machine, cartoons or MTV on cable, something microwaveable. When they first talk to me it's more often than not to ask for directions or a light.

The tourists are more business-minded. They ask about departure times and rates, and whether I can guarantee they'll see a whale. Preferably a killer whale, they add. We stand just inside the office, the words CHASE WHALING STATION painted in white-capped, sea-blue letters on the storefront window, "Chase the adventure!" and "Come chase the whales!" in smaller script on the wall behind me, which also features a bright seascape—a Jacques Cousteau's wildest fantasy—of all the creatures they might possibly see.

Some tourists gesture at the killer whale spy-hopping over the seascape while others point out the door toward the orca leaping over the rattling sign. Most have seen or at least heard of *Free Willy*, the Hollywood movie about the orca that was captured as a calf and kept in a tank so small that its dorsal fin became deformed, folding over nearly in half like some punch-drunk boxer's bent ear, until a kind and able boy helped to set him free. What are their chances they'll get to see an orca?

I smile and nod and describe to them what whales we saw yesterday—normally, resident grays feeding off Radar Hill or Combers or Long Beach or up in the kelp beds off Vargas Island or Flores—then add that every experience in the wild is different, and there are no guarantees. I smile again and hold their eyes with mine, hoping they'll understand. I say that we'll find the whales if they're out there, but they need to understand that these creatures are natural beasts and don't run on anyone's schedule, and when they don't want to be seen they do their best not to be seen. I try very hard to be cordial, respectful and polite. Along the way, I add, we'll likely view plenty of other wildlife: sea lions, harbor seals, sea otters, eagles, tufted puffins. Occasional minkes, harbor porpoises, humpbacks and even the odd basking shark. I tell the tourists that nearly all the orcas in these waters are transients—packs of three or four that stay in no set territory, unlike resident orcas, who are highly social and live in pods and sub-pods of six to sometimes as many as twenty, and who generally fish the same waters year after year—and there's just no predicting their whereabouts. But if they're out there, I repeat, we'll do our best to chase them down. Whenever Wayne is in the office, I use the operant word, *chase*, which suggests both pursuit and speed, and then, as I've been trained to do, and as I've done ten thousand times, I point to the picture on the wall of one of our Zodiacs.

What characterizes a Zodiac, I then explain, is the fat, bright orange or red inflatable collar ringing its fiberglass hull. They're our fastest boats. The one in the photograph on the wall is racing at a decent angle to the water, white jets of spray shooting up and behind the stern, CHASE WHALING on the port, as well as starboard, collar. A dozen or so smiling passengers in navy-blue knit caps and orange deck suits sit on the vessel's four benches, hands clenching the taped seat bar in front of them, like riders on a roller-coaster at an amusement park. A somewhat blurred Ignatius squints from the console at the stern, beneath the roll bar and radar. With its twin diesel engines, I tell the tourists, the Zodiac is built for efficiency and speed. That's more than enough for most people, I say, a good, hard ride in an impressively fast boat, a ride during which they'll see plenty of wildlife and likely get splashed with sea water, and sometimes outright soaked.

When the office is empty of tourists, Wayne tells me that even after all these years I still could use some help with my people skills. Wayne is a man of considerable size, pink as a newborn mouse, nearly as hairless as an egg. The belt buckles that hold up his pants are as big as tea saucers. "Shit on a shingle, Sansone"—as is his habit, he drops the third syllable of my last name, rhyming it with *sandstone*—"folks come up here from all over God's green earth to see with their own two eyes an actual living whale. Kindly assure them that they'll see a whale. They don't give a damn if a whale is a resident or a transient. They don't care whether or not a whale wants or doesn't want to be seen."

"But you know as well as I do that sometimes we have whale-less trips." It's in the small print on the bottom of our brochure. Free trip the next day if we don't see at least one whale. Wayne's printed up a batch of colorful brochures—"Chase the Experience at Chase Whaling Station!"—and keeps statistics on Clayoquot Sound whale sightings. He accepts travelers' checks and major credit cards, and after taking a course in Victoria he designed and maintains the company's Web site, which is accessible in French and German as well as English, and in high season gets hundreds of hits each day.

"Doesn't matter a tinker," Wayne says. "If they ask for a guarantee, give them a motherloving guarantee." When I stare back at him, unconvinced, he adds, "For the love of Pete just how many times do we have to go over this? A thing could be ninety-eight percent sure and you focus on the miserable two percent chance that it won't be."

I say nothing. I've learned that if I stay quiet long enough people eventually get tired of arguing with me and shake their heads and change the subject or walk away. He's right, though. I tend to obsess about that two percent. So I busy myself by straightening the pile of brochures on the table, restacking the release of liability forms, making everything on the counter parallel and perpendicular with everything else. Wayne knows I'm uncomfortable making the guarantee, even when he's right beside me in the office, and that I dislike the money word, *chase*. I've learned long ago the falseness of making promises. I know that apparently sure things often become the least likely outcomes in the end. I know that life has a way of twisting back on you sometimes and biting you hard where you least expect it, giving you the opportunity to do the most hateful things to the very people who least deserve them, despite what you've told them, despite even your most sincere intentions. I know because I've done these things, and worse.

"You really tend to make mountains out of molehills, Vince," Wayne says.

Then a crowd of tourists comes through the open door, asking about the orca leaping outside on the metal sign, putting an end to my conversation with Wayne. I nod and manage a smile as I tell them about the whales we saw yesterday, then add that every experience in the wild is different, and in nature, as in life, there are no guarantees.

ᘓ ᘓ ᘓ

As for the hippies and nearly everyone else who hangs out at The Last Crumb, a popular coffee slash bakery and sandwich shop a block and a half up the hill from our office, I'm reasonably well known. I'm the dark, usually clean-shaven guy with the Italian nose and longish dark hair (now beginning to gray) who works on one of the whale-watching boats. Came up from somewhere down in the States years ago, back in the old days, not too long after the road was built. Usually wears a faded blue work shirt, white T-shirt and jeans. Has a place that's an easy hike from the center of town. Word has it that he's the guy you look for if you need a place to crash for the night and don't mind sharing a tent with a few other homeless souls like yourself.

At least that's how things got started, years ago, not too long after I arrived up here and scored a steady job at the fish processing plant on Main and could afford an actual house to rent. Early one summer morning as I was leaving for work at the fish plant, I noticed a guy and girl about my age sacked out beneath the lean-to that kept the rain off my woodpile. This was after the government dedicated the national park and drove the squatters each night off the beaches. People used to live on the land that's now the Pacific Rim National Park Reserve, in greatest numbers down on Long Beach, like the Nuu-chah-nulth before them, hundreds and more at a time. There's even an old totem pole or two carved by the squatters whose tents and makeshift shacks once lined the beach, and near Florencia Bay there's a totem commemorating the spot where a hippie child was born.

When my squatters returned that evening and untied their sleeping bags and snuggled up beside my woodpile, I went out with three beers and introduced myself. They had a two-person tent rolled up in their knapsack, and after a while they asked if they could put it up instead of sleeping out in the open. I remembered what the church people had told me when I crossed the border, and so immediately I said yes.

One thing led to the next. Over time word of my hospitality spread. Eventually I put up three big RCAF tents in my yard for the kids—usually no more than five or six at any one time—who come up here and can't afford a campsite or who get too cold or wet crashing illegally on the beaches. All I ask in return is that they do an hour of daily work—picking up roadside trash, helping out at the Friends of Clayoquot Sound, aiding someone in obvious need—anything good that benefits others. Opportunities present themselves, I say. I caution them about the cougars and black bears they'll possibly encounter when they're hiking in the rainforest. I lend them bright yellow Smelly Hansens for when it rains.

It rains a lot here, more than just about anywhere else in North America. The average is nearly three meters of rain (about 120 inches) per year. In 1967 it rained an amazing 489 millimeters (over nineteen and a half inches) on a single day in nearby Ucluelet. Each winter, mainlanders wanting a break from city life come up here to watch the terrible, magnificent storms.

I remind them that everyone is responsible not only for the mess they make but also for the mess left behind by others. Hey, I say, listen, the world is unbelievably small—I make a bowl of my hands—and all the life clinging to it is delicate beyond our imagination. Even ten, twenty, thirty years after the fact, you do your best to try to clean the mess up, restore the balance and order, undo some of the negative consequences of your existence.

Even if no one else but you will ever know.

When I have the time and means, I feed them. Big pots of soup, mainly vegetarian, or fish and crab stews, which over the years I've become reasonably good at making. I use whatever I can catch or scrounge and is plentiful and in season. Most summers now I set out a couple of crab pots. I have a friend at the co-op who sells me buckets of scrap chicken parts, which I think are the very best crab bait around. Backs along with legs and thighs, anything that's bony and too big to be pulled directly from the bait box. These summers the kids in my tents eat their fair share of Dungeness crab. Sometimes they pitch in and make a big salad to go along with it, and when there isn't a red tide they dig for clams or pick mussels, and maybe someone else brings a nice crusty loaf or two of bread.

And eventually I extended my house's plumbing and put in a second bathroom, complete with sink and shower and claw-footed tub, and next to the bathroom I built some bookshelves to house a growing library of paperbacks. Both are on my back porch, which I leave open day and night for the campers in my tents. I have a lot of books by the Beats, both novels and poetry, along with the classics: Blake, Castaneda, Brautigan, Salinger, Vonnegut, Kesey. Lately I've been reading Toni Morrison, who's not easy. Ditto for Italo Calvino and García-Márquez. I'm fond of Fante, Algren, di Donato, Bowles, Carver, Bukowski. Lopez and Abbey. Momaday and Silko. Kundera and DeLillo. Atwood, Zora Neale Hurston, Edna O'Brien. I could go on and on. The rule with the books is that you can keep one if you want, but you have to add another book to take its place, preferably nothing too trashy, and none of that demonic horror slasher stuff, of which there is already far too much in the world.

Sure, some kids walk off with my books or one of the yellow sou'westers, and despite my pleadings some leave unbelievable amounts of trash in my back yard. Some laugh at me and my lectures about a daily hour of good work. Some get so strung out on drugs I have to sit with them and talk them down, or if they're in really bad shape I drive them into town to the clinic. Some are lying if they claim to have done even five seconds of volunteer work. But most kids, given half a chance, are cooperative and cool. They clean up without being asked. They tell me about books and writers I've never heard of. They send me postcards from all the new places they visit after they leave.

☙ ☙ ☙

People just wouldn't believe how many kids get messed up, or just fed up with their lives, whether it's because they don't have enough food or can't cut it in school or their father or mother or sister or brother beats them. Sometimes at night we head for the beach and build a fire, and I sit with a group of them and listen for hours to their stories.

There was the girl from Albuquerque whose father. There was the boy from Medicine Hat whose mother. There was the boy from Edmonton whose uncle who lived next door. There was the girl from Saskatoon whose two step-brothers.

Sometimes I think that with families who needs enemies?

After a while the kids grow tired of it, decide not to take it anymore, throw a pair of jeans, a spare T-shirt and their toothbrush into a knapsack, and head for the nearest highway, the thumb of their right hand sticking out into the breeze. I remember all too well what they want, how they feel.

I listen to their stories but don't volunteer any of mine. Though in group, under Big Ed's patient guidance, within the circle of chairs around the coffee table in the back room of Queen of All Saints, I'm learning to push out pieces of my story, though doing so sometimes makes me feel like a lifetime smoker hacking up bloody scraps of lung.

The kids eventually wind up on the streets of Vancouver, where an earlier version of me once wound up, where they eat out of dumpsters and panhandle or steal, doing what they can, what they must, to get by. Some get into things pretty deep and end up doing stuff that later they're none too proud of. Some grow sick and die as a result. Some try to take their own lives. Some resign themselves to fate and drift on back to the misery of their parents' homes. Others head up to Alaska or down south to Seattle, Portland, the California coast.

The ones I meet find the sea to the west inviting and hop the ferry at Horseshoe Bay or otherwise work their way to Nanaimo. Then once they set foot on Vancouver Island they just keep on going, like a stone rolling on a hill, following the road to Port Alberni, then heading up and over the mountains and then down again to the ocean, where the great stands of Western hemlock and old-growth red cedar and spruce—some of the oldest and biggest living things in all of North America—descend majestically to the edge of the sea.

You can see the kids dotting the roadside as far back as Victoria. Knapsacks and rolled sleeping bags leaning against their thighs, they raise a thumb to the rushing traffic. In their other hand they hold up little cardboard signs.

UCLUELET

PACIFIC RIM PARK

TOFINO

They follow the same road I followed when I first came here years and years ago, not too long after the highway to Tofino was paved. Though this—the long conversations over a fire on the beach, the back-porch bathroom and library, the Thursday night meetings with group and Big Ed and Lillian—is actually the story's ending. My story begins far earlier than that.

# 1

# Chicago 1963

MY STORY BEGINS back in Chicago, the stinking onion creek, with me at fourteen, and with a girl named Marie Santangelo.

One of our eighth-grade classmates threw a graduation party. Crepe paper in our school's colors looped from the basement ceiling. "Walk Like a Man," the Four Seasons' latest hit, spun on the record player, its turntable flanked by a pancake stack of 45s. The host's father eyeballed us abjectly as he puffed on a panatela. The host's mother, whose lipstick was fire-engine red and whose stiletto heels clicked sharply wherever she walked on the basement tile, paused to ask each child's name.

"Oh, you're Vincent Sansone." She said my name slowly, as if it were something her mouth could chew. "Isn't your mother the one with all the babies?"

I nodded.

"And your father, not that we ever met him or see him on Sundays in church, he's a fishmonger down on Lake Street's Fulton Market, right? Gracious, it must be ten years since we've driven down there. My Harry doesn't really like that part of the city. You must eat a lot of fish."

I pictured my father at work, the sides of his face weighed down by his usual frown, wrapped in his blood-stained apron, walking amidst rows of tubs packed with crushed ice and fish. I nodded again and gave the woman our standard line. "In our house, every day is fry day."

"Well, well, well," she said, "I must say you certainly don't look the worse for it." She grabbed both my wrists and shook my arms, then seized me by my cheeks and gave them a hard pinch. "There, that adds a bit of color to your face." With one hand she ruffled my hair. "You might be a bit thin for your age but in no time you'll fill out. And they say that fish is brain food. You must be very smart. Are you a bright boy?"

I smiled and shrugged, just smart enough to know not to answer that one.

As I tried to pull away she asked, "If you don't mind me asking, Vincent, exactly how many babies does your poor mother have? Whenever I see them all with her in church they never sit still in the pew long enough for me to count."

"There's seven of us kids," I said. "Nine altogether in my family, that is, counting my folks." I began ticking them off on my fingers. "Me, Tina, Carmella, Angelina—"

She waved the rest of the names away. "And those two elderly people I always see with her, they're your mother's parents?"

"My father's," I said. "Nonnu and Nonna. They live upstairs."

As soon as she released me I ran a comb through my hair, which earlier I'd greased liberally with Wildroot Cream Oil. I combed my hair straight back. I loosened the knot on my tie, hiked up my black stovepipes, and headed for the clear space in the basement's center, where I commenced to dance with every girl who'd agree to dance with me.

At the time I thought myself a jitterbugging fool. The jitterbug was the main step I knew, other than slow-dancing, having learned the basics some months earlier from Lucy Sheehan in the alley outside Ronny Cannon's garage. I pulled the girls toward me, then let them spin out and away from me like a top, then drew them firmly back, moving them here, there, this way, that way, all without conversation or intention or thought, in perfect time with the music, with only the unspeaking body, which is one of the true pleasures of dancing.

After two hours or so of this, as the last dance was announced, I grabbed the hand of the girl nearest me, who happened to be Marie Santangelo. Dion's "The Wanderer" had just ended a great string of fast songs, and I was still singing the words.

"Yeah, I'm a wanderer," I sang.

Then the last song started to play, Shelley Fabares's dreamy "Johnny Angel." Marie smiled sweetly as she fell into my arms, then dropped her head against my shoulder. For a while she sang the words of the song softly into my ear. Then she shifted her right hand and put both arms around my neck and we shuffled together there on the dance floor—wordless and pure—dancing serious and close.

Then the lights came up and everybody scrambled for their shoes. The mother stood on the front porch steps, highball in hand, telling us all to walk home safely. The maraschino cherry in her drink bobbed desperately as she waved. The girl's father leaned against the porch railing, draining a beer, pausing only to slap at an occasional mosquito.

The night was cool and dark, the air sweet with the scent of flowers growing in front yards and the peppery smell of automobile exhaust. In the dark gaps between streetlights, the yellow tracers of lightning bugs zigged and zagged. I sauntered along, momentarily happy. Then Marie appeared just behind me saying, "Hey, Vince, wait up." Her shoes scuffed the sidewalk. "Hey," she said again, "I didn't think you even knew I was alive."

"Huh?" I said. "Huh? I knew you were alive." Whenever surprised, which back then was often, my default response was to disagree.

She was out of breath and had hurried to catch up with me. She had thick, dark brown hair, combed back and away from her face, curled up at the ends in that Annette Funicello style all the neighborhood girls wore back then. But what set Marie apart from the other girls were her full lips and her exceptionally clear complexion that glowed in the light beneath the streetlights. Marie had olive-colored skin, the kind that looks ever-so-slightly oiled or as if she'd just been in front of a tanning lamp.

"Well," she said, slowing her pace to match mine, "maybe a person might just not know it by the way you act."

I've never been very comfortable with conversation. Words are slippery eels. No sooner do you think you have them in the boat than they give a twist and a flip and, *whoosh*, confusion, chaos, and far more trouble than if you'd kept your dumb mug shut in the first place. Marie kept staring at me, indicating it was my turn to speak. "I know everybody's alive," I said, "even all the Chinese miles down below our feet drinking all the tea in China," which seemed an incredibly odd and stupid thing to say a second or two after I said it.

She didn't seem to mind. "You only sat in front of me in class for eight years." She laughed gaily, in that free and open way young girls laugh before self-consciousness sets in. Then she said, "It won't be too long before you like oolong." She had dimples in her cheeks that grew deeper when she laughed. I'd never noticed her dimples before. Her teeth were exceptionally straight and white. "No, wait," she said, "I believe I should stand corrected. If I'm not mistaken that would be seven years. Weren't we in different fifth grades?"

Who I was in class with wasn't really one of the things I kept track of. But as we walked along I realized that, not counting kindergarten when we sat at little tables, and fifth grade, when she got the nun and I got the lay teacher, I must have sat in front of Marie during seven of our nine years of grammar school. I pictured our classroom, its neat rows of desks. Estelle Roberts, Walter Ryczek, me, Marie Santangelo. "I guess you're right."

"Of course I'm right," she said brightly. Her fingertips brushed against my hand. In a moment or so we were walking down the side street together, holding hands.

"Nice night," was all I could think to respond.

That made her laugh again, which pleased me. I turned to look at her dimples, which I realized I enjoyed looking at. "Yeah, sure," she said slowly, licking her lips and giving me another sweet smile.

☙ ☙ ☙

Marie's licking her lips reminded me of the day earlier that year when the Communion Host fell on the collar of her winter coat. I was serving that morning's eight o'clock Mass. Our parish had two Masses each weekday morning, the first at six-fifteen. Usually a couple dozen people, mostly old women and middle-aged factory workers, went to the six-fifteen. The women wore overcoats and babushkas and knelt in the first three or four rows. You could hear their rosary beads clacking against the pew in front of them as they prayed. Most prayed out loud, so you could hear their prayers, too, as if you were God. The factory workers knelt behind the women and were as silent as their gray metal lunch pails. You could see the impossible-to-scrub-out grease from the machines they worked beneath their fingernails and in the creases of their hands. Most left for their jobs immediately after taking Communion. At the eight o'clock Mass, which was for all the grammar school children, nearly every pew on each side of the center aisle was full. Each boy was dressed in dark trousers, a long-sleeved white shirt, a knit school tie. Each girl wore a pleated green plaid uniform skirt, white blouse with rounded collar, and white knee socks. From the altar you could hear the low rumble of feet and knees shuffling about, the occasional hiss of someone calling out *Sister*, the sharp snap of the teachers' crickets. Each nun and lay teacher had her own metal clicker, or cricket, which she clicked in special code whenever it was time for her class to walk in a slow and orderly fashion up to the altar rail for Communion.

This was before the Second Vatican Council, back when people knelt at the rail for Communion. Back then the Mass was in the universal language of Latin and the altar faced the back wall of the church. Or, as we were instructed, the altar faced God. Just behind the tabernacle was a huge white marble reredos featuring Christ the King flanked by a quartet of saints rising majestically toward the vaulted ceiling, and behind them on the rear wall three arched windows separating frescoes of the archangels Michael and Raphael. Their tremendous wings curved up in a manner that invited one's eyes to gaze even higher, at the round stained-glass window between them. The effect was such that anyone, even a non-Catholic, who looked at the altar couldn't help but feel his eyes being pulled up toward the lap of God.

We were taught that the church's steeple was the channel through which God's graces flowed down to us. As first graders walking from school to church, barely able to hold onto our winter mittens without the aid of elastic clips, the nuns had us pause on the sidewalk and crane our necks at the iron cross topping the steeple. God's grace enters through that cross, the nuns said, just like lightning through a lightning rod, and travels down past the painted angels and marble saints to the tabernacle, where in the gold monstrance the crucified Christ in the form of the Communion wafer lives. We were taught that when we folded our hands in prayer we made a miniature steeple for God to funnel grace down through our hands and arms into our souls. That was why when you prayed you held your crossed hands slightly higher than your heart, because your soul lay inside your heart. Grace flowed invisibly, like electricity, through the wires of your fingers and arms down to the soul in your heart.

That morning after the old monsignor consecrated the Host, raising it high in both hands up to God the Father, changing it from unleavened bread to the body of Christ, and after he raised the golden chalice, changing the wine within to Christ's blood, the crickets began clicking and the children commenced their soft shuffle up to the Communion rail. Since there were so many communicants, another priest normally came out of the sanctuary to assist. As second paten I worked at Father O'Reilly's side, my left hand on my heart, my right outstretched with my golden paten, which I positioned beneath each communicant's chin as the children tilted back their heads and opened their mouths and stuck out their tongues. My job, essentially, was to catch any fallen crumbs.

The priest's job was to say in Latin, "May the body of our Lord Jesus Christ bring your soul to everlasting life," make a miniature sign of the Cross before the child's face, then carefully top the child's tongue with Communion. Most priests compressed the blessing to its first two words, "Corpus Christi." Father O'Reilly was a fast worker, famous among the parish's altar boys for having said the shortest Mass—twenty-eight minutes—one Saturday morning while his golf clubs, each topped with a knitted cap bedecked with shamrocks, awaited him in the sacristy beside the wine closet. His "Corpus Christi" devolved into "Cor Crispy," a deft curl of the wrist and a sharp, two-fingered flip, like a cowboy snapping one playing card after the next off a fresh deck and flipping them in quick succession into his hat.

When we came to Marie the wafer skipped off the side of her slender tongue and onto the gold sheen of my paten, which I held in position beneath her chin. As the Host skidded away, she did one of those Little Rascals takes, where for a moment her eyes popped big as wall clocks. Her mouth formed a perfect terrified O. Despite my best efforts to juggle the wafer to a stop, it slid off the paten's slick surface and down onto the collar of her coat.

I cursed myself for failing to catch it. At once Marie's cheeks flushed with shame. I dropped to my knees in front of her. Father O'Reilly let out a sigh and lifted the Host from her collar, returned it to his ciborium, and walked heavily back to the altar. From practice with the nuns I knew that first he'd put the ciborium back in the tabernacle, then go into the sacristy to find a cloth of some sort—in the parlance of altar boys, this was known as the Sacred Rag—so as to cleanse the area where the body of Christ had fallen.

This was a situation for which all altar boys had been trained. Despite the incongruity of my kneeling, my role, in effect, was to stand guard. Should this be some sort of trick by an enemy of the Church, I was to defend the spot where the Host had fallen against any and all defamation or sacrilege. If necessary, I was to defend even the least part of the sacrament with my life. This wasn't a mock air raid or fire drill. This was real-world real. At the time I took these things dead seriously.

At the time I would have been more than glad to die in that situation. Who wouldn't? As a martyr I'd earn the immediate reward of Heaven through what was known as baptism of blood. In an instant my soul would be cleansed of all sin. One moment I would be in church, defending Marie's collar against atheists and communists, and the next I'd be in Heaven with God and all the saints, part of what the nuns called the Mystical Body. I'd get to see the Beatific Vision, which we were told was joyful beyond even our wildest imagination. I imagined it would be like gazing at an extremely beautiful woman— Marilyn Monroe or Grace Kelly or Sophia Loren—only even more intense. I'd be so joyous I'd vibrate and glow. Happiness more yellow than real butter would gush out from me, as if in a cartoon. More practically, I'd be free of my lousy life, which wasn't near as bad as some, I'm sure, but most days was no picnic in Lincoln Park. I looked about eagerly for any possible enemies of the Church, hoping to see one, hoping I could defend the crumbs on Marie's collar with my life.

By now all of the children waiting behind Marie had gone over to the other side of the communion rail. From the pews the nuns whispered to one another, trying to figure out what was what. "Did I do something wrong?" Marie whispered. She wasn't crying yet. She stared at me for a moment, then hung her head in shame.

"Nah," I whispered. "It was his fault. He flipped it off the side of your tongue."

"The side of my tongue?"

"He was in a hurry. You know how he is. He thinks he's The Flash. The guy from the comics. Fastest guy alive. Quickest flip in the diocese."

I didn't know if saying that was the right or wrong thing, but the conversation certainly opened the floodgates. All at once Marie gave out a stifled sob. For a minute or so I watched her tears plop onto the white linen cloth covering the communion rail. They made a pair of ever-widening splotches on the cloth. I hiked up the back of my cassock and handed her a clean handkerchief, which I kept in my back pocket. Head down, Marie nodded her thanks, then demurely wiped her eyes and cheeks and modestly, as only a young girl could, blew her nose.

Then Father O'Reilly returned. With the Sacred Rag he brushed the top of her collar onto my paten, then turned and retrieved the ciborium from the tabernacle and wiped any and all crumbs from my paten into it. By now everyone else in church had received Communion. Father O'Reilly faced Marie. She raised her head, then opened her mouth and tilted back her neck. Tears welled in the corners of her eyes like sparkling jewels.

"*Cor Crispy,*" Father O'Reilly said, and with a flip of his anointed thumb and first finger jammed the wafer down the back of the girl's throat.

～ ～ ～

All that was behind us, I thought, now that we'd graduated. Ahead lay the future and its many challenges. As we sauntered down the street Marie chatted about the party, which couples danced together during slow dances, and did I think that meant they liked each other and would go out? Then she asked if I'd deliberately saved the last dance for her.

Was there more than one answer to that question? "Of course," I said.

She said she'd hoped I'd say that, and added that I was sweet. We were still holding hands. Our legs had fallen into an easy rhythm of walking together. It was as if we didn't even have to think about walking together. Our legs just moved together all by themselves.

We walked to her house up on Farragut. As we neared the front of her parents' six-flat she glanced up at a trio of first-floor windows, then tugged my hand and said, "Vince, let's go in here." We scurried up the front walk and gently opened and closed the outside door to the hallway, so the people on the ground-floor flats wouldn't hear.

"Don't brush against those," she said softly when I stepped back from her in the vestibule, pointing to the row of doorbells beneath the mailboxes on the wall.

I smiled and made like I was going to ring all the bells. When I was a kid, sometimes on Halloween I'd go from six-flat to six-flat with a pack of safety pins, sticking them in the cracks just above and beneath the bells. That would make all the bells ring continuously.

I started to tell this to Marie but when I looked at her in the closeness of the hallway it suddenly didn't seem like something worth saying. It seemed childish and half-witted, as if saying that belonged to another world. For a while we just stood there, still holding hands, holding each other's gaze, and then our fingers untwined all by themselves and we held each other the same way as when we were slow-dancing. Then in the briefest slice of time our heads moved toward each other, and without thinking she tilted hers one way and I tilted mine the other way and we kissed.

When the kiss was over and I started to back away, she kissed me again. This time she opened her mouth a little and in response I opened my mouth a little, too, and for the briefest moment our tongues touched. Though I'd closed my eyes I suddenly saw quicksilver, as if the inside of her mouth were glistening and shiny. Like the mercury inside a thermometer, I thought, only more clear and wet and bright.

We were like a pair of third graders playing a slow game of tag out on the parish playground. Then she tightened her lips and sipped my tongue into her mouth, as if my tongue were a thing she could drink, and then I did the same to her tongue, sipping it softly into my mouth, and in this manner we teeter-tottered back and forth, until there was nearly no distinction between us, no difference between her mouth and my mouth, and all separation between our bodies simply fell away, as if we were shedding unnecessary clothes, and in that moment there was nothing at all playground about us.

Then a door clattered open above us and we heard the heavy footsteps of Marie's father, who owned Santangelo's Quality Meats on Clark Street. SANTANGELO'S QUALITY MEATS, the neon sign above his store would blink, one word glowing brightly after the next, until the sign would go dark and the middle three letters of the last word—EAT—flashed off and then on. The effect made the sign read as if it were a sentence, an eternally blinking command.

EAT

SANTANGELO'S

QUALITY

MEATS

The approaching footsteps called downstairs, "Is that you, Marie? What'sa taking you so long down there? Did you a-lose you key?"

I got out of there fast, whispering, "See ya," before fleeing into the darkness.

Walking home that dark night, I'm not sure my shoes touched the sidewalk. I wondered what in the world had I done to be so fortunate. To be taken by the hand! To be pulled into a hallway! To be kissed, not just once or twice but three distinct times by such a pretty girl! I could hardly tell if I were myself or someone else. It was as if I'd suddenly awakened and saw I was wearing someone else's clothes.

～ ～ ～

The downstairs light in the front room of my family's red brick two-flat still shone brightly. Unusual, since my father normally went to bed by eight or nine at the latest, given that his mornings at the fish market started at four-thirty, and recently my mother had taken to sleeping on the front-room couch in the darkness with a dampened rag over her eyes, due to the aggravation caused by the seven of us kids and her persistent, incurable headaches.

When people asked my mother if she'd been having headaches, she'd give them this insane laugh and say, "Yeah, about once every other year on average for the last fourteen years." Well, maybe you should take something for it, such as an aspirin, they'd tell her. "The only way an aspirin would help me," she'd answer, issuing her maniacal laugh again, "is if I held it between my knees."

I looked up at the black, moonless sky. It was ten, maybe ten-fifteen at the latest. I'd been given a ten-thirty curfew, but my ma usually paid it little mind. What mattered, she'd say, during the rare times when she wasn't tending to one of the babies and had a moment or two to speak, was that I was home safe. Nonetheless I opened and closed the hallway door as quietly as I could, slipped my key into the front door lock and turned it so slowly that it gave the least click, then tiptoed inside like a little bird.

Just beyond the hallway waiting for me was the shadow of my father, stretching from out of the front room. As I walked into the front room to greet him, all at once the windows clapped loudly, and the ceiling filled with stars.

It's nearly eleven, and what. Selfish son of a. No good for nothing. Your poor mother. In bed again, headaches, and where were you tonight to help? Now the walls nearest me clapped, too, and the floor rose up to kiss me. I stood, and the floor came up and kissed the side of my head again. Worthless piece of. I tell you, mark my words, keep this up and you'll put her in an early grave. She'll be lying dead in her coffin, and maybe then you'll regret. Maybe then you'll realize.

By then I was scurrying into my safe place, where I curled like a roly-poly into the tiniest possible ball. The wall behind my head enthusiastically applauded my efforts. The floor beneath me throbbed and pulsed with a sudden wild jungle beat. Work all goddamn day only to have to come home to. Expect from the oldest. What with all the aggravation. All the constant. Daily. Now there was an earthquake, which tossed me up from the floor and shook me back and forth, as if I were a doll. The wall beat a steady tom-tom against my head. Don't you ever think before. Don't you have even a shred of common. Whose son are you? About time you learned to face the music. Look, now you've woken.

She was standing in the semi-darkness of the hallway, holding a wet cloth up over her eyes, asking him what was going on. Nothing, he answered. Everything's fine. Go back to bed. He turned off the light. Then to me, embracing the floor again, get up and go to bed, too, you no good. You hear me? Get out of my.

He went away then, murmuring, the floorboards in the hallway moaning. The two of them talking and then falling silent. Then the toilet flushing.

After several moments I stood and gathered myself. I picked up an arm here, a leg there. In the corner I found part of my forehead along with a burning ear.

❧ ❧ ❧

If there was one lesson the good Sisters of Christian Charity taught us, it was that people got what they deserved. They taught us that according to God's plan whatever takes place follows if not directly stems from the course of actions that preceded it. Forget to study for a test and you fail. Miss attending Mass on Sunday and you spend eternity in Hell. *Go to Hell. Go Directly to Hell. Do Not Pass Go. Do Not Collect $200.*

The nuns were big on stories and had one for every occasion. Most stories focused on sin and what were called near occasions of sin. Sin was any act forbidden by God. Near occasions of sin were all persons, places, or things that might lead you to go against God's or the Church's laws. Near occasions of sin included just about everything that was or could be of any interest to anyone in the world. A piece of chicken lying on a plate in the refrigerator, a handful of change piled on the dining room table near your dad's keys, a brassiere on a back yard clothesline waving its softly puckered cups in a summer breeze.

You could be just walking along the street of life without a care in the world, with a prayer on your lips and a righteous hymn in your heart, when *bang!* all of a sudden you're on the verge of eating meat on Friday or stealing some of your dad's hard-earned money or having impure thoughts and coveting your neighbor's daughter or wife. Even at age fourteen, I was becoming an expert on sin and at recognizing its near occasions, and, given the arc that my life would later take, the knowledge I was acquiring wouldn't go to waste.

Other than A B C and two plus two, sin and its avoidance were what the nuns mainly taught us. They taught us the laws of God and the Church, and about the thoughts, desires, words, actions, and omissions forbidden by those laws. They described in explicit detail the realm where deeds and their consequences are set. How every flood begins with a single drop of rain. Each avalanche, with a lone flake of snow. How one seemingly innocent little sin leads to the next and then the next and the next, like the numbers on our rulers marching like good soldiers from 1 to 6 to 12 and then onward, to three-digit numbers, seven-digit numbers, eternity. The nuns taught us about the fall of man, our inherently evil, sinful nature, and how the only path to redemption was through the body and blood of Jesus Christ.

They were fond of telling us stories about good Catholic children just like ourselves who obeyed their parents and listened respectfully to their teachers and went to daily Mass and Communion and said their nightly rosary and made room at their desks for their guardian angels, how these kids grew up and became honorable priests and nuns and lay people, upright citizens of a great and magnificent land blessed by the Almighty, parents of the next generation of good Roman Catholic children, and so on down through the remainder of time, a string of unfurled smiling paper cutouts, little acorns growing into mighty oaks, straight and tall as the masts of the ships that first came to this New Land.

There was the story about the poor altar boy who found a wallet full of twenties on the sidewalk outside the sacristy, how he diligently searched the neighborhood streets for its rightful owner despite his own family's need for food, how when he returned to the cold-water flat where he and his mother and younger sisters and brothers lived he found that they were crying out of the pain of true hunger, but the boy resisted and gave the priests the wallet anyway, and in the savings and loan of God's eternal kingdom the boy's eternal soul grew richer than any millionaire.

There was the story about the beautiful prima ballerina, who one day after dance practice spotted somebody drowning in a pond, how she rescued the unfortunate soul even though the pond's murky waters were known to be teeming with polio germs, how the girl considered her risk a mere pittance when stacked against the sacredness of life, even a life dumb enough to swim in a pond marked by a sign bearing a skull and crossbones and the words WARNING! POSSIBLE POLIO GERMS!, how the young girl refused to cry, not a single tear, after the doctors measured her legs for the heavy iron braces that she'd be forced to wear until the day she died, but how up on God's stage her soul was performing perfect pirouette after pirouette in her little pink toe shoes and ruffled tutu.

There was the boy from ancient Sparta who stole a fox and hid it beneath his cloak, and didn't respond when people from town walked past him and questioned him about what seemed to be moving under his clothes. Sister explained that even though it was a grave sin to steal we should recognize the Spartan ideal to be stoic in the face of adversity and silently endure even the greatest pain, and that this ideal was shared by the Church's earliest martyrs. Sister described how the boy didn't even utter a cry when the fox clawed him and bit into his tender flesh with his sharp teeth, and finally began to eat his stomach and liver and intestines, and how in the end the boy died in the arms of a beautiful maiden who happened to be strolling by.

I loved that story, particularly the part about the beautiful maiden. At night as I lay in bed trying to fall asleep sometimes I'd pretend to be walking down Glenwood Avenue with a fox gnawing on my stomach, and I'd be so brave and strong that as people passed me by I wouldn't show my pain, my mouth not even making the slightest grimace, and they'd never suspect what was happening to me. Then, as I'd drift to sleep, Sophia Loren or Grace Kelly would take me up into her arms.

There were the stories of all the brave Catholic children who refused to deny their faith when they were tortured by the Russian, Chinese, and North Korean communists. There was the story of the saint in Sicily who took a vow of chastity and devoted her life to Christ, and who, after a rich young Roman fell in love with her, claiming that what drew her to him were her beautiful eyes, plucked her two eyes clean out of their sockets and handed them to him on a dish rather than break her vow. Another virgin martyr, threatened with a life of prostitution, cut off her own breasts.

It got so that you'd hope you'd find a wallet just to prove you'd give it back, too. As proof of your inner strength, you refuse to scratch your mosquito bites or take a sip from the drinking fountain even when it's hot and you're very thirsty. You'd be willing to hide a stray dog beneath your shirt and undershirt, that is, if you could catch a stray dog. Entering the dark, sweet-smelling church on mornings when you're assigned to serve the six-fifteen, you look twice at the statues because you both hope and fear that their saintly eyes are following you. You're certain that their mouths whisper their heavenly secrets in Latin. You pause before the side altar devoted to Mary, who stands in a recessed cove, eyes down, palms open and raised slightly at her sides beneath the folds of her blue cloak. You slip a nickel out of your pocket, listen to the echo of its fall in the iron collection box, and light a votive candle, then genuflect before the Virgin and pray, "Holy Mother, please protect me."

ॐ ॐ ॐ

"Are you all right?" her voice asked me from the hallway.

I froze, not knowing if she'd actually spoken or if I'd only imagined the voice. It always took me a long time to come back out of it, after I'd fled to the special place. I was still looking for one side of my head, which must have slid beneath the sofa or some other piece of furniture. I stood where I was, listening intently, at the same time pretending I couldn't hear her. Tears fat as bumblebees stung the corners of my eyes.

I stood as still as a statue in Grant Park until she went away. Had she come into the room then, she would have found that I'd turned as hard and solid as bronze. Had someone tipped me over then, I would have fallen to the floor and shattered into a million pieces.

But no one came into the room. The hallway floorboards groaned. My parents' bedroom door slowly swung shut on its squeaky hinges. The latch on their door gave out a final click. After a while (how long? a moment? several minutes? a full half hour or more?) I allowed the spinning atoms in my body to turn back into bone and flesh and blood, then moved my stiff arms and dried my cheeks and wiped away a thick strand of drool glistening eerily in the streetlight glow that had snuck into the room from between the imperfectly shut slats of the venetian blinds.

I hated crying. Crying was for babies, for losers, for morons and weaklings and mamma's boys, and I did it too often back then, nearly all the time, it seemed. Never during, but always after. I wondered why. Anyway, I was a regular Niagara Falls, a genuinely sappy crybaby. You could sell tickets. Maybe I could join the circus the next time it passed through town or work in the freak show at Riverview, the amusement park out on Western and Belmont, where the slogan was "Come and Laugh All Your Troubles Away." *Step right up, ladies and gents, only fifty cents! Come see the Crybaby Boy!* I could share a cage with Allie the Alligator Girl and keep her in saltwater.

I was nearly as bad as my littlest sister. I was weak and pitiful and ashamed. Still, as I crept down the hallway to the bathroom to brush my teeth, part of me disagreed and allowed them, or at least anyone with ears still awake, to hear me crying.

Let them hear me, for all I cared. Who cares if he can't get to sleep? Let him stay awake the whole damn night, and then the next morning at work while he's filleting some fish maybe his knife will slip and he'll gut himself. Let her stay awake all night, too. What gives her the right to sleep? Why wasn't she in the front room to greet me? Who cares if she has headaches? And while we're on the subject, who cares about her having so many kids? It wasn't me who gave her a job on the new-kid-every-other-year assembly line. It wasn't me who asked to be born to her. As far as I knew, I had nothing much really to do with it. In all likelihood, there was a mix-up in the hospital and I belonged to some other family.

I brushed my teeth and washed my face, then shook away my sadness, like a wet dog shaking out his fur, splattering water and bits of toothpaste foam all over the bathroom mirror. Let it dry there. Who cares if it spots the mirror and she has to clean it up? I lifted the seat on the toilet and let loose a mighty stream, right in the middle of the bowl, loud enough to wake my six sisters as well as my grandparents upstairs. I watched the bubbles race toward the sides of the bowl, and then I peed on the biggest ones to make them break, in the process sloshing a good squirt or two of piss right on the floor. Let it dry there. Then I pictured her the next morning down on her hands and knees beside the bowl—my sisters crawling up over her back, and at least one of them needing a diaper change, another crying, a third whining for her bottle—so I got a couple of squares of toilet paper and mopped up most of my piss before I flushed.

☙ ☙ ☙

And then there were the stories about the bad Catholic children, the kids who did the dumb things nearly all of us had considered doing at least once. The girl who went to Communion and bit down hard on the Host just to see what would happen. (Her mouth filled with blood that gushed so copiously that the church's marble floor was quickly covered, not stopping until the priest made the sign of the Cross on her forehead as she begged for the crucified Christ's forgiveness.) The boy who spat into the church's holy water font as a joke. (His lips, neck, and face at once froze, in a manner similar to the story of Lot's wife, and from that day on he could never gaze up at the sun or the sky, and all he could eat were those tiny jars of pureed baby food, sucked through a straw.)

That my nature at the time was sinful I had not the slightest doubt. According to my father I was worthless, lazy, and a pitiful excuse for a son, particularly a first-born son, who, damn it to Hell, by this time in his life should know better. According to my mother my father was right, and who was I to question him, he who worked two and sometimes three jobs each day to feed and clothe a family of nine along with both of his aging parents, who wouldn't know gratitude if it smacked them in the face. According to the nuns I was willful, disrespectful, too smart for my own good, and marred by a dozen bad habits, not the least of which included cracking my knuckles, tapping my feet, not paying sufficient attention to the blackboard, snorting during examinations, and bad penmanship, which every nun from third grade on indicated was an unmistakable sign of a weak and untrustworthy character.

At the top of each of my themes my teacher Sister Ascension would write, *"Sloppy! Chicken scratchings! Don't rush! Take the time necessary to form each and every letter!"* All of the nuns had such perfect Palmer-script handwriting that I imagined they did little else but practice it when they weren't eating or sleeping or doing the priests' laundry or kneeling on the marble floor of their convent chapel praying for the conversion of the Jews.

*"A sloppy hand is a sure sign of a messy, untrustworthy mind,"* Sister would write at the end of each of my themes, her o's perfectly rounded, p's precisely looped and tight.

The nuns told the story of the boy who lied about his sins in confession and as a result made a bad confession, and then went to Mass and Communion and further compounded his sin, inviting the body of Christ into a house that was twice unclean. The evil boy continued in this manner for three years, his sins swirling darkly, like a muddy whirlpool spiraling his soul ever downward, ever closer to Hell, until his mind snapped like a bent yardstick and he was placed in a home for the insane, where he was made to wear a straightjacket, his mouth repeatedly babbling the opening words of confession, "B-b-bless m-m-me, F-f-father, f-f-for I h-h-have s-s-sinned," which no one could understand due to the severity of his stutter.

There was the girl who rolled up the waist of her uniform skirt beneath her belt, thinking that exposing her legs and knees to the world would make her more attractive. This girl couldn't walk past a mirror without pausing to admire her reflection. One morning on her way to morning Mass, after again rolling her skirt beneath her belt as soon as she was free from her mother's eyes, the girl paused to gaze at her image in a storefront window and at that moment a sudden explosion from a gas leak inside the shop shattered the glass window into millions of shards, each thin as a needle, each sharp as a surgeon's scalpel. The shards flew at her with incalculable speed, everywhere piercing her skin and in the process blinding and deafening her. After her wounds healed, the girl ended up on an island out in the Pacific, where she worked as a nurse changing bandages in a lepers' colony since her unseeing eyes couldn't object to the sight of the lepers' bodies, and her unhearing ears couldn't register their complaints and moans.

There was the boy who touched himself impurely each night, until he caused himself to spill his seed. The first night he did so his emission was white, and in the next room in her sleep his poor mother cried out in pain. On the second night his emission was gray, and his mother's arms and legs grew paralyzed. On the third night his emission turned black, and his mother gasped and called out Christ's holy name. As she died, the boy's black seed stained his palms with an ink more indelible than a merchant marine's tattoo, and from the day of his poor mother's funeral until the day he died wherever he went everyone knew what the boy with the black palms had done, and no paint or bleach or pair of gloves could possibly disguise him.

There was the boy who stole money from the class's overseas mission box as it was being passed around. Not only did the coins burn a hole in his pants pocket but the wood of his desk and seat caught fire, too. Curiously, the fire didn't spread to the other desks, and even though his teacher immediately grabbed a fire extinguisher and sprayed the burning boy with foam she couldn't extinguish the flames that consumed him, nor could the school janitor or the firemen from the fire department. Then all at once the flames disappeared, and the boy's body collapsed into a trickle of ash that puddled on the suddenly restored seat of his desk along with the coins he had stolen.

And if you think for a moment his suffering was bad, Sister told us, his torment and pain was *nothing* when compared to the intensity of Hell's fires. We were told to imagine the world's hottest flame and then multiply it by ten thousand. Take that number and multiply it again by ten thousand, and do so again and again, ten thousand times. That heat would approximate the intensity of an atomic bomb, Sister claimed, the kind we prepared for each Thursday morning at air-raid time as we crouched beneath our desks, one hand protecting our eyes and the other the back of our necks, imagining the H-bombs the godless communists might drop on us at any moment.

Multiply that bomb by another ten thousand, and do that again ten thousand more times, and you approximate the heat of the sun. Now multiply the sun's heat by ten thousand and imagine that heat is a single grain of sand. Picture all of the sand along Chicago's long lakeshore, then all the sand on all of the world's deserts and beaches. Then take that heat and think of it as a droplet of water, and carry on the multiplication process until you've imagined every drop of water in every river, sea, and ocean in the world. That does not even *begin* to represent the heat of the fire that Almighty God has created for those who would rather dwell with sin than embrace the broken and cruci-fied body of his beloved son, Jesus.

Sister Ascension illustrated this lesson one morning by bringing to class a votive candle inside a glass jar. She lit the candle and held it before us in her outstretched palms. "Imagine how long you can hold a finger in this fire," she said. "Consider just how quickly you'll feel the fire's pain and want to pull your hand back. Understand, children, that here on earth, in this realm of existence, we have the choice, the *free will*, to pull our hands away, just as we have the choice to avoid sin and its near occasions. But the unhappy souls condemned to Hell can *never ever* escape its fiery punishment." She put the candle on the corner of her desk and asked each of us to come up and, if we dared, stick one of our fingers into the flame.

The other kids who accepted her dare brushed the flame with one fingertip and gave out a little "Ouch!" or "Zowee!," then shook their hand hard, as if trying to shake their fingers off. Several sucked on their fingertips as they walked back to their seats.

But me, I put my first finger directly into the dancing teardrop of fire, surrounded by its clear pool of melted wax, and I held it there, in the center of the flame for so long that Sister Ascension shouted out my name, rushed around her desk, the oversized rosary beads cinched at her waist audibly clacking, and slapped my arm away. Then she sent me to Sister Superior's office, where the lady who types and answers the telephone greased my finger with salve.

Later out on the playground, all the kids wanted to know what was behind my trick.

I told them there wasn't any trick. I had guts and they didn't.

But there is a trick. There's a place I can go where I feel no pain.

It's a simple enough thing to do, really, like finding yourself trapped inside a locked room with nowhere to escape, then discovering that the back wall of the room has a secret panel that opens up onto a little shelf where everything is calm and safe. The next time you find yourself inside that room you just hold yourself still and press against the back wall, feeling for that secret shelf, that safe place where your body perfectly fits, sliding yourself into it as easily as a folded sheet of paper slips into an envelope, leaving behind the shell of your body to face the music.

ᘛ ᘛ ᘛ

My bed was near the front door, in a sort of makeshift room where there had once been a hallway closet. The back wall of the closet separated our flat from the front steps leading up to my grandparents' flat on the second floor. My father punched out the wall between the closet and the steps, under which he placed my bed. In the space remaining he put my dresser and a lamp. This was after Josephina was born, when they kicked me out of Tina and Carmella's room. Our flat had only three bedrooms: one for my parents and two for my sisters, who slept three to a room in bunk beds and trundles and always got in one another's way and always whined and complained. My bed lay directly beneath the upstairs steps, on a platform over the steps that led from our flat down into our basement. So as to be able to get into and out of our basement, my father put in a trapdoor, which lay beneath my bed.

"You sure that platform's going to be strong enough?" my ma had asked.

"What do you think?" my father said. "It's strong enough. I'm standing on it. Come here, squeeze yourself in and stand on it, too."

"But it's so dark and dank in here."

"It'll air out. Come on, get over here. Suck in your gut. As for it being dark, it's supposed to be dark. Christ's sake, it's a place to put a bed. We've both slept in worse."

"You'll have to do something about these nails." From past attempts at laying carpet, half-inch tips of nails protruded in jagged rows from the bottom of each stair.

"Not a problem for long. Just hand me that hammer."

It took me a while to get used to sleeping there. I imagined the blunted nails as teeth, the stairs as a giant mouth that one day might decide to eat me, the trapdoor beneath me as the gateway to Hell. I imagined the steps falling, crushing me against the plywood platform and breaking through to the steps below, where I'd be squished inside a staircase sandwich. The firemen would pry up the top staircase and there I'd be, smeared like tomato paste all over the lower stairs. If I lived, my body would be bent and crooked like something out of a cartoon. When I walked I'd resemble a staircase, my head and shoulders only a foot or two off the ground but several feet behind my shoes. Playful mice and frisky cats would run up and down my length. As I grew older everybody would call me Mr. Stair Man. I came to call my room "the stair room," and after a while everybody except my father called it that, too.

Beneath the lamp on top of my dresser I kept my two most precious belongings: a five-gallon aquarium and a plastic figurine of Ernie Banks, the great Chicago Cubs shortstop. In my aquarium I kept a pair of guppies along with a couple of neon tetras and a lone spotted catfish, whose job was to patrol the tank's bottom and keep the gravel clean. Stuck in the gravel by the corner box filter was a small plastic sign.

PEOPLE FRY

SAT. NITE

I clicked on the lamp on my dresser and watched as the fish swam up and toward me. I had dreams then of creating what was known as a balanced aquarium, a tank whose perfect mix of plant life, fish and light would never need cleaning or water changes. I'd checked out several books from the public library and read all about it. The fish's secretions along with bacteria in the filter and a good source of sunlight would nourish the plants as they emitted enough oxygen to enable the fish to breathe. It was a utopian dream, a perfectly enclosed, self-sustaining world. All life within it would be balanced, harmonious.

I gave my fish a pinch of food and watched them as they ate, darting up to the top of the tank from between the broad, yellowing leaves of a sadly dying Amazon sword, and then I gently lifted the plastic brown bat from the circle of Ernie Bank's locked hands and swung the bat softly near his hands fourteen times (his uniform number), hitting deep, centerfield, scoreboard-shattering, bases-loaded home runs.

Then I said an Our Father and a Hail Mary, making the sign of the Cross three times between each prayer, doing my best to recite the words of each prayer slowly, with meaning, so that the words really meant something, rather than just saying them by rote. I turned off the light and slipped beneath my blanket and sheet.

The toilet tank was refilling, trickling to a stop, then after a few moments again refilling and stopping again. In the next room, one of my sisters mumbled something in her sleep.

The stairs wouldn't fall, I reassured myself. The mouth wouldn't swallow me.

In the darkness I reached up and touched the stairs, then ran my fingers over the blunted, protruding tips of the nails. For a while I pretended I was blind and with my sensitive fingertips I was reading some secret message in Braille, a message written by the stair gods for me and me alone, a message that someday I'd come to understand.

Outside on Glenwood Avenue there was a siren. At first it grew louder, drawing close, then drew closer and still yet closer, but then suddenly it waned and went silent, as if it had never been anywhere near.

# 2

# *Tofino 1974*

"SURE," I TOLD THE SQUATTERS crouching beside the lean-to over my pile of firewood, who'd asked if they could pitch their tent beside it for the night, "that would be fine with me." I remembered what the church people who'd helped me cross the border told me, as I stepped out of their van, the wound on my chest still fresh, as they gave me two sandwiches and forty dollars, Canadian. "But I've only recently rented this place and don't know how cool it would be with my landlord if someone crashed here for, say"—I paused to let them know I wanted them to fill in the blank—"a week or a month or the rest of summer."

This is the beginning of the Tofino half of my story, the night when I met Roxanne Parker and sort of stepped back into my own life.

"Oh no," Roxanne said, eyes smiling, "we plan to be here only for a few days."

"Three or four days max," the guy, whose name was Josh, added quickly, "and then we're heading back over the mountains and up to Port Hardy."

"So you're going to see the whole island," I said.

"That's the plan," Josh said.

"Fine," I said, nodding. "You're more than welcome to crash here, but please try not to bother my neighbors beyond those trees." I pointed to a row of Douglas fir just beyond a tangle of salal and salmonberry. I didn't even know my neighbors but I said it because I wasn't comfortable around people. I wasn't very good or pleasant company.

Part of me was still scrounging out an existence in the parks and back streets of Vancouver. I imagined people could just look at me and see all I'd done.

"We'll be as quiet as mice in fur slippers on Sunday morning," the girl, Roxanne, said as they began setting up their tent.

They seemed a nice enough pair. Roxanne was a student from some small town in Montana, a major in art therapy at the university there, a big, ripely lush girl whom some would judge as verging on plump, a girl with a round face and lips and large, dark, expressive eyes. Attentive and watchful and sort of wary, as if at every given moment she were keeping track of which direction she'd run so as to make her escape. I liked that. She made me want to touch her hands, hold them down, somehow assure or still or soothe her. Immediately I sensed that she was Josh's better, that it was likely he hardly deserved her.

Josh was a manically thin, impressively nervous guy who wore his hair in a bushy white-man's Afro, and whose chest and arms were covered with so much hair that at a distance you thought he was wearing a sweater beneath his T-shirt. He said he was from Salt Lake City and was working on a degree in political science and philosophy. Though don't get me wrong, he added, I'm not a Mormon, as if you couldn't guess from my major, har har har. He had a goofy way of pulling the ends of his beard when he talked, and by the way he kept interrupting Roxanne and bringing the conversation back to himself he seemed the kind of guy who noticed fewer things than she did. In any event it was clear that he enjoyed the sound of his own voice. At one point he said his favorite philosopher was Marx. Karl, he added after a beat, you know, the German, like in *Das Kapital*? I prefer Harpo, I answered, honking an imaginary horn on my belt and then winking at pretty, shy Roxanne.

I may not have gone to university but I'm no dummy. I may live in an obscure little fishing village out on the western edge of nowhere, but that doesn't mean I don't know music and books, women and men, art and life.

Roxanne asked me what I did for a living, and so I told her and Josh about the fish plant where I worked, that for eight hours each day I stood beside an assembly line, gutting fish. Salmon, mainly, caught by the area's many trollers. After the crews out on the trollers cut the salmon's gills and bled them, I and a handful of others back on land finished the job, slitting open and ripping out the fish's entrails. Then we iced and packed the fish in totes, which were driven over the mountains to Nanaimo and processed, I believe, back on the mainland in Vancouver. The job was repetitive and unpleasant and more mind-numbing than anyone can possibly describe. It was precisely the kind of work I wanted then and needed, a purely routine sort of self-administered anesthetic. By their silence I could tell that my description of standing all day in fish guts put a damper on the conversation and so after a minute or two I nodded, drained my bottle of beer and split.

The next day after work I forced myself to be sociable and brought Roxanne and Josh a nice piece of fresh halibut I picked up from a friend at the Fourth Street Dock. I think I was genuinely pleased then not to be alone. I told them they could cook it on the pot-bellied grill I kept next to the woodpile but seldom used. Roxanne was very happy with the fish. She'd never eaten or even seen truly fresh halibut. I gave them charcoal, utensils and plates, and showed them where I keep my garbage can, reminding them to put the lid back on tight unless they wanted to be roused from their sleep by raccoons.

On the third night there was a hesitant knock on my back door. I was in the front of the house, reading and listening to music, Miles Davis's *E.S.P.*, I remember, because later on Roxanne remarked on the fetching woman gracing the album cover, and I told her that the woman was a former model and the second of Davis's many wives. Anyway, at the back door stood Roxanne apologizing for her boldness and asking if maybe, if it wasn't too much trouble, could she please come in and take a shower. She said it had been weeks since she'd showered, and she'd be quick and not use too much hot water, promise.

"Sure," I said and invited her inside. "Forgive me for not offering you one earlier." I didn't know what sort of things I should say. I wasn't much used to visitors. "Shower for as long as you'd like," I told her. I went to the hallway closet and returned with a fresh washcloth and a couple of towels.

Josh was in town, she told me as she sat at the kitchen table, unlacing her boots. They were sturdy, waterproofed, sensible boots, the kind someone interested more in utility than fashion would wear. I liked her for that. He'd run across some old college buddies, she continued, and they'd gone off drinking and smoking some of B.C.'s finest.

"And they left you all alone?" I opened the refrigerator and offered her a beer, then took out a bottle for myself and pulled up a chair across from her.

No, she said, she could have gone with them but she didn't want to. They can get so boring, she said, sipping her beer. She was wearing tiny pearl earrings and smelled so faintly of perfume—something jasmine, I decided—that I wanted to nuzzle my nose against her soft neck and hold her for a moment and just sort of breathe her in.

I saw it all then, what she wanted, at least in possibility if not in deed, in that moment when I recognized that she'd put on perfume and earrings to come to my house to ask for a shower. The earrings and perfume disclosed her intentions. I leaned forward in my chair and laughed at her stories about her boring boyfriend. She continued talking about what she and Josh and his buddies had done that day—where they'd gone, all that they'd seen—and as she tilted back her beer I stood and walked from the kitchen and returned with the leather dopkit in which I kept my stash of dope.

"Your boyfriend had better be careful with B.C.'s finest," I said as I sat again at the table. With a pair of bathroom scissors I snipped small pieces off a few choice buds, then licked two Zig-Zags together and rolled a fat joint. "The THC level in some of the local stuff can get pretty high." I licked the joint closed, twisted its ends, then lit it and sucked down a good hit and offered it to her. She took a good hit off it, too.

"Why's that?" she said, hissing, eyes wide, doing her best to hold the smoke down.

I explained what I knew, that for years some who came here in the early 1960s grew marijuana out on the edges of the forests, cultivating it like a crop. They kept the seeds from the best plants and experimented, crossing one strain with another, learning over time how to grow increasingly better and more potent plants. We drank two more beers as we shared the joint. I didn't realize then that people were already cloning female varieties from cuttings as well as taking the industry indoors and growing marijuana hydroponically. All I knew was what every amateur pot grower knew: avoid open areas that might be spotted from the sky, cull the males, and when the time is right harvest your crop before someone else does.

"I grew this myself," I said, proudly, as we finished the joint.

I'd leave things up to her, I decided. If anything was to proceed, I thought, it would do so at her initiative. Maybe she'd put on the perfume and earrings out of politeness, not desire. Maybe she was simply tired of feeling grungy. Of course that was it, I realized. I was foolish to think anything else. Then the first side of the album ended, and I walked to the stereo in the front room to flip the LP. Roxanne trailed me, blissfully stoned, beer bottle in one hand, the clean towels and washcloth beneath her other arm.

We talked for a while then about the music, and she remarked about the beautiful woman on the album cover. As she turned toward the light to study the cover more closely, I caught a whiff of her jasmine perfume and had the sudden urge to smell her hair. For the briefest moment I leaned forward and did so. Her hair smelled dark and warm, of earth and flowers. Then I stepped back. Though I'd washed when I came home from work that night, I wondered how badly I still stank of fish. Living alone, one tends to grow used to one's own smell. In those days, working at the fish plant, no matter how often or how diligently I washed I always smelled of fish.

There was that awkward moment as the first cut on side two started to play when it seemed obvious that we each wanted to continue talking but were just too stoned to think of anything coherent to say. So we did that little stoners' thing where one person smiled and nodded as the other person smiled and nodded, with the silliest of grins plastering our faces. Then, like a gracious host, I pointed toward the bathroom and nodded and smiled some more and went on with my business.

I went back to the book I'd been reading, Lawrence Ferlinghetti's *The Coney Island of the Mind*, the poem about the penny candy store beyond the El, where the guy in the poem first falls in love with unreality. For a long, stoned moment I wondered what *unreality* might mean. Reality was a hard enough concept to get your mind around. But unreality? Whew. In that moment the distinction between the two words was the most important consideration in the world. Understanding it seemed to hold the answer to every question I'd ever had, everything I'd ever been seeking. I pictured myself standing beneath the tracks of the Bryn Mawr El station back in Chicago. I tried to connect the line in the poem to my own life.

I could hear the water from the shower running and the end of Tony Williams's long and brilliant opening drum solo on "Agitation" when she opened the bathroom door, dripping wet, holding up one of the towels over her body. She walked across the room toward me and, wordless, took my hand.

"But I smell of fish."

She pressed a finger against my lips, then pulled me toward the running shower.

☙ ☙ ☙

The second side of *E.S.P.* was playing for the fourth time on the turntable—moving from the shifting, up-tempo "Agitation" to the lovely, haunting ballads "Iris" and "Mood"—when Josh returned from drinking in town, much earlier than Roxanne and I had expected. We were still in bed, lying back on the pillows in my bedroom in the front of the house, blanket heaped on the floor, sheets still slightly damp from our shower, when I thought I heard something unusual outside. We listened for a moment but heard nothing. I quickly dressed and walked around the house, senses on alert, listening, then decided it was probably only the wind or a raccoon or two rooting in the garbage. I changed the album as Roxanne got up and made a pot of herb tea and carried it and a pair of mugs to the bedroom, and then a rapid riff of knocks exploded on the back door.

"I've brought Roxanne's things," Josh announced. At his feet on the back porch were her knapsack and sleeping bag along with a couple of paperbacks, four or five drawing pads, a bundle of colored pencils, a hairbrush, some toiletries, three or four stamped postcards, and a bright orange Frisbee.

"Josh," Roxanne said. She stood behind me, barefoot, frantically tucking her T-shirt into her jeans. Her dark hair fell about her face, loose and wild.

"I looked in all the windows," Josh said, "but when I didn't see either of you and I heard the music. . . ." He pulled the ends of his beard and shrugged.

"This Frisbee," she said, leaning over and picking it up. "Josh, I bought it for you."

"And I'm giving it back." He nudged her belongings closer with his foot. "Hey, don't underestimate me. I mean, it's not like I'm into being possessive and all that, but I'm not clueless. I can connect the dots. I'm not without imagination." For a moment he listened to the album playing from the stereo in the front room, cocking his head toward it like the Victrola dog. "Herbie Hancock?"

I shook my head. "Ahmad Jamal."

"But before, that was Herbie Hancock."

"Playing with Miles Davis, yes."

He smiled, as if he'd won some prize, then nodded and stepped past us and inside. Roxanne and I moved back to give him room.

"You were probably looking for this," he said to Roxanne, pulling something from his jacket pocket and flipping her a flat plastic case it took me several moments to understand was for her diaphragm. "It was mixed up with my stuff. Imagine that, Roxie, your stuff and my stuff all mixed together. Really, it isn't like you to leap into something unprepared."

"I wasn't unprepared," she said, opening and then showing him the empty case. A bit of the corn starch inside snowed onto the floor.

"Wow," Josh said, as if someone had punched his stomach. "So you two really—"

"Yeah," Roxanne said, "and when or when not I put in my diaphragm isn't anybody else's business but my own."

He let out a long breath. "Wow. I'm like totally blown away." He laughed weakly. "'Bump, bump, bump, on the back of his head.'" His eyes met mine. "Hey, man, like you know what I mean? Are you hip with that? Do you get it?" He laughed again, nearly snarling. "Like, oh my God, wow. I cannot believe it."

"Josh," she said, drawing out the sound of his name.

"Whoaza," Josh said. He bent at the waist and held his sides, breathing through his mouth in long, exaggerated gasps. I wondered if he was hyperventilating. I knew I'd need to find a small paper bag. "Whew," he said. "Whoa. Like fucking wow."

"You two would probably like to talk." I grabbed my boots along with a jacket and moved past him toward the back door when I realized I wasn't wearing socks. No matter, I thought as I pulled on my boots, then knelt alternately on one knee as I laced them. He smelled of cigarettes and beer but didn't seem drunk or stoned to me. Given the situation and the suddenness of everything, I figured that backing off and leaving the pair alone for a while would be the best thing I could do. I slipped on my jacket. "Take all the time you need."

"No," Roxanne said. "Vince, you stay. Josh and I can talk in the tent. We don't want to put you out. This is your place."

"Well," I said, "it's late, and the two of you are already here, so you might as well stay here." I gestured to indicate the kitchen, in which we were standing. "Just let me ask you to put things back where you find them. And if you listen to any more albums, please put them back in their liners when you're through."

Josh was still bent over but was breathing regularly. "Wow," he said again. "Whew. Bump, bump, bump. Heavy."

I'd transformed into an innkeeper. "I keep the tea in that cupboard," I said, pointing to a cupboard to the right of the stove. "There's sugar in a bowl on the shelf below. What's left of a six-pack of Canadian is in the fridge."

That revived Josh sufficiently to move him toward the refrigerator. "Cool," he said, "maximally cool, because, let me tell you, man, I am fucking starving." He gave his last two words four strong, equal beats and opened the refrigerator door and bent, rummaging around, then tossed onto the counter a packet of Genoa salami wrapped in white butcher paper, a wedge of cheese, a jar of mustard and another of mayonnaise.

"By all means," I said, "help yourself."

I watched him, doing my best to gauge his mood. The worst he'd do was become whiny and sarcastic. Still, what with the surprise and tension in the last quarter hour, I felt an overwhelming desire to leave. In the face of energy like his I get a heightened fight-or-flight response, which often finds me running away. As I've gone over with Big Ed and Lillian in group, one of the things I've been best at in life is running away.

"The bread's in the same cupboard as the tea," I told them. "Plates are on the middle shelf in the cupboard on the left. Utensils, in the drawer just below them. You'll find an opener for the beer in that drawer in the slot furthest to the left."

Josh tsk-tsked me and smiled and shook his head.

My eyes held his gaze. I didn't feel I needed to defend myself. Order relaxes something within me. Mess tends to make me vulnerable and tense. So why not separate the forks from the knives, the jazz LPs from the rock and the folk, the books of poetry from the novels and story collections and the nonfiction, the hardbacks from the paperbacks? In my pantry all the canned and boxed goods stood in tidy rows—soups with soups, beans with beans, grains with other grains—with their labels right side up and facing out.

Roxanne stuck her postcards and books and things inside her knapsack and hunched against the kitchen's far wall, staring down at a square of tile, idly brushing out her hair, which was still slightly wet. It seemed as if she were trying to make herself as small as possible. I wanted to tell her to stand tall.

On the wall behind her hung one of the remnants from my other life, a framed black-and-white photo of the 1969 Chicago Cubs. Back in the summer of '69, when it appeared as if the Cubs were certain to capture the National League pennant, I found the team photo in a Vancouver sports shop. Even though I was in Canada I did my best to follow the pennant race, all the way up to the New York Mets' miracle surge, the Cubs' heartbreaking, graceless collapse. I was living in Vancouver then, doing things I don't talk about. In a way the picture was a last link to my past.

"You're up here because you dodged the draft," Josh said suddenly to me. He said it more as a statement than a question, like a bright student who felt he'd suddenly stumbled on the answer. The color in his face had returned, and his eyes had grown steady, even steely. He'd been studying me, I realized. He stood at the kitchen table, watching my every move while the steak knife in his hand generously slathered mayonnaise on a piece of bread.

"No," I said. "I didn't leave because of the draft."

He gave the air a derisive snort.

"Josh drew an outrageously high number in the lottery," Roxanne said. "What was it, three hundred something?" She turned to me, slowly brushing her hair. "I wasn't with him then—that was back in

'69, four or five years ago, wasn't it?—but he still talks about it, you know, the night of the big lottery."

"Three fifty-eight," Josh said, as if his high lottery number were a personal accomplishment. "And, you're right, it'll be five years this December." He scattered things noisily for several moments in the silverware drawer, then nudged it shut with his hip and opened one of the Canadians by banging the edge of its cap down against the wooden lip of my counter. "Let me tell you, man, that lottery, it was nothing short of surreal. I got so stoned I could hardly see the TV. Listening to them call out one date after the next, like the next number in Bingo. I thought they'd *never* get around to my birthday."

I picked the bottle cap up from the floor, assessed the damage to the counter, then moved past him to the drawer and set the bottle opener on the kitchen table, in his sight.

"Were you in the lottery?" Roxanne asked me. She stopped brushing her hair and was now sorting through the things in her knapsack. Her hair shone in the kitchen's light. "What number did you pull?"

"I'd already come up here," I answered. By here I meant Canada, not Tofino. I made my escape from the States in 1967, a month or so after I graduated from high school, crossing the border with the help of some church people. By 1969, when the first lottery was held, I was living in Vancouver.

"You split from the draft early," she said.

"I split for other reasons. Personal issues. That sort of thing."

"So you're our age," Josh said, slicing a wedge of cheddar with the same knife he'd used with the mayonnaise. "You seem older somehow." He looked down, then wiped the knife on the side of his pants and tossed it on the table. "So tell us, man, what gives? You flunk out of school? Lose your student deferment?"

I shrugged. "How does any of that matter now?"

Josh tore a big bite from his sandwich, chewing as if he were working out some mathematical equation in his head. With his free hand he began pulling the ends of his beard. My question must have triggered something in him because even before he swallowed he took in a deep breath and nodded and smiled. "I can understand where you're coming from, man, but let me tell you, it does matter. Nixon fucking divided the anti-war movement with that lottery. I knew dudes who pulled really high numbers—I'm talking solid two-eighties, two-nineties, anything in the three hundreds—and the next day they quit doing anti-war work so they could spend all their time in their cribs smoking weed and listening to Jimi Hendrix. Speaking of which, if you have some, a little reefer sure would go mighty nice with this *cerveza*." He smiled impishly, then mimed toking hard on a joint.

I raised my hands, indicating both were empty.

"And I knew dudes who drew these outrageously low numbers and then did all sorts of crazy things, everything from chopping off their trigger fingers to taking pills to whack up their blood pressure to getting their home-town honeys pregnant."

He was making me feel anxious. "You don't say."

"So what's your story, man?" Josh said. He wolfed down more of the sandwich, then took a long slug off his beer.

From the animated way he talked, I thought he was recovering nicely from Roxanne's indiscretion. She sat calmly at the kitchen table, picking at the open wedge of cheese.

Then I wondered if maybe this was a thing between the two of them, something they did, that perhaps had happened before. He'd leave her alone and she'd cheat on him. Then he'd get all hurt and quote lines from *Winnie the Pooh* before they'd argue over which one of them owned a Frisbee and precisely when she'd put in her diaphragm, and then in an hour or two they'd end up all lovey-dovey in bed. As I'd learned during my days in Vancouver, the world was vast and strange and made up of all kinds. In any event, I'd learned to distrust before I trusted. Trust was earned, over time, and as a result it was quite rare.

For a moment I wondered if they'd set the whole thing up, from the time Roxanne knocked on my back door asking for use of my shower, to now when she sat beside her boyfriend nibbling on a wedge of cheese. I wondered if during the time she and I had been together he'd been listening or maybe even watching from outside my bedroom window.

Roxanne stood then and walked back to the bedroom, return-ing with her mug and the pot of herb tea, which by now had prob-ably grown tepid. Nonetheless, she sat at the table and held the mug with both hands to her chest as if it might warm her. No, I thought, she seemed without guile. Her boyfriend was a selfish jerk. She was a sweet, lush, generous girl who deserved better. They hadn't arranged anything. I must have left the arm on the turntable up because sud-denly a smatter of applause broke the silence and the teasing opening notes of "Ahmad's Blues," the first cut on the LP on the turntable, were playing again.

"So tell us your story, dude," Josh said.

I smiled, then grabbed my jacket and opened the back door. "Let me give you two some time to talk. I'll be back in a couple of hours. Don't do anything foolish here"—I looked at Roxanne to check again that she was okay, then back at Josh—"or I'll have to hunt you down and kill you." I gave Josh a nod and held his gaze until he looked away. "And kindly use the opener with the other bottles of beer."

ରଧ  ରଧ  ରଧ

I decided against walking and took a drive instead, heading down toward the Park Reserve and then turning around and going back up toward town, where I eventually parked by The Last Crumb. The lights in the restaurants on Campbell Street were dimming. As usual at this time in summer the sky was bright with stars, with a sense of depth and darkness I'd never noticed when I lived back in the States. Up here you can actually see which stars are closer, which are farther away. There are nights when the stars seem so close you nearly think you can make out features on their surfaces, like the moon. Or were they planets? I never learned how to recognize stars and planets. Being from Chicago, I didn't much look up at the sky.

I smelled the water before I could see it. The sea's edge has always smelled dark to me, some color between green and brown, of brine and shell and weed, of wet wood and sweet sea grass. I saw the tide was rising, a rolling, foamy pulse.

Outside the co-op a group of kids smoking cigarettes nodded at me, then asked if I knew where they could cop some dope.

"Sorry," I answered, though I knew the town's dozen or so dealers, at least by sight, and I knew that if the kids kept asking around sooner or later they'd connect with one of them. At the time I smoked only on occasion and, like many of the reefer smokers here, grew my own in secret spots in slashes adjacent to the rainforest, in groups of no more than five or six plants, which I marked with strings of green yarn and harvested in late summer, always in an amount modest enough that any objective observer or lawman would conclude was solely for my own individual consumption. I was wary of being busted, and particularly wary of the big growers. Whenever I stumbled on one of their patches—normally a stretch of at least two dozen or more plants—I steered clear and didn't touch a single bud or leaf. There are those who graze and outright raid others' plots, letting others do all the preliminary work, waiting until the buds are thick with resin, but I am not among them.

One local grower, prominent in these parts, drives an old green pickup that sports a bumper sticker flanked by a pair of marijuana leaf decals.

GOD MADE POT     MAN MADE BEER
WHICH DO YOU TRUST?

That evening I would have enjoyed smoking another joint. It had been a while since I'd been intimate with a woman, and for all I knew it would be an even longer time until I'd be with a woman again. I wanted to mark the occasion with some celebratory gesture, something more than a walk to the water's edge.

The only woman I'd been with since crossing the border into Canada I came across in the forest not too far from where I grew my modest patch of weed. We connected nearly wordlessly, while standing, against a rotting, fallen tree.

She was a hippie out hiking with her girlfriends. At the time it seemed that they'd lost track of her, or perhaps she'd lost track of them. As we were doing it, her friends called out to her in singsong. "Em-i-ly?" they called. "Em-i-lee?" Three distinct female voices. Their proximity made the coupling all the more exciting for her, as if she and the voices were playing a game, some variation of hide-and-seek.

She was wearing a long, flower-patterned, many-buttoned dress, what the girls today call vintage, and was reclining against a nursery log off to one side of the trail when I came up on her. I was a good fifteen yards off trail. All I was doing was checking on my modest garden, which grew near a broad stretch planted by the big-scale marijuana grower with the old green pickup. When she saw me, her hands pulled at the sides of her dress and her face broke into a wide smile.

I stopped where I stood, and something sparked between us. For several seconds we stood still, staring into each other's eyes. I kept expecting her to open her mouth and speak but she only stared at me and smiled. I imagine that if I'm ever allowed to look upon the face of God it won't be much different from the way I sometimes feel when I'm with a woman and things suddenly click, like flipping on a power switch. She leaned back against the fallen tree, lifting the folds of her dress, then ever so slightly opening her legs. If I took a step toward her she frowned and stopped. When I stepped back she lifted her dress again.

I remember the shocking sheen of her calves and thighs above the darkness of her work boots. Her trippy, dreamy smile. Then she stretched back on the tree and opened her legs wide, as if she were doing so for me, then flashed her eyes and spun off and then stopped and looked back at me and smiled so that I'd come after her, which I certainly did, with an intensity and hunger that surprised me. She pulled her dress up again as I reached out and touched her arm, as if it were a reward or consequence for my having caught her, then spun away again and paused until I pursued her again. It was as if she were teaching me the rules of a game she was spontaneously inventing.

We chased each other through the brush, through wide patches of skunk cabbage and deer fern, wordlessly, with me stretching out a hand and touching her arm or shoulder with my fingertips, with her lifting her dress ever higher. After several minutes of this after I'd reached out and caressed her shoulder with my hand she paused and leaned back against a smooth section of another fallen tree.

My mouth swallowed hers, and hers mine. Her bright, glassy eyes. Fingers furious at my belt and zipper as she opened her legs. Then she swung them closed to free one leg of her white underpants, which drifted down her tanned thigh and fell in a loop over the laces of her boot. The way she drew in air between her clenched teeth, then strung out a rising series of sound—"Ha, ha, ha, ha, ha"—that was more breath than voice. The smile again flashing on her face. All the while the ever-closer triangle of voices called out, "Em-i-leee?"

Then it was over, and her eyes fell from mine, and she turned away from me and ran off into the rainforest. After a few seconds all was silent.

Remembering all this I let out a long breath, then walked down to the end of the dock, where I squatted and looked out at the dark sea and spat three or four times and then sat down and for an hour or so listened to the incoming tide spend itself rhythmically against the pilings and the shoreline.

❧ ❧ ❧

I fully expected Roxanne and Josh to be back in each other's arms when I returned home later that night, but Roxanne was sitting alone at the kitchen table, sipping a steaming cup of tea and playing with the bowl of purple olive snail shells I keep on the kitchen windowsill.

"I don't know if you'll take this as good news or bad," she said as I unbuttoned my jacket and hung it on the hook by the back door, "but Josh and I have decided to travel separately from now on." Eyes cast down to the surface of the table, she grabbed a handful of shells and tumbled them into her open palm, then spilled them back into the clear glass bowl. The shells made a pleasant clacking sound as they fell against one another in her palm and then in the bowl.

"Is that what you wanted?" I asked.

"After what happened, sure." She tumbled the shells in and out of her hands again. "I just made a new pot of tea, if you'd like some."

"Thank you, no. And where's Josh now?"

"Out in the tent, sleeping, I suppose. He said he'd be gone by late morning. He and his friends plan to head back over the mountains to Port Alberni and then some beach—"

"Qualicum Beach," I said.

"—and then from there hitch their way up to Port Hardy." She blew on her cup of tea, then sipped it hesitantly. "He made sandwiches with your bread and cheese and cold cuts, and told me to tell you that he liberated a few cans of fruit and beans."

I opened the pantry door. Its shelves were nearly empty, save for a tin of anchovies and a can of red beans that had rolled back against the wall. I righted the can, label out.

"He also said he regrets chipping your counter when he opened his beer."

Chipping my counter? It was definitely more of a gouge, but I said nothing.

"We didn't play any of your albums, and I put away the one that was on, like you said. I hate it, too, when people leave records out and they get all scratched. So, tell me, do you want some of this tea?"

Her hands were shaking. "Sure." I smiled. "I'll have a cup with you." I took a handful of the shells and trickled them into her palms. "You've sure had a full evening."

"I've had worse."

I got a cup from the cupboard. "This thing between you and Josh—"

"Let's not talk about it anymore tonight, okay?" After I sat down at the table she took a fistful of shells and held them in the air and then dropped them into my open palms. "So," she said, "you think maybe I can crash here for a couple of nights?"

"Of course," I said. "I'm surprised you think you have to ask." We sat together for a while in silence as I drank some of the tea, and then I got up to wash the dishes and told her that she could have the bedroom, that I didn't want to assume anything or take anything for granted, that I'd be happy to sleep on the front room couch.

"Do you normally sleep on the couch?"

"Only when I get so drunk I mistake it for my bed."

"And are you drunk right now?"

I didn't think I had to answer that.

"Hey, I know we've just sort of met, but you should sleep in your own bed. In fact, if it's all right with you, I'd prefer that we both slept in your bed."

"Sure," I said, hoping to disguise my delight. I'd never slept in a bed with a woman before. This would be my first time. I rinsed the last plate. I always wash the utensils first, when the soapy water is at its hottest. Roxanne grabbed a towel and started to dry. "Sure, that would be fine. I only mentioned the couch because I wanted to give you the choice. You're my guest. I don't mean to assume anything, you know, or be presumptuous."

"I like it, that you're concerned with that."

"Good," I said.

"I like it that you're not making assumptions."

I nodded.

"I like being a guest."

"And I like having one."

"Then everything's copacetic." She drew out each of *copacetic's* four syllables, as if it were a word she'd just invented, then folded the dish towel neatly into thirds and draped it over the back of one of the kitchen chairs. Then she walked across the room toward me and put her arms around my neck. She'd lost the wariness I'd noticed when we'd met. "Hey," she said, "don't worry about being presumptuous with me. I'm a big girl. I'll let you know if there's something I want or don't want."

"Sure," I said, then added, "copacetic."

*❧ ❧ ❧*

Her major, art therapy, was going to transform education, she said. It was the coming thing, she said, a new revolution in how to reach troubled children, particularly those suffering from trauma or autism, both of which, she told me, scientists were now studying and have yet to understand. We were sitting one night at the kitchen table, drinking beer, and Roxanne was doodling in one of her big drawing pads. She said that giving challenged kids crayons and pencils and paper allowed them to tap into the various feelings of anxiety and sorrow and guilt and anger that often seethed unconsciously within them. Art therapy was healing and life-affirming, she said, particularly as it helped children work through traumatic experiences. As she talked she sketched a drawing of a mountain, then transformed it into a volcano, then gave it a jagged top from which issued steam and lava. Imagine if we could learn how to tap active volcanoes, she said, to relieve some of the pressures building inside them. Then she drew a tiny woman and man wearing oversized hard hats drilling a hole into the mountain's side so as to release some of its pent-up pressure before it blew.

When I asked her if scientists could really tap volcanoes by drilling holes into their sides she smiled and said it was a metaphor. Still, she said, pictures tell stories, often more extensively than words. For example you could tell a great deal about a child if you asked him or her to draw a house, she said. You could read their self-image as they sketched a figure beside it. Like rubbing a clear space in a cloudy window with the side of your hand and then putting one eye up to it, you'd be able to gaze right into the child's soul. She described pictures drawn by children who'd survived the trauma of war or imprisonment in refugee camps, or who were witnesses to unimaginable violence done to their families. Art was one way for these children to express some of their life experiences, some of their suffering and pain, and self-expression of any sort—be it drawing or music or song or role-playing or even telling a made-up story—could be a step toward their recovery.

I sketched a picture of a person's head about to explode, then a stick figure with a drill tapping the head's side to relieve some of its pressure. Roxanne said that what my drawing portrayed was actually an operation practiced by ancient peoples as well as many around the world, even to this day. Scientists have found ancient skulls with holes drilled in their foreheads, she told me. The holes were called trephines. Lobotomies aren't entirely unrelated to this practice, she said, though in a lobotomy the surgeon doesn't so much bash a crude hole through the forehead as slip up through the eye socket and disconnect the frontal lobes from the brain. Rather than knock a hole in the wall— she drew a wall and in its center a jagged gaping hole—they slide up behind the drywall and clip some of the internal wiring. She sketched a scissors and a pair of snipped wires. One moment you're connected to your emotional affect, she said, and then the next—she snapped her fingers—the light in the room housing your emotions goes out.

I didn't really understand the rest that she told me. She said scientists were working on drugs that would affect the brain's chemistry, sort of chemically rewire things, so to speak, so that brains could function more smoothly. These drugs would turn on or turn off various chemical taps inside the brain. She drew a pair of faucets, one dripping chemicals and the other tightly shut. At the other end of the spectrum, she said, there was R. D. Laing, a British psychiatrist who believed that schizophrenia was more often than not a healthy response to an insane and fragmented society, a society that prompts people to repress, deny, and split so much healthy self-awareness in order for them to appear normal that many people, under the stress of trying to act sane, behave as if they are insane. Their insanity, Laing claimed, was actually a rational response to the demands of an irrational world.

She drew a second volcano, then with her pencil allowed it to explode. So Laing bought an old settlement house in London and opened its doors to schizophrenics, who could go there and be tended to by its doctors and staff but not treated by surgery or mind-numbing drugs. I drew a bowl of nuts—peanuts in the shell—and smiled. Roxanne shook her head at this drawing and told me to stop being silly.

One woman with a past history of schizophrenia went to the house and regressed so far back into her past that for a while she had to be fed like an infant. She began drawing on the walls of her room with her feces, then with paints and oils, and now she was a fully functional adult, known all over England as a highly regarded painter. It was as if the woman were somehow able to crawl back inside the womb, Roxanne said, then come out a second time, once again clear, with a capacity to be whole. Through her paintings, Roxanne said, the woman was able to be reborn and tell her story.

As I listened to her, I drew various faces on my peanuts. Some screamed in horror or outright lunacy. Others lowered their eyes and wept.

"Don't make fun of me," Roxanne said. "This is going to be my life's work."

"I'm not making fun of you," I said. I couldn't tell her how serious I was, how at that moment something inside of me ached to work itself out.

※　※　※

It was sweet having another body in bed with me. Not sweet like sugar or candy or pink flowers and hearts but sweet like the ripest of berries, made full and dark by the rain and sun, the ones that have swelled to completion the moment you come up on them in clearings in the forest. You don't so much pick these berries as lift them with your fingers and allow them to fall into the palm of your hand. If you have to pull at the berry it's not ripe yet, not yet ready. When you put the berry into your mouth rather than mash it with your teeth you roll it around and caress it with your tongue, softly pressing it up against the roof of your palate. Then the berry's many chambers rupture and burst, and the fruit's juices seep into your mouth, and you make a sort of suction in your mouth and draw the pieces of berry and its juices down across your tongue and down your throat as you swallow. Yes, sleeping with Roxanne was every bit that sweet.

Sometimes at night when we'd go to bed I'd only pretend to fall asleep. I'd close my eyes and breathe softly and evenly until I could hear Roxanne breathing deeply and evenly, and then I'd open my eyes to the room's darkness and take a deep breath and just try to take everything in. I'd try to hold onto the moment, freeze time, or at least slow it down, savor it. I'm in bed with this lovely other human being, I'd tell myself, and she trusts me enough to fall asleep beside me. I'd edge closer to her so as to be able to feel some of her body's warmth. When I lived out in the parks of Vancouver, I never trusted anyone enough to fall asleep near them or beside them. No, I felt it was best if no one knew when or where I slept, if I always kept to myself and slept alone.

Sometimes I'd slip out of bed and put an album on the stereo, set the volume down low, so low the sound was nearly beneath hearing. I'd creep back into bed and lie with my hands crooked behind my head and smile as I listened to the music and Roxanne's breathing. She'd shift about, a big and restless girl, and sometimes mumble things as if somewhere deep inside the cobwebs of her dreams she were having a serious conversation. Sometimes she'd seem to argue. Once, in the middle of Thelonious Monk's *San Francisco Holiday*, as Monk was tinkling out the opening notes of "Rhythm-A-Ning" and outside the bedroom window it was softly raining, she laughed ever so sweetly and shook her head and said clear as day, "No, not now." Now I'm unable to listen to Monk's song without remembering her and smiling.

I never touched her during those times, never disturbed her, and often didn't even look at her as she slept in my bed just to the left. I simply tried my best to hold onto the fact that at that moment I wasn't alone. I tried to *realize* it, make it so real that all its sensations would be impressed indelibly on my mind, imprinted in my memory.

Of course I'd be tired from my day's work at the fish plant, and sooner than I'd wish I'd fall asleep. I'd never remember falling asleep, and on some mornings the same side of some album I'd selected the night before would be replaying over and over again on the turntable of the stereo. "Did we leave this on last night?" Roxanne would ask me. I'd shrug, say that I must have put it on just before we went to sleep. She'd tell me to be more careful, that leaving things on all night was a fire hazard, a waste of electricity. At the bathroom sink we'd stand, hip to hip, and together brush our teeth.

Can I admit now that these intimacies were deeper than the physical intimacies we shared? Of course back then I could never have even come close to saying such a thing. I knew back then what was manly and what was not, and it was extremely important to me to always be manly. It was important that I distanced myself from my feelings, that I hold them at least in reserve if not in contempt. Cherishing the moments we held each other in our arms was a womanly thing, I thought at the time, and my desire for and appreciation of it were signs of weakness. Men share no fear greater than to be called a mamma's boy. My job was to be like my father: a stern and uncaring rock, the stable, hard-working anchor of a family. That I'd failed so miserably at achieving this role was all too evident to me.

One night while I was listening to Stan Getz and Charlie Byrd ease their way through "Desafinado" Roxanne woke up with a start and turned toward me.

"What's wrong?" she said. "Is something wrong?"

"No," I answered. "Everything's fine. Nothing's wrong. Go back to sleep."

"Why is the stereo on?"

"Because I wanted to listen to some music. Go back to sleep. If it bothers you, I'll turn it off."

"No," she said, "I think I like it."

She settled back down as we listened to the music playing in the other room. That was the way life was supposed to be, I thought, effortless and unforced, the way Stan Getz coaxed sound from his horn. The way Lester Young and Ben Webster played. Ever so cool. So easy. As if the music they made was merely an extension of their natural breath. I rose from bed and walked into the front room.

"What are you doing?" Roxanne called.

"Putting on a different album." I looked for Ben Webster's *King of the Tenors* and walked back to bed as the needle dropped on the first cut, "Tenderly."

As I slipped beneath the sheet she turned toward me, arms open, and then we made love. And for some reason as we finished and as I held her and thought she was again falling asleep she began to cry, suddenly and so copiously that after rocking her in my arms for several moments I reached toward the nightstand for a box of tissues, which was empty, and so I rose from the bed to get another box from the hallway closet. I knew enough not to ask Roxanne why she was crying.

From the dark front room Ben Webster was playing the final cut on side one, "That's All," a ballad I'd heard done so often it sometimes seemed stale and tired. But Webster's version was so feathery and full of reed and breath, his notes so round and ripe, it seemed as if you could reach out and hold them in your hands as they hung around you, like bubbles, like living things, pulsing and breathing in the air. I had to stop and gather myself for a moment in the darkness of the hallway, locate myself in the spaces between the big, round notes, for fear of losing myself or bumping into them.

# 3

# Chicago 1962

I WAS A GOOFY KID, more a loner than someone embraced by class-mates and friends, a dreamer who spent as much time as possible outside my house in Chicago, walking up and down the alleys and softly shaded tree-lined streets. In temperament I bounced between moments of wormlike insecurity and unwarranted bravado. My favor-ite joke was about the ant lying on his back, fingers laced behind his head, floating on a leaf down the mighty Mississippi. As the ant gets an erection he shouts, "Raise the drawbridge, raise the drawbridge!"

Back then I amused myself in dozens of ways, but by far the most lucrative was for me to walk around my neighborhood, eyes down, scouring the ground for dropped coins and unbroken pop bottles. Each bottle was worth two cents in deposit. After I had a reason-able armful I headed for the grocery store on the corner of Glenwood and Bryn Mawr, where I cashed the bottles in. I'd peruse the comics in the circular rack near the counter, partial to *Iron Man*, *Sub-Mariner*, and *Human Torch*, whose flaming red body had the potential to destroy everything around him since he burst into flame whenever he was in contact with oxygen. I would have liked to have had that power. If there wasn't a comic I hadn't read I'd pick out a bar of candy instead, and then when I was in an alley somewhere and couldn't be seen I'd rip open its paper wrapper and devour my bounty in two or three bites, ripping off chunks savagely, as if I were a wolf. Sometimes I'd tilt back my head and howl like a wolf until the neighborhood dogs behind the chain-link fences in the yards behind the garages barked at me. Sometimes I'd imitate the neighborhood dogs. I could do all kinds of dogs: a dog barking at a trespasser, a dog begging for food, a dog being beaten with a stick.

I liked nearly every kind of candy—Chuckles, Snaps, Dots, Jujubes, Mary Janes, Sugar Babies—but the one I bought most often was Turkish Taffy. On the candy wrapper was a picture of several smiling men in fezzes pouring taffy batter into a huge vat. The candy was less a taffy and more of a nougat, nearly like the ones from Italy my nonna kept during holidays in the right top drawer of her china cabinet. The store kept its Turkish Taffy in a freezer along with popsicles and ice cream bars. After you paid for a frozen Turkish Taffy, you laid it on the flat of your hand and slammed it down hard on the store's counter so that the candy inside the wrapper shattered into dozens of pieces. Then you ate each piece one by one. A single Turkish Taffy could keep your jaws busy for an entire summer afternoon.

Wolves don't like people to see them eating, so I prowled the alleys whenever I had some taffy to consume. Even then, if someone appeared suddenly in his garage or back yard I immediately stopped chewing and acted as if nothing was in my mouth, transforming myself into the boy from Sparta walking around in denial of the fox beneath his cloak. I greatly envied the boy from Sparta and wanted to be as brave as he was. Nobody would ever call the boy from Sparta Crybaby Boy. "No, there's nothing inside my cloak," I'd say aloud when no one was around, while the imaginary fox beneath my T-shirt viciously clawed and bit me. "Pain? You must be mistaken. Pain and I are complete strangers." I'd stumble forward. "Oh, you think that what my eyes are doing is wincing?" I'd wince and wince like mad. "And you think the liquid welling in my eyes is tears? It's actually a nervous tic, see?" Then for the next half block or so I'd blink my eyes and twitch in imitation of a tic.

Sometimes I'd have a prizefight with myself. With my right hand I'd punch my left shoulder or the left side of my chest, as hard as I could, and then with my left hand I'd punch my right shoulder or the right side of my chest, and so on and so forth, until my arms ached and were too heavy to lift. Sometimes I'd do this while walking down the alleys looking for unbroken pop bottles. Sometimes I'd do it at home in front of the bathroom mirror when my father was at work and my mother was napping due to one of her migraines. I'd take off my shirt and punch myself until my skin purpled and bruised. I'd seen *The Great Escape* and would pretend I was one of the escaped Allied prisoners toughening himself up before trying to make his way undetected through Nazi Germany. My favorite movie in the entire world was *The Great Escape*. Everywhere I walked I whistled or hummed its theme.

Sometimes I'd be walking undetected through Nazi Germany and pretend a pretty French girl just ahead was struggling to open her father's heavy garage door. Maybe it was stuck or she couldn't lift the door by herself. The girl would be part of the French Resistance and after seeing me for who I was would do everything in her power to help me escape. But first I'd need to come to her aid. Standing in the alley beside some garage door, I'd make up my side of the conversation.

"Oh, here, *mademoiselle*, allow me to help you with that heavy door so that you don't stain or soil your pretty hands. . . . Why, of course it's no trouble, no trouble at all. . . . Think nothing of it, and you say you are new to the neighborhood and your family only just today moved in? . . . *Oui*, I attend the parish grammar school. . . . *Oui*, I am an altar boy, what the nuns in my native country refer to as a server, and in fact this coming Sunday I'm scheduled to serve the ten-fifteen High Mass. Perhaps I'll see you there? . . . Perhaps I'll be first paten and at your side when you receive Communion? . . . *Oui*, I would like very much to see you stick out your tongue."

And if she asked me my name I'd tell her it was Victor, Victor Sands, and my true family was from England though now we lived somewhere deep in the Sahara, in the exact spot where *Lawrence of Arabia*, my second favorite movie in the entire world, was filmed, and where my grandfather once owned a herd of camels and a lush farm on which he grew dates and figs.

"You wouldn't be so kind as to have, perhaps, a small cup of water?" I'd ask. "Growing up in the desert has given me an unquenchable thirst. . . . Yes, your conclusion is correct. I am an orphan. Feel no pity for me, please. I've never known my father, and as for my mother, well, it was the headaches, you see. We had to bury her one night in a shifting dune of sand. . . . Why did I leave the desert? Well, thieves came and stole my grandfather's herd of camels, then seized his farm, then hanged him, arms outstretched, in a tree until he grew old and the birds of prey descended upon him and picked his bones clean. . . . That family living in the brick two-flat on Glenwood Avenue? You think I belong to *them*? Oh, no, they only pretend I'm their son, and I pretend to go along with their foolish game. . . . Yes, yes, you're right, I consent to live with them merely as an amusement. They are an amusement to me. Like an afternoon at Riverview, where I laugh all my troubles away. . . . *Oui, oui,* you heard correctly, those two old peasants who shout down to me from their windows do refer to as me Vincenzo Antonio Sansone, but that's only because they're poor and uneducated and cannot speak proper English, as do you and I. . . . Yes, they live upstairs from my pretend family, up in the second-floor flat. The older man used to be a fisherman in Monterey, California. Or so he claims. The marbles in his head have come loose, you see. Whenever he tilts his head you can hear them rolling. Sometimes he talks in a language known only to fishermen. He claims to have taken his living from the wide blue African sea, as did his father and his father's father, and all the generations before them. That was before the evil Nazis forced him to move to the desert. The old woman he shares a bed with used to sharpen the hooks on his lures. Tiny angels live on her shoulders. Yes, you can actually see them. Each is exactly two inches tall. At night when she sleeps she dreams of eating meat. As for the brute who pretends to be my father, well, he has nothing to do with me. He's only a smelly fishmonger whose boat crashed into pieces one day upon the rocky coast."

Then I'd bolt and run away as quickly as I could, pretending there was a bomb inside the garage that was about to blow up, and if I didn't run fast enough I'd be blown up, too. Sometimes it would be a hydrogen bomb placed there by the Russians, who, along with the Chinese communists, wanted to rule the world. The nuns in school taught us all about the Russian and Chinese communists. The bomb would blow up all of Chicago if I didn't run fast enough. The fate of the entire city would be up to me and only me. At the same moment in Wrigley Field the immortal Cubs shortstop, Ernie Banks, would dig in at the plate, bottom of the ninth, bases full, and swing on a full-count fastball.

"That's pretty well hit," I'd say as I ran, imitating the way Jack Brickhouse, the announcer on WGN, would describe it. "Back she goes. Back. Back. Hey, hey! A home run!"

But my efforts would be all for naught since my legs would never run fast enough. I would never be quick enough to save Chicago. The bomb inside the garage would always explode, and though the ball would bounce into the centerfield bleachers Ernie Banks would never make it all the way around the bases. The Cubs would never win. The escaped Allied soldiers would always be tricked into answering in English and be returned to the POW camp inside Nazi Germany. The Nazis would always take away my grandfather's house and boat and banish him to the desert, where he would mutter in a strange language while marbles rolled around inside his head. And then the bomb would explode and the entire city of Chicago and, most importantly, my family and our red brick two-flat on Glenwood Avenue would buckle and melt into nothingness inside a hotter-than-the-sun mushroom cloud.

᪥ ᪥ ᪥

Ronny Cannon's garage was a good six blocks north of my house, past the grocery store on Bryn Mawr, all the way up on Hollywood Avenue, and always open, it seemed, at least every time my alleyway wanderings took me past it. For a few years when he was my age, Ronny worked for my father at the newsstands my father operated each weekday after he finished work at the fish market. The newsstands were downtown on Adams Street, on four corners flanking the north entranceways to Chicago's Union Station, where each day thousands of office workers caught the late afternoon trains back to the suburbs where they lived.

Ever since the fifth grade I, too, worked at the newsstands after school, catching the El at Bryn Mawr and riding it downtown, then taking a bus west until I reached the bridge spanning the Chicago River. In the teeth of the wind that blew steadily off the river, on Canal Street directly across from Florsheim Shoes and down a short block from Café Bohemia, I worked each weekday from three-thirty to six, furiously making change as I sold the latest editions of the *Chicago Daily News* and the *Chicago American* to the dark-suited men and perfumed women who raced past me in furious lines on their way to their trains.

At first the men and women only trickled past, and I'd be able to look into their faces and nod as I accepted their coins and occasional dollar bills and made their change. I'd keep stacks of three pennies for change for a dime; pyramids of a nickel, three pennies, and a dime for change for a quarter. As the afternoon stretched toward evening, the *Daily News* truck would squeal to a stop behind my stand and I'd grab bundles of the latest editions from the curb, replacing the Red Flash with the Red Star and then the Two Star, Three Star, up to the final edition, the Five-Star Red Streak.

"Final markets?" the men in their business suits would ask me. "Final markets," I'd respond. "Red Streak! Final markets!" Quickly I'd count the newspapers in each bundle as I broke it open, to learn how severely the driver had shorted us. Each bundle was bound with wire, and it was all too easy for the *Daily News* driver to have his assistant, who rode in the open back of the truck, slip a paper or two out of the middle of each bundle. One paper here, two papers there, five days a week, month after month: before long it was real money. It was my job every day to count how much we were being cheated, then report the numbers to my father, who'd take the issue up with the driver later that night when we gathered inside the station to go over the day's totals. It was a rare windless day in the Windy City when the bundles tossed at our stands were true.

It was my job to make sure the newsstand in front of Florsheim Shoes had the latest editions. It was my job to keep up with the rushes, which swelled at my stand in waves. The heaviest rushes began at a quarter to five and slowed down only at five-thirty. During those forty-five minutes, thousands of commuters rushing to make their trains hurried past my stand. It was my job to collect their money, hand them a newspaper, make and give them the right change. During the rushes it was all I could do to keep up. The coins fairly flew at me. All I could see were newspapers, coins, and open hands.

The stand on the corner of Canal and Adams had been Ronny's back when he worked for my father. Each evening as we drove the Kennedy Expressway and then Ashland Avenue home, my father never failed to let me know that of all the boys who ever worked for him Ronny was far and away the best. Ronny was one of those teen idol lookalikes. He had blazing dark eyes, a strong chin, black hair combed back perfectly in a pompadour, a frame nearly as skinny as the young Frank Sinatra but with hammers for fists and biceps like cue balls. Later, after I began listening to jazz, I'd think of Ronny as a darker version of Chet Baker. A Lucky Strike usually dangled from Ronny's lips as he bent over whatever car sat parked, hood yawning, awaiting his repair in his spacious three-car garage on Hollywood Avenue. The smoke drifting toward his eyes made him squint, made him seem every bit as tough and aloof as James Dean.

Of course my memory romanticizes him, but without doubt Ronny was the coolest guy in the neighborhood. He wore sleeveless white T-shirts that today the kids call wife-beaters but back then were called dago-Ts, along with baggy, dark blue work pants from Sears

Roebuck, the kind factory workers in our neighborhood wore, with deep side pockets and full one-inch cuffs, and durable creases ironed into the ridiculously wide legs. The guys called the pants baggies so as to differentiate them from the skin-tight, front-pocketed, cuffless dress pants we called stovepipes. Baggies were so loose that whenever a guy was fishing around in his pocket for keys or some change he'd say, "I got so much ball room in here I could hold a fucking wedding reception," and even though everyone had heard the line a thousand times all the other guys around would laugh and laugh.

I never knew if Ronny was Italian—whether Cannon was a shortened version of some longer name—but Ronny always acted as if he were a *paisan* and smiled broadly whenever one of the guys called him Cannone, which in Italian meant cannon, or something goofy and playful like Cannelloni. That set Ronny up for his favorite joke. "Cannelloni this," he'd say, grabbing his crotch or his forearm. Sometimes he'd say, "Cannelloni nothing," along with a crotch tap, then add, "Hey, we're talking sweet cannoli here, and don't you know the girls just line up every night outside my window begging for a taste."

My hanging around his garage began the summer before eighth grade, one afternoon while I was working the alleys, three or four pop bottles tucked under my arms. "Hey, you, alley picker!" Ronny called from inside his garage. With him were a couple of guys I didn't yet know. As I neared, Ronny's face softened with recognition. "Hey, ain't you Alfonso Sansone's kid? Little Vincie, right?"

"Vince," I snapped. Since Vincenzo was my grandfather's name, around the house I was sometimes called Little Vincie, a nickname I deeply despised.

"Sure." Ronny nodded. "Vince it is then. So, how goes the friendly fishmonger?"

He meant my father. "He's all right."

"His old man sells fish down on Fulton," Ronny told his friends. "Man oh man, you should meet the guy on a summer afternoon. Phoooee. Smelliest fucking job in the world."

"It puts food on the table," I said quickly. Even though I was three or four years younger than these guys, I knew enough to respond to a put-down with a come-back. I knew enough to stand up to a cut. If you didn't it was like handing people a permission slip to walk all over you. If you showed people any weakness they were sure to take advantage of it later. Nonetheless I was wary, ready to drop my pop bottle stash and run. "It's honest work," I added. "He feeds nine mouths. Eleven, counting my grandparents."

"Sure, Vince." Ronny laughed and raised his hands. "Don't start foaming at the mouth or pretty soon we'll have to call a vet for your next rabies shot. I didn't mean you no offense. I was only stating a fact."

I nodded.

"Me and your old man, you know, we go way back, and we got along real good, even though sometimes he can be a real son of a bitch." Ronny grinned and gave me a wink. "He even made me his lieutenant. He ever tell you that?"

I nodded. Whenever my father was in a playful mood, which with me was rarer than Leap Year, he called his oldest and most responsible worker his lieutenant.

"But, hey," Ronny continued, "you yourself got to admit, the smell of your old man when he's fresh off work, it could make a dead man roll over in his grave."

"You hear what the blind man said as he walked past the fish market?" one of the other guys said. Later I'd learn that the guys called him Chick. He was wiry and muscular, with small eyes that bounced everywhere and blondish eyebrows and hair. He raised his head in the air and fluttered his eyelids and made like he was tapping a cane. "'Hello, girls!'"

I didn't understand and later that night and all through the week thought long and hard about it and still didn't understand it.

"Hey," Ronny said when the guys were done laughing, "somebody hand this kid a paper bag. And give him those empties we got over here." He gestured magnanimously toward a pile of empty pop bottles in the corner. Within minutes I stood between a pair of shopping bags overflowing with perfectly returnable bottles.

"Get a load of Vince here with his matching set of Polish suitcases," one of the guys called out, and everybody burst out laughing again. That spurred among them a run of jokes.

The reason why there were so few Polish suicides in Chicago was because it was impossible to kill yourself jumping out of a basement window. A rocking chair set out in a gangway was Polish air conditioning. The three most difficult years in the average Polish kid's life were second grade.

"I know one about an Italian," Lenny, the guy who handed me the shopping bags, said. He was slight and fair, with rimless eyeglasses and a face sprinkled with acne. "Did you hear about the dago girl who was so stupid she took her Smith-Corona to the doctor? She told him it skipped a period."

After they laughed, the quietest guy of all shook his head and said, "Hey, that ain't very funny." Then all the others loudly sang, "Daa dum-da-dum, daa dum-da-dum," the opening notes of "Here Comes the Bride."

"And do not ask for whom the funeral bell tolls," Chick said, "it tolls for thee."

Then they tossed me a couple of singles and a list of things—candy bars, packs of cigarettes, ice-cold bottles of pop—to get for them from the corner store on Bryn Mawr after I turned in my pop bottle stash, and told me I could keep the change. Ronny wanted a pack of Lucky Strikes, Chick and this big, hulking guy they called Dandoo wanted Chesterfields, and for Lenny I was to get the only brand he ever smoked, OPs.

"Let me hear it out of your mouth what you're supposed to get," said Dandoo. He towered over me, big as a grizzly bear.

"Three packs of cigarettes. Luckies, Chesterfields, and a pack of OPs."

"You got that right," big Dandoo told me with a wink.

"Stop messing with Junior's brain," Ronny said as I picked up my shopping bags and started to leave. He then explained that OPs stood for Other People's, get it?, and all the guys, even the sad one about to be married, who later described how the pregnant girl's father actually brought out a length of string to measure his ankle for a ball and chain, laughed and laughed. In its place I was to get a pack of Parliaments.

"Don't run out on us now, kid," Chick warned me with a menacing glare. "We know where you live. Fuck us over and we'll hunt you down and kill you." He pointed at me from the garage's far corner, where a speed bag hung from the rafters. On the floor beside him were several gasoline canisters and orange crates standing up on their sides along with some cartons of motor oil on which rested various tools, engine parts, fan belts, and open boxes of spark plugs. Behind Chick's head on the wall beside a ledge that held a radio was a calendar featuring a blonde with a blank expression tumbling out of her bikini top while straddling a big blue rubber beach ball painted over with green continents so as to represent the world.

"He won't run out on us," Ronny said, squinting from behind the smoke of his cigarette. "He's no thief. I'll vouch for him. The kid's old man made me his fucking lieutenant. Their whole family is as square as the day is long."

It was all I could do to unglue my eyes from that bikini top. *Bappada bappada*, went the speed bag, in response to Chick's fists. Punching the bag, Chick's forearms swelled as big as Popeye's. *Bappada bappada bappada. Bappada bappada bap.* The bag blurred in a marvelous swirl of sound and motion, exactly like in the cartoons.

〜 〜 〜

Since I returned promptly with their cigarettes and sodas and candy and went to the store whenever they wanted me to and kept my yap shut and didn't ever think about shorting them on their change, the guys tolerated my hanging around the garage, even when they didn't have any errands for me to run. They normally gathered in the garage each day at noon, grunting a few words to one another about what they'd done the night before. There were long stretches when no one said anything, or one guy would ask another if he had a match and the other guy would answer, "Not since Superman died" or "Sure, your face and my ass." Then someone would start off on some unrelated topic, usually involving the right way to do something, such as opening a pack of cigarettes (you tear open the foil at the bottom so that your unclean fingers don't touch the end you put in your mouth) or the efficacy of lighters versus matches (neither was ideal since lighters frequently leaked fluid through your pants pocket onto your leg, whereas smokers who relied on matches often ran out and were forced to bum lights). At other times the guys would recite, apropos of nothing, lines from their favorite movies ("I am Spartacus!" "No, I am Spartacus!" "No, *I* am Spartacus!"). Their repetition of lines would sometimes go off and on for hours.

Each day I left the garage promptly by a quarter to three to catch the El downtown to work at the newsstands. Over time I laid claim to an orange crate nobody seemed to be using and dragged it some distance away from the other crates, where I'd sit silently, ready, at their bidding, should ever they need me. Eventually the guys came to refer to the crate as mine. "Hey, leave that one be, that's Vince's seat," they'd tell a new guy who'd try to kick it over nearer the others. And over time they taught me how to scrape and gap spark plugs, soak out carburetors, change a car's motor oil and replace its oil filter tightly enough not to leak, but not so tight as to strip its threads. Over time they became my older brothers. My teachers. They were my masters, and I served happily as their eager apprentice.

ॐ ॐ ॐ

One day I was under a car draining its oil into a paint roller pan when a fantastic pair of legs in black pedal-pushers and flats meandered by, only to be immediately surrounded by the baggy blue legs of Ronny,

Chick, Lenny, and Big Dandoo. Those legs were my first glimpse of Lucy Sheehan.

Lucy Sheehan didn't come around the garage regularly, but she did so often enough not to be a stranger and was always, always a pleasant surprise. She was Ronny's main girlfriend, *numero uno*, he'd say, in his little black book. She was every bit as shapely as the blonde on the garage wall calendar, if not even more so, with wide green eyes and curly hair the color of old pennies and more freckles on her face and neck than anyone I'd ever seen, so many that after a while you'd forget that she had freckles and think that was just the way she looked. She was a couple of years younger than Ronny and worked up on Clark Street near Peterson at a pet store that also featured as a dog grooming parlor, where behind a big glass window she gave dogs shampoos and flea baths, and on a high, stainless steel table she cut and shaped the dogs' coats. I'd seen her a couple of times working away in a white lab coat since the store was where I bought my tropical fish food. Lucy always seemed to enjoy her work, even when it involved clipping the nails of snarling German shepherds. She had a big, sweet smile for everyone. She kept a roll of masking tape in her purse and, at the garage, frequently peeled a loop of the tape off the roll and pressed it methodically against her sweater and slacks to remove the dog hair that clung to her, like stray metal filings on a magnet. All of the guys envied the tape, saying when she wasn't there that they'd give just about anything to press themselves all over her sweater and slacks, too.

She came by late one Saturday afternoon while Ronny and the other guys were busy with a job they'd promised would be done by that evening. I was killing time, sitting on my crate just outside the open garage doors, watching a cloud of flies buzz around a nearby garbage can. The flies would settle down inside the can for a while and then for some reason known only to flies leap up and scatter, only to buzz over the can in a swarm and then settle down again inside where I couldn't see them, and then after a minute or so repeat the whole process. The guys ignored Lucy until a tune she really liked came on the radio and she turned it up and started doing jitterbug steps. She tried dancing with Ronny, who shook his head with disapproval and held up his greasy hands, and so for a moment or two she danced alone. Then all of a sudden she twirled toward me and with a smile grabbed my hand.

At first Ronny and the other guys ignored us, but later they paused and gave us a laugh and a good razzing. Though I did my best to imitate her steps, I had no idea what I was supposed to do. I felt clumsy and exposed and nearly bolted and ran off. Then another song started and she said, "Here, like this. Watch my feet. One, two, back step," and after a while, by the middle of the second song, I began just a bit to hold my own.

"She's teaching the kid how to dance," Ronny announced, unable to resist pointing out the obvious.

Lenny nodded. "He's got two left feet like me."

"Nah," Chick said, "only a clubfooted epileptic could be *that* spastic."

"Slow, slow, quick quick," Lucy instructed. "Start with your left. That's it. Left, right, back right. Left, right, back right. Good, good, that's it. Keep your steps quick and small. Dance with the beat. One, two, back step. One, two, back step. Hey, that's it, Vince. That's it. It's a body thing. Don't think. It's all in the body. That's it. Hey, you got it now."

That night, as I lay in my bed beneath the stairs, I could see Lucy's face and feel her warm hand in mine. I could picture her sweet smile and the way her breasts pressed against the soft fabric of her blouse as she danced, as I raised my arm to give her a spin, then pulled her back and closer to me. "Excellent," she'd tell me as I twirled her, then pulled her toward me and took both her hands and twirled her again. "That's it. You're the boy. That's it. Take charge. Be the boy. Be in command."

Then in my imagination the others disappeared and the buttons on Lucy's blouse melted and she was straddling the green world, leaning toward me, smiling, nearly falling out of her top, leaning further toward me, one two one two, slow slow quick quick, that's it, be the boy, take charge, good good, that's it—

⚮ ⚮ ⚮

One day I went over to the garage early, when only Ronny was around. He was sitting behind the wheel of an old Packard, staring out its windshield, blowing smoke ring after smoke ring that collided with the windshield and then drifted out through the open driver's door. On the wall behind the Packard hung dozens of evenly spaced hubcaps, their emblems aligned, shiny like sightless eyeballs even in the dim late-morning light. I sat down on my orange crate and looked out at the garage doors, resuming my study of the habits of garbage-can flies.

"Hey, Vince," Ronny called. "Let me look at your mug."

"What?" I said, shrugging and turning away.

"How'd you get that welt over your eye?"

"What welt?"

"What do you mean, what welt? The welt on your ugly face. Look at me."

"Oh, that." I turned.

"Jesus Christ Almighty," he said.

"I walked into a door."

He got out of the car, flicked his cigarette butt to the floor, and ground it out slowly with the toe of his shoe. "So you walked into a door?"

I nodded.

"He knocks you around pretty hard sometimes, huh?"

I looked away and said nothing. Part of me wanted to talk, only I didn't have any idea what I might say. Another part of me wanted to run away.

Ronny could be just another person sometimes when you were alone with him. When the other guys were around, nothing seemed to matter—everything was cool, no big deal, no sweat off his balls—but when the guys weren't there he could be a regular human being.

"You know, my old man used to knock me around," Ronny said after a while. "Yeah, when I was younger, you know, he knocked me around plenty. Never needed a reason. It was just something he'd do."

I wanted to say, "Oh yeah?" and nod, but I thought about the boy from Sparta and forced myself to remain motionless and stare at the ground.

"Then I got bigger, see, and in the meantime the only thing he got was older. You gotta remember that. Sooner or later even the meanest son of a bitch gets old." He smiled and winked. "You see that two-by-four over there?" In the corner by the calendar and the gasoline canisters and speed bag was a four-foot length of two-by-four. "You see it? One night when he came for me, all pissed off over something I did or didn't do, who knows the reason, I smacked him right in the fucking gut with it. I said, 'You ever hit me again and I'll break open your fucking head.' That was the last time he laid a finger on me."

I still didn't move, though for some reason a couple of stupid crocodile tears slid their way down my Crybaby Boy cheeks.

"Yeah," Ronny continued, "I heard that in China a kid becomes a man on the day he's strong enough to pick up his father and throw him down the village well." He laughed. "Hey, that'd sure be one place where I wouldn't want to drink the water."

Several more tears joined the first pair, forming tiny puddles on the ground. If I sat there long enough, I thought, I'd create a second set of Great Lakes.

"You know," Ronny said, "I think it's like with a dog. Unless you raised it from the time it was a puppy, you never know what happened during the time you weren't there. You give a pup a halfway decent life, three squares a day, a warm place to sleep, maybe a tennis ball or old shoe to play with, and it turns out pretty decent and friendly. But if a pup gets kicked around most of the time, it learns to snap and bite. You follow what I'm saying here? I mean, it's no excuse for the old ones, but like the saying goes, you know, we haven't walked a mile in their shoes."

I remained silent and still, even though a huge gob of snot was drooling its way out of my nose and threatening to obliterate Lake Erie.

"But hey, what do I know?" Ronny said. "Maybe that's all just a crock of shit. Maybe there's no excuse on earth for knocking a little kid around, let alone your own kid, your own flesh and blood." He was lighting a cigarette. I could hear the clank of his lighter opening and then closing, him taking a deep drag, then letting out a long breath. "Hey, just so you know, you're welcome to come over here any time. I mean here, to the garage. I'll give you your own key. It can be, like, you know, like in *The Hunchback of Notre Dame*, sort of like your own little sanctuary. Sound okay to you, Quasimodo?"

I nodded and wiped my nose. Ronny walked back to the speed bag and slipped something off the shelf, then returned to me and pushed the key to his garage into my hand.

"And what I told you before about the two-by-four," he said, patting my shoulder, as I had to force myself to stop from leaning into him for a hug, "just between you and me, that was all bullshit. Though in my mind I've murdered him a million times."

🐋 🐋 🐋

"She's getting sweet on you," Ronny told me the next afternoon, with a face so serious that for a moment I almost believed him. "Let me tell you, Vince-a-rooni, my little freckled-faced sweetie pie's gotten all soft and gooey and sweet on you."

Then Lenny, standing by one of the back windows, pushed his eyeglasses back up the bridge of his nose and gave the air a pair of kisses, and I understood it was all a joke.

"I'm just a gigolo," Chick sang, in imitation of Louis Prima. Chick ran his fingers through his slicked-back hair, then in the center of the garage opened his arms wide.

"You'd better be real careful from now on," Dandoo cautioned Ronny, wrapping one of his big arms around Ronny's shoulders, "or your *numero uno* will be telling you *sayonara*."

"Gigolo, gigolo, gigolo," Chick sang.

I laughed along with them, not knowing what else I could do, but for some reason they wouldn't let it drop.

"How could you betray me like this?" Ronny asked, his face a sudden study in pain.

"Yeah," Lenny said, "after Ronny took you in off the streets like he did. After all the pop bottles he gave ya. He loved you like you was his own little brother. He took you in like an orphan out of the cold. Taught you everything a guy needs to know."

"*Et tu*, Brutus," said Dandoo, his arm stabbing forward to Ronny's guts.

"Next time try the back," Chick said. "You *et tu* a guy in the back."

"Cradle robber," Lenny said.

"Has life surrounded me with morons?" Chick said. "That's backward, too. If anyone's a cradle robber, it's good old L.S.M.F.T."

"Maybe," Ronny started, "I should get her one of those, what do you call it, you know what I mean, those things the knights of old used to put on a girl's snatch."

"Chastity belts," Chick said.

"Yeah, I should get her a chastity belt. You know, the kind you lock with a key, and inside there's this little spring-loaded guillotine."

"Yeah," Chick said, "they did that once to Lady Guinevere back when King Arthur went off to fight some ancient battle. When the king got back, he lined up all the knights of his Round Table and had them drop their pants. Dickless, dickless, dickless, dickless, each and every one of them dickless, until he came to this one knight, Leroy—"

"They didn't have any knights back then named Leroy," Lenny said.

"Who's telling this?" Chick said. "Are you telling this? Are you fucking telling this? Are you suddenly an expert on ancient history?" He gave Lenny a long stare. "So anyway Leroy's cock was just fine, smooth as a baby's cheek, not a scratch on it, and so King Arthur slaps both of Leroy's shoulders and says, 'Finally, at long last, a loyal subject,' and Leroy answers, 'Rrrank rru.'"

Ronny smiled. "I don't know if old Vince here has graduated to that yet."

"Clam on the half shell," Dandoo said, smacking his lips. "Mmmm mmm! I can hear the dinner bell ringing! Pass the Tabasco sauce, the wedge of lemon."

"The kind I get," Ronny said, "comes with the juice already splashed on."

"You hear about the girl who wore only a pair of black gloves and two black shoes to the costume party?" Chick said. He spread his feet and threw up both hands. "She went as the five of spades."

"What's L.S.M.F.T.?" I asked. I knew L.S.M.F.T. was the slogan on the bottom of packs of Luckies—the abbreviation for *Lucky Strike Means Fine Tobacco*—but here, in the context of Ronny's garage, it clearly meant something else.

"Lucy Sheehan Means—" Lenny began.

"I'm positive old Vince here hasn't graduated to *that*," Ronny said, and Lenny didn't finish what he was saying as all the guys laughed. I kept my eyes on them, wary. Though I understood it was all a joke, some part of me feared it wasn't and that I'd done something wrong. Back then I spent a lot of time thinking I'd done something wrong. I spent nearly every moment of my life expecting that something bad was about to happen to me. But then big Dandoo was suddenly next to me slapping my shoulders and back and laughing, and the guys were lighting cigarettes and Ronny offered one to me, too, and Chick kicked my orange crate closer to the circle where they kept theirs, and

Lenny lit my cigarette with his Zippo, and even though the fag made me so dizzy I wanted to lean down and puke that was one of the best moments of my life in Chicago.

∞ ∞ ∞

"We've got to get this kid in fighting shape," Ronny announced to the others the next day, "you know, so he can get in the ring, spar a little, work his way toward going the full twelve rounds." He was leaning against the car they were working on, a rusting blue-and-white Chevy sedan, and then straightened and threw a flurry of jabs and uppercuts into the air.

"Give me five minutes," Lenny said with a cackle, "and I'll call Doreen."

"I don't mean that way," Ronny said. "I mean mentally. I mean we got to fine tune the kid's attitude. At least three quarters of it's attitude, you know what I'm saying here?"

"Yeah," Lenny said, "and believe you me, the other half's pure balls."

Chick wagged his head at the garage rafters, then opened his arms and shouted into the air above, "Zeus! You've surrounded me with idiots!"

"Besides," Dandoo said, "I heard Doreen moved up to Milwaukee."

"Waukegan," Chick said. "I got the address, and so does the state Board of Health. Bet on it, northeastern Illinois will never be the same."

Thus began the lessons these four young men gave me. Quickly it became a contest of sorts, with each guy trying to outdo the others by giving me his best warped advice about how to meet and impress girls.

I learned that the main rule of thumb was to be cool and bide your time, never sweat or rush or panic, go slow and steady and sure. "It's just like stealing from a store," Dandoo claimed. "It's all in the attitude. If you act guilty, expect to get fingered. When you pick something up and put it in your pocket, make like it's already yours."

"Act like you belong there and you've been there before," Ronny said. "And once you get it there in front of you, own it. Take a deep breath and enjoy it. Every second you find yourself in the land of milk and honey, remember to take your sweet time. Don't become one of these guys with Roman hands and Russian fingers."

I nodded, pleased that I understood the pair of puns.

"No girl likes a jackrabbit," Chick said. "You know, in the hole one second, out of the hole the next."

"Fucking A," Lenny said. "Truer words were never spoken."

They told me that in order for anything to develop between a guy and a girl there had to be a special tension. This line of tension was like the monofilament used on fishing rods or the rope held by opponents in a tug-of-war. The thing to keep in mind was that it should never be allowed to go slack.

Your first goal was to get the girl to pick up the rope, and your second goal was to pull it taut. If you see a girl you like and you want to go up to her and talk to her, make eye contact and walk past and then away from her instead. Approach her before she's checked you out and you risk scaring her off. Approach her with a lame line and you'll remind her of every milk-breathed mamma's boy who's tried to move in on her at every boring parish sock-hop she's gone to. So you've got to act as if talking to her is, like, no big deal. Acting eager in front of a girl is never attractive, the guys said. Eager is for beavers and Boy Scouts. In fact, nearly every single virtue the Boy Scouts uphold—being trustworthy, loyal, helpful, friendly, courteous, kind, obedient, cheerful, thrifty, brave, clean, and reverent—works against a guy's getting a girl's attention.

Being trustworthy, loyal, and helpful is safe and boring, for banks, credit unions, and department stores. Whether they'll admit it or not, the guys said, most girls like things to be a little bit dangerous, a little bit out there in the land of uncertainty and distrust. Distrust is exciting and keeps her alert, on her toes. It lends the moment possibility. It's like putting a jar of hot red pepper flakes on the table, the guys said. You don't have to sprinkle any on the pizza, but the meal's automatically more spicy simply because the jar is there. As for loyal, that's why God made dogs. If a girl needs helpful, hand her the Yellow Pages.

The last thing a girl wants is a boyfriend who's friendly, the guys told me. Being friends with a girl means that the two of you can't imagine ever making it together. It means she doesn't feel that line of special tension. Being friendly, as well as courteous and kind, is for tea drinkers or bag boys in their aprons and bow ties at Jewel or the A&P. A girl wants a guy who has an edge, who's strong and unpredictable, a bit crude, even occasionally snarly, somebody capable of acting out of righteous anger in the right time and place. In order for that line of tension to stay taut, a guy has to act like a guy, not like one of her girlfriends. Still, the guys told me, that doesn't mean you should go around all Neanderthal, kicking kittens or knocking over baby strollers, or that you shouldn't open doors for her or touch the small of her back now and then or walk beside her on the outside of the street. Those were decent things to do, the guys said. Just don't be a fucking waiter about it. Ditto for obedient, cheerful, and thrifty.

The only Boy Scout traits girls warm to, the guys said, are being brave and clean. A stand-up guy rises to any danger when he's out with a girl, and that includes muggers and rapists and thugs with knives and guns. You take the bullet or get your belly slashed before the rotten son of a bitch touches the least hair on her head, and you let the asshole with the gun or knife know it, big time, in no uncertain terms, *abso-fucking-lutely* loud and fucking clear. Without question the single most important thing a girl needs to feel when she's out with a guy is that he'll protect her with his life in the face of any and all danger.

And in the event things come up, so to speak, as they often do, and the girl decides to take matters into her own hands, or elsewhere, as you so desperately hope and pray she does, a guy has to keep his dipstick clean—not so clean it smells of soap or perfume, mind you—but definitely clean enough not to be rank. If he's uncut, he's got to pull back that turtleneck and scrub out the Gorgonzola. The same goes for armpits, though for some girls, Chick claimed, there are few aromas more enticing than a little good clean manly sweat.

As for reverence, the guys said, well, ask ten girls on the street if they'd rather go out with a saint or a sinner. If the girls are truly honest, eight out of ten will choose the sinner. Though they'll never admit it, the guys said, girls absolutely love the bad boys.

When I looked up from my orange crate, thoroughly confused, the guys explained that in the world of romance this falling for another person was literal. A girl *falls* for a guy in every sense of the term because everyone knows she's better than him, literally *above* him, to begin with. When she falls for him it means she agrees to come down to his base level. Just like angels and men.

That's the whole secret, Chick explained. From the lowest whore working her corner on Division Street all the way up to the Queen Mother of England, women know they're superior to men. But what they fail to understand, Ronny added, is that most guys really don't give a fuck. Bingo, Chick said, because when the rubber hits the road the only thing that matters is that it's all pink. Hey, are we giving Junior here a good education or what? He should be paying us tuition. That's over the fence, Lenny said, and out onto Waveland Avenue. I hope we're not casting pearls before swine here, big Dandoo said, because whether you know it or not we've just handed you the Holy Grail. Tilt at windmills no longer.

# 4

# Chicago 1965

EVER SINCE MARIE AND I KISSED in the front hallway of her six-flat, I felt peculiar whenever I went into Santangelo's Quality Meats on Clark Street. Not that I was sent there often, since, under my mother's always busy hand, the broiled remains of some unsold portion of fish normally lay in semi-charred splendor on a platter on our table, accompanied by a pan of boiled potatoes the color of the February sky and a bowl of some heated vegetable set free of its tin can. But my grandmother had, in my father's words, a "sweet tooth" for meat. My nonna would snare me with a crooked finger whenever her carnivorous urges grew too strong to resist and instruct me to fetch her pocketbook, inside of which her gnarled fingers would roam until she drew out her coin purse, a dark rubber oval that resembled a flattened egg. She'd pinch the egg's slit and pick out a coin or two. "Get some nice meat," was her basic instruction.

After all, we were living in America, and while it might not necessarily be the land of milk and honey it certainly was the land of meat. And Chicago, don't forget, was hog butcher for the world. To listen to my grandmother describe the old country, the peasant immigrants from southern Italy were fortunate if they ate meat twice a year, on Christmas and Easter Sunday. Nonna's Sicilian family survived mainly on lentils and fava beans, onions and escarole, wild fennel and chicory and dandelion leaves. And since they lived along the sea, on fish.

In the history of my family, fish cannot go unmentioned, particularly the humble sardine, which my grandparents and their ancestors grilled, fried, salted, baked, and mashed into a clot that they spooned into their mouths or spread on a crust of bread whenever they were fortunate enough to have a crust of bread.

As a result, to my father's parents, meat was the rarest delicacy. Bring my grandmother a piece of red meat and she'd do the most miraculous things to it, slicing it this way and that way on a special cutting board she kept wrapped in a white cloth alongside the icebox, a board she used only for meat, working with a knife that she forbade me to touch and which she sharpened routinely. When her artistry was complete, she'd pound the fillets so flat they were nearly as transparent as windowpanes. She'd hold each piece up to the light and smile at me and say, "Eh?" She was nowhere near five feet tall and every article of clothing that she wore was black, from her stockings and shoes to her dresses and shawls, down to the roots of her hair, even though her husband was still alive (that is, if life can be defined by continued breathing). My grandfather spent his last twenty or so years like a spirit or a ghost, a house whose occupants had moved away, a creature gutted, void of heart and spleen, in the upstairs front room of our two-flat, sitting in an overstuffed armchair, staring blankly for hour after endless hour at the empty space before him, or sometimes holding his face in his hands, refusing to move, even when told it was time to eat, or on the dangerous days when he grew more active, pacing the back porch that faced east toward Lake Michigan and muttering dark curses out the windows.

My grandmother's wearing of black began, as far as I could tell from overhearing bits and pieces of the old stories, the day she and my grandfather and G.I. father made the long trip to Chicago from Monterey, California, where my father was born. My grandfather wasn't able to talk about the past—he could hardly hold a conversation about what was plainly in front of him—though when I was a child we'd play a game on the back porch in which he was a boat's captain and I was his crew. He'd order me around in Italian and together we'd motor out into the sea, riding the swells, then unwind our lines and troll slowly as we waited for slack water. Our catch was always plentiful. As the gurdies brought in our heavy lines we'd unclip the leaders and haul them in by hand, then gaff our catch with mighty hooks and laugh. We'd sort through our bounty, picking up pretend fish from the floor and tossing the best into the hold. As we worked he'd tell stories that had no clear beginnings, middles or endings. One moment we'd be on the deck of his boat out in the Pacific, the next moment back in *bedda Sicilia* stepping onto the ship that would take him from Palermo to New York, doorway to the new, golden world. And then, inexplicably, we'd find ourselves inside some sort of prison, locked behind a high fence topped by spirals of razor wire, and my grandfather would fall to his knees, pleading that he wasn't a spy or a friend of the enemy, that in God's name he had done nothing wrong. I'd do my best to distract him, change the subject, pretend I was pulling in a fish too big to get into the boat.

"It's a whale," I'd say.

"Let it go," he'd tell me, his face pale with fear. "Cut the line. Let it go."

"No," I'd protest.

"It's too big," he'd respond. "It's too much. Too full of power. Cut the line. Let it go." Then his eyes would shift and he'd be somewhere else again. "I've done nothing," he'd tell the air. "Untie me. Let me go. I'll do anything, say anything. Please. I'll obey."

I'd remind him that we were out on his boat and hand him a smaller fish, miming its size, struggling only a bit as I lifted it, until he'd wipe his tears and return to the game in which he was the happy captain and I was his joyful crew.

My grandmother brought out the old stories only rarely, like a woman with her finest tablecloth, drawing it out only occasionally from the locked chest in which it was kept, fondling its folds, giving it air, perhaps even spreading it partially on the table, only to quickly refold it and wrap it tightly in the thickest paper and plastic and put it back beneath lock and key. What happened to the family back in California was a subject I learned never to raise. Whenever I tried to bring to light specifics about what came to a tragic end out there on the West Coast during the mid-1940s, my grandmother would raise her right hand and push my words to the ground, then bend at the waist slightly in obvious pain, as if someone had stabbed her with a knife and was now pressing the blade's sharp tip against her heart. The creases in her lined face would deepen, and she'd look as if she were about to rend the air with moans and wails. The look she gave you nearly made you cry.

But bring her a nice piece of meat and her nearly toothless mouth would grin like a carved Halloween pumpkin. "Here you go, my little black bat," I'd say. She understood only the least bit of English—or at the time that's what I thought—and so whenever my parents weren't around and Nonnu was in one of his dark moods in the front room I felt free to say to her whatever foolish prattle would pop out from my head.

She'd drizzle the windowpanes of meat with olive oil and massage them lovingly with minced garlic and fresh basil and other herbs either chopped or mashed in her mortar, then sprinkle the meat with coarse sea salt. Sometimes she'd slice and sauté some strips of peeled carrots and zucchini along with a couple of hard-boiled eggs, and these ingredients sprinkled with grated Pecorino Romano cheese would make their way inside the tissue-thin pieces of meat, which she'd roll like cigars and then tie off with loops of string topped with the daintiest of slip knots. She'd brown these rolls carefully in olive oil and then place them in a casserole dish and top them with her own tomato sauce and then cook them slowly in the oven, so as to serve them later on a plate of homemade pasta. Take my word, a person could die of happiness just from the smell.

She was particularly fond of pork. It was the sweetest of meats, she said. Pork chops made her smile. A rack of pork ribs caused her to laugh out loud. Hand her a nice lean loin pork roast and she'd make the sign of the Cross and hold her wrinkled hands to her heart as tears welled in her eyes.

But perhaps her favorite meat of all was pork neckbones, which the butcher, Marie Santangelo's father, on occasion would give to his regular customers for free, Chicago being the world's hog butcher and all of that, with endless pens of pigs slaughtered daily at the busy Union Stockyards down on the South Side, and Mr. Santangelo not wanting even the boniest pork neckbone to go to waste.

When the history of food in the New World is written, some astute researcher will record the importance of pork neckbones to Midwest America's children from southern Italy. Take an impoverished population deprived of meat, expose them to an inexpensive and plentiful source, and watch them use it to transform one of their most cherished dishes. What I'm leading up to saying is that my grandmother used pork neckbones in her Sunday pot of *sugu*, or sauce (what those on the East Coast of the U.S. call gravy), whenever she made spaghetti and sauce, or *pasta cu sugu*, as it was properly called, or, around my house, shortened to a simpler, terser *pasta cu su*.

Whenever the question, "Hey Ma, what's for supper tonight, fish again?" was answered by "Nonna's upstairs making *pasta cu su*," it was an occasion for the greatest joy and celebration. My happiest memories of life inside the red brick two-flat on Glenwood Avenue involve coming home from work at the newsstands to a steaming plate of *pasta cu su*. I was a fully grown adult before I realized how the words were formed and spelled since my child's ear never heard *su* as an abbreviation for *sugu*. I conflated my sense of elation over this marvelous meal with the tube-shaped musical instrument you held up to your lips and hummed into. Whenever my mother would announce that we were going to eat *pasta kazoo*, the cherubs within my soul trumpeted and their fat little feet danced with joy.

My sense of what happened is that since pork neckbones were the cheapest meat, as soon as the poor Southern Italians could afford meat they purchased them and immediately put them into their sauce pots. That is, after they parboiled them. I learned about the importance of parboiling neckbones before I reached my grandmother's knee. Raw bones make an ugly foam that ruins the sauce's delicate marriage of tomato, onion, and garlic. So before adding the neckbones to the sauce, they must first be brought to a furious boil and thoroughly rinsed in cold water. The partially cooked neckbones then not only are able to change the color of the sauce, taking it from the tomato's deep red to a softer shade that approaches orange, but also soften and make much more complex and profound the sauce's tomato and onion and garlic flavor.

To this day, offer me a plate of pasta covered with bright red tomato sauce and I'll smile and politely decline. My grandmother's cooking has forever ruined me. I've been spoiled by the truest realization of tomato sauce's potential, sauce made with pork neckbones, my dear, blessed Nonna's *pasta cu su*.

🐚 🐚 🐚

Procuring the neckbones, however, was another matter.

It wasn't that the butcher didn't have an ample stock, because he always did, but it was that on only rare occasions did he give them to the women in the neighborhood for free. As a result, whenever my penny-pinching parents learned that I was going to Santangelo's Meats to get a pound of this or that for my grandmother, my mother would always add, "And ask for some free neckbones while you're at it." Upon my return from the shop I'd be greeted by, "Did you remember the neckbones? Did he give you any for free?"

If my answer was a pair of yeses, even if the neckbones were so scrawny a dog roaming the alley might pass them by, my family would praise them to the heavens. "Good neckbones," someone would remark during the meal. "He got them for free," someone else would respond. "They're really very good, aren't they?" "Yes, they're delicious." But if I were made to pay a nickel or dime for them or, God forbid, all of fifteen or twenty cents, my parents would find a thousand faults with the bones, and the world's most delicious meal would be ruined.

"What did you say he paid for these? Twenty cents? This one's just bone and gristle. And this other one, just look at it. Would you just look at it? Sweet Christ on the Cross, it has hardly any meat on it at all."

That's exactly what a neckbone is, I'd think as I'd sigh and put down my fork, as the pasta in my belly would congeal into a lump. It's a bone with a bit of gristle, with hardly any meat.

"You remember the ones he got last week for free? Now they had a lot of meat."

"They were a meal in themselves. You could fill yourself up just eating one or two, never mind the sauce and pasta."

"Eat. Don't get upset. It'll ruin your digestion."

"I just can't believe Santangelo charged the stupid kid twenty cents for these."

"It's highway robbery."

"You sure he wanted you to pay for these? It wasn't one of his idiot assistants? Santangelo himself said the words, 'That will be twenty cents.' You heard him say that? The actual words came out of his mouth? You didn't just hand him the coins like a stupid, lazy, daydreaming imbecile or put them on the counter like a little dummy before he told you himself that he wanted you to pay?"

"I've always told him not to offer Santangelo money for neckbones until Santangelo himself asks. He's to say, 'I'd like a pound or so of neckbones, please,' then wait to hear if there's a charge."

"You're a big talker. You should have gone to the butcher yourself. What did you do all day, lie on the couch watching your damn soap operas?"

"Yeah, and four loads of dirty clothes jumped all by themselves into the washing machine, then hung themselves on the clothesline in the back yard to dry. Meanwhile, the breakfast dishes walked themselves over to the sink and went for a soapy swim."

"You know him well enough. He's worthless. You can't depend on him for a damn thing."

"And while I strolled over to the butcher shop, exactly who do you think was going to watch your daughters? The maid or the babysitter? Ha ha ha ha ha."

"I'm just saying, these are the kind of neckbones Santangelo gives away for free."

"You think the clothes folded and ironed themselves? You think the girls changed their own diapers and made their own lunch? You think their lunch jumped on the table and their dirty dishes rinsed and dried themselves?"

"You sure you didn't just put the two dimes down on the counter, like a stupid fool? Because he'll sweep them into his palm every goddamn time if you do that."

"I've always told him to pay nothing until he's asked."

"You go back tomorrow and tell Santangelo that your parents weren't too happy with these neckbones."

"He should get our twenty cents back."

"Tell him we're simple, honest, working-class people, and that, at least in our house, money doesn't grows on trees."

"God only knows how hard your father has to work to earn twenty cents."

"Tell the son of a bitch he shouldn't take advantage of stupid children."

"Alfonso, the girls. Little pitchers have big ears."

"I'm serious. I'm dead serious. Have Worthless here march down to the butcher shop tomorrow after he's done with school, before he takes the El down to the newsstands. I don't care if he's late. Let the little dunce learn a lesson about hard-earned money. You got that? Damn it to Hell, I'm not joking around here. By dinner time tomorrow night I want to see those two goddamn dimes on this table."

༄ ༄ ༄

The bells over the shop door jangled as I walked in, and my shoes slid in the thick bed of sawdust covering the warped slats of the shop's wooden floor. As always, I shivered from the cold. Mr. Santangelo stood behind the counter in his white apron, crusted with bits of bone and dried blood, working today without the assistance of either of his helpers, ringing up a customer's purchase on his antique cash register.

On both sides of the counter were refrigerated display cases of meat. The larger case in front of the side wall was full of brilliant reds: sirloins and porterhouses and T-bones, prime rib roasts and rump roasts, shimmering livers and kidneys, mounds of ground chuck and round, soft pink sections of veal. The smaller case in front of the back wall was packed with fresh poultry, several still connected to their feet and heads, assorted cuts of pork along with a herd of pigs' feet and things I could only imagine were actual ears, along with salt-cured hams and slabs of bacon as well as mouth-watering rings of various sausages coiled like some Arabian charmer's sleeping snakes. Play the right tune on your flute and the snakes would raise their heads and dance. Someday, I thought, as my eyes fell on the fennel-flecked lengths of the snake marked *sweet Italian*, I'd eat as much sausage as I wanted for breakfast. Someday I'd eat pork chops for lunch. Then I'd eat an inch-thick porterhouse for dinner, and if I ever had a son I'd never ever ever ever order him to embarrass himself in front of a nice girl's father for a measly twenty cents.

Mr. Santangelo was short and dark, with a tangle of curly black hair that he combed back and away from his face. Even though Marie had told me that he shaved twice a day, his beard was so heavy that the sides of his face along with his chin and upper lip appeared blue. His chin was slightly dimpled. I wondered how he managed to get his razor in there. What did he do, I wondered, core it out, like an apple? I saw in his olive-colored face a darker, more masculine version of Marie. Mr. Santangelo was impressively thick and seemed as fit and strong as a light heavyweight boxer in his prime, though with soft eyes and long, dark eyelashes, the kind that curled up visibly at the edges, the kind that all the mascara ads were encouraging the women of America to aim for.

When you walked into his shop, you took a number from the metal stand just to the right of the door. The numbers were on rectangular plastic cards and hung there on a hook. I drew 42. Mr. Santangelo kept the called numbers on a smaller stand beside the cash register.

"A-forty-one," he called out, slightly rolling the r. The woman he'd just waited on smiled and tucked her roast in the crook of her arm like a halfback would a football and said, "Thank you so much, Angelo. Until tomorrow." He nodded and again called out forty-one.

Since there was no one else in the shop, I shuffled through the sawdust toward the counter. "I'm forty-two," I said, showing him my card.

"Where's forty-one?" he asked the empty shop.

I looked around. We were the only people there.

He shook his head and wiped his hands on his apron, then shook his head again.

"You remember those neckbones I bought here yesterday," I began.

"Oh, here's a-forty-one. Stuck to the back of number forty." He showed me the two cards, raising each in the air as he pronounced their names and smiled.

"Yesterday's neckbones," I said.

"You want pork neckbones. How much? A pound? Pound and a half?"

"No. I, uh. That is, my parents. . . ."

"You're the boy my Marie meets sometimes at the parish dances."

I gulped and nodded yes.

"Vincenzo, no? Vincenzo Sansone?" He reached out over the counter and beckoned me closer, then laid one of his powerful hands on my shoulder and gave it a slight squeeze. "You're a good boy, yes? You go to church, to the Catholic school. The nuns they teach you right and wrong. My Marie, she talks about you some of the times with her mamma."

"I hope she says nice things," I said.

"Sure," he said. "All of the time from her mouth she says such nice things about this boy Vincenzo I think maybe he's so good he must already have his own feast day." For a moment he laughed softly at his joke. "So let's keep it that way, okay? This is just between you and me. You behave. She's a good girl, you understand? You be a good Catholic boy. You know what I mean?"

"Sure."

"You know what I mean," he repeated and nodded. "My Marie, she's my only baby. I love her like no other. You have a lot of brothers and sisters, no?"

"Sisters," I said. "No brothers. I have six sisters."

"Six sisters!" He stared up toward the ceiling as if he could not imagine such a marvelous thing, his hands and arms flying open as if he wanted to embrace them all. Then his expression changed. "Your poor papa, each night he must pray for six more pairs of eyes! Seven children, and six of them girls!" He said something in Sicilian, some proverb or folk expression, that I didn't fully understand. His smile beamed down on me like a spotlight, as if I'd had something to do with it. "And you're the firstborn, no?"

I nodded.

"The only son, and the firstborn to boot. You must be his right hand, his steady rock, his Gibraltar, the one he all of the time leans on and depends on."

"Oh, sure. You hit that right on the head. That's me and my pop exactly."

"Tell me, Vincenzo, my mind it forgets, what part of *Italia* does your family come from?"

"Some little fishing village on the west coast of Sicily," I said, "where the people were poor and mostly ate sardines. M something. My nonnu was a fisherman there."

"And your nonnu, he's your father's father? What again is his name?"

"Vincenzo. The same as mine."

"Vincenzo Sansone, *il pescatore*," he announced slowly to the ceiling, his jaws working as if chewing. "San-son-e. San-son-e. I think some years ago I had a conversation with your nonna. That village, it wouldn't by any chance be Menfi?"

"Yeah," I said. "That's right. Menfi. In Girgenti."

"Yes, Girgenti, now Agrigento. That makes us neighbors!" His smile burst like a Fourth of July rocket creasing the dark sky. "My own family, when I was a boy, we come to this country ourselves from a small village not too far from Menfi! I first saw Menfi when I was a young boy not much older than you."

"Oh," I said. "How nice."

"I go back to visit my family maybe every two or three years." He thrust forward his thumb and then one and then two of his thick fingers, nodding enthusiastically with pride.

"The neckbones," I said.

"Menfi." He wagged his head. "And all these years every Sunday at Mass I see your nonna outside of church, we exchange hellos but don't take the time to pause to talk."

"The neckbones," I said again.

"Sure," he said suddenly, as if remembering. "I got plenty. How much you want? A coupla pounds?"

"No," I said, "thank you, not now, nothing today. I just wanted to tell you, my parents, that is, they sent me here to tell you, um, they wanted me to tell you. . . ."

"They like the neckbones I sell them, yes?"

His face was full of such kind eagerness that I didn't have the heart to say anything except, "Of course."

"That's good. Your nonna she told me once how she likes to cook them nice and slow in her sauce, and I agree. The meat, it just falls off of the bone, know what I mean? And how is your nonna? And your nonnu?"

"She's fine. Nonnu stays mostly inside the house now but he's fine, too."

"Tell them I say hello. Tell your nonna I look for her on Sunday." I nodded. "Say that Angelo, the butcher up on Clark Street, he says to her hello."

By now a few other customers had entered the shop and were wandering about the sawdust like lost lambs in search of their shepherd. "They said for me to tell you they were delicious."

"What?" He glanced beyond me at his waiting customers, and after looking down at his plastic cards called out in a strong voice, "A-forty-three."

"My parents." I didn't know what else I could possibly say. "They sent me here to tell you that those neckbones you sold us the other day, they were simply delicious."

❧ ❧ ❧

Much to my chagrin, at the time of this conversation I was doing a bit more than merely meeting the butcher's daughter at parish dances. Marie and I were also seeking out dark nooks and crannies where we could be alone to hold hands and kiss. Marie loved to kiss. Kissing was maybe Marie's favorite activity in the whole world. She'd say there was nothing sweeter than to be held in someone's arms and kiss, and to hold someone in return and kiss him. So when we got together, we'd kiss and kiss and kiss. And I'd fall into each one of those kisses. Our dates would begin with dancing, two or three furious sets of sweat-inducing jitterbugging punctuated only by an occasional slow song, during which we held each other as closely as the chaperones allowed, trembling with expectation for the sweet kisses to come.

By now, the mid-1960s, most of the kids on Chicago's North Side had moved beyond the jitterbug to steps that didn't involve touching their partner. Kids did the twist, the swim, the jerk, the watusi, the monkey, the mashed potato, and the pony, along with an assortment of novelty steps they saw performed on TV's *Shindig!* and *Hullabaloo.*

Most would combine aspects of each of these dances, ending up doing none of them well. They'd stand flat-footed and crook their elbows and hold their hands level to their heads and rock back and forth, then go into a loose twist or a couple of cha-cha steps, then make like they were climbing a rope or doing the breaststroke, then push out their elbows and shudder and gyrate like someone trying to work out a kink in their lower spine.

Marie was fond of dancing and did an exquisite pony step that showed off the perfect musculature of her calves and thighs. She often wore a dark, pleated skirt and a light-colored blouse with a Peter Pan collar, bobby socks and dark, plain shoes. Around her neck she wore a red coral horn, or *corno*, given to her to ward off evil by some well-meaning relative when she was still an infant in her crib, along with a small gold heart on which was etched her name in the finest Palmer script. She wore no makeup and only a hint of red lipstick, which she'd carefully wipe off on a tissue each night before going home. After we saw *Gypsy* at a movie theater downtown on State Street, I realized how closely Marie resembled Natalie Wood. Of course she shrugged off the comparison and told me I was being silly, but that's how I saw her then and how I remember her now.

Call me old school, but I preferred the jitterbug and often danced its familiar steps by myself while Marie jerked and ponyed away the evening. My preference had nothing to do with actual or considered taste and everything to do with the way Lucy Sheehan had twirled me off my orange crate outside Ronny's garage. That moment injected the jitterbug into my veins. It made the jitterbug my dance.

Whenever I jitterbugged I could still feel Lucy's soft hand, see her red hair, the blush of freckles splashed across her face, the soft sway of her breasts beneath her dog-hair-specked sweater, the smile on her full and generous lips.

How was it that I could be with one girl yet sometimes think of another?

I spent more than a few hours daydreaming about Lucy, recreating that dance in the alley in my mind, then fleshing it out with a dozen subsequent fantasies, each of which grew bolder as I grew older. Lucy would have some problem with one of her classes in school, and she'd ask Ronny to help her. The guys in the garage would laugh and crack jokes, but I'd know the subject and volunteer to help, and so we'd meet in the public library, where we'd sit at a back table and after a while hold hands and, when the librarian wasn't looking. . . .

In another she would have injured her leg, likely at work at the pet store, and needed someone to help her get home. Ronny would be busy working on a car and tell me to take charge of it. He'd slap my back and call me his lieutenant. So I'd help Lucy walk home, and after we got there she'd insist on showing me where the injury was, on the inside of her thigh just above the knee. Then she'd ask me to carry her in my arms to her bedroom. . . .

Or maybe she'd be angry at Ronny, sobbing hot, bitter tears because she'd overheard what he had told the other guys about her. She isn't stupid, no, far from it, she wasn't born yesterday. She knows which way is up. We'd catch him bragging again and I'd come to her defense and tell Ronny to knock it off. I'd say just the right things, things that put Ronny in his place, really shred him, that silence him and make him hang his head in shame. Her honor restored, Lucy would smile and thank me, and then. . . .

This is my Achilles heel, the key to what happened later and more or less led to everything else. All the while that I was going out with sweet Marie, I knew that I had some connection with Lucy. I felt it the moment she looked me in the eyes and twirled me off my orange crate. Somehow we were kindred souls, in a way that made Marie and the rest of the world seem nearly foreign. The connection meant I was fated to try to rescue her, the girl of L.S.M.F.T. fame. This was after I came to understand more of what was being said in Ronny's garage, after I figured out that the T in the phrase stood for the word "tonight" and the F for the fancy Latin word that rhymes with Horatio.

ᜁ ᜁ ᜁ

I often wore a jockstrap when I ventured out into the world because my arousal trigger was so hair-sensitive the slightest provocation could set me off. I'd be working at the newsstand on Canal and Adams and a secretary's coat would fall open and I'd see the soft outline of a breast beneath a white blouse. I'd catch a whiff of the woman's perfume and a bulge would blossom beneath my change apron. Walking around the neighborhood, I'd cut through the alley and notice a black brassiere dangling alongside a dainty pink slip on a clothesline in someone's yard. My stovepipes would resemble the crow who swallowed the bullfrog.

I kept the key to Ronny's garage always with me, and often went there with Marie after we'd been to a parish dance. Nearly always one or two cars were parked inside, under repair. Ronny kept their keys in an empty clay flowerpot near the calendar. One night as we arrived there we saw that Ronny was just leaving, and so I introduced them. The two stood still as statues, smiling at each other, as if they each were sizing the other up. Later Marie admitted to me that she thought Ronny was very cute.

"Cute?" I said.

"Dreamy, if you want to know the truth. You know the feeling you get when you eat really really really good dark chocolate?"

"You're not supposed to find my friends dreamy."

"Vince." Her tone was stern, as if I were suggesting something obscene. "Vince, how can you even think such a thing? I mean, he might be absolutely groovy and drool-worthy but he's so *old*."

We'd unlock one of the cars and sit in the back seat, roll down the back windows so that we could hear the radio on the ledge near the gas canisters and speed bag, and hold each other in our arms and kiss. After a while, when my arousal became too obvious to ignore, Marie would let out a sigh and say, "Well, well, well, well, well, how very sad. It seems the two of us are no longer alone."

"Sorry," I'd say, as any good Catholic boy would. Like boxers obeying the bell marking the end of a round, we'd retreat to opposite sides of the back seat to cool down. Marie and I would nod our heads to the music, whatever was playing that night on WLS, the coolest radio station in all of Chicagoland, listening over and over again to the loop of the era's most popular songs—the Beatles' "Help!," the Supremes' "Stop! In the Name of Love," the Four Tops' "I Can't Help Myself," Beau Brummels' "Laugh, Laugh," the Righteous Brothers' "You've Lost That Lovin' Feeling," Freddie and the Dreamers' "I'm Telling You Now," Herman's Hermits' "Mrs. Brown, You've Got a Lovely Daughter," Gary Lewis and the Playboys' "This Diamond Ring," and the Rolling Stones' "I Can't Get No Satisfaction"—before either one of us would talk.

"I don't really know that I have a whole lot of control over it," I admitted one night as we sat in our separate corners in the back seat.

"You mean you can't just decide it won't happen and then it won't happen?"

"I wish."

She frowned. "Then it's not something you can will, like there's not some sort of mental control you can exercise?"

"You mean can I turn it on and off? Like the switch to a light? No way."

Her mind chewed on that for a while. "Aren't you supposed to recite the alphabet backwards in your head or something?"

"Where'd you hear that?"

"I don't know. Somewhere."

"I'd always heard reciting the alphabet was for a different situation, to prevent the occurrence of something else."

"The Sisters told us that in situations like this we should fold our hands and pray," Marie said. She was attending an all-girls Catholic high school taught by the Benedictine Sisters. "What did the Brothers tell you?"

I went to an all-boys Catholic high school taught by the Christian Brothers. "They told us we're supposed to do something physical and athletic," I said. "Such as, say we're in a parked car, like we are now. I'm supposed to come up with an excuse to physically remove myself from the situation. For example, that I just remembered that I urgently need to check the pressure on the tires. Then I should go out and pretend to be doing that but really hide behind the car and do twenty-five push-ups—fifty, a hundred, whatever it takes—until any and all vestiges of the urge go away."

"That's strange," Marie said. "What in the world would the girl left all alone in the car think?"

"We didn't discuss the girl's part. I guess she's supposed to just sit there. But the idea is that the boy is supposed to work it out physically."

"But her just sitting there in the car doesn't make any sense. I mean, he's only checking the tires' air pressure. Wouldn't she volunteer to go out with him and help?"

"We're to jog, run, sprint, shoot baskets, lift weights, do calisthenics. Afterwards, if we still have lingering vestiges of desire, we're to exercise even more. 'Spend it on the field, not on the sheets,' the Brothers teach us. By the way, this is the main reason why all-boys Catholic high schools and colleges are so good at football."

"Actually, the Sisters' main recommendation is that we immediately stop whatever we're doing and engage the boy in question in a diverting conversation."

"A diverting conversation," I said after a few beats. It took a while for that to sink in. "Such as the one we're having right now."

"See?" Marie said, beaming. "Now you don't have to get out of the car and check any tire pressures."

Then Marie talked about wanting someday to get serious with a boy, the right boy of course, and settling down with him, getting married, having a family, a big family, plenty of kids, so many that you could hardly keep track of their names. They'd still live in the neighborhood, of course, but they'd have their own place separate from the six-flat where her parents lived, which her father as of late was considering buying now that the butcher shop was making money hand over fist, and he thought he could get it reasonably cheap and even if he paid market value her mother said it was still a good investment. Then maybe after a while, after she and this boy were married, say, for a couple of years, the guy could help her father run Santangelo's Meats. It was clean, honest work, she said, in demand six days a week, every day but Friday, that is, unless Protestants moved into the neighborhood, and he'd be sure to make a good living—butchers who knew how to cut a side of meat made pretty decent money, she said—and in time he could be like the son her father never had, and the shop would be his when her father got older, that is, as long as the boy was sweet and honest and loved and honored and respected his daughter and he learned how to cut meat and did it honestly and faithfully and well. But he had to be the right boy, you understand, not just some everyday slob off the street, and certainly not one of those goons like the ones she'd sat in class with back in grammar school, the kind of guy who drops his pencil in class so he can lean over in the aisle and sneak a look up a girl's skirt at her underpants, or who stares at a girl's breasts, or has dirty hands or fingernails, or unclean teeth or foul breath, or who lies or cheats. No, he would have to be somebody respectful and kind and compassionate, the sort of boy who without even thinking does genuinely thoughtful and considerate things for others, particularly in times of extreme embarrassment and stress and need, such as giving a young, frightened, crying girl at the communion rail his clean white handkerchief.

Marie went on about her hopes and dreams, but I stopped listening. I suddenly understood why she'd trailed me after that graduation party when I danced the last dance with her, why she'd pulled me into her front hallway and gave me the three sweetest kisses I'd ever received in my life. I understood something then about the power of small gestures, and of return, how everything in life ultimately connects with everything else. It was because that morning in church I'd offered her my handkerchief.

But then I stopped thinking because all of a sudden Marie was on my side of the back seat and in my arms, pressing herself against me, giving me a deep, long, sensational kiss.

❧ ❧ ❧

As for the neckbones and the twenty cents, at the newsstands that afternoon I did something I'd never done before, something all too easy, and something I'd continue to do from that day on. I slipped a pair of dimes from my change apron into my pants pocket, and then after a moment's hesitation I thought what the heck and pocketed four quarters as well. At dinner that evening I dropped the two dimes on the table and announced that they were from Mr. Santangelo, as a refund for the inferior neckbones he'd sold us. Plus, I said, Mr. Santangelo extended his hellos to nonna and his sincere apologies to the entire family along with his assurance that the problem would never happen again.

"He actually apologized?" the two shadows asked me, after they'd scooped both dimes into their hands.

"Yeah. He told me he was sorry and it wouldn't happen again."

"He said that? Those were his words?"

"Whose else would they be?"

"He actually apologized?"

"I've never heard of such a thing. A butcher giving refunds."

"Well, you've heard of it now."

"Unbelievable."

"I guess there's a first time for everything."

"I still can't believe it. He apologized?"

"Well," I said, "I mean, there were other customers in the store. He didn't get down on his hands and knees."

"What did he say again? His exact words?"

"I told you a hundred times already, that it wouldn't happen again."

"Don't get smart or I'll give you some of this."

"I'm only telling you what he said."

Later that night, as I helped my father count the newsstands' totals, sitting across from him at the now-cleared kitchen table as we did each evening, having spilled the coins from each apron into the mounds that we would sort and count and then slip into paper tubes that later we'd take to the neighborhood currency exchange, he let out a long, disapproving hiss and shook his head back and forth. Then he announced that my day's apron was a dollar five short.

"A dollar five short?" I fell back in my chair in mock surprise. "There must be some mistake."

"You didn't take out your tips, did you?" On a good day I averaged fifty cents or up to a dollar or so in tips. "How many times have I told you not to take out your tips?"

"I never touch my tips."

"Did you count each of the bundles you got from Jack?" Jack was the *Daily News* driver who routinely shorted our bundles.

"Yeah, at least as many as I could. But you know how crazy it gets during rush. I can't count them all. You know that some people take a paper without paying."

"But tips always balance out shortages and thefts. Are you sure you left your tips in?"

I nodded.

He was dividing some numbers on his pad of paper. "Son of a bitch. That comes to fifteen papers. Son of a bitch." His furious pencil scratched his paper, like a chicken chasing a flea. "A dollar five per day, five twenty-five a week, over twenty dollars a month." Like a radiator in winter, he let out another long, steamy hiss. "Over two hundred and fifty dollars over the course of a year."

He was starting to fume, starting to unwind the anger that would lead to his raging and shouting, so I eased back my chair and plotted where I would run. This is the part of the movie where the not-too-bright caveman realizes that the rumbling he feels beneath his feet isn't thunder or a herd of passing dinosaurs but a reliable indicator that the mighty volcano towering over the cave where he lives is about to explode.

Fortunately for me, the molten rocks and lava rained down the next evening on Jack, who gave back every bit as much as he was given. We stood by the pinball machines and coin lockers on the ground floor of the Union Station, where we always gathered after work to settle the day's totals. No sooner had Jack relit the stub of his cigar than my father ripped into him about the shortages, and within no time the pair stood jaw to jaw, fingers pointed and poking the other's chest.

I didn't care if sooner or later my dumb father would figure out the truth and I'd have to take it in the moon. With each poke of my father's finger into Jack's chest, I patted my pants pocket, inside of which nestled three or four more quarters for me to spend on whatever in the world I wanted, along with a couple of shiny dimes I'd keep in reserve for the next time I was told to humiliate myself and beg for neckbones.

# 5

# *Tofino* 1974–75

ROXANNE STOOD NEAR the back door, tossing her things into her knapsack. "I hitchhiked in," she said, "I'd really like to hitchhike back out."

She'd had a fine vacation. In the weeks she'd stayed with me she'd grown tan and more finely muscled, and her dark hair had lightened from the sun. The sun drew out tints of red in her auburn hair that now shone when she combed it out. Her face had a warm, healthy glow. She no longer appeared shy or apprehensive. Maybe the change was due to Josh having left her to travel up-island with his friends, or maybe it was due to the time we'd spent together. Whatever, her direct, even gaze made her seem self-assured and at times even bold.

"I told you," I said, "I can drive you to Nanaimo. I'd be delighted to do it. We could even take the ferry together to Horseshoe Bay."

"I want to do this by myself, Vince."

"But you never know who'll stop to pick you up. Anything could—"

"Vince," she repeated, patiently.

I raked a hand through my hair. Maybe she was right to split, I thought. I knew that as far as my relationships with women went I was toxic. Seven weeks together was more than enough. The less time I spent with a woman, I thought, the less chance I'd have to mess up her life. "Sure, no problem, whatever suits you." I walked over to the counter and rubbed the gouge Josh had inflicted on it, as if touching it might somehow make it go away.

"Don't look at me like that. It's important to me that I do this by myself."

"I'm not looking at you like anything."

She shook her head and laughed. "You most certainly are. You should see yourself, the expression on your face." She pushed her hair back and away from her face, then ran her fingertips down behind her ears. She had a habit of doing that, and sometimes when she was day-dreaming she bit down on her lower lip. She was wearing the new pair of silver earrings she'd just bought in town. The shiny silver spoons on her earrings resembled tiny fishing lures. She wore a soft cotton blouse and faded jeans with an American flag patch sewn over a tear on the right rear pocket. There was another patch—purple paisley—on a rip above her left knee. If she allowed me to accompany her, I thought, she could travel the rest of the way by herself after we hit Horseshoe Bay. I didn't want to go back down to Vancouver, back to the mainland. "You're looking at me like someone lost."

"I'm not lost." I placed a folded dish towel over the gouge so that I wouldn't notice it. "It's just that, you know, I'm really no good at goodbyes."

"I'm not good at goodbyes either but, hey, consider the bright side. We had this time together. What a vacation. I can't thank you enough. And look at what Josh and I evidently started." She was refer-ring to the hippies who were hearing about me in town and now were making their way to my back door asking if they might crash here for the night. "I don't think you're going to have any problems from now on making new friends. Whether you intended it or not, you've become the host of an ongoing party."

I shrugged.

"Don't worry. I know you'll find a way to make it work. The guys respect you, since you're a local and you're pretty good at putting on the tough-guy act. And as for the girls. . . ." She laughed. "I'm sure if they knock on your door you'll find a way to settle them down."

I turned away, not wanting her to see my sadness. I edged my hand down my T-shirt and touched the smooth outline of my scar. "I don't know what you're talking about."

"Do you need me to spell it out? I watched you today talking to those two new girls. You're obviously a guy who likes and appreciates women, and you let them know it. You look them in the eye, and when they look back you smile and hold their gaze. You listen to them when they speak. You wouldn't believe how many guys don't. And if a girl responds, like I did, you deliver on the promise. In bed you're very generous, maybe even too generous."

"I didn't know there could be such a thing as 'too generous.'"

"Of course not. You wouldn't be half as charming if you did." She slid a flat box out of a paper bag and handed it to me. "Here, when you were at work yesterday I came across something in town that had Vince Sansone written all over it."

Inside the box was a pair of midnight-blue boxer shorts. The shorts were bedecked with white cartoon whales, grinning knowingly, with a healthy fountain of gush spurting from their blowholes. Enclosed was a card on which Roxanne had drawn another smiling whale with a big V on his forehead, and beneath the gentle waves through which the whale was spy-hopping she'd written, *To Vince, From your grateful guest, love forever!* Beneath the word "love" was an R and a row of tiny hearts.

I didn't know how to react to the gift. I had no idea how to tell her goodbye.

In the end Roxanne agreed to let me drive her to the highway, but not an inch beyond. Within minutes a car driven by a lone driver stopped for her. I returned to my house and went out back and grabbed my ax and split wood ferociously, ignoring the campers lounging in my back yard, even the two new girls, until my shirt was soaked with sweat and I'd split my woodpile to matchsticks and it was too dark to see.

☙ ☙ ☙

After Roxanne left, I smoked a lot of dope.

I kept a lid of passable weed in the glove compartment of my car, and each afternoon when I got off work at the fish processing plant I rolled a joint in the parking lot. I'd sit behind the wheel and gaze out at the splendid blue water of Clayoquot Sound and the lush expanse of trees covering the mountains on nearby Meares, nodding silently to my coworkers as they passed on the way to their cars, and lick the joint tight and twist shut both ends, then run my mouth briefly over it and strike a match and fire it up, sipping the first biting hit as deeply as I could into my lungs. The sweet marijuana would fill my nose and head, and with the second and third hits the weed would begin to wrap my head in its warm embrace. I'd hold the smoke in and stare out the windshield and smile. Ahh, cannabis. Only after I was back home working on my third or fourth beer—I normally drank a beer or two for every joint I smoked—would I decide to throw my clothes into the washer and take a shower, scrubbing stray fish scales off my arms and neck and out of my ears and my hair. Then I'd stand over the sink and lather my face and neck and slowly shave, a towel wrapped around my waist, music pulsing from the stereo, depending on my mood often Clifford Brown's full and expressive trumpet or Art Pepper's pure, fluent alto sax. When I was lucky, I'd forget about everything for a minute or two and feel like a normal fucking human being.

I don't think it was so much loneliness, though in the years before I'd met Ignatius George and learned how to spend part of each day on the water with the whales I was truly, profoundly lonely. And I don't think it was longing for the physical intimacy I'd had with Roxanne, or with any of the other women who in the days that followed consented to be intimate with me. As Roxanne had predicated, after she left there were occasional others, nothing very serious—interludes, really—

mutually cordial connections that lasted an hour or so or at most one or two nights.

If anything, the main feeling that pervaded my soul was something close to outright fear. I suspected that even though I'd traveled thousands of miles, an entire country, and several time zones away from my narrow bed beneath the nail-studded stairs in the brick two-flat on Glenwood Avenue, I'd hardly gone anywhere. If it makes any sense I still felt *there*, in my past life, in Chicago, in my father's house.

The fish smell on my clothes was a constant reminder to me of my father. Sometimes I'd walk into a room and there it would be, waiting for me, his very smell, as palpable as an intruder sitting on my sofa. The fear that my father was physically there in the room with me would wash over me in a hot, sudden rush. If I was stoned I'd whirl about, searching for him. It wasn't anything rational. Of course he wasn't there in my house. He had no idea where I lived. No one I knew from Chicago did. The North American continent is vast, and I'd covered my tracks carefully. Still, knowing all this did little to slow my racing heart.

More than once at night I sat at the kitchen table, the ceiling light gauzed over by a haze of marijuana smoke that hung like a blanket in the room, my mind slowly making the connection that by working at the fish plant I was repeating and somehow replicating him. For some perverse reason, I'd picked a job that insured my father would always be there alongside me. But even after making the realization, I did nothing to break the cycle.

One night I woke in a sweat, dreaming I'd physically become him. My fear was so strong that my body shook. I stood by my bedroom window in the moonlight and stared at my hands, turning them palms up and then palms down, again and again, trying to convince myself that the hands I was looking at were mine. I gazed at the reflection of my face in the windowpane while repeating my name.

Roxanne had left behind a few of her things: a brown barrette, the orange Frisbee over which she and Josh had argued, one of her drawing pads, a few colored pencils, and a tortoise shell hairbrush in whose bristles there remained a snarl or two of her hair. I kept the pencils, brush, and barrette inside the shallow bowl of the Frisbee, which I set atop the drawing pad and placed on top of a bookcase in the front room, as if someday she were going to come back to claim them.

Sometimes late at night when I was alone and couldn't sleep, I'd walk over to the bookcase and touch her things. I'd pick up the hairbrush and smell it, with the hope that I could remember her more vividly. I'd open the drawing pad, which was new, unused. On the inside front cover she'd written her name. *Roxanne Elizabeth Parker* she'd written in a cursive so distinct and letter-perfect that she would have earned an A+ in penmanship from Sister Ascension.

One night I took the pad and the handful of colored pencils to the kitchen table, and in my best cursive I wrote my name opposite hers.

*Vincenzo Antonio Sansone*

It wasn't that much of a leap before I pressed the pencil's point onto the first blank page. There I wrote a line of loopy zeroes, then the outline of my scar—the letter A minus the crossbar—and then I smoked a joint and opened a cold beer and allowed myself to draw.

I sketched a house with a cement walkway leading up to the steps of its front porch, and just as I was about to top the house off with a smoking chimney I saw that it resembled my parents' red brick two-flat on Glenwood Avenue. So instead of a chimney I gave the house a second floor, then drew a window at ground level to suggest a basement. I changed the shape of the first-floor windows so they looked more like my family house's windows. Our porch was topped by a metal awning, so I drew a metal awning. In summer my mother put out a long wooden box of geraniums on the front porch; I drew the geranium box, too. I used a red pencil for the geraniums after pausing for several moments to remember what geraniums looked like. I worked for a while on the porch steps, then sketched several bricks to suggest the building's facade. Then I drew the first bomb descending through the air.

My bombs were fat winged torpedoes full of raging, red-hot atoms aching to split and release their deadly, white-hot nuclear energy on whatever they hit.

A cluster of three bombs would fall on the house, as well as on all the other versions of their house I was to draw over the next several months. I sketched a small airplane that had dropped them, then added wavy lines behind its wings to suggest just how fast the plane was speeding away.

A lone bird watched all of this as it took place, so I drew a bird hovering in the air a safe distance away from the house. My rendition of a bird was weak—more a deformed chicken or turkey than anything that might be capable of sustained flight—so with the red pencil I set its wings on fire, and with one of the darker pencils I X'd out its eyes.

I put steel bars on the house's first-floor windows, in case any of its occupants tried to escape. For my grandmother up on the second floor I sketched in a fire escape. I drew her escaping: a stick figure in a black dress, not much bigger than an ant, running safely away toward the horizon line. Then I let the bombs fall, red-penciling in their powerful, earth-shattering explosions.

The next night I drew another version of my house, a third version the night after that. With practice and time I came to draw increasingly realistic porch steps and awnings. The fourth or fifth house merited wrought-iron porch railings and bright sprigs of green ivy. I let the ivy grow between the red geraniums in the flower box and trail down to the ground and sidewalk. Subsequent houses featured shadows behind the barred windows. After a month or so the ivy grew so thick that one side of the porch resembled the outfield walls at Wrigley Field, which are covered famously with ivy. Shadows in the first-floor windows developed red mouths open in terrified, Munchesque screams.

The lone bird observing the whole mess continued to trouble me. No matter how hard I tried, the bird always turned out monstrous, more a feathered freak with head and beak than anything resembling an actual bird. Mornings when I arrived at the fish processing plant, I'd stare up at the sky with the hope of observing a bird in flight. Whenever I saw one I quickly traced its outline on my thigh with my finger. Evenings at the kitchen table, as I put pencil to paper, I'd close my eyes and try to imagine that I was seeing it again.

In one house I drew my mother on the front porch watering the geraniums and ivy. I returned to the best of my old drawings, detailing and embellishing them. The ivy grew so thickly over the porch that it covered everything but the wooden steps. When the bombs fell I allowed my mother to remain there on the porch, watering can in hand, so she could see them. The can's head was as big as a sunflower. It was the kind of watering can you see in movies and cartoons on TV. It was what a woman watering flowers on her front porch was supposed to use. When my real-life mother watered her flowers she used a dented aluminum pot that for years had been under the kitchen sink catching drips from the slow leak in the S-trap. In subsequent drawings I let my mother face the viewer from the porch, but I placed a folded rag (for her headaches) over her forehead and eyes. Since the rag blinded her, in some drawings she watered the porch steps instead of the geraniums and ivy, and after a while, unbeknownst to her, I began drawing her watering can as empty.

The months passed. One night a large bubble popped out beside my mother's head along with a pair of lines pointing to what would have been her mouth. In none of the drawings did my mother have a mouth. She did have a nose—a short, straight line between a blind pair of dots—which stuck out beneath the rag and which enabled her to breathe. For some reason it was important to me that my mother be able to breathe. It was important that she be shown as blind, that her watering can be empty. It was important that she be drawn without a mouth. The bubble beside her head remained empty for several drawings until one night just before the bombs fell her bubble filled with several lines of illegible scrawl.

My mother's bubble filled with jagged, illegible lines, M's and N's joined at the ends, or what looked like rows of W's and V's, the kind of scrawl a seismograph might produce after recording a long, powerful earthquake. The marks were what she would have had to say if she had been born with a mouth, a mouth which she could have opened and through which she might have pushed air up from her diaphragm through her trachea and vocal cords and which might have created actual sound. Of course, had the woman been able to do that, she wouldn't have been my mother. The choppy scratchings in my mother's bubble broke into variously lengthed segments that, seen from a distance, could be considered words.

As a result, I realized, it appeared at long last that my mother was saying something. But as the grotesque bird flying by aptly observed, her words were a bit too late since the bombs falling on the house were already whistling their way down upon her and everyone else with complete and promised destruction.

∽ ∽ ∽

All the while I was smoking considerable amounts of marijuana—more than I'd ever smoked in my life—cloudfuls thick and wide enough to fill the sky, blot out the sun and moon, and cause the seven oceans to ice over. I smoked so much weed that I exhausted the plentiful stash I'd carefully cultivated and dried myself, and come spring I found that I needed to contact one of the local growers.

Tofino's most visible dealer, the one who drove the old green pickup decorated with marijuana leaf decals, was bearded and thin, with wild, feral eyes, like Charles Manson's. Everyone I knew referred to him as Mr. Zig-Zag because he physically resembled the French infantryman whose face adorned the packets of rolling papers nearly everyone used. I often saw him at The Last Crumb, drinking tea with a table full of laughing hippies. Though he sometimes nodded when we passed on the street, we'd never talked. Normally I kept my distance from Tofino's commune crowd. I gutted fish at the processing plant. When I talked with others in town, they were guys out of work or blue-collar types like me.

But one day after work I approached Mr. Zig-Zag as he sat alone at one of the Crumb's outside tables, scowling at a newspaper folded open to a crossword puzzle. I introduced myself and told him I was sorry to interrupt but I was looking for someone who might help me buy a lid.

He smiled broadly. With his pen he motioned to the seat across from him. His pen was one of those old-fashioned kinds, thick and ornate, the kind you bought from a fancy stationery store and refilled manually from an ink bottle. All but a handful of the squares of his crossword were neatly filled in.

"Not a problem," he said. "I'm pleased to meet you. Just put twenty beneath this napkin." He pushed the napkin he'd been using beneath his cup of tea toward me. "Don't do it right now. Wait a while, several minutes if you can. We're in no rush. Either palm the cash or let the napkin fall down into your lap."

"Sure." I folded my arms, then after a while put my hands in my pockets. I'd anticipated the price and had two tens in the front pocket of my jeans.

"I thought you grew your own," he said after a while, sipping his tea. "You know, the neat arrangements of six, with the outside plants marked with loops of green yarn?"

That set me back. Not only did he know what I'd been doing but he'd counted the number of plants I grew. "I do, or at least I did, but I've run out," I said, nodding and at the same time placing the palmed bills beneath the napkin, as if doing so were the most natural thing in the world. I weighted the napkin and bills down with my hand.

"That's been known to happen," he said and laughed. "All that labor, all those months of protecting the little sweethearts from interlopers and weeds and marauding bears and mountain lions and the next thing you know it disappears in a puff of smoke."

I smiled.

"Are you letting kids from the mainland crash at your place again this year? That hairy dude with the pseudo Afro"—he leaned forward until his eyes gripped mine—"didn't make himself very popular here last year. No, in fact you could say that he and his friends made themselves outright unpopular. The thing is, they ripped off one of my comrades the morning they split."

"I'm sorry to hear that," I said. "He stole from me, too."

"Thieves have a tendency to do that." He nodded. "They're equal opportunity. They seldom discriminate."

"He may have stayed in a tent out in my yard for a few nights but he was no friend."

"I know that. I know where he crashed, and for how long, and I guessed that he wasn't exactly your friend. I've heard about the others, how you've earned yourself a nice little reputation as a good Samaritan."

I shrugged. Being a good Samaritan had nothing much to do with it. People camping in my yard was a sort of entertainment, something to look forward to, keep my mind busy with during the long hours of mind-numbing work at the fish plant. It was also payment on a karmic debt, something I was told to do by the people who'd helped me enter Canada.

I didn't know what I was supposed to do with the napkin, whether I should push it toward him or not, so I left it where it was, beneath my arm on the table in front of me. As for his knowing my business, well, in a town as small as Tofino nearly everyone knew everybody else's business, or at least some version of it. There were few secrets in Tofino and even fewer locked doors. Then a long-haired guy walked up from the street and without a word or a glance at either of us tapped my arm and cleared our table of everything except Mr. Zig-Zag's pen and cup of tea. All of this was taking place out on busy First Street, with the season's new crop of tourists tromping up and down the sidewalk and a steady crowd of people going in and out of the coffee shop and bakery.

"Do you enjoy your job?" Mr. Zig-Zag asked. "Gutting fish?"

"You know how tight jobs are around here," I answered. "I'm lucky to have it."

He let out a long breath. "Lucky? Doing something anyone with half a mind would despise?" Again his eyes held me. "Like, why waste the precious moments of your life on something you don't enjoy?"

"Why do you think? I work for the money. The paycheck. So I can live."

"You'd live regardless of whether you worked or not, wouldn't you? You don't need a job to be able to live. And as for money, it has no intrinsic value. It's only a means to do something else. With the right amount you could do, what? Buy yourself a boat? A decent car? I've seen what you drive. What would you do with real money? Buy a nice, isolated piece of land around here you could have all to yourself?"

"I like living in town," I said. "If I had real money I guess I'd buy the place I rent."

"Patron saint of the homeless." He nodded. "Whose calling is to gut fish."

I didn't like his tone. "There's no dishonor in what I do," I said. "It puts bread on the table. It's what my father did for a living. My grandfather years back was a fisherman, too."

"Hey, man, relax. I'm just fucking with your head a little." He smiled, then after a beat asked me, "Do you think there's any dishonor in growing and distributing weed?"

"No. I didn't say that."

"I guessed that but I wanted to ask you anyway, to hear you say it out loud. Of course I agree. I like to think that I'd never do anything dishonorable." He sipped his tea. "So where did your old man and his people fish?"

I told him about my father, how he worked in Chicago's central fish market after his father's family was forced to move to the Midwest from the West Coast. "My grandfather was the real fisherman," I said. "He grew up on the western coast of Sicily and after he came to the States he lived in California, in Monterey. That is, before he lost his boat."

"Rough weather?" Mr. Zig-Zag said.

"For my grandfather and the other Italians living there at the time, sure." It was a sad, involved, and to them a very shameful story, something no one in my family ever spoke about openly, something I didn't want to go into right then and there.

"You sound as if you're still really into your family."

"In some ways, yeah, I guess I am. In other ways. . . ." I gave a shrug.

"But still, you're not the type who runs much with the pack."

"No," I said, shaking my head.

"Hardly a team player."

"I guess not."

"You don't mind working alone."

"Not at all."

"In fact, you might prefer it."

I laughed, wondering where the conversation was leading. "I might."

"You enjoy your own company, sort of like the lone wolf."

I nodded.

"You think you could occasionally drive a truck?"

"Sure. If it wasn't too big a rig."

"And you have a boat license?"

"No," I said, "but tell me. What's all this about?"

"Just consider me curious." He greeted some hippies passing by on the sidewalk, then turned back. "But, hey, I've seen you run a skiff."

I nodded. A guy at the fish plant had a skiff he wanted to sell, but in the meantime let me use it as long as I kept it clean and full of gas. I took it out on Grice Bay now and then, and in season used it to run a few crab pots. But I hadn't yet taken the official course that led to a license.

"So you wouldn't have any objections to getting your license," he said, as if he were reading my mind.

I stared at the waxed, twirled ends of his mustache and noted that it seemed he darkened his eyes ever so slightly with eye liner. For a moment I saw how hard he worked to achieve the effect he gave off. "You do that intentionally," I said, raising a hand and rubbing together my first finger and thumb, "that thing with your mustache, so that you resemble—"

"Sure," he said and laughed. "And why not? Isn't it all finally a matter of costumes and roles? Think about it. Step out of the here and now for a moment and consider it from a distance. In the end, isn't it all theater?"

I'd lost track of where the conversation was heading. "Beats me."

"I mean the dreamy illusion before us, what we think of as life."

"I suppose that's one way of looking at it."

"From my perspective, man, it's the *only* way to look at it. Unless you want to go fucking crazy." He gave the air a sudden cackle. "You're certainly serious, and yet at the same time you're honest. Diligently so, if you want to know the truth."

"Honest?" Now it was me who was leaning back and laughing.

"Honesty's not something to laugh at, my friend. To tell you the truth, I find it exceedingly rare."

I wagged my head and thought about all the dishonest things I'd done back when I was in Chicago. "Let me tell you, man. If you only knew."

"I know enough to be able to judge you," he said, leaning forward. "And you know enough to keep your hands to yourself. Most people don't. Their first impulse is to open their hands and take. Their eyes fall on something and they think that just because they see it it's automatically theirs, as if their perception of it, you know, somehow grants them rights of ownership over it."

"I don't follow you," I said.

He raised his thin fingers and looked up at the blue sky, as if he meant everything and nothing, everyone and no one. For a moment he looked like a religious figure, like Christ in the pose of the Sacred Heart. Now I understood how he could command the attention of so many others. It wasn't only his flashy looks. Once you got past the waxed mustache and eye liner there was something appealing, even charismatic, about him. He folded his hands and held me with his dark eyes.

"The slashes rimming the forest," he said with a smile. "For a couple of years now you've been growing your crops directly alongside mine, responsibly culling out the males, then later on harvesting only and precisely what you planted. That's *exceptionally* rare, my friend, particularly in a business where those who care for as many gardens as I do are forced to factor in certain margins of loss due to theft. Are you following me here? Your plants grew within easy sight of mine, my garden within sight of yours, and in this world where borders between objects more often than not blur you didn't touch a single leaf that wasn't yours."

"Well," I said, "of course not. Your plants weren't mine. I'd marked mine with yarn."

"Dude, that's *precisely* my point."

He smiled and pushed his cup toward me and then stood and walked away, and I sat there as the setting sun stretched the tourists' shadows down the sidewalk and across the bakery's windows. For a while I watched the shadows play against the glass, until a young woman with blonde hair strode up to me, smiling as if we shared some joke and were the oldest, dearest friends.

She was wearing a brown, ankle-length hippie dress and hiking boots, and as she smiled she sat across from me on the curved seat Mr. Zig-Zag had just vacated. Her dress was an old-fashioned flower print with a long row of dark, tiny buttons that went from its scooped neck nearly down to her knees. Looking at the dress I felt a sudden sense of *deja vu*, and yet when I studied her face I was certain we hadn't met before. In one hand she held Mr. Zig-Zag's newspaper, folded open to the crossword puzzle, its blank squares now completely filled in. Inside the newspaper's folds, I was to discover a few moments later, flattened ever so neatly, ends taped to the newspaper so that they wouldn't slip, was a plastic baggie inside of which was a generous lid along with my two tens.

"Peace," she said as she placed the newspaper on the table.

Several ornate silver rings adorned her fingers. Her nails were clean and unpolished, cuticles perfectly maintained. A sudden breeze blew her long blonde hair back and away from her face, which was warmly soft and tanned. The color of her eyes was nearly washed out, the palest icy shade of gray or blue, depending on the light and the way she held her head. She reached forward and touched my arm, then took Mr. Zig-Zag's cup and smiled a second time before she walked away.

❧ ❧ ❧

One afternoon later that week after my shift at the fish plant as I headed for my car, I saw her standing at the top of the hill near the road. She was wearing a bright tie-dyed T-shirt, jeans and sandals, and had pulled back her long hair and tied it in a loose ponytail with a strip of leather, its tips adorned by knots and beads. Before I turned away toward my car she gave me a wave, as if she'd been waiting for me.

"Hello," I said as I walked toward her up the hill. I did my best to contain my hope that she was there because of me. Main was a busy street. She could have been waiting for anyone. "It's nice to see you again."

She smiled and shook her head. "How can you stand being cooped up inside there all day? Don't you simply *hate* it? I think I'd lose my mind if I worked inside there day after day."

With her blonde hair pulled back she was even prettier than the day we'd met. The blue of her eyes was darker than I'd remembered,

more the color of the early morning sky, though I'm sure I'm romanti-
cizing and allowing my impressions to be shaped by my certain attrac-
tion to her. She had a slightly upturned nose and a pert expression on
her lips. The skin on high cheekbones was red from the sun. She
seemed the kind of girl who, if I tried to talk to her at a parish dance
back in Chicago, wouldn't have had anything to do with me.

Though I did my best not to stare at her chest, it was obvious
that she wore nothing beneath her T-shirt. The gusts of wind off the
Sound taunted me, repeatedly pressing the thin fabric against her
chest.

"Oh, the place isn't that bad," I said, nodding at the fish plant at the
bottom of the hill. "It pays the rent. There are plenty of worse jobs."

For a while we talked, both of us smiling, dancing around safe
topics like the recent nice weather, until I asked if she needed a lift
and we walked down to my parked car.

"It's not much," I apologized as I opened the passenger door.
Back then, even though I knew about women's lib, I still opened doors
and walked on the outside of the street and stepped back so that the
woman could precede me. My car was a pitiful beater. I drove what I
could afford: a bile-green '62 Oldsmobile Ninety-Eight Town Sedan
spotted with so much rust that on first glance some people thought
the body was two-tone. As we pulled out of the lot and up the hill, I
asked where she wanted to go.

"What do you usually do when you get off work?"

"Bennie and the Jets" played on the radio. I lowered the volume,
then turned the radio off. "To tell you the truth"—I hesitated—"I
usually smoke a joint."

She laughed. "Well," she said, "then let's smoke a joint."

At the stop sign on Campbell I reached for the lid I kept in the
glove compartment. "Don't bother," she said, "I've got a couple already
rolled right here." She held up a small suede purse with beads hanging from the knotted ends of its fringe. The beads matched the ones

on the leather strip that tied back her hair. She opened the purse and took out a glass vial that held three fat joints.

"This is really primo," I said after I pulled in the first hit.

"Better than yours?" she said. "I mean, than the stuff you grow yourself?"

There was hardly a comparison. It was even better than the lid Mr. Zig-Zag had sold or, since he'd returned my twenty dollars, given me. "Yeah," I said, taking a long second hit off the joint and doing my best to be cool and not choke or cough.

"So what do you usually do after you smoke your after-work joint?"

"Nothing much." We were on the main road now. "Drive home and drink a beer, take a shower, clean up, you know, that sort of thing. Why do you ask?"

"No special reason," she said. "Mind if we hang out?"

I shook my head no.

"I'm just curious," she continued, "and I don't want to put you out, so what do you say we do all that, all except for the shower part, I mean. I mean you can take a shower, but I, well"—she gave me a pretty smile and then laughed—"well, you know what I mean."

We passed the joint back and forth as I drove, and with each hit I got more stoned.

My house sits sideways to the road on a large rectangular lot, with a tangle of salal in the front and a big mowed field of grass in the back, which is where I park my car and where I let my occasional campers pitch their tents. As a result I nearly always enter my house through my back door. The field it looks out on is edged with Douglas fir and spreads of salal and alder. That day the field was empty, and as I stared out at it she paused to admire the various things I'd found and collected on my back porch. At the time I had a pair of old buoys hanging by their gray, frayed ropes, various pieces of driftwood, and an assortment of rocks and shells, mainly moon snails. In seaside towns like Tofino, it's a rule of design to decorate the outside of your house with things you've scavenged from the beach. I'm fond of large, flat-bottomed barnacles and converted several into candle holders, which I displayed on a shelf by the back door alongside clusters of shells and rocks and sand dollars. She seemed to find my barnacle candle holders amusing, picking them up one by one and smiling at me as I unlocked the door, and it was then that I realized that I didn't know her name. In another minute we were inside. I took a couple of beers out from the refrigerator and introduced myself.

She took the beer from me and said her name was Harmony. Then she sat at the kitchen table, one ankle demurely crossed over the other, sipping her beer as if she didn't really like its taste. I refused to let my eyes wander over her T-shirt. I stared instead at her sandals and the frayed bottoms of her jeans as I leaned back against the sink. The room was reasonably spotless, though an unwashed coffee cup sat behind me on the counter. Across from me on the wall hung the grim faces of the '69 Cubs. Above the stove, the second hand of my wall clock loudly ticked.

"Is that really your name?" I said after a while. "I mean, out in the real world—"

What I said amused her. "This is the real world," she responded.

"I mean, you know"—I turned sideways and let my hand stroke the gouge in the edge of my counter, as if my touch could smooth it—"when your parents gave you a name, back when you were born, what did they call you?"

"'Sweetheart.' Sometimes 'our darling little girl.'" She laughed. "As for my birth name, what does it matter?" The beads on her pony-tail swung back and forth. "It's a Gatsby thing, you know?"

I shook my head. "I'm not sure I follow."

"You mean you never read *The Great Gatsby*?"

"Of course I've read *The Great Gatsby*. Junior year in high school. Good old F. Scott Fitzgerald. The big pair of eyeglasses overlooking the valley of ashes."

"Doctor T. J. Eckleberg," she said proudly.

"The green light on the end of what's-her-name's dock."

"That's the one," she said. "The great American reinvention of self."

"Ah, yes," I said, as if I were a student back in Brother Jerome's classroom and understood the point she was making. I nodded for several moments, like one of those plastic, red-beaked birds you see in the windows of toy shops, the weighted kind pretending to drink, that once nudged into motion tips its head forward and back for hours. Good God, I realized, was I ever stoned.

"Please," I said, after what seemed to me to be an incredibly long and intense stretch of silence, "make yourself at home. In the other room"—my hand rose in the air by itself and pointed down the hallway—"I have some books. A lot of poetry and fiction, none of which I had to read in high school." My throat gave out a twisted laugh. What was I saying? Why did I feel the need to distance myself from high school? Why was I thinking about English class with Brother Jerome? "I also have a lot of music, which I often listen to." My arm fell back to my side. What an incredibly dumb thing to say. My arm felt heavy, made of wood. I was saying all the wrong things.

She stood and walked down the hallway to my bookcase. "You read poetry?"

I trailed her. "Yeah. At least the stuff that doesn't rhyme. I like the Beats. Blake. Wait, he rhymes, doesn't he? And he isn't a Beat. Still, I like him. And Walt Whitman. And Ferlinghetti and Corso and Ginsberg and di Prima. I like John Berryman. Basho. Frank O'Hara. I like William Carlos Williams."

"Do you write?" she asked.

I laughed and shook my head no, then felt really stupid for laughing. My oatmeal-filled brain searched for a polite return. "And what about you? Do you write poetry?"

"Some," she answered with a sigh. "I'd very much like someday to write full time."

"You'd probably be very good at it." Another wrong thing.

"If wishes were horses," she replied.

I knew there was another half to the expression but my mind was too sluggish to come up with it. "Why don't I take a quick shower?" I said. Like a dog my nose sniffed the air. "I must smell something awful."

"You don't smell that bad, but a shower might be a nice idea." She pulled a slim book of poems off the shelf. Plath's *Ariel*. "Especially if we go out later on. Want to go out later on?"

"Sure," I said, "a shower. But first I need—" I hesitated, knowing there was something that I needed. For the life of me I couldn't think of what it was.

"Soap," she said. "Shampoo. A towel. A washcloth."

"Of course," I said, feeling as if there were a wooden sign around my neck informing everyone that I was the village idiot.

୨୧ ୨୧ ୨୧

When I emerged from the bathroom after the shower and a shave I could hear music, the album I'd left on the turntable, Art Pepper's *Intensity*. The third cut, "Come Rain or Come Shine," played from the speakers, Pepper's wistful alto sax phrasing the song beautifully with long, achingly pure notes and perfect hesitations. Harmony was in the middle of the room, her back to me, weaving side to side, slow-dancing with herself. The physical desire I felt for her at that moment was as strong as a lion's roar.

The shower helped to clear my head. It also allowed me to remember the second half of her expression. *Beggars would ride*, I wanted to say but didn't, knowing that the timing was wrong, realizing that with a girl like blue-eyed Harmony I did feel like a beggar.

"This place," she said after the song ended and she noticed me standing in the doorway, "it's like really incredibly spare. Everywhere I've ever lived has been so cluttered. I mean, everything here is like totally organized and clean."

I looked around. In the front room I had an old but well-made sofa and a stuffed armchair that more or less matched it. Near the armchair stood a wooden end table and, upon it, a lamp. On the other side of the room was a floor lamp. On the wooden floor, which I regularly waxed and polished, lay a small area rug. Atop the rug near the sofa was a pine coffee table, which I'd sanded and stained and varnished. Against the walls were matching pine bookcases and a cabinet in which I kept my stereo and my records. Plath's *Ariel* lay on the armchair. I picked it up and returned it to its shelf. "Well, I live by myself," I said. "After I put something away, there's no one else to make a mess."

"There isn't a book or album out of place."

I didn't know whether to take that as a criticism or a compliment.

"I guess that's what I find so amazing," she continued. "That you have a concept of, like, where things go, like where to put things. You know, like you have this idea that there's an actual place where things belong."

I nodded. I not only had a concept of where things belonged, I had an actual need for things to be in their place whenever they weren't in use. Don't ask me why. I feel strangely out of sorts and even physically uncomfortable when I don't put things back in their place. The feeling is so different from the good feeling you have, say, after brushing your teeth. You're somehow square with the world right after you brush your teeth. But to dare go out into the world without brushing. . . . That's how I felt when I didn't put things away.

"And you really don't have much stuff," she said. "I mean, look at this room. Except for the sofa and armchair, you're nearly a Shaker. You couldn't have bought a plainer set of lamps. And did you notice that you've lowered each window shade precisely the same length as the others? You have nothing hanging on your walls except that old picture in the kitchen and the crucifix in your bedroom. And in your bedroom there's only a bed, a dresser, a night table and another plain lamp. The edges of that book you're reading"—she pointed to a copy of *In Watermelon Sugar*—"are nearly perfectly squared with the edges of the table. And your bed is actually made. There's hardly any dust beneath it or anywhere else on the floor. All the hangers in your closet hang in the same direction. And that pantry—"

"Order helps me find things."

"I've been in messier libraries."

"My back porch is cluttered," I said in my defense.

"Maybe, but it's an organized clutter. Even your barnacle candles are set on the shelf symmetrically."

"Well, there's dirty laundry inside the washing machine. There's a dirty coffee cup sitting out on the counter."

"Hey, I'm not rapping you. I mean, I'm just trying to tell you I'm really impressed."

We went to get something to eat, fish and chips at Daniel's place, down near the First Street Wharf overlooking the harbor. Daniel's restaurant is clean and decent and nothing too fancy, one of Ignatius George's favorite places to eat, I'd find out later, a place where locals and the smarter tourists ate, the Tofino equivalent of what back in Chicago would be a really good neighborhood diner. The fillets of fish were thick and fresh and fried to perfection. Harmony and I sat at a window table looking over the Sound. When our plates came, we leapt on them as if we were starving. Not pausing to speak, we ate and ate. As I picked through the last of my fries, Harmony asked if I wanted to drop some mescaline.

That stopped me short.

It was organic mesc, she said, the genuine article as opposed to bad acid in disguise, truly good stuff, no lie, trust me, she said, I should try it, it would be enlightening as well as great fun. She ruffled through her purse and in plain sight at the table in Daniel's took out another small glass vial, inside of which resting among variously colored pills were three or four round blue tablets speckled with little purple flecks like confetti.

"You've got a regular pharmacy in there," I observed.

"We could drop this stuff now and then head over to the beach. It'd be a great way to spend the rest of the evening." In the light of the restaurant her eyes were deeply blue.

"I've never taken mescaline. Or, for that matter, acid."

"You mean you live here year-round and you've never tripped?"

I shook my head. I knew plenty of people who lived here year-round and never tripped. Though they certainly did drink. Nearly everyone I knew who lived in Tofino year-round drank. The joke was that half of Tofino's resident population was in AA and the other half needed to be. Some drank a little beer every day, like me, and some blew their entire check in the liquor store each payday and then commenced to do some truly serious drinking. I mean some of the locals drank for *days*. They drank and drank and drank, for as long as their paycheck and their friends' charity could sustain them. That was how I'd gotten my job at the fish processing plant. I started there by filling in for the workers who didn't come back to work the day after payday.

Harmony held one of the tablets of mescaline in her raised palm. I was so attracted to her I might have swallowed bits of ground-up glass if she'd asked me, but still I had a host of suspicions. "Okay," I said, "sure, but before we go any further I need to ask you something." I took a deep breath, then locked into her eyes. "Why?"

She dropped her hand to the table. "What do you mean, why?"

I decided to lay it all on the line. "I may have led a somewhat limited life," I said, "but I don't ordinarily meet many girls who seek me out after work, get me high with killer weed, dance to Art Pepper while I take a shower, evaluate my belongings and housekeeping skills, share a great meal with me, then ask me to trip with them. I mean, not that I mind, don't get me wrong, I'm having a great time with you, but I have to ask you, has this got anything to do with Mr. Zig-Zag?"

"Mr. Zig-Zag?"

"You know who I mean. Your dealer friend."

"Oh," she laughed, "Clarence. I guess I get so used to him looking the way he does I forget how he appears to people who don't really know him. So everybody still calls him Mr. Zig-Zag? I thought that was so last year."

"You haven't answered my question."

She let out a sigh. "You're right. I have ulterior motives. Clarence wants you to work for him, Vince. Tend his gardens, protect them from thieves, maybe drive down-island to Nanaimo and Victoria on occasion. But he didn't ask me to deliver the message, he asked Jeremy"—she waved a hand in the air—"you know, the dude who picked up your money that afternoon outside the Crumb. I overheard Clarence talking about it with Jeremy later that day and said I'd be glad to talk to you. You seemed like a nice guy."

"So you live with Mr. Zig-Zag?"

She nodded. "Only during summers, when I'm not at university. We all do. I mean. Like, everybody does. I thought you knew that. It's like, you know, a commune."

So all of this was business. Her interest in me was all business. My heart fell.

Then she told me that Clarence had been having trouble with thieves—locals, he was convinced, grazers—who'd let him do all the work up until the last minute when then they'd sweep in like vultures or a swarm of locusts and harvest all the ripe colas and buds. It was as if the thieves tracked him, striking wherever he wasn't. He needed someone honest, someone he could trust. He also owned a van that he used to take kilos to Nanaimo and Victoria. His grass was known as far away as Vancouver for its killer-high levels of THC. On a scale of one to ten, if the local grass was three Clarence had developed seed lines that were seven or eight. Ever since she could remember he'd been interested in growing things, she said, and he'd studied botany and genetics and had been experimenting with clones—rooted cuttings from female plants—and marijuana seed lines for years. He was revolutionizing the industry. What Gregor Mendel was for peas, she said, Clarence was for marijuana.

"You must really like him a lot."

"Like him?" she said. "Sure, what's not to like? He's intelligent, witty, well-read, and an absolute genius at what he does, which serves only to bring other people pleasure. Like him? I love him. I've loved him for years, ever since I can remember."

I said nothing, since obviously there was nothing to say.

She stared at me strangely, as if suddenly recognizing that we weren't speaking the same language. Then a smile turned up the corners of her eyes, and she tilted back her head and laughed. She laughed hard and long, and with such unrestrained volume and glee that Daniel poked his head out from behind the counter and looked at us. Then she told me that I was so dense it was mind blowing and that Clarence was her older brother.

# 6

# *Tofino 1975–78*

"FOR YOUR MAIDEN VOYAGE," Harmony said, "we'll just split a tab, take it slow and easy. But first we'll need a nice piece of fruit." Apparently the best way to drop mescaline was to take it with fruit. So we said goodbye to Daniel and drove up the hill to the co-op.

"Ideally we're looking for a small pear," Harmony said as we entered the store. She'd dropped mesc more times than she could remember and always had the mellowest trips when they began with ingesting the drug on half of a soft pear. The pears at the co-op were hard as hand grenades, so we checked out the other fruits, deciding finally on some overripe apricots.

The evening was beginning to cool. If we were going to the beach, she said as we returned to the car, we should stop at my place for something warm to wear. At my house she chose one of my hooded sweatshirts, a black one, and I grabbed my old blue-jean jacket off the hook near the back door. She slipped on the sweatshirt, which came down to the top of her thighs, and then rolled up her sleeves and washed one of the apricots at the sink and split it in two with her thumbnail. Then she cut a tab of mesc in half with a sharp knife and sprinkled the speckled shards of the drug on the soft, fleshy fruit.

"Say a prayer as you take it," Harmony said as she handed me my half, "because unlike acid mescaline is a holy drug."

I opted for *Oh Lord, help me, for I know not what I do* and made the sign of the Cross as we each ate our half of the fruit, then shared the remaining apricots.

"Ever read Aldous Huxley?" she said, back in the car. I drove toward the highway, slowly, well beneath the speed limit. "He wrote a wonderful book, *The Doors of Perception*, all about his mescaline trips, how mesc opens up and heightens the senses."

"The *Brave New World* guy took mescaline?"

She nodded. "Religiously. So did all of the Beats you're so fond of reading. The native people down in the American Southwest use peyote in their religious practices."

Now I kept pace with the rest of the traffic on the highway, driving about five kilometers over the speed limit.

"Why isn't acid a holy drug?" I asked after a while.

"Because it was invented by the CIA. Down in the States in their secret labs, as a weapon to fuck with people's minds. You didn't know that, that it was governmental pigs who invented acid? I mean I'm not saying that in the right doses it's bad or evil. I've taken some really mellow acid trips in the rainforest with my friends. It's just not sacred, you know, since it doesn't come from the earth."

"So the earth—" I began.

"Whatever comes from the earth is sacred. Whatever comes from man more often than not is not." She leaned back against the passenger door, nodding her head. "It's literally profane, you know, as in 'outside the temple'? That's what *profane* means. Before, or outside, the *fanum*. Did you ever study etymology or read the italicized origins of words in the dictionary? My mother was an absolute fanatic about words, anything that had to do with language. Clarence and I would still be in our diapers and she'd be like correcting our grammar and teaching us the proper use of the subjunctive mood."

"Oh yeah," I said. "Those were lessons my mother taught me, too."

"Anyway," she continued, "it all goes back to that first moment, you know. I mean the true First Moment, the time before the serpent, when man lived in connection with the earth and forests and the seven seas. In the beginning there was peace and congruity, and then humanity's foolish pride gave rise to discord and confusion. Our challenge now is to get back, you know, to that pure state."

I nodded, focusing on my driving and monitoring my response to the drug. So far I felt nothing.

"Take a newborn baby," she said. "All of its instincts are natural and pure. Infants have a curiosity and attitude toward life that in an adult we'd consider genius. You were brought up Roman Catholic?"

I nodded again. "How could you tell?"

"Call me psychic." After a beat she added, "Of course, the rosary and gruesome crucifix in your bedroom sort of give you away, not to mention your habit of crossing yourself and kissing your thumb before eating."

"Very perceptive. You're a regular Sherlock Holmes."

"But even if I hadn't been inside your place," she continued, "I'd take you for a latent believer in original sin. Maybe you can't see it, but it's written all over you. It might as well be a letter you wear on your chest."

I drove in silence, not mentioning my scar. Then I had to touch it, so I slipped my hand down the front of my work shirt and inside my dago-T and touched it.

"As for me, I believe that babies are born pure, then are muddied by contact with their parents and society. Actually, the phrase I used before, 'brought up,' is backward. I think most kids are 'brought down,' if that makes any sense."

"I can relate to that."

"What we do to kids as they get older simply reduces them, you know, bit by bit by bit, wearing them down like a lead pencil pushed into one of those metal sharpeners hanging on a classroom wall."

"Amen to that."

"We grind them down until they get smaller and smaller. We call that growing up. We grind them down to stubby nubs. Then when they're as small and uncreative as the rest of us, we slap them on the back and call them adults."

I hung a right at Chesterman Beach Road and eased the Olds into the public lot. The sun was just dipping into the treetops ahead. We stood outside the car in the evening's cool air, and as Harmony walked toward me I took her hands.

"How dangerous will it be if I work for your brother?" I asked. "I don't know what else you can guess about me, but back in the States I ran away from a lot of things, I mean in both a personal but also a legal sense. If I get caught and sent back I could be looking at a lot of jail time."

She gave my hands a squeeze. "Do whatever you think is best, but don't think you need to decide now. Tonight's just for us. And later, if you think it's too great a risk or it doesn't feel right, don't do it." She studied me for several moments, then placed the flat of both of her hands on my chest. "You know," she said softly, "there's a darkness here that I'd prefer not come with us to the beach. Don't you feel it?" She smiled. "What do you say we get rid of it?" She poked my ribs. "Come on, let's lock it in the trunk."

She took the keys from my pocket and unlocked the trunk of the Olds and tossed in her beaded purse. Then she flattened her palm against my chest and told me to imagine my darkness. "Close your eyes. Breathe. That's it. Slow, deep breaths. Are you seeing it?"

Even though it was lame and dumb I did what she asked of me. I closed my eyes and breathed and as I did so I tried to imagine that some great, dark thing lay on my heart.

"Now imagine that each time you exhale you're letting it go."

I exhaled loudly, still trying to imagine it.

"That's it. Push it out."

"There," I said, "that's all of it."

"Push out more."

I exhaled.

"Done? Are you sure?"

"I'm sure," I lied.

"It's all out of you?"

"It's all out of me."

"And now it's lying there in the trunk. Keep your eyes closed. Can you see it?"

I nodded. "Sure."

"What's it doing now?"

"I don't know," I said. I imagined the empty trunk and tried to think of something. "Sniffing the air with its tongue. Coiling around itself, like a snake."

"You feel lighter and freer inside, don't you?"

I nodded. "Sure."

"It'd be dumb to lock it up here, wouldn't it? So why not just let it go?"

"I don't follow you."

"Release it. Let it crawl out on the road. Maybe it can get run over on the highway."

I played along and imagined the snake-like thing crawling out of the trunk onto the gravel parking lot and then back toward the road and highway. As I turned my head to follow it, Harmony pressed her hand against my chest, then undid a couple of buttons on my work shirt and slipped her hand inside, pressing her palm against my dago-T. She leaned toward me and dropped her forehead against my chest. Though she whispered a few words into my chest, I didn't hear them. I still hadn't opened my eyes. I felt her fingertips trace the out-line of my scar, and then I heard her whisper my name.

"There," she said after a while, after everything around us had grown silent except for the surf sounding softly on the nearby beach. "There, now it's out and you're free."

I opened my eyes as she buttoned the button she'd undone on my shirt. How I wanted to believe her. But then we were running across the road and down the public accessway, past newly planted pines and through a hedge of salal in full berry—its branches clacking as our shoulders brushed against its thick leaves—as the sound of the pounding waves grew louder and we could smell the brisk, salty fresh-ness of the sea.

❧ ❧ ❧

"Well, my friend, here we are," Harmony announced as we stepped onto the sand. "Down the rabbit hole. From here on out things just get curiouser and curiouser."

The mescaline was just starting to kick in. I felt a warm, rippling glow at the base of my neck followed by a flurry of electric blue shivers that skittered across my shoulder blades and back as if I were the keyboard of some piano being played. It took me a while to realize that I was shivering not so much in response to the cool, early evening air blowing in from the ocean but because I was so jacked up, because of all the adrenaline surging through my body. So I stretched my arms, rolled my neck, took several deep breaths, and did my best to calm down. My senses were opening up wide, sudden and fast, like the petals of a flower in one of those nature movies where the hours collapse into seconds and clouds speed by in the sky in expanding, furry blurs. Suddenly I could feel each and every sensation outside my body: the texture of the passing breeze as it fluttered across my cheeks and forehead, the soft weight of my clothing as it brushed against my arms and chest, the wet caress of my eyelids as they passed down over my newly opened eyes.

As Harmony and I neared the water, my eyes snagged and stumbled down into the intricate mesh and weave of my denim jacket, and the sheer marvel of its complex, grid-like stitching. What a truly tremendous thing this was, I thought as I gazed at the arm of my jean jacket. I realized that for all the years I'd owned the jacket I'd simply taken it for granted and never before actually *seen* it. What an astounding thing the sleeve of my jacket was! How blind I had been to all the things in the world around me! Certainly I'd never appreciated the intricacy of the weave of its cloth let alone the extraordinary complexity and beauty of its incredibly symmetrical stitching.

I have to study this jacket, I thought, I really have to examine it in detail, and then my gaze tumbled further down onto the most incredible arrangement of sand, seaweed, and shell that lay before me on the ground, an absolute marvel on which, in my profound inattention to the world, I very nearly stepped. At once I stood still and dropped to my knees. There before me snagged in a drying clump of kelp was a thatched barnacle no thicker than my little finger, a discarded fragment of Dungeness crab shell, an entire starfish, a broken bit of mussel shell. The sight before me was nearly too much to take in, particularly since at that moment a busy squadron of sand fleas leapt from it and onto a nearby sandhill like a herd of miniature wild horses. The tiny horses leapt again, then again. I nearly fell backward in surprise. From my chest poured out a long cry of splendor. I would have knelt there in the sand fully entranced for an hour or more studying all the colors and textures of the world had Harmony not pulled me up and forward, toward her and the amazing golden ball of light glowing off in the distance like the face of some ancient god.

Her touch on my arm set off another wave of blue shoulder shivers, and as her fingers slid down to my hand a hot white spark pulsed in my chest and then my groin.

"Pretty great, huh?" she said.

"Wow!" was all I could say. The sound of my voice rippled strangely in my ears.

"I wish I had a camera," she said. "Like, you wouldn't believe the expression you have on your face right now. You're wearing the biggest grin."

"If you say so," I grinned.

"I take it everything's cool with you now." We walked, arm in arm, toward the fantastically burning sphere slowly sinking toward the water on the horizon.

I nodded. To my left suddenly a dog with a furious long brown coat ran effortlessly along the darker sand at the water's edge, pink tongue happily lolling, paws splashing the foamy spill of the receding waves. *Plash! pa-plash! plash!* exploded across my eardrums, a sound so thick and wet I imagined that if I closed my eyes I could reach out and touch it. Beneath that was the rolling, ever-changing pop and crash and hissing whisper of the waves. How the sea speaks in such a complex language! I thought. How its sounds nearly resemble words! I tipped my head sideways to allow the liquid sounds to splash about in my ears as the dog raced forward, toward the sun.

A wisp of Harmony's long hair lashed my cheek. With one hand she'd untied the strip of leather and beads that bound it, and now her hair tossed freely behind her in the wind as if it were something alive. Another swatch of hair brushed my face. My tongue leapt sideways to greet it.

Salt. In the corner of my lips. The corner of my lips tasted distinctly salty. I glided my tongue across the fleshy roll of my bottom lip, then my top lip. Such a complexity of taste and feeling! My tongue tasting and simultaneously feeling, my lips being felt by the soft, erotic lick of my own tongue. Then, from somewhere else in my mouth, or perhaps my throat, came the sudden and distinct tastes of fish and fries and ketchup.

Harmony locked my arm more tightly with hers as she plunged her hands into the front flap of her hooded sweatshirt. "It's kicking in real nice, isn't it?" she said, as the wind reached between us and snatched her words and nearly ran away with them before I could grab a piece of their sound and make sense of them. I think she meant the drug we'd taken. "I'll have to remember the apricots," she added.

Again I nodded, only to feel a thousand sensations run down my neck and along the length of my spine. The sensations had a golden color about them and ceased whenever I stopped moving. "Apricots," I heard my voice say, and then I laughed because for a moment the sound that came from my mouth made absolutely no sense to my ears, and *apricots* seemed the funniest, most absurd word in the world.

Harmony slowed and pulled me toward her, choosing that moment to kiss me there on the sands of Chesterman Beach, with the big sun setting gold-orange beside us, twenty or so yards away from where a group of kids stood around a bonfire, whose flames were just beginning to leap past the top of its tented logs. The wind was in my ears as she pulled me toward her, toward the full flesh of her lips. The playful tip of her tongue sought out mine and then quickly retreated. I tasted the cool taste of her mouth and found it pleasing.

Her arms draped my shoulders as she gathered her hands at the nape of my neck and pressed her fingers into my hair and onto my tingling scalp, pulling me down and forward to her mouth for a second kiss. Her hips fit themselves against mine. I allowed my hands to outline the graceful dip and curve of her waist and then my right hand held the small of her back, pressing her body firmly against mine, and my left hand ran up and over the soft, bunched hood of her sweatshirt into the luxurious thick tangle of her hair, which swirled magnificently about her head in the wind. Then her lush mouth rose up again to mine.

Along with all of this there were at least a thousand other sensations, but these are the ones I can most clearly remember, as the waves limned gold from the sun broke gently beside and beyond us and the wind filled the hollows of our ears, as some guy ran past us and then paused to reach up for a floating yellow Frisbee, and I thought of Roxanne's Frisbee, how maybe I should throw it away, as a child with a blue tin bucket on which were painted orange starfish squatted to pick up and inspect a purple snail shell, as the sharp white beam from the lighthouse on nearby Lennard Island flashed and swung confidently over the water, as the retriever mix raced happily back and forth along the edge of the shore, as the flames of the bonfire leapt without the least thought of consequence into the coming night, and the bright sun in the distance dipped into the shimmering waves.

༄ ༄ ༄

At Harmony's insistence we progressed from mescaline to acid, which was not really a move forward in my eyes.

If being straight was like living inside a muted photograph of half-tones punctuated with occasional streaks of sharper blacks and whites, and being on mescaline was like stepping into a Japanese watercolor in which life's finely brushed hues bled delicately from one to the next, dropping LSD was like leaping feet-first into a full-screen Technicolor cartoon complete with Dolby surround-sound cranked up to near eardrum-bleeding levels.

Watch out before the falling safe rushing through the air above you descends on your head, before the wild-eyed rabbit chomping the carrot ties the double barrels of your shotgun into a knot and the gun explodes in your hands. Just when you think you're walking on firm ground, you gaze down and notice that you've taken several steps off the side of the cliff. Momentary take to the audience, as the whites of your eyes throb once, then twice, in shock and sheer panic. The receding sound of a whistle screeches in your ears as you dive-bomb into a tiny cloud of dust below.

Wile E. Coyote has booby-trapped every curve on the trail ahead of you, and you're no Road Runner, able to escape his bag of tricks. No, just like the fat stuttering pig in the ill-fitting vest and bow tie, you fall for each and every one of his pranks: the cigar that on third puff explodes and leaves your face a blackened cinder, the handshake with the electric buzzer that causes you to vibrate and writhe until the viewer can make out every glowing bone in your skeleton, the steamroller that runs you over from behind, making you so flat you fit neatly inside an envelope, which is promptly airmailed to an insane asylum, where three men in white coats and butterfly nets chase you down. Your head turns into a lollipop on which is written the word SUCKER! The dark tunnel on the path before you is really only a painted backdrop on the side of a mountain, against which, after you smash into it full speed, you flatten into a manhole cover and then wobble about on the ground. *Wobble wobble wobble wobble*, goes the soundtrack. Ever so gingerly you try to step away after you light the stick of dynamite, which always goes off in your back pocket or your hand. Another dark office safe drops on your head, followed by a grand piano, an immense boulder, a giant anvil, a slew of bowling balls, a two-ton hydrogen bomb. After they smash your toes with the sledgehammer, a weight rises through your legs and chest and clangs the bell of your forehead, and you see a pair of twirling mobiles featuring tweeting bluebirds and twinkling yellow stars. Cream pies from right and left simultaneously smack you in the face. The barber then decides to shave you, yanking out your tongue to strop his razor, and when he's through you end up with no nose, no mouth, no ears, no hair, no eyes. Acme has sold you another rocket ship, which runs out of fuel midair, and you plummet down once again into an exploding mushroom cloud. *Ca-ching!* rings the sound of a cash register, as rectangular black tabs saying NO and SALE pop up in the empty sockets of your eyes.

You keep falling into the same rabbit hole, the one where, when you look out at the world, it's as if you're gazing through the wrong end of binoculars. I'd be tripping on acid at the commune with Harmony, sitting on the floor with my back leaning up against a wall, and then all at once the wall behind me would rush backward thirty, forty, fifty feet from the rest of the room, taking me along with it. The commune was an old ramshackle place, vintage Tofino architecture, with uneven floors and a leaky roof and a near-endless maze of rooms added at various times onto the primary structure with no real thought given to symmetry or design, as if the place had been constructed by a speed freak with a hammer and a chainsaw. In theory the commune was meant to be like my aquarium, an attempt at a perfectly balanced, self-sustaining environment. In actuality it was haphazard, chaotic, arbitrary. "Are you all right?" someone an inch tall would ask as the wall behind me fell away. I'd be receding fast, spinning off like a rudderless ship in some outer-space movie, a hundred, two hundred, three hundred yards away from them.

I'd be unable to open my mouth or move, even raise a finger. Then a voice from somewhere inside my head would tell me, *Well maybe this is it, the really bad acid trip you sometimes hear about, the one you don't come back from, the one that leads you straight to the padded white walls in the windowless room from which you never ever escape.*

"He's cool," someone else would say. "Not to worry. Capone's cool."

Around the commune there were nicknames for everyone, as if our actual birth names were embarrassing or off limits. Apparently my being both Italian and from Chicago was too much to resist.

"You're cool, Capone, right?" the voices would ask as I tumbled further and further back toward the room with the padded walls.

"Sure," someone would answer for me. "The dude's fine. He's only spacing."

If the voices only knew how absolutely unfine I was, I'd tell myself, how absolutely terrifying the space separating me from the rest of the world was, and how utterly impossible it seemed at that moment to bridge that space, they'd help me. They'd do something about it, I'd assure myself, as I would, if any of them were in my place.

At times like these—moments of sheer heart-thumping panic—I'd sit back and do my best to ride it out. I'd stay where I was, my back against some solid object, whatever was there to support me, and try to remember to breathe. That was the secret, I told myself. Remember to breathe. Pull the next breath in, push the air in your lungs out.

I was more than familiar with the routine. Go numb. Ride it out. Face the music, as my father would say. Try not to acknowledge any feeling or pain. Remember that the present moment will end eventually. Remember that nothing goes on forever, that eventually even the very worst situations come to an end.

∾  ∾  ∾

The acid trips dredged up memories I'd done my best to forget.

When I was just a kid, a neighbor who lived a few houses down on Glenwood apparently disapproved of the noise I made while outside playing. Supposedly he worked nights and needed to sleep during the day. Whatever, there were times when he'd find me and grab me, then drag me from where I was playing and lock me inside his wooden tool shed, which stood adjacent to the alley beside his two-car garage. Since the neighborhood had rats and we kids sometimes saw rats slinking in and out of the shed, in our neighborhood the place was known as the rat shed.

I've gone over this in group with Big Ed and the others and don't have any real memories of being inside the rat shed beyond the sensation of being shoved into its darkness, its awful, musty smell, the door behind me slamming shut against the bright light. I don't know if the man came into the shed with me or merely thrust me inside and closed the door. I do remember the roughness of his hand squeezing the back of my neck as he pushed me toward the shed. He always did that, always grabbed me by the back of my neck. Whenever he caught me my neck would ache for the rest of the day.

I can remember crouching inside the shed's dank, dusty darkness, wiping away my tears, brushing spider webs from my face and hands, afraid to go back out into the light. So I'd simply crouch there, crying. After the longest time, after I was certain that everyone in the world had forgotten about me, I'd hear Nonna's voice calling my name. "*Veen-chen-zo, Veen-chen-zo,*" she'd cry, over and over, like the cry of some ancient chant.

For some reason I never could answer her back. I'd be unable to open my mouth or move. Nonna would have to come all the way down our rickety wooden back steps from her second-floor flat to search for me, and as her voice grew louder she'd hear my whimpers and rattle open the shed's wooden door, flooding the shack with so much light that to gaze into it and try to make out the features of her face was painful. I can remember her hands pulling me out from the darkness, then shaking me out of my stupor, sometimes cuffing the side of my head until I'd come to and say her name. Then she'd cover my cheeks with kisses and embrace me inside her dark smell.

She'd always tell me to scream with every ounce of my might should the man ever push me inside the shed again. I was to scream my throat raw, scream and scream and never for a moment stop screaming. Then she'd show me how it might be done by releasing onto the neighbor's house such a string of dark curses that I imagined the earth itself would open up and swallow the brutal neighbor's two-flat with a fiery roar.

Though I was shoved into the shed repeatedly—over a period of a few years I'd guess at least a dozen times—I never once screamed out for help. I can remember that after the man banged the door shut and after I wiped my tears and the sticky spider webs from my face, I'd grow quiet and lean back against something, an old barrel or perhaps the shed's far wall, and wait in the darkness for my grandmother to rescue me. Sometimes I'd stand beside a dusty table littered with tools—hammers with rusting claws, screwdrivers with wooden handles, monkey wrenches with jaws so big you imagined that if you touched them they'd leap up and talk—and stare at the tools. Despite what my father told me about myself, I was a reasonably good boy and mainly did what I was told, stayed where I was put, obediently, patiently. Yet at the same time I believed all the things my father said about me, and I knew from Sister Ascension and the old monsignor to whom on Saturday afternoons I routinely confessed my transgressions that I was born in sin and that in all likelihood even being an altar boy and serving thousands of Masses and lighting ten thousand votive candles before the statue of the Virgin wouldn't keep my soul out of the fires of Hell.

I knew that I aggravated my mother and often failed to help around the house. The house was always a mess. As the oldest child, it was my duty to help her clean up the mess. To pick things up and put them where they belonged. Things in our house were always not where they belonged. As the firstborn and only son, it was my duty to work. To open my eyes and see work. Not to have to be told what to do. A true man opens his eyes and sees what must be done! Then he does it without hesitation or complaint. At school I was often reprimanded for daydreaming or fidgeting in my seat or having little dialogues with myself and, as a result, disturbing my classmates. Surely there was little hope for my soul.

"*Veen-chen-zo! Veen-chen-zo!*"

"Hey, Capone, you all right over there? You're whimpering like a damn dog. Nod your head up and down for yes, side to side for no."

"*Veen-chen-zo, Veen-chen-zo,* what did he do to you again? *Mischinu!* Get up! Wipe your tears."

"Capone, if you're joking it's not funny. Snap out of it, man."

"*Veen-chen-zo, Veen-chen-zo,* come to me, *Veen-chen-zo.*"

"Like, I mean *really*. You're really fucking freaking us out."

I think they preferred nicknames because they wanted to alter or erase the pasts they'd left behind in the lousy world beyond our narrow western peninsula that jutted out into the sea. These were the kids who could no longer tolerate their families, the kids who'd been driven out or just got too sick and tired of things and split, who threw a T-shirt and an extra pair of jeans and a toothbrush into a knapsack and headed out to the nearest highway, the thumb of their right hand poking up in the breeze. They were just like me, and I was just like them. We did this even though we knew that in the end the past couldn't be erased, even by changing your name and pretending you're Jay Gatsby. Deep in our hearts we knew how things really turned out. The past is fixed and absolute, so real and inescapable it's like that image in Dickens of Jacob Marley's chain: a great iron weight that we drag behind us, that we forge daily from our own greed and selfishness, heavy link by iron link by iron link.

"*Veen-chen-zo, Veen-chen-zo,* come here to my arms."

"Snap out of it, Capone. Don't make us have to take you to the hospital. Come on, dude."

"*Veen-chen-zo! Veen-chen-zo!*"

Eventually the wall against which my back rested would inch forward and return me to the others in the commune. I'd be able to move a hand, nod my head, grunt. I'd be able to stand, to run to my Nonna's arms.

"Capone," they'd say, "hey, welcome back to fucking planet Earth, dude."

And I'd do my best to smile, though if I closed my eyes and thought hard enough I could still feel Nonna's hands clutching my shoulders and brushing my cheeks and hair, still smell the suffocating comfort of her dress as she pressed me to her chest, still hear her curses at the neighbor rip and splinter the air.

∾ ∾ ∾

"Did the neighbor ever go in the shed with you?" Big Ed asked the first time that I talked about it in group.

We sat around the old coffee table, sipping mugs of bitter coffee we'd brewed in the church's big stainless steel coffee urn. Long shadows of the bushes and trees outside the church stretched sideways through the side windows and across the room. Beyond them, the sun was setting over the Sound. "I don't know," I said.

"You're always so sure about everything else," one of the guys in group said. "Seems like something this important, you'd remember."

This drew the guy a couple of red cards.

"I think if Vince doesn't want to talk about it he doesn't have to talk about it," the guy who threw the first red card said.

"I agree," said the other red card. "Though we don't need to go into the specifics."

"Yes, we do," said the first guy. "We always need the specifics. Like Big Ed says, the truth is in the details. So lay 'em out. Spill your guts, Vince. We're not going to judge."

"But what if he can't remember any more?"

"Yeah, what if he's telling the truth?"

"The bad things," the first guy said, "they're the things you can't possibly forget."

"That's not always true," Big Ed said. "Sometimes the very worst experiences are the ones we disassociate from, the ones we don't remember, that we repress."

"What I can't understand," said the first guy, "is that this happened a dozen or so times over a period of a couple of years. Am I right? So it was more or less routine. Seems if it happened that many times he'd remember something."

"Talk to Vince," said Big Ed. "Tell Vince what you think."

The guy turned to me. "It seems to me, man, that you'd remember something."

"No, really," I told him. "Really. I just don't know. Believe me, I wish I did."

☙ ☙ ☙

The first thing I learned from Clarence was the locations of his gardens. He had them all over the islands, wherever the forest had been clear-cut a decade or so ago and the sun could still make its way down to the forest floor. He chose spots where the land was spotted with salmonberry and alder, fireweed and bracken fern, where shoulder-high spruce and cedar could provide his marijuana plants with cover. I'd clear the land of bracken and fireweed before he came in to plant. We'd use the roads cut by the lumber companies though Clarence preferred that whenever possible I access the areas by boat. Boats were less noticeable, he claimed. I was essentially his security guard, protecting his crops from thieves. Though I worked during the day I thought of myself as a night watchman whose job was to make his rounds rattling the lock on each shop door to insure that all was safe.

Upon maturation the plants would be harvested and dried, then pressed into kilo-weight cubes wrapped in glistening plastic and bound tautly with tape and cellophane. The bound kilos, or keys—sometimes called bricks—were then placed in black plastic garbage bags and sealed with more tape. Then the keys were picked up at certain locations outside of town or trucked with all due care to their intended destinations.

Clarence's distribution system offered the big wholesalers the option of delivery: a rarity but understandable given Tofino's remoteness. Whereas most dealers purchased product directly from growers, Clarence was willing to truck product to his highest volume clients in

Nanaimo and Victoria. It was these processed keys along with stacks of wooden totes, the rows closest to the back end of the truck filled with iced salmon, that I drove at irregular intervals down-island to Nanaimo and Victoria, often at twilight or during the dead of night, in addition to my regular duties as security guard.

Hauling the crates of salmon along with the keys was my idea, brainchild of my paranoia. I could imagine a thousand things going wrong—a flat tire or non-functioning taillight, or perhaps a fine for speeding or failing to yield—and then as a result being asked if my vehicle might be inspected. The crates of fish might offer me sufficient camouflage to survive a cursory inspection. In the event I was busted, the totes of salmon could give me the defense that I was unaware of the van's actual contents. Of course the excuse was lamer than a pirate with a wooden leg, but given my status in Canada I felt that something was better than nothing. After a while Clarence saw the wisdom behind the guise, and so we added at least two rows of crates of iced gutted fish on every run I made to Nanaimo and Victoria, the smell of my father trailing me like my shadow.

During my years of making these runs I was never once pulled over, and the one time I had a roadside emergency (a worn fan belt gave way and snapped) the cop who drove by set up safety flares on the road to warn passing motorists of my whereabouts, then leaned alongside the van with me, smoking a cigarette and chatting about his wife, the old ball and chain, and his three kids, with a fourth now on the way, and my fortunate lack of both, while I did my best to stay calm and keep up my end of the conversation as I feverishly waited for the tow to the garage for repairs.

What I gathered from everyone was that the RCMP were more concerned about B.C.'s finest making its way down into the States along the various roads leading to Seattle and beyond than its growth or internal movement, particularly in our relatively remote part of Vancouver Island. The highways leading from Canada down to Seattle were called "the corridors," and while we guessed that some of our crop made its way down the corridors we were comforted by the knowledge that we weren't the ones taking that risk. We knew that most of the keys sold to the Nanaimo wholesalers were taken to Vancouver. The keys we dropped off in Victoria were likely re-processed (de-twigged, sifted for seeds, sometimes diluted with less potent strains of marijuana or filler herbs such as marjoram), then weighed and broken down into single-ounce lids.

We were safe, in other words, or at least that's what the others told me and what I chose to believe. During late September, when it was time for Tofino's gardeners to harvest their crops, I'd occasionally see police helicopters sweeping the sky, on the lookout for the most obvious patches of marijuana. I'd run Clarence's boat parallel with the shoreline and watch them fly over, raising a hand to shield my eyes from the sun, at my feet the chainsaw (for cutting cedar shakes) I carried with me as cover in case anyone ever wanted to know why I was where I was. Cutting cedar shakes was my excuse for being near the clearcuts in the forest. The others shared stories about growers who diligently tended their crops all spring and summer, who took all the risks and did all the labor, and then just before harvest found their entire crop gone, the stalk of each plant hacked by the police four or five millimeters above the ground.

Or by thieves. Grazers, Clarence called them. Despicable low-life grazers, who come in like hyenas after the long hunt with the hope of stealing the entire kill. Clarence cared far less about the RCMP than he did the grazers. After a while I came to understand that my true job was to safeguard Clarence's crop against the grazers, whom Clarence maintained were among the most vile and reprehensible creatures in all of the world.

᠁ ᠁ ᠁

To supplement my earnings I took a string of jobs bussing tables at the restaurants in town during the busiest parts of tourist season. I worked aboard fishing boats whenever the mood to get out on the open sea and carry my father's smell home again struck me. I hung drywall for a sub-contractor whenever there was a sudden flurry of work. I hunted mushrooms in the forest, and cut cedar shakes from logged-out stumps. I harvested mussels, Dungeness crab, and gooseneck barnacles: whatever I could legally obtain and sell.

Even though Clarence paid me generously, I learned there were ways a driver might supplement his earnings. As the old saying goes, a little butter always sticks to the dish. Try doing anything in Chicago and you'll see that the middleman's hand seldom goes ungreased. I learned that one of Clarence's former drivers deliberately broke open keys and pocketed an ounce or two from each, much in the same way that Jack, the *Daily News* driver, routinely skimmed papers from the bundles of newspapers sold to my father. Another popular way to steal involved fudging the count of keys loaded on a truck, then selling the surplus gained by the undercount. One former driver, along with a friend in Port Alberni, developed a system which involved trading a few of Clarence's keys for a greater number of inferior ones grown elsewhere, with the mixed batch sold in Nanaimo and Victoria at the higher price Clarence's keys were demanding. Of course at nearly every stage of the operation there were graders, experienced smokers who sampled and evaluated product.

Despite these temptations I refused to touch whatever wasn't mine.

∾ ∾ ∾

Harmony kept fairly thick walls around the boundaries of our relationship, and I really didn't push or question them. Essentially what we did was what we held in common, and what we held in common was sharing drugs and occasional sex.

In bed she had a practiced, regal air, a way of lying back, posing like a Vargas girl in *Playboy*, arms crooked casually at the sides of her head, her long blonde hair splayed across her pillow like a peacock's fan, her expression confident and yet slightly bored, as if she expected not only to be serviced but serviced appreciatively and well. She wasn't aggressive or even very active or inventive, preferring to lie back quietly while we were intimate, which was two or three times a week and almost always up in her room in the commune during the summers and her occasional fall and spring visits to Tofino.

I concluded that her passivity came from her being so conventionally pretty. I guessed that the guys with whom she'd been involved were so grateful just to be with her that they demanded little more of her than her physical presence. It seemed to me as if her mind were made up in advance about what a sex partner could and couldn't do for her, and one evening during our third summer together she volunteered that she'd never once met a guy who satisfied her as much as she could satisfy herself.

"Don't you find that's true," she asked me one night. We were very stoned, the topic of our conversations drifting lazily from one subject to the next. "I mean, for yourself?"

I didn't have to think about that for long. "No," I said.

We were in the commune up in her attic room, lying on a mattress and box spring set like a futon along the wall opposite the door. On her writing desk and dresser, and the four wooden crates positioned near the corners of her bed, were scores of scentless candles, some squat, some tapered, all of them white or tallow, at least a dozen or so lit at any given time. They cast everything in the room in a warm, soft, saffron glow. Other than sunshine from the windows, candlelight was the only source of illumination Harmony used in her room. She'd left the planked wooden walls of her room bare but covered the angled ceiling with an immense tie-dyed sheet tacked up along the edge of the exposed rafters. She'd dyed the sheet years before and was fond of gazing up at its swirled patterns of colors whenever we ended in her room after we tripped. That's what our relationship consisted of, what we mainly did together. We'd get high and have sex. That night we'd just had sex, and now, as was her habit, she unscrewed the cap on her glass vial and took out another fat joint.

"Well," I said, smiling, resuming the conversation she'd started, "then you must be pretty damn good at satisfying yourself because this is the first time in my life I've gotten any complaints." I was bluffing, verbally thumping my chest, trying not to show that I felt hurt and insulted. I didn't realize she was telling me something about herself.

She asked me to hand her another tissue. After she lit the jay and took a long hit, holding the smoke deep down in her lungs, with the joint crackling and popping and flaring bright red, she slowly exhaled and said, "Now don't get me wrong, Vince, you're a good lover, even better than most. But maybe you're not hearing any complaints doesn't mean. . . ." She hesitated as I took the joint from her hand. "Let's just say that some girls learn how to touch themselves in special ways, and most guys are too rushed or clumsy or just don't want to take the time—"

"Are you telling me I'm rushed or clumsy?" I asked.

"No," she said. "Not at all."

"Or that I don't want to take enough time?"

"I didn't say that. In fact, you actually take a lot of time. You're very patient. Very strong and steady. And the absolutely best thing about you"—she laughed and reached for the joint—"is that you're not a talker, do you know what I mean?" She pinched the joint to her lips and took in another deep hit. "I mean I absolutely hate it when guys talk or ask questions, you know, like they're an announcer at a sports event or some reporter doing an interview. I mean, talkers just make me want to pull out my hair."

I nodded.

"You know what I mean," she continued. She stubbed the joint out in an ashtray on one of the end table crates, then lay back and pulled the bed's top sheet against the cool air to just over her breasts, meticulously tucking the sheet around herself.

I normally didn't sleep over when we had sex at her place. In fact the only times she and I slept together were the rare times when we hooked up at my house back in town.

I couldn't leave it alone. "I'm steady and patient?" I said.

She nodded.

"You make me sound about as exciting as a clock."

"Very funny. But you forgot strong. I said you were strong."

"Or maybe I'm as steady as an interest-bearing savings account. Or life insurance." I was like an old dog worrying a bone. Instead of simply asking her what she'd intended by what she'd said, instead of listening to what she was saying and trying to understand, I pressed on. In hindsight I guess I was trying to exert my own importance, applying some of the faux wisdoms I'd been taught back in Ronny's garage. "You make me sound about as sexually exciting as life insurance."

She shook her head, becoming irritated now. "What would you like me to say? That you're all firecrackers and sparklers on Dominion Day?"

"Considering the fireworks I've seen here in Tofino, I would think I'm much better."

"This isn't about you," she said. "We were talking about how I felt about something, and I told you the truth. You asked a question about me—"

"I never asked—"

"—and I tried to tell you about something I was feeling. I tried to share something. Something about my own life. Don't take it so personally. It wasn't about you. I don't know why you can't just leave it alone."

I didn't know why I couldn't leave it alone, either, why as a result of the conversation I felt I had something to prove. A day later, when we got together again up in her attic room, I finished the act as quickly as I could, handed her a tissue, pulled on my T-shirt and jeans, declined a hit off the ritual joint, and promptly departed. I did it without imagining or considering consequences, without turning back to see how she took it, or how she felt.

❧  ❧  ❧

Then the next time when we were together, I took my time sweet time, kissing her for longer than I'd ever kissed anyone. Every time she pulled me toward her, trying to tell me she was ready, that we should do it now, I kissed her until she grew still again, and then I got on top of her and slowly spread her legs with my knees. Then I paused.

Around the bed the flames of Harmony's candles hovered in the air like rows of votive candles in a church. From a nearby room of the commune a stereo played loudly enough for the sound to pulse through the floorboards: "Born to Run," Bruce Springsteen's voice raw, rugged, and, to me, angelic. Then a stereo in another part of the house rocked the walls with the opening guitar riffs of Aerosmith's "Toys in the Attic," and elsewhere in the house someone was repeatedly blasting Patti Smith's "Horses." I lay lightly atop Harmony, pushed in the tip of my sex, and said, "There."

"Don't tease," she said, moving against me.

"I'm in all the way," I said, pulling myself back each time she pushed herself up against me. This went on for several minutes, with her thrusting herself up toward me and me pulling myself back, only to push myself a bit forward each time she stopped thrusting.

"Do it," she said.

I held myself still. "I thought you didn't like to talk."

"Shut up," she said. "Please."

"No problem," I said as I again pulled myself back.

"No," she said, "please," her hips writhing up and forward against me. "Vince, don't make me ask."

"There," I said, easing my sex inside her a bit deeper, "I'm in you all the way," though in truth I was in only halfway. I moved an arm beneath her bent leg and slipped her leg up onto my shoulder, then slipped her left leg up onto my other shoulder as well, so that her feet were behind my head. "There," I said again. Now she could hardly move.

She thrashed her head from side to side as I moved slowly within her, gently back and forth, still with only about half my length. I wanted her to value me, to think I was the best lover she'd ever been with. I wanted to prove something, not only to Harmony and to myself but to the whole world.

Just as Harmony seemed about to resign herself to my teasing, I thrust into her more deeply and then pulled back slowly and pushed myself again inside her more fully a second time, then back and again even more fully and deeply, until I was stretched forward inside her as much as possible. Something inside her seemed to open up then: a tiny mouth, the wet petals of a flower. It was then that she began to express her desires, as her eyes met mine and she said the three words she'd once admitted she'd never told any lover.

Victorious, I smiled and said, "I love you, too."

# 7

# *Chicago 1966*

ON SATURDAY AFTERNOONS in Chicago whenever I had a couple of hours to spare I'd put on a clean shirt, run a comb through my freshly greased hair, and head up Clark Street to Peterson where I'd stop by the record store and thumb through albums and listen to jazz and then go next door to the pet store, where I'd pretend to browse for tropical fish.

The jazz playing in the record store would help me to work up my nerve, get me in the right mood. The shop was run by a man named Hank, a beatnik—I could tell—since he normally wore a black beret and greeted me with a hearty "Hey, man!" On display on the counter beside the cash register were the latest issues of *Down Beat*, and spinning on the turntable behind him were Hank's personal selections of the finest recent jazz. Miles Davis's *Kind of Blue*, John Coltrane's *A Love Supreme*, Don Cherry's *Symphony for Improvisations*, Duke Ellington's *The Far East Suite*, Bill Evans's *Waltz for Debby*, Herbie Hancock's *Maiden Voyage*, Lee Morgan's *The Sidewinder*, Grant Green's *Idle Moments*. I spent many an idle hour in Hank's record store, browsing as I listened to Hank discuss music with his customers, as I waited for just the right moment to leave and go next door to the pet shop.

There, I'd walk nonchalantly down the aisles displaying boxes of fish food and water treatments, and then I'd check out the glistening rows of tanks lining the store's rear wall. I'd admire recent shipments of golden dwarf cichlids, rainbow and red-tailed sharks, big black sailfin mollies, and elegant Siamese fighting fish, each in his own small round bowl. I'd gaze at the tank holding a pair of splendid blue discus surrounded by their fry. The tiered rows of tanks would give off a moist, warm, green smell that I was fond of inhaling deeply. I imagined it was the smell of the open sea. The air stones bubbled with a soothing regularity that both calmed and reassured me. I'd study the tanks full of aquatic plants: broad-leafed Amazon swords, lithe corkscrew Vallisneria (whose scientific name was *Vallisneria spiralis*, a name that lay light on the tongue and which I seldom grew tired of repeating), banded bunches of deep-green American waterweed, graceful lengths of *Cabomba* and *Sagittaria subulata*, as well as squat banana plants, whose tuberous roots remain above the gravel and resemble a miniature bunch of green bananas. If only my father allowed me to run an all-day grow light on my tank in the stair room, I'd think, I could cultivate a true tropical paradise for my neons and guppies.

In one tank I'd watch a darting shoal of zebra danios; in another, a gang of tiger barbs. I'd study the Harlequin rasboras, a cloud of recently hatched angelfish, a dozen or so bleeding heart tetras, each looking as if its side had been stabbed by a tiny dagger. When the pimply salesclerk shuffled toward me with his dripping fish net I'd tell him in a firm voice, "Thanks, but no thanks, nothing for me today, I'm only browsing." Then and only then would I allow myself a glance at the grooming room's glass partition, behind which in a sweater, dark slacks, and starched white lab coat would be the copper-haired Lucy Sheehan.

I'd always act surprised to see Lucy, as if I'd forgotten that she worked there, as if she weren't the main reason I'd walked all the way up Clark Street to the pet store in the first place. I'd say, "Oh, hello!" and offer her a nonchalant wave, which at home on weeknights when there wasn't a line of hundreds out in the hallway waiting to use the toilet I'd practice in the mirror above the bathroom sink. My wave was really more of a loose-fingered point to the ceiling or sky than something done with an open hand and wrist. (My open-handed wave made me appear feminine, while the direct finger point reminded me of recruitment posters featuring Uncle Sam.) Then I'd turn back to the fish tanks, timing my turn so that it would take place just as she was saying something—likely nothing more than a simple hello or how are you—through the glass window to me.

"What?" I'd mouth as I raised a cupped hand to my ear, as if I could neither hear nor lip-read. This would permit me to take several steps closer to the glass. Invariably one of us would look at the grooming room's doorway, toward which I'd point as if I had no idea of its function. With the same expression I'd point to my chest, then again to the door, repeating the sequence until she nodded. Then I'd walk to the door and step into the grooming room, where if I'd timed everything just right I'd get to talk to her for a minute or two, sometimes even five or a delicious ten or fantastic fifteen, just the two of us, Lucy Sheehan and me, in a room together, all alone with the dogs.

We'd never say much of any real importance, but we'd smile a lot and do a good deal of nodding. "How are things?" she'd ask, to which I'd answer, "Fine, and you?" I'd restrict further comments to the obvious. "I see there's a new shipment in of pearl gouramis," I'd say, or "Boy, doesn't that tank of silver hatchetfish look marvelous?" She'd nod and smile in response. "So," I'd say, if it appeared she'd just finished bathing a dog and was now drying the shivering mutt down with a towel, "I see you've just given old Rover here a bath." Lucy would tilt her head to one side and say, "Aren't you the perceptive one?" I'd nod at that and then say something else banal and obvious.

One Saturday afternoon I'd timed my visit so that it occurred just as she'd finished sweeping out the room and was wiping down the stainless-steel grooming tables. After she motioned me over, I talked to her from just inside the door. As we talked she took off her long lab coat and started to work on the front of her sweater with a loop of masking tape, pressing the sticky length of tape first here on her chest, then there, to clean her sweater of stray dog hairs. Her sweater was the kind a girl in grammar school might wear: soft pink with a ribbed collar and a long row of tiny white buttons shaped like candy hearts. In it Lucy looked like anything but a girl in grammar school. The thin fabric stretched across the soft mounds of her breasts with a magnificence I found utterly dizzying. She was just about to leave for home and before I could think of what I was doing I said I was about to leave, too, and suggested that we might walk back to the neighborhood together.

"All right," she said. She looked me suddenly up and down, then laughed. "You've sure grown up. How old are you now? Sixteen?"

"Seventeen," I said quickly, even though I was still a month and a half shy of my birthday. I stood as tall as I could. "I'm an upperclassman, a junior, at Saint George."

"Saint George," she said, "up past Howard Avenue, on Chalmers, right?"

I nodded.

"I dated a boy once who went to Saint George." She smiled and wagged her head.

"Lucky him."

"The Dragons, right?" she said, in reference to our school mascot.

What other mascot was possible for a school named for the original dragon-slayer, Saint George? "You got it," I said.

"I think you might be about the same height as Ronny now," Lucy said as we walked out of the pet shop and onto sunny Clark Street. She clutched her small dark purse beneath one arm, then paused to unclasp it and draw a pair of sunglasses from its depths. "Definitely thinner, but maybe just about as tall. Really, it's as if you shot right up overnight."

She put on her sunglasses. They had dark red lenses and red plastic frames that perfectly complemented her freckles and hair. Sweet Mary in Heaven, what a peach!

"How tall is your father?" she asked. "Are you taller yet than your father?"

With that I stumbled and nearly tripped on the sidewalk. "We're about the same height," I lied. I knew I'd never be as tall as my father, despite the fact that he wasn't a big man. I remembered what Ronny had told me the afternoon he gave me the garage's side door key, that someday I'd have to throw my father down the village well.

"Then you're bound to grow another inch," Lucy said and then expounded on her theory that nowadays most guys normally grew about an inch or so taller than their fathers. This was due to a combination of the average American person's diet and people's genes. Look at a girl's mother, she said, and you'll see the girl in twenty years. Look at the boy's father, subtract fifteen pounds, add a bit to the hairline, an inch or two of height. She was a student of human behavior, she told me, the type of person who had theories about all sorts of things, being that she was observant due to what she'd learned in school as well as at work in the pet shop's grooming parlor, where from behind her glass partition she was able to observe more than anyone could possibly believe, and where inside she was able to meet all kinds, and believe you me, she told me, when I say all kinds I mean *all kinds.*

Now don't get me wrong, she said as we walked down the street, I'm not some kind of egghead or even junior-college material, not that I couldn't make it in junior college or even four-year college if I wanted to. But at the same time, she continued, I know you don't need a PhD to have eyes and ears and the ability to use them. The trick, she said, is to keep your eyes and ears open while at the same time keeping the nemesis of actual learning, your big mouth, tightly shut. I could tell she liked that word, *nemesis,* by the careful and deliberate way she pronounced it. As if pleased with herself, she gave the air a proud smile.

It was as if she'd stored all these ideas in a closet and had decided to crack open the door and let a few of them spill out. *The nemesis of actual learning,* I thought, as I stared at her perfectly shaped lips that were covered with just the slightest touch of pink lipstick. Not only was she fetching but she was quick-witted and bright.

179

I don't mean that you or anyone else in particular has a big mouth, she added quickly, it's just a figure of speech, if you know what I mean. There are two kinds of people in the world, she continued, the ones who are book smart and the ones who are people smart. As for her, she definitely fell into the latter category.

"Ahh, yes," I said. "Uh-huh," I said. "Yeah, that makes a lot of sense," I said. "Yeah," I said, "you're sure right about that."

As for me, she said from behind her snazzy red sunglasses, she could tell from the first day she met me that I was people smart, too. She could tell from first sight that I was the type of guy who kept his mouth shut and his eyes and ears open. She could tell I had ideas.

"Oh no," I said, raising my hands, "not me, absolutely not," as a hot blush spread across my face and neck. I was ready to swear on all that was holy and good that not once, even in my wildest fantasies, had I ever had ideas about her.

"Don't kid yourself," she said, "and don't kid me either. Life's too short. I see and know things, and if I do say so myself, I know quite a bit more than a certain someone who for the sake of our conversation shall go nameless gives me credit for. No knock against this particular someone, but brains really aren't his long suit. But you, Vince, you're cut from a different cloth. You're a thinker. Things aren't lost on you."

I liked the tone of that and nodded vigorously.

She stopped on the sidewalk and lifted her sunglasses to her forehead for a moment, then winked at me conspiratorially. "You ever really look at this place?" she said. "These streets, these houses, the factories, the shops? This whole lousy stinking neighborhood? Let me tell you, Vince, it's all a trap. One big mousetrap." She raised her eyes to the sky and laughed. "Only this mousetrap doesn't just snap your neck and kill you, like the spring-loaded kind they sell at Ace Hardware." She shook her head. "Oh, no, that would be the easy way, wouldn't it be? No, this trap doesn't do anything quick and merciful like that. This trap likes to close its walls slowly around you instead and then keep you confined inside, just barely alive, until it's too late to do anything different and you realize you're never going to escape. You stay in it too long and you never get out, are you following my drift? Blink and overnight you've turned into your parents."

"God forbid," was all I could say.

"Or, at least in my case, seeing as how my mother passed away when I was twelve, into what my parents might have been." She looked wistful for a moment and then sighed. "Anyway, you know what I mean." She nudged me with her elbow. "We're tuned into the same frequency. We get the same station. You catch my drift."

"Man oh man," I said. "I do."

We walked in silence for a while, crossing busy Ashland Avenue and then heading up Rosehill toward the cemetery and its imposing Victorian entranceway and the nearby row of houses on quiet little Hermitage Avenue where she lived.

"You must think I'm morbid," she said and then paused. "Believe you me, I'm not. In another month I turn nineteen. I have my whole life ahead of me." She turned toward me and laughed. "At heart this girl is a card-carrying optimist. See"—she tapped the frame of her sunglasses—"I even walk through the world wearing rose-colored glasses."

We stopped in front of a small frame house with peeling siding, enclosed by a rusting iron fence. Inside the fence a few scrawny pansies were doing their best to try to push their little purple and yellow faces toward the sun from amidst a tangle of dandelions and several crushed cigarette packs and semi-flattened soda cans. "Come on," Lucy said as she swung open the gate. We sat on the second from the bottom front porch step.

We talked then about the guys, about Lenny and Dandoo, who'd both been drafted the year before, what we gleaned from their regular letters when they were both going through basic training at Fort Ord, but now that they'd been shipped overseas not even Ronny, who wrote back to them both religiously, was hearing from them anymore. A guy

I didn't really know named Pete had moved out to one of the north-west suburbs with his wife and their third kid. Pete was the guy who learned he'd knocked up his girlfriend at the time I started to hang around Ronny's garage. I remember him as the hapless soul whose face collapsed in his hands while the others circled him and hummed "Here Comes the Bride." But the pregnancy was a blessing in disguise, she told me, since if he hadn't put the bun in Maggie's oven, well, who could say where he'd be now what with all that was going on over in the war in Asia. Still, Lucy said, having a third so soon after the second was most definitely overdoing it. She nudged my arm again and told me that in her opinion when a girl gets caught unawares she has only two choices: dump it fast and shut up or have a second right away to prove to both sides of the family that the first wasn't an acci-dent. But popping out a third while the other two were still crawling the carpets in diapers was most certainly overkill.

Ronny's getting into the Illinois National Guard was going to save his ass, she told me, as was Chick's rheumatic fever. Chick has rheu-matic fever? I said. No, Lucy said, pardon me if I misspoke. When Chick was a kid he had rheumatic fever, or at least now he so claims, and anyway it gave him a slight heart murmur, nothing real serious, mind you, but enough to earn him a 4F deferment. Though of course these things can be faked, she said, and when it comes to Chick who can ever know what's on the up and up? She'd heard about guys who, a week before their physicals, drank a pot of coffee each day along with a fistful of dexedrine to raise their blood pressure, guys who ate fifty bananas the night before to throw off the levels of nutrients and minerals in their blood. Then she leaned toward me and said that she knew I came around the pet shop on Saturday afternoons mainly to see her.

"No," I said. "That's not at all true."

"Well, let's consider the facts. You never buy anything. You always wear clean clothes. You spend all of maybe three minutes looking at the fish. Then you turn toward me with that big grin."

"No. You must be confusing me with someone else. I never grin."

"It's okay, Vince. You don't have to deny it. I'm not saying it's not okay. I know it's because you've been wanting to talk to me. You're a thinker, just like I am. I'm guessing you sensed that, too. I'm flattered to have a friend like that."

"Well." I shook my head. "I guess you've got my number. You sure pegged me square. I suppose I can't keep any secrets from you, can I?"

She laughed. "Saint George is an awfully good school, isn't it? I mean, you can really learn some useful things there, can't you? Things that can get you out of here, out of this lousy neighborhood, take you far away. Get you into college, and I mean a real college, not just some diploma mill operating out of a storefront on south State Street. That guy I dated, the guy who went to Saint George, he went on to a real college, the University of Notre Dame." She gazed off into the distance. "I never heard any more from him after we broke up, but sometimes I still think about him. And when I do I wish him well."

Then one of Lucy's older brothers stepped out onto the front porch. Lucy had a pair of older brothers. As he opened the vestibule door there was a rush of music from inside, the song "96 Tears" by Question Mark and the Mysterians, a tune that was popular then and bounced around in my head for the rest of the day.

*Too many teardrops*, I kept thinking for the rest of the day.

Lucy's brother didn't meet our eyes. A lit cigarette dangled from the side of his mouth. He was wearing a sleeveless T and baggy grays and in one hand held a dark barbell, which he curled in slow sets of ten reps before switching arms and repeating the same slow, deliberate motions. After he was through he turned to Lucy and said in a flat voice, "We're getting pretty hungry in here, Luce, and supper's not cooking itself." He squinted his eyes from the smoke wafting off his cigarette and tossed back his head in the same way that Ronny squinted his eyes and tossed back his head while simultaneously smoking and leaning over the engine of some automobile. Then he lifted his

T-shirt and with the hand that wasn't holding the barbell scratched his flat stomach. A two-inch scar ran between his ribs.

I took that as my cue to nod a farewell to Lucy and exit out the iron gate, though while doing so I was unable to resist picking up and carrying away a couple of the crushed soda cans from the pitiful bed of pansies.

☙ ☙ ☙

My relationship with Marie Santangelo then took a decided turn.

It began with her being asked to be a bridesmaid at a cousin's wedding, and would I come with her early one Saturday morning to a fitting at a fancy dress store down on Lincoln and Belmont? Sure, I said, not realizing that Marie's mother would be accompanying us and Marie's father would be doing the driving, which was an enterprise all by itself.

Mrs. Santangelo was a nervous wren of a woman, small and squat, with quick, dark eyes that looked down the long beak of her nose inspecting and immediately disapproving of everything they fell on. Despite her small stature she enjoyed smiling down on things, particularly things she didn't like, and particularly me. She kept the books for Santangelo's Quality Meats, recording countless columns of figures in a distinctive, crimped hand, and filing and cross-referencing receipts into a separate red ledger that was half her size. According to Marie, after a decade or two the work had made her eyes go bad, and so she visited an optometrist who issued her a pair of spectacles with chestnut-colored frames, through which she commenced to gaze on the world with obvious discontent. She never ventured far from their flat without her big black pocketbook, a squarish thing nearly the size of a suitcase. It was a purse a clown might carry in a circus act, and open to allow a midget clown to climb out of. Her pocketbook was linked to a pair of thick shoulder straps that she ignored, preferring to lug the thing in front of her, like a shield. Sometimes I'd look at her and then at Marie and then back over at her in her big brown eyeglasses that seemed to see everything, trying to do that twenty-year projection thing Lucy talked about, but it would make me feel dizzy and creepy and so I'd stop.

As for Mr. Santangelo, since he was able to walk every day to and from his butcher shop on Clark Street, to and from the grocery store and pharmacy, to and from church over on Gregory, he seldom used his car, a pristine four-door black-and-white 1956 Chevrolet Bel Air sedan, which rested beneath a patchwork quilt of blankets and sheets in his garage. After the four of us removed the sheets and blankets, which Mrs. Santangelo insisted we shake out in the alley, Mr. Santangelo felt compelled to walk around the auto checking the pressure on his whitewalls, and then he fumbled beneath the hood in search of the dipstick.

I stared in awe at the Chevy's charcoal gray and ivory interior, which formed a zigzag pattern on the backs of the wide seats. Never in my life had I seen a car so clean. Marie and her mother stood patiently in the alley, chatting away like a pair of magpies. When Mr. Santangelo emerged from beneath the hood muttering and shaking his head, I knew it was time to intervene.

"Not to worry," I told him, taking the dipstick from his hand. "You're getting a low reading on the oil since the car's been sitting here idle. You have to check it after the car's been running a while, when it's hot."

I stood beside him, gazing down at the shiniest, most meticulously cared-for engine in all of greater Chicagoland. If someone had told me that every morning a dozen Sicilian elves climbed down from the rose of Sharon bush in the back yard of the Santangelos' six-flat and spent the rest of the day beneath the hood polishing the Chevy's engine and parts, I'd have said, "Only a dozen?" This engine was beyond clean. It suggested some other world's definition of purity. You could eat off this machine. You could perform surgery on it. You could allow a newborn baby to sleep on it. Forget about gold, frankincense, and myrrh; this car was a gift you could offer the golden Child on the first Christmas.

"You don't drive this car very often, Mr. Santangelo, do you?" I said.

"Why, no," he answered reluctantly, as if I'd accused him of some crime. "How can you tell?"

I eased the dipstick back into its tube and smiled. "Just a lucky guess."

He took Ashland Avenue south, driving in the right lane at a steady fifteen to twenty miles per hour, never accelerating quickly, never braking with a touch that came anywhere near harsh or abrupt, sliding up and down through the gears like a musician playing a song on a well-oiled trombone one full count behind the beat. The rest of the traffic flowed around us like a rushing river around a boulder. On the visor above his head was pinned a large medal depicting the Sacred Heart, and at a red light, when I inquired about it from the back seat where I sat beside Marie, Mr. Santangelo explained that he'd placed it there years ago for protection, to keep his car safe from damage and theft. Mrs. Santangelo had suggested the Virgin Mary, perhaps Our Lady of Fatima or the Virgin of Guadalupe—

Simply the Madonna, Mrs. Santangelo interjected. Everyone knows she would have been a much better choice. Look at how well she cared for the Christ child.

—but after due consideration, he continued, he decided it would be better to go one step higher, nearly to the very top, to the son of God, to Jesus Christ. This was followed by a pause, during which I realized that I was supposed to agree with him or at the least comment on the merits of both sides.

Instead I heard myself announcing that if his intention was to protect the Chevy, the Sacred Heart seemed a somewhat risky choice. Risky? he said. Yeah, I said, risky, seeing as how during Christ's relatively brief lifetime he allowed his body to get broken and battered and bruised, crowned with thorns and crucified with nails in his hands and his feet, and how on Easter morning Mary Magdalene thought he'd even been stolen, whereas Mary's body was not only immaculately conceived but remained virgin pure up until the moment she ascended into Heaven. Mrs. Santangelo's head rotated toward me suddenly. Though I couldn't see her mouth I had the distinct sense she was smiling.

"You make a good point," Mr. Santangelo said after a while.

"Of course," I said in a sudden panic that I'd made a mistake, "the Sacred Heart, well, after all, I mean, come on, the Sacred Heart is the Sacred Heart, you just can't go wrong with that, no sir, since everybody in the whole world knows nothing can protect you better than the Sacred Heart."

Mrs. Santangelo said something in Sicilian that caused Mr. Santangelo to laugh. I couldn't hear all the words due to the noise in the street. He responded, also in Sicilian, and in another moment both were laughing.

"What?" I said, leaning forward toward them.

Mrs. Santangelo turned sideways to speak. "Only a fool tries to refill the hole he's just dug." She stared at me through her enormous glasses and nodded. "In the translation it loses some of its flavor."

"But what did he say about Giufá?" I asked.

"That you were just like him, when his mother told him to pull the door shut after him and he pulled it off its hinges."

There were worse things to be called. In Sicilian lore Giufá was a likeable fool. At least I wasn't a *cafone*. I relaxed and basked for a moment in the feeling that I was being accepted, working my way toward their good graces. Since I wanted to impress them further with my wit I asked them if they knew who was the very first priest.

"Is this a joke?" Mrs. Santangelo asked. "I don't like jokes about priests."

"It's a serious religious question," I answered. "Something we discussed in high school."

"Then it would be Christ," Mrs. Santangelo said, almost immediately.

"So most people think," I said. "But what about the Virgin Mary?" I gave them a few moments to consider it. "After all, wasn't she the first person to take bread and wine and turn them both into Christ's body and blood?"

"Oh, listen to him," said Mrs. Santangelo after a moment or two. In her voice was a near-chuckle. "Now he's a theologian."

"But he has a point," Mr. Santangelo said and laughed.

Then we were passing the bridal shop, in front of which Mr. Santangelo double-parked to allow Marie and her mother to hop out. Before we drove off in search of a parking space, he told me to get into the front seat. For the next half hour or so we cruised the nearby neighborhood, rejecting one potential spot after the next (too small, fire hydrant, too close to the pedestrian crossing lane, another fire hydrant) until we neared the corner of a quiet, distant sidestreet, where he promptly pulled over, shut off the ignition, set the hand brake, and then turned to me suddenly and asked me to show him my hands.

I did as I was instructed, offering him first the backs, then the palms.

"That's good. Hold them out straight before you. That's it. Relax." For a while he stared at them. "They're steady? They don't shake?"

"They're like a rock," I said.

"You care for these hands? You depend on them?"

"They're the best pair I ever had."

"And your fingers. You care for them?"

I nodded.

"Count them."

I did as he asked.

"And they're all there?"

"Yes. Every single one, present and accounted for."

"Are there any that you don't like?"

"Not that I can say. As far as I know I like them all."

"You must be sure."

"I'm sure."

"Look at my hands," he said, holding them up.

I looked at them.

"Take them into your own," he said, offering them to me. "Inspect them."

They were big hands, impressively strong, with a laborer's hard calluses on each of the fleshy pads surrounding the palms, which themselves were soft and surprisingly smooth. His fingernails were meticulously manicured, each cuticle pushed back evenly, each nail perfectly rounded and clean.

"Lean forward," he said, "and I'll tell you a secret."

Without thinking, I did as I was told.

"You have to love your hands," he said, "more than anything else. More than any woman, any child, any other thing on this earth living or dead. That's the first rule. The saws, you can be cutting a side of meat and the saws they can take a piece of your finger away so clean and fast that it will be entire minutes and a pool of spilled blood before you realize it, before you come to understand that the cold wetness you feel running down onto your leg or into your shoe is the blood of your own life. You have to remember that your hands are pieces of meat guiding the cutting of other pieces of meat. The saws you use recognize no difference. Also remember that your work is in the cold, and in the cold your hands they have less feeling. One slip of the handsaw. . . ." He shrugged. "The saws don't care if the meat they cut is yours or the pig's. Do you follow what I say? You never want to cut the meat of your own flesh."

I nodded, not really sure of what he was telling me.

"I like it that you're a friend of my Marie. You seem like a good boy. She talks all the time about you now. Too much maybe, but these days with the whole world upside down and sideways what do I know? She's a bit too boy-crazy for my taste, but better the noisy tongue in the kitchen than the silent one in the grave. Your nonna, too, we talk after Sunday Mass about Menfi. She remembers a woman, my own

Zia Marianna. You come from good stock, a good family. And also I like it that you have the good sense to know that my shop it's a place of business and not the Goodwill or the Catholic Charities. You're not like the others, asking me all the time for free this or free that. When you come into my shop, you take a number and wait and show your respect."

I nodded.

"So if you can learn to love your hands, I wish to ask you a question."

"Shoot."

"I may have an opening for an apprentice. Not tomorrow or next week, but maybe soon. In a year maybe, in eighteen months, maybe just about the time you finish with your high school. I can teach you how to break down a side of beef, how to cut the loin off the leg so that you don't ruin the sirloin, but deep enough so as to preserve the rump roast. In two, maybe three years you can become a journeyman. These days, especially here in Chicago where there is so much meat, a good butcher never has a want for work. And his family never has an empty table."

"But I have school," I said, "and I work at my father's news-stands."

"Sure," he said. "I understand. But I said in six months, maybe a full year. Maybe after you finish with school and you put on your long pants."

"But my father—"

"What about him? Is his shadow so long you can't step out from under it? God gave you two legs. You weren't born a tree."

"I know that."

"My papa used to tell me an old proverb. *Nienti mi ratta a manu como mi ugna.* 'Nothing scratches my hand like my own nails.' You understand? Think about it. Nobody knows your own needs and wants better than you yourself." He paused. "Your father grew up and away from his own father. I buried mine. My father buried his. In their own

190

time we all leave our fathers, one way or another, whether with our feet or our will or at the grave as we turn over earth with a spade."

He glanced at the gear shift on the column and then pushed down the clutch and turned on the ignition, softly revving the engine until, at his prodding, it let out a velvet whirr. "It's hot enough now, no?" he said, pointing beyond the windshield at the car's hood. "We'd better check the level of that oil."

⌇ ⌇ ⌇

Mrs. Santangelo stood waiting for us at the curb outside the dress shop, scanning the passing traffic with her enormous, all-seeing eyes. "What did the two of you do," she said, "drive all the way to Indiana?" Motioning back to the shop, she told us, "She says she won't change until he goes in. She wants him to see her dress." I turned to Mr. Santangelo for approval. He set the hand brake and let loose a long sigh. "And don't take all day in there," Mrs. Santangelo called out after me.

The tinny chime of wedding bells sounded over my head as I entered the doorway. My shoes sank into the nap of a carpet so deep and plush it felt as if I were wading through quicksand. "He's here," a woman's voice called out from behind a display of white veils. "Tell her that he's finally here. At long last, he's here."

Then Marie stepped out from between the folds of a curtain, clad in a shoulderless peach-colored gown, her dark hair pinned up and entwined with sparkling rhinestones and sprigs of baby's breath. Her lithe body filled the soft curves of the gown so magnificently that I grew suddenly weak in the knees. She smiled at me and registered my reaction and then looked demurely down and began walking toward me in that way that brides do as they approach the altar, taking one slow step forward and then pausing for a beat before stepping forward again, her hands at her waist, holding a linen flower bouquet.

Time itself stopped. The hands of the shop clerks froze mid-applause. On the sidewalk outside, passers-by gasped as they stared

191

through the windows. In the sky above, planets paused in admiration in their orbits around the sun. Hovering low over the Chicago skyline, the moon's full just-visible face became envious, turning a sudden green.

෩ ෩ ෩

That afternoon when I got home I learned that Nonnu had died.

He'd passed sometime that morning. At first all that Nonna could tell us, when she wasn't sobbing into the handkerchief which she'd wrapped like a bandage around her right hand, was that he'd spent all day yesterday complaining. He was talking in that crazy way he did sometimes, Nonna told my father, you know, mumbling and gesturing wildly, as if he was getting ready to board his troller back in Monterey. He was worried about his gear, concerned about his lines and the lures and spoons he was using.

"Be quiet, Ma," my father told her. His face bore little expression other than exasperation with the situation. "You know as well as I do that we don't talk about that anymore." His voice had the tone that signaled sooner or later someone or something would be hit. As he spoke my mother scrambled about, the barnyard hen who sees the shadow of a hawk. Inside a minute she'd gathered my six sisters in a tight circle around her.

We stood upstairs, in Nonna's front room. It was a room cluttered with too many things, couches and chairs and end tables and lamps and a mirrored wall box displaying countless dusty knickknacks: a glass girl in a frilly skirt holding a blue umbrella, a spotted leopard about to pounce. On the coffee table in front of the wide sofa squatted an ashtray, four pewter penguins standing sideways on the lip of a bowl, each with its bill open and ready to hold someone's cigarette. The room smelled of dead air, closed and stale, of dust and age and Nonnu's occasional cigars, as well as something faintly sweet that perhaps had rotted. I wondered if maybe something sugary hadn't burned on the stove, or if perhaps an apple had fallen behind the overstuffed sofa and chairs, the backs of which Nonna had covered with so many overlapping doilies they resembled bunting.

She wouldn't come down to our flat as long as his body was still there, in their bed in their bedroom where earlier she'd found him. He woke up early that morning, Nonna told my father, at dawn, like he did every day, as if today would be like any other day. Usually Nonnu made a pot of coffee and walked back and forth from one end of the house to the next while it boiled, but this morning instead of his usual pacing he stood by the windows on the back porch, gesturing and mumbling into the air like he did all day yesterday. He'd get that way sometimes, she said, as if he didn't know where he was.

"I asked him if he wanted me to make him an egg," Nonna said, "and he said no, he didn't want an egg, he didn't have time. He wanted to know about the moon. He kept asking me about the moon, when it would next be full or new. 'There's no moon,' I told him, over and over. 'Drink your coffee,' I said. 'I'll make you an egg with black olives.' But he kept asking me about the moon, and then whether or not he had enough leaders. You remember how much your father used to worry about breaking leaders."

"Get the kids out of here," my father barked to my mother.

I hung back in the hallway as my ma marched down the front steps to our flat with the girls. My father paced the room like one of the big, bored caged cats at Lincoln Park Zoo, each time pausing to look out the blinds on the front windows for the ambulance that would take his father's body away and put an end to his mother's talking.

"You remember how he'd get on the mornings he set out. I told him all of his lines were fine and that I'd make him an egg. His favorite way, sunny side up, you know, with garlic and black olives. I was squeezing the pits out of the olives when he started. 'No!' he shouted into the air. 'Don't take me! Stop! You have no right!'"

"Ma—"

"'Take your hands off me!' he was screaming, as if all around him there were things he could see. He was slapping the air with his hands. 'You don't understand,' he yelled. 'I am an honorable man! I have a wife and son!'"

"Enough," my father said.

I stood in the hallway, where I couldn't be seen.

"You don't know," Nonna said, suddenly looking up from her handkerchief. "You don't remember because you were already gone away into the army and you weren't there." She pointed a finger at him. "After they came through the front door, they pushed me aside like I was nothing. They knocked me down, hard, into one of the chairs. Like they didn't even see me. I fell right over and hurt my arm." She rubbed a spot near her elbow, as if it still hurt her. "They yanked the plug on the radio right out from the wall and took it with them. Two of them went through the chest of our things and all the drawers. One of them kept asking me where I had hidden the guns."

My father stopped pacing and took a step toward her. "They took that pair of binoculars Dominic gave me just before I reported for service," he said. He shook his head and hissed in disapproval. "I never even got to use them. You remember Dominic?"

She nodded. "Who could forget Dominic?" She muttered a prayer for the dead and made the sign of the Cross and kissed her thumb. "We told them you were in their army. Your father and me both. We shouted and shouted to them that our only son was already in the service in their army."

"Ma, we've gone over this a thousand times. That didn't matter. We were at war. They did the same thing to all the Italians in Monterey."

"But I still don't see why, after we gave you up into their army."

"You didn't give me up, Ma. I enlisted." He pushed aside the coffee table and squatted in front of her and took her hands in his.

"Then why did they take your father away and lock him away in prison? They already had you. You know that after they took him away he was never the same."

My father let out a long sigh, as if he were genuinely weary. "It wasn't a prison, Ma. It was an internment camp."

"What does it matter, they still locked him up. You know how much your father loved his boat. Why did they have to take it from him?"

"Ma, let's not go over all this again." He dropped her hands and stood. "They took all the boats that were owned by Italians. There was a major world war, you understand, and Japan had just bombed Pearl Harbor. That drew the U.S. into the war, and that made Italy the enemy, too. That stupid fascist Mussolini had sided with Hitler, and then Pearl Harbor was bombed. They were afraid we might be spies, that the boat might be used by a ring of spies."

"But your father was only a fisherman."

"That didn't matter to them, Ma. He was Italian. And they were the enemy."

"But you were in their army."

"I told you, that didn't matter. After Pearl Harbor, nothing mattered."

"He was never the same after that," Nonna said. "Even inside the house, he was afraid to speak his own tongue. You should have seen him after they let him out, pulling the blinds shut even during the day, all the time worried and afraid. Hushing me whenever I spoke Italian. He'd say somebody from the government would hear me and they'd arrest him again."

My father stretched his arms and back, and for a while my grandmother sobbed into her handkerchief. As she cried my father returned to the windows, peering down at the street while bouncing on his toes like a heavyweight champ in the corner of the ring just before a fight. That was all you could hear for a while, her sniffles and sobs and the squeak of the floorboards from his bouncing.

I stepped back and looked past the cracked door into their bedroom, where my grandfather's body lay on the bed. In the darkened room the angle of his head and size of his nose made him look like some ancient fallen bird, something from the days of the dinosaurs. A pterodactyl, I decided. I edged closer to the body. If it weren't for his utter stillness and open mouth, you'd think he was asleep.

I crept back into the hallway. In the front room my father made a long hissing sound and was wagging his head. "We called them hours ago. What has it been, four or five hours now? Jesus Christ, it's taking them all damn day."

"Even after we came all the way here," Nonna was saying, "to Chicago, your father was afraid to walk outside."

"Drop it, Ma."

"You know he was afraid every time someone strange came to the door. He'd hear knocks. That's why he wanted to live up here. Because it was farther away from the front hallway door. 'Don't answer,' he'd tell me whenever the doorbell would ring. The telephone would sound and he'd jump off the couch. He was scared of everything after that."

"He was born afraid, Ma."

"You remember how upset he'd get when he couldn't find that card he had to carry? He thought he had to take it with him everywhere, even to bed."

"Ma, I said drop it. Let it go. What's done is done. You can't undo the past."

"You can look in his pants pocket even now and you'll still find that card."

"We were all affected," my father said, turning toward her. "How do you think I felt, coming home to all that? After being gone for two years, in the war for fourteen months?"

"Your father loved that boat."

"You don't hear a word I say, do you? I had plans, big plans, for that boat, for my own life, my own livelihood, and all you can talk about is his cowardice and yourself."

"That boat meant everything to him."

"It meant everything to me, too. I tell you, I had plans. How else do you think I got through the war? But why am I even telling you this? You're as deaf as he was."

"Losing it nearly killed him."

"Then maybe he should have died then. What else can you expect? When a boat's impounded because they fear you might be spies, you can't very well fish with it, can you?"

"Don't put the blame on him. You sound like you're blaming him."

My father said nothing.

"Your father did everything he could."

My father said nothing, bouncing back and forth again before the front windows.

"A lot of the old Italians lost their boats."

"Then maybe they didn't deserve them in the first place," he said.

"Don't be so bitter. Oh, I know when you got back you were so heartbroken. But believe me, there was nothing else anybody could do."

"Oh, yeah? After all these years, you really think that, Ma? With all the lawyers in the world now, Ma? All of them just itching to file lawsuits? Look at the Jews and how they stand together and file lawsuits to get back what was stolen from them during the war by the Nazis. You expect me to believe that the only thing the Italians could do was to accept it, then keep their mouths shut up about it for, what has it been now, twenty-five years?"

"You don't know how it was. You weren't there. You were away, in the war."

"All because that fool Mussolini had to side with the Nazis."

"All these years," Nonna said, "all these years your mouth has been shut, too."

"They're here," my father said suddenly, clapping his hands. He turned from the windows toward the hallway door, as if the bell sounding the start of the round had just rung.

My grandmother let out a wail.

"Finally," my father said as he rang the hallway buzzer. "Ma, don't just sit there like a bump on the log. Open the door for them. Let them in. They're here."

⁓ ⁓ ⁓

Color the funeral in black and gray, as the coffin rests in the center aisle outside the open gates of the communion rail at Saint Gregory's church.

Though Nonna made no hysterical leap upon it, issued no dramatic cry to God and the saints above to strike her dead, to wrench the breath from her body, to allow the living among us to bury her, too, she was far from mute. For most of the Mass she sat like a pile of sticks, rocking back and forth, forth and back, darkly, like something ancient and foreign. In the air hung the sweet, heavy smell of incense. Every now and then she lifted her head toward the altar, its domed tabernacle and towering display of saints, the titanic frescoes on the rear wall of the archangels Michael and Raphael, each with one raised wing, and let loose a piercing scream.

While part of me admired her ability to grieve with such openness and ferocity, another part of me was embarrassed and wished to silence her. Part of me cringed and felt ashamed every time her screams disturbed the proceedings and echoed in the nearly empty church. Another part of me broke off from what was happening, as if the family involved in the drama before me were someone else's and not mine. I abjectly watched the entire proceedings, which were led by the speed-talking Father O'Reilly.

Some part of me tingled with the knowledge I'd gained while lurking in the hallway. *Why, of course!* I thought, as Father O'Reilly hurried around my grandfather's casket and anointed it with incense. *It only makes sense.* The silences, the occasional snatches of stories about their having left California. My grandfather's peculiarities and back-porch games. Perhaps the depth of my father's rage. No one in America, at least no one whose entry into the New World began on the Atlantic, voluntarily migrated from west to east. (This is why, when I left Chicago, I knew it was my fate to head west.) *Now it all makes sense*, I repeated, as my mind added the muscle of detail to the skeleton they occasionally dragged out from the closet of their anger and shame.

I imagined my grandfather on the deck of a modest troller, a screeching flock of gulls overhead, the magnificent California sun glistening over the waves, harvesting the fruit of the sea. At the time I didn't much think about his being imprisoned, or my father coming home from the war to find his parents' home boarded up. Only later would I learn that some Italians spent as long as two years in the camps, that there were several suicides, that afterwards many families refused to speak Italian even inside their own homes out of fear. I learned that the night in February 1942 that the knocks sounded on the Italians' doors would become known as *la male notte*, the bad night, and that eventually the entire affair would be called *una storia segreta*, or a secret story or history.

## DON'T SPEAK THE ENEMY'S LANGUAGE! SPEAK AMERICAN!

ordered the placards displayed in the public places, a stern Uncle Sam towering over a cowering miniature trio of Hitler, Mussolini, and Hirohito. I learned that Americans of Italian descent were the largest ethnic group to serve in the United States Armed Forces during the war. I learned that over ten thousand Italian Americans on the West Coast were forced out of their homes, that thousands were arrested, and that hundreds, including my grandfather, were interned in military camps. Hundreds of thousands were forced to carry identification cards and suffered from travel restrictions. Over fifty thousand were subjected to curfews. Even the American-born parents of the great Joe DiMaggio were photographed and fingerprinted and forced to carry "enemy alien" registration cards, and due to the travel restrictions placed on Italian Americans they couldn't even drop in on their famous son's restaurant on Fisherman's Wharf. Even Enrico Fermi, the Italian physicist who helped to create the atomic bomb, was prohibited from traveling freely along the East Coast.

And then after the war was over, instead of protesting, or even making what happened public, the Italians said nothing about it! Of course their deep, historic mistrust of government was one reason for this response, but nonetheless *they said nothing.*

How very Italian of them, I'd later think. To equate silence with a sense of honor! How stoic! How the boy from Sparta would have approved!

Some Italians denied that anything had happened. Some didn't even tell their own children the stories of what had happened. But at the time I learned of all this, after our line of cars had made its slow way to the cemetery and Father O'Reilly had sprinkled my grandfather's coffin with holy water and the men with the ropes began lowering it into the ground, as we stood amidst the silent limestone crosses and angels and the autumn leaves swirled around our shoes on the browning grass, all I could think of was the lost troller.

All I could think of was my father as a young man fresh from war working out on the open blue sea instead of traveling with his parents and new wife inland to defeat and shame and finding work inside the dank underbelly of the Fulton Street Fish Market and the bowels of Chicago's Union Station. How my father might have turned out differently! I thought. How he might have been content, perhaps even fulfilled and happy. How my life might have been different as a result. I could have been out on the sea with him, working beside him, son with his father, actually doing what I'd pretended to do with my grandfather years earlier on the back porch when I was a boy. As we filed to the grave to throw a handful of dirt on the coffin, I tried to imagine what might have been.

Marie stood beside me through all of it, silent, eyes brimming with tears, and that evening we slipped out of the depressing reception at my house and made our way over to Hollywood Avenue and

Ronny's garage, where, parked in the soothing darkness, was a true gem, someone's vintage 1958 Studebaker Starlight. I turned on the radio near the speed bag and calendar girl. The Lovin' Spoonful's "Summer in the City" came to an end, and then the DJ played the Rolling Stones' "Paint it Black."

"You know, they don't make these anymore," I told Marie as I pointed to the car.

But instead of listening to me go on about the Starlight she pulled me onto the car's wide back seat. In the blink of an eye we were kissing, then fumbling with the buttons and zippers on our clothes. And there on the dark back seat of the Studebaker, for the first time for each of us, we did our best to make love.

# 8

# *Tofino* 1979–80

BEFORE I KNEW MUCH of anything about the whales, they came to me.

This was back when I was hauling reefer down-island for Clarence and tending his dozen or so gardens strategically placed along the edges of slashes on several of the islands. I'd hike about the islands, on the lookout for others who'd scattered their seeds near our patches, particularly those who were too ignorant or lazy to cull their male plants. Male marijuana plants produce pollen, which can fertilize and as a result ruin the valuable females, turning them from producers of premium bud into virtual seed machines. Most of Clarence's plants were sinsemella clones: rooted cuttings off other females. Even though male plants tend to be tall and spiky, while females are shorter and more full and round, a male can look like a female until late July or early August. I'd pull other growers' male plants out by the roots whenever I came across them. I'd check our gardens for damage by wind or rain. I always carried my chainsaw, and in the pocket of my flannel shirt a spare chain: cover should anyone stop and ask me why was I hiking up and down the edges of the slash. My answer would be that I was looking for logged-out cedars so as to cut shakes out from the remains of their stumps. Indeed, sometimes while checking the gardens I cut out shakes from the remains of cedar stumps, which later I'd bundle and sell.

I ran a fourteen-foot aluminum hull skiff equipped with a 35-horsepower outboard capable of pushing me against respectably strong tides and yet small enough that I could lift the vessel up for beaching when the tide was rising. When the tide was falling I'd toss out an anchor and back toward the beach with the motor partially tilted up, then take a stern line ashore and tie it off. After the tide had risen, I'd pull the skiff toward me, hop in, and pull anchor. I seldom strayed very far from land. Whenever I was out on the sea I paid careful attention, constantly scanning its surface for rocks and reefs and other hazards. I understood that all the maps and charts in the world can reveal only so much. Nothing replaces the experience of going over the same stretch of water in a variety of weather conditions and tides. Over time I became familiar with the peculiarities of the Sound, the intricacies of its many shorelines, even its swirling, often unpredictable and dangerous tides.

Early one morning as I headed for Siwash Cove on the ocean side of Flores Island, coming out of Russell Channel just past Bartlett, I saw something dark and big—something I'd never seen before— splash portside. It snagged my attention as I wove my way carefully through the rocks in the waters north of Bartlett. Allow me to admit that I'm a timid sailor, ever on the lookout for rocks or logs, and par- ticularly deadheads: old logs lying hidden in the water, at their worst bobbing vertically, one end up, just at or below the water's surface. I'd rather be timid and living than intrepid and dead.

Since I didn't wear an insulated deck suit, I knew I wouldn't last very long if the skiff were to strike a rock or deadhead and I were to tumble into the sea. Hypothermia would set in within minutes. I didn't want to die that way, lost at sea, a floater, no one ever knowing my fate unless my bloated remains washed ashore. Particularly when I was on the ocean side of the islands, I ran my skiff as cautiously as a blind man making his way down an icy street, taking one small step at a time, tap-tap-tapping his cane.

The splash off port must have been a breaching whale, likely a gray. I'd seen their blows, mostly in spring when they migrated up the coast, sometimes in impressive groups of eight to ten, but I'd never had a close encounter. Back then the best word to describe my relationship with the whales was *wary*. Since they were far bigger than me, even bigger than my skiff, I gave them plenty of room and hoped they'd return the favor. I never sought them out and didn't really understand the people who did.

Then the darkness splashed again, and out in the blue I saw first one, then two, then three shimmering black dorsals slicing toward a point off my bow. My heart thudded hard and fast, and my breath snagged in my throat.

The dorsals were easily five feet high, racing on an angle toward the same part of Flores I was heading for. Orcas, I suddenly realized, as a fourth and then a fifth dark dorsal fin broke the surface of the chop, speeding from a different angle toward some central point ahead. Only then did I understand that this was a group of transients pursuing something. My eye strained to make out in the water, thirty or so yards ahead of the two groups of whales, something brown and furious and frantic. Yes, the orcas were chasing it. Then the whales and I merged on it at nearly the same moment, as if this were something we'd agreed on beforehand and deliberately choreographed. The orcas were chasing a Steller sea lion, a young female, not yet fully grown though easily five hundred pounds, every ounce of which rattled my teeth as she leapt from the water squarely into the bow of my skiff.

I don't know how it was possible that the skiff didn't upend. The orcas swarmed around me, their black sides and white saddle patches magnificent and shiny in the morning sun. Lead whales from both groups struck the skiff with their broad heads, likely less out of aggression or anger, I thought later on, than sheer confusion. Their echo-location must have indicated that one moment directly ahead of them was the sleek form of a juicy sea lion, and the next moment their prey was no longer there. Two or three of the whales made sharp dives, splashing the water's surface with their broad flukes, then a few moments later again circled and surrounded the skiff. One dorsal came so close to the side of the skiff that I could have reached out and touched it. Another orca surfaced and chuffed so close to me that for several moments I could smell what I guess could only be considered its breath. The whale's breath was greasy and nearly thick enough to chew though not entirely unpleasant, a mix of sewage and low tide, fatty oil and the stench of rotted fish. I sat within the oily cloud of the smell and despite myself inhaled deeply.

*Glorious.*

Then my nose curled suddenly in revulsion. Amidst the confusion of the circling whales, I'd swung the skiff away from the shoreline just as the sea lion in the bow unleashed a copious stream of shit. In consistency the shit was somewhere between oatmeal and bean soup, and by my rough measure the creature had let loose gallons of it. I gagged and headed directly for land as a line of the liquid oozed back nearly to my gumboots. Perhaps in the grave or the bowels of one of the circles of Hell there are worse smells.

Shit or no shit, I would have dumped the sea lion back into the water and let the orcas have her if I could. If I'd had any choice in the matter, I certainly wouldn't have gotten in the way of their hunt. I'm no animal lover, no bleeding heart, no sentimentalist. I imagined that the whales labored long and hard to separate the sea lion from the groups of other sea lions that hauled out on one or more of the various outcroppings that made up the nearby reefs, then worked to drive her toward shore. Or perhaps the sea lion had strayed from the herd. Maybe she was ill. Whatever, she should have been theirs. And now not only was she in my skiff but she'd smeared it with a souvenir that would take me hours and hours to clean.

By now the killer whales had disappeared. They'd vanished before their exit even registered on me. I wondered what they thought about what had just occurred, if indeed they thought consciously, and as I steered the skiff into Cow Bay I guessed that they concluded that I was just another predator, some noisy boat-shaped creature who at the last moment had come up on them out of nowhere and stolen their prey.

Since the sea lion was in the bow of my skiff, and not in their jaws and bellies, I imagined as well that they thought me the better hunter.

❧ ❧ ❧

He was standing back of the sedges and dunegrass, near several sprays of seashore lupine that led back to a narrow trail hacked out of a tangle of salal, watching me from beneath the visor of his dark Adidas cap. Thin, wearing blue jeans and sneakers, blue T-shirt and open, untucked cotton shirt. I saw him just a moment before he called out to me.

"Need some help?" he shouted as if there could be any doubt about my answer. He took a step toward the beach, hesitated, then gave the air a friendly wave. By now I'd partially lifted the outboard, headed backward into the bay. I dropped anchor and stood beside the skiff in the shallows, wondering how in the world I was going to induce the sea lion out of my boat and back into the water where it belonged.

I returned his wave and grabbed the stern line. "Yeah, I could use all the help you can give me."

Ignatius George was a good two inches taller than me, likely a few years older, with piercing brown eyes and a warm light-brown complexion the color of a culturally modified cedar, where someone has sliced away a section of its bark or cut out a board or plank. There were several culturally modified cedars here on Flores—trees that the Nuu-chah-nulth had used for making clothing or baskets after they'd peeled away its bark—a fair distance away from the salty water, most of them deep in the forest, where the quality of the wood was better than that of trees living nearer the sea.

He motioned for me to throw him the stern line, which he tossed further upshore, and then walked toward me into the shallows. We introduced ourselves and shook hands. His gaze below the visor of his cap was level; his hand, big and calloused; his grip, firm and warm and strong.

"I see you've been out fishing," he said with a nod. He smiled, then gave out a soft laugh.

"Yeah," I said, "without even putting a hook into the water."

"Hope somebody doesn't come along and ask to see your seal license."

I smiled.

"She's still spooked, but if we tilt your skiff a bit to one side she's likely to crawl out." As he walked toward the skiff he said something to the sea lion, then smiled back at me, shaking his head. "I guess you already noticed she's scared shitless."

I followed, lifting the portside edge of the stern as Ignatius tilted up the larboard, all the while talking to the sea lion in a low, soothing voice. I couldn't make out his words, but within a few moments as we rocked the skiff back and forth the creature got the general idea and rolled inelegantly out into the sand and soft surf and then pushed herself forward into the deeper water, where at once her movements were sure, graceful, and swift.

As for the shit, I'd have to hose the skiff out after I returned to harbor. I could check on the garden Clarence planted near Siwash Cove another day. Ignatius and I secured the stern line on a log and then walked toward a tumble of driftwood and debris—old, broken buoys, torn sections of nylon rope knotted with lengths of kelp—and talked about the whales. He'd seen the entire incident from shore, he told me, after having noticed the first group of dorsals. He knew the whales were pursuing something, but from where he stood on land, he said, he couldn't see what that something was. When he noticed the second group of orcas converging on the first, he realized they must be out hunting big game.

"I've seen them take sea lion bulls off Lennard," he said, nodding, "right off the rocks there." Lennard Island was the site of the lighthouse near the entrance to Tofino Harbor, the source of the flashing light seen on Chesterman Beach. "You know, they must have been just playing with this one," he said, gesturing out toward the water where the sea lion had swum away. "Just having some fun. Or maybe they were teaching their young to hunt. The bigger orcas can snatch a bull clean off the rocks. Some of those bulls weigh over a ton."

I nodded even though I didn't know that.

"Then you came along, as if out of nowhere, with perfect timing, like in one of those old movies about the cavalry." He laughed. "You're American, eh?"

"Used to be," I said. "But as for my timing, it was a complete accident."

"An accident?" He smiled. "Don't tell me you believe in accidents?" He asked the question as if the concept was maybe a step beyond the edge of rational belief. It was as if I'd said I'd seen Sasquatch or the Loch Ness Monster or one of those big-eyed aliens fond of dropping in on New Mexico. "Do you think that creature out there believes her rescue was an accident?"

I didn't know what to say, so I said nothing.

"A used-to-be American who believes in accidents." He rubbed the palms of his hands together slowly. They were big hands, and no strangers to hard work. Their thick calluses made a rasping sound, like the rustle of fallen leaves. "I tell you, that animal doesn't believe in accidents. You were the answer to her animal prayers. Right now her heart is singing your praises to her God."

I laughed. "You're Ahousaht," I said, more statement than a question.

"Sure"—he nodded—"at least the last time I checked."

"And so you believe. . . ."

"About the sea lion?" He smiled. "Oh, I don't put anything past Creation. But I know there's something inside that creature that's still saying hallelujah." His smile grew broader as he gazed out at the sea.

"Well, I guess I'm glad I could be of some small service to her."

He nodded. "And you can see how she showed her appreciation." He motioned toward the skiff. "There's a life lesson in that."

We talked then a bit, about ourselves, about our pasts, about who we were and are and where we were from. When I mentioned that I'd attended Catholic schools he said that he'd been raised Roman Catholic, too. My surprise must have registered on my face because he said, "Sure, part of taking over a land and its people is having them conform to your religion. When I was three or four they put me in a white gown that went down to my ankles. They held me under the water until I nearly drowned. They sent me to their school."

"Here in Ahousat?" I said. Ahousat was the Nuu-chah-nulth village here on Flores.

He nodded, his hand gesturing out toward the ocean in a wide sweep. "I used to work these waters back before the Sound was all fished out, ten, twelve years or so ago, just about the time you said you came up here. I ran a thirty-seven-foot double-ended salmon troller. In the fish plant back then you probably gutted some of our catch."

I nodded.

"Anyway," he continued, "every now and again we'd pull in our sets and come across an old survivor, you know, a grizzly old fish with a piece of broken hook caught so tight in its jaw that the bone had grown over it." He crooked a finger and held it up beside his jaw.

I smiled.

"It's amazing to think about, how bone can grow right over metal. Creatures learn to take things in stride. They adapt. Either that or they die. The stress kills them. But if they can get past the stress they can get used to just about anything, even a broken hook sticking out of their jaw."

I didn't fully understand his point. Though we were talking about the fish, he seemed to also be telling me something about himself and the Ahousaht. "So what did you finally do with it?" I said after a while. "Pull the broken hook out?"

"No, we cooked it on a plank of cedar, like all the others." Now both of us were smiling. "Speaking of which, I saw you up here before, here on Flores and down on Vargas, as well as the main island, hiking with your chainsaw, only you nearly always come back out empty handed, same as when you went in."

"Well," I said, worried for a moment that I was trespassing, "there aren't many cedar stumps here." I never knew what land was public and what was native owned or controlled, and I doubted that Clarence knew either. He simply planted along the slashes, where he was reasonably sure crops would grow.

"Sure," Ignatius agreed. "And I suppose that's a good reason to check back every couple of weeks. Because you never know when a new cedar stump might pop up."

My mind scrambled for some other excuse as to why I returned again and again.

"Don't be concerned with me," he said, as if reading my thoughts. "You're fine here. Your business is your own."

"You're all right," I said after several moments of silence.

"That sea lion leaping into your skiff," he said, "it'll make a pretty good story. You'd better show that boatful of seal shit to all your friends so that when you tell them the story they'll know you're speaking the truth."

"I really don't care about proving my stories. Or even whether I tell them."

"Then you're even smarter than I thought."

"Sometime when you're next in town," I said, "in one of those bars, we should get together, you know, talk again. I'd be happy to sit down with you, buy you a drink."

"I'd like that, as long as you make mine coffee."

"Coffee, then."

"Fine," he said. "Coffee." The tide was just beginning to rise. I thought about all the shit I had to clean. "I'll hold you to it," I said to Ignatius, then again shook his hand.

❧ ❧ ❧

By then Harmony and I had been together for several summers. Each fall she'd return to the university in Vancouver, where, with the exception of occasional weekend trips to Tofino, she'd remain until spring when classes let out. As a result we had an on-again, off-again arrangement that neither of us cared to define or analyze. Our unspoken understanding was that when she was in town we were a couple, boyfriend and girlfriend. Partners, I suppose, faithful and true. But when she was down-island and back in Vancouver, well, she was her own person then. And during her absences in Tofino, I was my own person.

Not setting things in words was fine with me. I believe that the sunset you watch with someone else is more beautiful when neither comments on it, when viewing it wasn't planned in advance and you come up on it more or less unannounced. When neither person has to say to the other, "Hey, in an hour or two let's make sure we're in this spot or that spot so that we can watch the sun set." If you live that sort of life, you spend it gazing at the clock.

And each of the falls I was with Harmony the grazers hit us, and with each passing season they grew worse. They'd graze some of the buds and colas from one garden, several more from a second, all of the choicest parts from a third. We couldn't be everywhere at once. One garden would lose eight or more plants overnight; another would be reduced to a few plants surrounded by stumps cut a few millimeters above ground level.

Clarence was certain it wasn't the RCMP. We'd seen no helicopters or agents. Besides, the RCMP didn't cherry-pick. They cut down a field clean. No, Clarence was dead certain it was the work of grazers.

❧ ❧ ❧

I haven't yet described winters on the Sound, the time when even many long-term residents shut their houses tight and pack their trucks and cars and drive down-island to Nanaimo or Victoria or the mainland, to some place, any place, with a reasonable degree of human activity and interest. For it is in winter that those of us who live in Tofino and Ucluelet come to realize why the area is called a temperate rainforest. In fall and winter in Tofino it rains. And rains. And then it rains some more. And then when you think the rain is finally letting up, when you think that there could be no more rain possibly left in the sky, no more rain in the incessant, never-ending series of storm fronts rolling in from the open waters of the slate-gray Pacific, storm fronts that pound the shore, your windows, siding, roof, hands and face, right then at that moment it begins to rain all the harder, with an impressive insistence that becomes background to your thoughts, your mood, the very marrow of your life.

Need I explain more why many here spend winter inside a bottle or a sweet cloud of smoke or both?

It's as if all the day is a gray, wet funeral. Good Friday at noon, when the church bells toll and everyone in the neighborhood pulls their blinds and drapes tightly shut and for the next three hours you kneel, as you've been taught by the nuns, in homage to the crucified and dying Christ. Only here there is no neighborhood. Here there are only trees and shrubs and ferns, liverworts and mosses and lichens. Here there are banana slugs as big as the yellow bubble-gum cigars sold on the counter of the corner store on Bryn Mawr. You pull on your gumboots and Smelly Hansen and slosh among the slugs sliming the muck of the forest floor because if you spend even one more minute inside your house reading the same books and listening to the same records and dusting the same furniture and vacuuming the same wooden floors you'll go absolutely fucking batty, and there's nothing left to clean or straighten.

The kitchen floor is swept, washed and polished; the counters (particularly the section bearing the gouged-out scar) scrubbed with baking soda. All the books are alphabetized, dusted, and categorized—fiction alongside fiction, poetry next to poetry, nonfiction with nonfiction—each thing grouped with its complements in its proper, logical place. If you spot a piece of lint on the front room rug, you bend and pick it up. The books on the coffee table in front of the sofa sit at right angles with the corners of the table. All the jars, bottles, and cans in the pantry stand brightly on their shelves, labels front and forward—apple sauce, baked beans, creamed corn, green beans— soldiers awaiting inspection, tops washed and dried, not a single thing out of place.

You dust the faintest of spider webs off the frame enclosing the photo of the '69 Cubs, then recite their names before you hang them back in their place on the wall. Starting from the top left: Don Kessinger, Ernie Banks, Jim Hickman, Ferguson Jenkins, Glenn Beckert, Kenny Holtzman, Ron Santo, Billy Williams, Willie Smith, Ted Abernathy, Randy Hundley. You smoke another joint, trying not to think about Ronny, Lucy, and Marie, and then decide to make a master list of your jazz albums, which are sorted by name of principal artist, then arranged by date of recording. You light two or three of the candles you've put in flat-bottomed barnacle shells and try to shake the ghosts—Lucy, Marie, Ronny—from your head as you work on your list. Inside your chest, your heart tightens like a fist. You add recording dates to the list (month followed by year) then pick up another piece of lint from the rug on the front room floor. You take the crucifix down from the nail on your bedroom wall, then hang it back up again. You slide the sketches you drew years ago of your house in Chicago into the wood-burning stove, watching as the sheets of paper curl and blacken. You toss Roxanne's tortoise-shell hairbrush and brown barrette in the trash, think better of it and take them out, then picture Harmony's smile and put them in the trash again. You drink a glass of water and wash and dry and put away the glass. You lean the orange Frisbee up against the wall on the shelf in the small room off the kitchen, where you've now put in a washing machine and a clothes dryer. You do a load or two of wash, separating the whites from the colors. As the cycles spin, you put on some hard bop, Art Blakey and the Jazz Messengers, and crank the volume up high. You decide to give all your LPs a thorough dusting. Sliding the albums back in their liners, you make sure the A side faces you and that the printing on the label is right side up. Some albums are in the wrong liners, so you put them in the right liners. You decide which liners are the wrong liners and which are the right liners. You stare into the flames of the candles in the barnacle shells. Ghosts jitterbug around you—Marie, Lucy, Ronny—their shadows swaying wildly on the walls. Your chest tightens. Your next breath is hard as stone. The hard rain falls. You hold your fingertip inside one of the flames, re-creating the moment back in Sister Ascension's class, then look in the medicine cabinet in the bathroom for some salve. You could have held your finger in the flame longer, but what do you have to prove to anyone? You smoke another joint. Some of the album liners are frayed or torn, so you repair them with a bit of tape.

All the while it rains.

The rain is Art Blakey at Birdland, at the Café Bohemia, Live at the Village Gate, keeping time on your roof. Playing cross- and poly-rhythms, thunderous press rolls and hi-hat snaps. Brightly splashing the cymbals. Laying down woodpecker rat-a-tat-tats on the edge of the snare. Working the bass and the bell of the cymbal with a furious swagger, and then driving the beat up-tempo with drum rolls so explosive that Ronny, Lucy, and Marie slip from any past or present existence. Crack open a beer. Have you eaten today? No matter. Roll and smoke another joint. Turn the music up louder. Loud, louder. Loudest. Loud enough to drive the dancing ghosts away. All the while the storm raging over the fragile edge of the Pacific where you live rises to higher and then even higher intensities.

෨  ෨  ෨

Harmony would never tell me in advance when she planned to return to town, or even when she was heading back to Vancouver. Things with her were always unspoken, cool, moment to moment, day to day.

Sometimes she'd simply show up at my door. Sometimes I'd go over to the commune expecting to see her, and as I walked in the others would tell me she'd gone. "Are you the last to hear everything?" they'd say. *"Dude!"* They'd pronounce the last word as if it had two syllables, as if saying it like that meant everything obvious in the world. "You mean like she didn't fill you in on her plans? Bummer."

I'd nod and mutter thanks.

"Cool," they'd say. "I was just going to roll one. Want to get high?"

Then a few weeks or a month or two months or three months later, some rainy afternoon or evening, I'd be in my front room reading a book and hear a knock on my back door.

"Anybody home? It's just me," she'd announce.

As she'd unlace her boots I'd take two mugs from the cupboard and put on water for tea. Harmony and I would sit on the sofa and armchair in the front room and sip our tea, seldom saying much of any real consequence, listening to whatever was playing on the stereo (she was partial to alto sax—Johnny Hodges and Benny Carter, Charlie Parker and Art Pepper and Paul Desmond—and when she was away I'd sometimes listen to Art Pepper and recall the image of her dancing in the late afternoon light of my front room when she thought she couldn't be seen), and then we'd head for the bedroom where we'd pass our time wordlessly for a few hours.

With the exception of the time when we told each other I love you, we said nothing about our feelings or what we expected or wanted from each other or what we thought we were or could or should be. It was like the saying on the poster in the head shops in Victoria, the one with the white dove and the open-palmed innocent watching as it flew away, that if you really loved something you let it go. *And if it truly loved you, it would return.*

I always knew that one day things would come to an end between us. So whenever Harmony and I made love I delayed my own orgasm for as long as I possibly could, trying to prove myself as the best lover, ever, as well as wordlessly let her know that we were a good, true thing and hoping that she saw and felt that, too. I hoped it would suggest to her that she and I should stay together and she should never leave me. Over time I came to value simply being with her more than our sharing the act of sex. The feeling frightened me because I realized that I was tiring of being by myself, living alone. I was afraid of the feeling because I knew that if I ever let it show it would reveal me as needy and clingy and desperate, traits I was certain were among the uncoolest in the whole world.

❧ ❧ ❧

I was in my kitchen one rainy afternoon making *pasta cu su*, at the point where I'd finished parboiling the pork bones and was rinsing them and adding them to the sauce, when Harmony and one of her girlfriends pulled up behind the house and knocked at the back door. Outside, the rain was washing down over my yard in visible, pulsing waves driven by a strong wind. Since the co-op in town didn't have any neckbones I was using pork spareribs, which I'd cut in two-rib sections. A pound of ground chuck sat in a bowl, waiting to be made into meatballs. The room was beginning to smell like Nonna's kitchen, warm and sweet.

"This is a surprise," I said.

"Well, aren't you Chef Boyardee," Harmony said. As she shook out her sou'wester and hung it on a hook on the back porch I could see that she'd cut her long hair. She and her girlfriend stepped inside. "Wow, it smells great in here."

Harmony's hair was cut to about chin level. It made her look older, more mature. It was a haircut that belonged to an office worker in a big city, someone stylish, professional, certainly not someone in torn jeans and a ragged sweater who seldom wore a bra and who lived part of the year in her marijuana-dealer brother's commune.

"You've cut your hair," I said.

"He's making spaghetti sauce," Harmony's friend said. She stood over the pot on the stove inhaling deeply, then gave the pot a stir with a wooden spoon.

"Like it?" Harmony pirouetted slowly, then gave her hair a flip and smiled.

"Yeah," I lied. "You look great."

"So," Harmony's friend said, "what's the occasion? Are you having a party? You've got enough here to feed an army."

"It's my grandmother's recipe. I only know how to cook it the way she taught me."

"Can't you just cut quantities in half?" the friend said, putting the wooden spoon down on the stove between the two sets of burners. The friend was dark and shapely, shorter than Harmony, with coal-black hair that fell nearly to her shoulders. She wore jeans and a sturdy black cable-knit sweater and smiled at me every time I looked her way. Her eyes were bright and playful, as if she were privy to some joke. I wondered if I'd ever seen her around before, then moved past her to put the spoon upright in the empty tomato sauce can that sat beside the pot of sauce.

Nonna always put her wooden spoon upright inside an empty can of tomato sauce. Later, after she'd browned the meatballs and they'd cooked in the sauce for a while, she'd siphon the shallow puddles of fat off the top of the sauce and carefully spill the fat into the can, then lay the spoon across its rim. I followed her example exactly.

"No," I said to Harmony's friend, "I always do it the way my grandmother did. I'd be afraid I'd ruin it if I changed it."

"Oh," Harmony said, "forgive me. I should introduce the two of you. Emily, Vince. Vince, Emily. Emily's a very dear and old friend, from Vancouver."

"Not that old," Emily said with a laugh. She shook my hand firmly and smiled, then glanced past me at Harmony and nodded her head as the two of them exchanged a laugh.

"Hey," Harmony said, "we caught you right in the middle of things, didn't we?" She gestured toward the kitchen table, to the bowl of ground meat and some day-old bread I was soaking in water. "Listen, there are some things I need to tend to in town, so, I hate to say it, but I need to split. But you don't mind if Emily hangs out here for a while, do you?" She looked past me, at Emily, who was smiling. "That is, if you don't have other plans."

"But you just got here," I said.

"I'll swing by later or else give you a call."

"Sure. That's cool. Whatever."

"Vince," Emily said, "why don't you show me your grandmother's recipe?"

Harmony opened the back door and stepped out with her raincoat onto the back porch. I followed her. "What's going on?" I shouted to her through the rain but she was already in the yard shielding herself from the torrent coming down with her Smelly Hansen, which she'd tossed over her head and shoulders like a cape.

It was as if she couldn't get away from my place fast enough. And she hadn't even given me a kiss. Or maybe everything was cool like she'd said and she merely had a lot to do in town. I comforted myself with that thought as I stood on my back porch. Sure, I told myself, in a couple of hours when the sauce was ready she'd return, likely with a bottle of wine, and we'd sit down together and share a good meal, maybe lose the friend, and sit down together and catch up on our lives as we resumed the one we had together here in Tofino.

After she opened her car door and got inside she hesitated and waved, holding the wave so long that my misgivings made me feel foolish and petty, as the wind gusted audibly, driving the rain down in angled sheets.

❧ ❧ ❧

"So what are we going to do about this meat?" Emily said as I stepped back inside.

She'd pulled her hair back and up into what girls called a high ponytail, one that began its arc near the crown of her head. The dark arms of her sweater dangled over the back of a kitchen chair. Now she wore only a white dago-T, one so new and bright you'd think she'd just bought or bleached it. "I should get you an apron if you're going to help me," I said. At once I could imagine the front of her white T-shirt splashed with sauce.

"You have an apron?" she asked as if my having one was the most contradictory thing in the world. "I mean, here you are, this tough Yank from Chicago"—she made a machine-gun of her hands and rat-a-tat-tatted me—"and Mr. Alphonse Capone has an apron."

"Second drawer on the left," I said, pointing to the cabinet. I knew that there she'd find two of my most beloved belongings, a pair of white butcher's aprons, folded neatly alongside a stack of dish towels.

"That's right," she said. "Harmony mentioned you knew where everything was."

I frowned. "I just like to keep things in their place."

"And why is that?" She put on one of the aprons, then tied the strings on the back.

"Because things take up physical space," I said, "and since they do they might as well take up the same space consistently rather than inconsistently. Then everyone will know where the things are instead of having to search for them each time they need them."

Now it was her turn to frown. "That doesn't sound like much fun."

"Do you enjoy looking for lost things?"

"Some things"—she laughed—"sure."

"Well, what might be fun for you might not be fun for another. Would you like a beer?" I walked over to the refrigerator. I didn't know how I could explain to her, or anyone for that matter, the comfort and reassurance that I found in order, in something being there for me when I needed it. I didn't know if I could explain the pleasure—or was it relief?—that I felt while rearranging something. It was as if seeing things organized neatly and in their place eased an ever-present tension in my mind. Disorder in a room set off alarm bells inside me and made me feel vulnerable and anxious. True mess tightened my throat and stole my breath. There was pleasure and reassurance in expecting a thing to be in a specific place and then entering that place and seeing it still there.

"I'd rather smoke some bud," she said.

"No reason we can't do both." I opened a bottle of beer and sipped it, and she took it from my hand and smiled and sipped it, too. "Keep it," I said and got another bottle from the refrigerator, then went to get the leather dopkit where I kept my stash of dope.

She cut up some of the bud and rolled a couple of joints while I made the meatballs. Then we browned the meatballs in a skillet and began dropping them one by one, ever so gently, into the pot of simmering sauce. Just as I'd anticipated, as she plunked the second-to-last meatball into the pot, some of the sauce splashed up on her apron. We laughed, then went into the front room with our beers and fired up the first joint.

I'd seen her around before, I was certain, but couldn't figure out precisely where. As we smoked the first joint, I kept stealing glances at her. She had exceptionally clear, white skin and high cheekbones, and an impressive air of confidence about her, as if she were very used to being in charge. She wore no jewelry that I could see, not even earrings. She had a compelling, no-nonsense, clear-eyed gaze. As we shared the joint I could tell she enjoyed wearing the butcher's apron.

"You don't recognize me, do you?" she said as I sorted through my albums for something appropriate to listen to. I squatted on the rug on the living room floor beside the record cabinet. She sat a foot or so away, Mr. Santangelo's apron spilling down between her crossed legs, close enough for us to pass the joint back and forth. I hesitated over Horace Silver's *Blowin' the Blues Away*, already hearing Blue Mitchell's sweet trumpet smoking its way through the title track, but then opted for something wilder and pulled out Pharaoh Sanders' *Karma*. I lowered the needle onto side one, "The Creator Has a Master Plan."

"Of course I remember you," I lied. Sanders's sax trilled and squawked its way through the rippling waves of the opening percussion, quickly joined by James Spaulding's dreamy flute. I adjusted the volume. "You're one of Harmony's friends. We met a couple of years ago at the commune."

"Nope," she said, standing. "You're cold."

I moved across the room, to the overstuffed armchair near the front windows where I often sat when I read.

"I'm trying really hard not to take this personally." She was only half-smiling. "I *am* one of Harmony's best friends, but you and I didn't meet a couple of times. We met precisely once, several years ago, during my first trip to Tofino, and it wasn't at the commune."

"We had coffee together at the Crumb," I guessed.

She took off the apron, balled it in her hands, and dropped it on the floor. "Imagine me in work boots and a long brown, flowered dress, one with about five million antique buttons, all running down the front." In the air her hands described the vertical row of buttons.

"Harmony has a dress like that," I said.

"You're getting warmer. In fact, the dress I was wearing that day was Harmony's. Get it? When you first met me I was wearing Harmony's dress."

"You're sure this wasn't in town at the Crumb?"

She laughed. "No, we definitely weren't in town."

"And I didn't meet you at the commune?"

"I'm really disappointed that you don't remember. The whole ride up here I was hoping you'd remember. But then again, I don't really know you. Maybe you fuck a lot of girls you just happen to meet in the rainforest."

I didn't know what to say to that. After a while I said, "Oh," and then, ever so slowly, what she was saying began to make sense.

"Well, you didn't fuck me in the rainforest, exactly," Emily said and smiled.

"Oh," I said again, "of course," feeling like the stupidest guy in the world, unable to even recognize a woman with whom I'd once been intimate. I stared at her face. The balled-up apron on the floor suddenly nagged at me, so I stood and retrieved it, and on my way out of the room I picked up our empty beer bottles. I went down the hallway and back to the kitchen, where I set the bottles on the table and then began rinsing the spaghetti sauce stain from the apron. The aprons meant a lot to me. They were once Mr. Santangelo's. If I soaked it now maybe I could bleach it later, I thought, and it would be all right.

She followed me. Behind me, as I stood at the sink, I could hear her lighting the second joint. "Well," I said, folding the wet apron and then setting it in the sink and drying my hands on a dish towel, "small world."

"Well water," she said, inhaling. "Want some of this?"

I took the lit joint from her hand. "I really don't know what to say."

"Don't feel bad, honey. It was a long, long time ago. And I mean it's not exactly like we exchanged numbers and names."

"Allow me to introduce myself." I extended my hand. "Vince Sansone."

"Emily Fournier," she said. We shook hands, formally, like two diplomats meeting at the United Nations. "Hey, don't bogart the jay."

I handed it back to her. "French Canadian?"

"*Mais oui.*" She took a long sip from the joint as we sat. "And you're a Yank from Chicago. I know all about you. The conscientious Mr. Capone from Chicago's wild and wooly North Side. Clarence's right hand man. Harmony's told me all about you."

The rest of it—snippets of picture and sound, what I imagine could be the clutter on the floor of a film editor's studio—was falling quickly in place, punctuated by the marijuana and the beer. The dark-haired girl in the forest, several years before, flirting with me, playing a variation of catch-me-if-you-can. Not too far from my garden of plants, marked with green yarn, which at the time grew alongside Clarence's vast garden of plants. The shocking white of her calves and thighs as she lifted her dress. She and I chasing each other, like children. Her glassy eyes. Panting breath. The white loop of her underpants around her ankle, as she leaned back against the fallen nursery log. The long, lovely stretch of her leg and thigh. The chorus of other girls—three distinct voices—calling out her name as if they were playing hide-and-seek. *Emily! Em-i-lee!*

"Was Harmony there?" I asked suddenly. All at once things became clearer. "I mean, back then, was she one of the voices calling out to you?"

"That afternoon when we fucked in the forest?"

I nodded.

"Of course." She hesitated, then laughed. "You mean Harmony never told you? I thought you knew."

"Knew what?"

"That she was there, of course, silly."

"You mean, she saw—"

Emily laughed. "I don't know what all Harmony saw, but, oh, the girls took notice of you, believe me." She smiled broadly. "They were very impressed. Apparently we put on quite a show. Besides, Harmony had noticed you hiking around the forest before. You went there a lot. So did she. You know, it was originally her idea for you to work for her brother."

"I don't follow."

"I think it was the next spring. One day Clarence was complaining about how people were always ripping him off and how there weren't any honest people left in the world, even all the way up here, in mellow-yellow hippie-dippy Paradise beside the sea, and Harmony said what about that loner dude we sometimes run into in the rainforest. So

Clarence said he'd try to figure out a way to meet you, and then one day you just dropped into his lap."

I wagged my head.

"I guess he always knew about you but hadn't ever actually thought about you working for him until Harmony suggested it. When we mentioned where we were going the day we tripped, he even said we might run into you. He told us to keep an eye out for you. He'd spotted you around. He knew you were a Yank who lived in town but didn't know if you were a thief."

"I never touched his plants," I said. "I'm not—" I paused and looked at the apron drying on the sink. "I steal only from my family and a handful of old friends."

"Well, by the time Clarence hired you he knew for sure."

I got up and stirred the sauce and took two more beers out of the refrigerator, opened them and let their caps fall and rattle on the tile floor. Who cared if they fell on the floor? I thought. Side one of *Karma* had ended, due to the length of LPs, in the middle of the song. I wanted to flip it over and hear the rest of it. Then I couldn't resist the bottle caps any longer and bent and picked them up.

"You mean you thought that all of these things just happened?" Emily said. "That the whole arrangement between you and Clarence and Harmony just simply fell into place all by itself?" Her voice was edged with patience and condescending sympathy, as if she were explaining bad news to a child. "Don't you know that nothing happens in isolation? I mean, every single event in the world, every single detail, like it's all like one gigantic nexus. If just one detail changes, then all the others. . . ."

I was aware at that moment of the rain, how during all the time Emily had been here with me the rain was firmly and constantly pounding the roof, and I hadn't paid attention to it. I hadn't heard it. It was right there all the time, pounding against my ears, and I hadn't heard it. And now everything between me and Clarence and Harmony. . . .

It was a classic stoned thought, the gradual uncovering of connection. So Harmony watched me as I was intimate with Emily in the rainforest. So she set up my current job. I nodded to Emily, grateful for what she'd told me, and began walking past her to the front room to put on a new album, but then her free hand snagged my arm, and as I turned back toward her I stepped into her kiss, her marvelously soft lips, her wet and open mouth, her playful and invitingly tempting tongue.

It took away my breath. I stepped back. "What was that for?"

"What do you think?" Her free hand fell to my thigh, then brushed the crotch of my jeans. "Or do you only like to do it in the forest?"

"But Harmony—" I began.

"Never mind about Harmony. You don't see her here, do you?"

She circled around me and nudged me backward, until the back of my legs bumped against the seat of the kitchen chair on which she'd draped her black sweater. My mind was still buzzing from the reefer and beer, turning round and round, as if in a maze, trying to process all that Emily had told me. She set her beer bottle on the table and pushed me back so that I sat in the chair, then dropped down to her knees before me.

The high knot of her ponytail bound by a doubled-over piece of green elastic swayed as her fingertips touched my belt buckle, then the button on the waist of my jeans.

"Don't worry," she said, her dark eyes gazing up at me. "Harmony's not coming back here, at least not tonight. Didn't you understand that?"

"No," I said.

"You will," she said.

"Hey," I said.

"Does someone have to spell out everything for you?" Her voice grew low and fell to a whisper as she looked down. "I mean, are you so dumb you can't connect the dots?"

I said nothing and leaned back in the chair, then let out a sigh and closed my eyes.

"Well," she said.

"Well water," I said.

She smiled, and then I understood, at least in part.

∾ ∾ ∾

Later, after we'd eaten, after it grew dark and the rain seemed to abate, Emily and I drove over to the commune. Going there was my idea. All I knew was that I had to talk with Harmony, to tell her what I'd done, to say I was sorry and confess.

Cut to the chase, or should I say the discovery scene.

You move past the commune's mismatch of furniture, its spray-painted walls, its incredibly cluttered kitchen, where piles of week-old unwashed dishes teeter like miniature Leaning Towers of Pisa, the commune's Babel of competing stereos each loudly playing a different LP—Pink Floyd's *The Wall*, The Clash's *London Calling*—and up the darkened back staircase to Harmony's attic room, where you're certain you'll find her since her car's parked outside and she isn't in any of the rooms downstairs.

You've prepared the explanation—or is it a confession?—since years ago you learned your lesson about the timely telling of truth. Now you know the importance of getting things like what just happened between you and Emily out in the open, in the light and clear air, immediately, like an adult. You're an adult, and you don't want to repeat history. You've learned from your mistakes, or at least you're still trying to. Your mistakes have burned you and ruined the lives of others in the past, but so far at least you've learned this much. You know what you need to say, that even though you've made no real promises or commitments you know that you each expect the other person to be faithful, at least when you're both in town, as you've been now for years, and now you're ashamed and sorry to have failed her in that regard.

You take the steps to the attic three at a time, knock twice on the wooden door, and when you think you hear an answer you swing it open.

What was it that Emily said about connections? What was it that Ignatius George told you back on Flores about there being no accidents?

There before you, on her box spring and mattress, in the bedroom filled with gauzy, golden light from a score or more flickering candles, the room whose ceiling is covered by a magnificently tie-dyed sheet that fills with air when the side windows are open and the wind is just right, that billows like a topsail on some mighty ship, there before you is Harmony with short hair in a hot, shiny sweat, wearing only sparkling silver earrings and a black choker, straddling some strange dude, fucking his brains out, you see clearly, working him hard and slick and fast.

The room reeks of sweat and dope, and the scene imbeds itself indelibly inside your consciousness. The black velvet choker caressing her neck. Her shiny earrings. The lines of sweat glistening on her back. The dude's twisted face, his beard and dark eyebrows, the dark mass of his hair, long dreads splayed wildly like a black hand across the white cotton of her pillowcase. The flexed muscles of her thighs. His hands holding her bouncing hips.

What was it that Josh said years ago, after finding out about you and Roxanne? The line he quoted from *Winnie the Pooh*?

*Bump, bump, bump, on the back of his head.*

# 9

# Tofino 1980

BUMP, bump, bump.

Here's where things in the Canadian part of my story unravel, or should I say come together and return, hand me the karmic payback I deserved, as I turned from the doorway of Harmony's bedroom and ran down the stairs, head bouncing like Christopher Robin's stuffed bear.

My main thought was that I should find Emily. I sensed that more was going on than I understood, and Emily was the best person who could explain things. So I banged open doors and shoved my way past whoever stood in my way as I searched for her among the knots of hippies roaming about, drinking beer and wine and listening to music and rapping in the various rooms and nooks and crannies of the large house.

Then I bumped, literally, into Clarence. He was dressed in full-blown Mr. Zig-Zag regalia, wearing a khaki shirt with epaulets, his dark hair meticulously slicked back, the waxed tips of his mustache curling magnificently in the air. We collided in the dark-paneled hallway leading to the commune's oldest section, referred to by most as "the great house," the section of the commune where Clarence kept an office and where, behind locked doors, he lived. I didn't care that I was invading his private quarters, off limits to everyone unless specifically invited. Since I couldn't find Emily anywhere else, I figured she had to be there. I began to push my way past Clarence, who in response clamped his hands on my shoulders and did his best to hold me at arm's length, and for a while we did a clumsy back-and-forth dance in the hallway.

"My good man," he said.

His eyes were bloodshot and rimmed with red. He rocked back on his feet, as if drunk. On his breath was the sweet, cloying smell of whiskey.

"Let me past."

"Whoa, my good man, where's the fire? What's the rush?"

"Emily," I began.

"Listen, dude, she's not—"

"I need to talk to her."

I tried to brush him aside. His hands tightened, an eagle's talons. They hurt, and for a beat or two I stared unbelieving at him as he deliberately dug his nails into my shoulders. Then I raised my hands, clenching my fists six inches or so in front of his face, then swung both forearms sharply outwards so as to break his hold on me, at the same time stepping close to him and lifting a knee up into his groin. It was a trick I'd learned back in Ronny's garage, when the guys would practice ways to get out of various holds, rehearsing the best moves in the event someone grabbed you. I didn't knee Clarence very hard, but his face warped as the breath rushed out of him. Then with both hands I shoved him in the chest as I swept my foot against the back of his ankles so that he'd fall.

As he stumbled backward and down onto the floor my eye caught Emily, in the far room he was blocking, rising from behind a wooden table. On the table stood a bottle of whiskey and a pair of glasses, each half full. Next to the glasses, as if they were on display, sat a bowl of multicolored pills. From what I could see, the walls of Clarence's quarters were paneled in a warm, rich cherry wood. On a waist-high bookcase stood a half dozen or more shining trophies and loving cups. Topping the trophies were gilded figures in the shapes of curlers or bowlers. From the distance I couldn't tell. Amidst them stood a rubber Godzilla, her outstretched hands cradling a hash pipe.

On Clarence's stereo a Leonard Cohen album was playing, *Songs From a Room*, "The Story of Isaac" coming to its end and then melting into the beginning chords of "A Bunch of Lonesome Heroes."

"Hey," Emily cried as I stepped over Clarence and grabbed her hand, pulling her out of the room and out into the hallway. "What's going on here?"

Clarence lay sprawled on the floor, like a broken toy, a Nutcracker marionette, a pile of Pick-Up Sticks, all bony knees and splayed fingers and elbows. "Yo," he called from his position down on the floor.

"I take it you went up to her room," Emily said to me with a drunken smile.

"Dude, let's think this over," Clarence said, his phrases punctuated by half-breaths. "Rewind the tape. Let's pause, put this thing in reverse while there's still time."

"In your dreams." I pulled Emily further toward me out into the hallway.

"Harmony—" he began.

"I don't give a fuck about Harmony."

"You do, too. You wouldn't be here otherwise. Let's all go inside my rooms and sit down and have a drink and peaceably talk about it."

"I don't want to talk. I came here for Emily."

He groaned and mumbled something I couldn't understand to the wall.

*"I'd like to tell my story,"* sang Leonard Cohen from the next room.

All at once I wanted to kick him. I felt curiously strange, outside myself, as if the drama unfolding in the hallway was an image I was watching in a movie theater, some *film noir* in which a drug dealer and one of his men fight during the third reel over who gets the girl. Was that what Clarence and I were fighting over? Were we fighting over Emily? Or maybe, because he was Harmony's brother, was I taking out on him what I really felt toward her? Why were we fighting to begin with? And what was with the shiny trophies?

I continued to hold Emily by the wrist, and by the way she was responding—not resisting, smiling glassily whenever I glanced at her, as if she were enjoying her part in the scene—I sensed that my claiming her was not only agreeable to her but something she was enjoying. I sensed that she wanted to leave the commune with me and go back to my place, where we'd spend the night. That's right, I thought, I was laying claim to her. I'd take her back to my place. All the while the image of the black velvet choker around Harmony's neck played on the screen in my mind, blurred by Josh's hurt face at my back door, Roxanne idly brushing her wet hair, Marie smiling at Ronny after I'd introduced them, Harmony grunting as her earrings glistened in the soft glow of candlelight.

Her newly cut hair, wet with her sweat. The room's smell: candle wax mixed with the funk of sex. Breasts swaying in the candlelight. Her face blurred with pleasure as she turned toward the sound of my footfalls on the stairs and opened her mouth, as if to gulp air or speak. The other man's long, dark dreads on her white pillowcase.

I stepped closer to Clarence, a tangle of angles, fallen hangers on a closet floor, and pressed his side with the toe of my shoe, not hard enough to hurt him but hard enough to let him know I was absolutely serious and didn't want anyone to interfere with me.

"She's leaving with me, you understand?" I nudged his side with my foot a second time. "What do you say to that? Huh? You have a clever answer for that?"

"Dude, dude, dude," he said, each word drawn out longer than the last, "calm the fuck down. Mellow out. Let's sit down and get this situation under control." He tucked in his arms to cover his ribs and raised both hands meekly in surrender. "Let me get you some valium or a couple of 'ludes. Come on, man, let's move past this. Sit down like a couple of old friends."

Now, suddenly, all the violence was making me feel nauseous.

"Think about it, dude," he continued as he sat up, "take a deep breath and think about it. Do the right thing and we can both forget any of this ever happened. As for me and you, we're comrades-in-arms, remember? Over the past years we've made some considerable jack together, haven't we? Just think of your house in town that jack built."

I nodded and bent at the waist, feeling as if at any moment I might throw up.

"Why mess with a good thing? You know, man, if it works why fuck with it? Why break the symbiosis? Shatter all we have? You've been getting what you want from me, haven't you? Have I ever refused you anything? I've never refused you anything. I took you out of that horrible fish plant, didn't I? I brought you outside, I gave you nature, and now you can work out in the open, in God's pure and clean air. You're part of my family, man. You know you're always welcome here. We're a family, man. You're getting what you want from me, and I'm getting what I want from you, and all of that makes things between us very mellow. Very cool, *capisce?* You and me, we work together, tongue in groove, hand in glove. Why screw it all up now?"

It was an excellent question. I wanted to answer *because screwing things up is what I do best, and if you think this is something wait until you hear what I did back in Chicago.* Instead I said, "I don't have to explain. Not to you or anybody. I can do whatever the fuck I fucking want."

"Ever the articulate one, aren't you?" He shook his head sadly. "But your point is well taken, my good friend. Of course you may do whatever you want. I've only shown you doors. I've never forced you into anything."

I leaned forward and offered him a hand.

"I'm disappointed in you," Clarence told me as he stood. "Deeply disappointed." He wagged his head and began putting himself back into order, raking his greased hair with his long fingers, tugging and straightening his shirt, curling the ends of his mustache with the tips of his fingers. "I found you promising, Vince. The yarn on your plants was so charming, I was fooled into thinking you had wit and charm."

I said nothing and looked away.

"Let's go," Emily said, and so I turned away from Clarence and made my way down the hallway, past a large peace sign embroidered with bright cartoon flowers painted on the wall. Beside it was a drawing of R. Crumb's Mr. Natural. From a stereo in the first room in the addition came the sweet, familiar strains of Bob Marley and the Wailers.

༄ ༄ ༄

The day's storm had blown over.

Emily and I walked onto the commune's wide front porch, its wooden planks slick and dark from the rain. The night had turned uncharacteristically mild, with the bright, hard edges of ten thousand stars rippling the black fabric of the sky. The air smelled of the impending spring. Soon the sky would fill with wings and Tofino's mudflats would be covered by thousands of migrating shorebirds: western sandpipers, whimbrels, black-bellied plovers, greater yellow-legs, sanderlings, dunlins, least sandpipers, black oystercatchers. Soon the fields would pop with wildflowers and the land would be ripe again for planting.

"So you knew all about it?" I asked. I was still feeling sick, as if I might vomit. Violence does that to me, makes me want to vomit. Then the feeling passes and I either get a headache or grow depressed and numb. "Ahead of time, earlier today, you knew?"

She didn't answer. Her full lips were slightly parted; her dark eyes were lacquered over from all that she'd smoked and drunk.

"Listen," I said. "This is important to me. Earlier today, when you and Harmony stopped by my place, did you two have all of this planned out?"

Still she said nothing as she began walking toward my car.

"I understand," I said in soft voice as I followed her, "that you're really ripped."

"Yeah," Emily said after a while. She leaned against the passenger door. "She knew ahead of time that he'd be here."

"You mean the dude she's with?"

Emily nodded. "Totally. His name's Travis. He flew up this afternoon on a float plane. The dude's loaded. Harmony met him two months ago down in Vancouver."

I tried to make sense of it. "So why didn't she just get together with him up here, I mean, just the two of them, hooking up, without involving me? I wouldn't have had to find out about it."

"That's not the way Harmony does things."

I said nothing.

"You don't know her as well as I do."

"Apparently."

"I mean, that's her way of breaking up. That's her M.O. She finds another guy and then lets the first guy, like, sort of discover by himself the fact that he's been replaced. You were the guy she used to break up with Jeremy."

I remembered Jeremy from the Crumb, from the day I bought the lid from Clarence.

She shrugged apologetically, licked her lips, and took a deep breath. "She was getting close to you, I guess, really close, and she didn't like it. Plus she said she'd never been with someone as long. So when she told me that she'd met this new guy and he was maybe going to fly up and things were, like, over with between the two of you, I said if it was okay with her maybe I wouldn't mind seeing you again. That is, as long as she thought it was cool. You know, like I wanted sort of to play it by ear, like we did earlier today. To see if maybe the energy we had back in the forest was still there."

I stared at her dark eyes.

"The day we met you were giving off this tremendous amount of sexual energy. It was unbelievable. You came right out of nowhere and were absolutely glowing, all bright yellows and really intense shades of orange, like your aura was made of this tremendously hot fire." She offered a smile. "You came at me as if you'd just walked out of a fiery blaze. I never had visuals like that on acid before. So, anyway"—she hesitated—"the plan was, like, this afternoon Harmony and I would stop by your place and either I'd feel some of that energy again and dig you or maybe there'd be nothing there and I wouldn't. If I didn't, I wasn't going to tell you we'd met before. Like I wasn't going to reveal to you who I was. Harmony and I decided on the drive up that if you recognized me and there wasn't a vibe I'd just deny it, and she'd back me up and both of us would say you were like confusing me with someone else. The plan then was for me to split with Harmony when she left."

"I see."

"But if the energy was there and I did dig you then I'd give Harmony the high sign and I'd stay. It was Harmony's idea that if I stayed I should blow you. No guy ever refuses." She let out a long breath. "That way, she said, later on when you found out about Travis if you tried to come down on her she could call you a hypocrite and say things were even."

"It's so nice when girlfriends are able to help each other out like that."

"Don't look so glum," she said. "And don't be so sarcastic. You can't say that this afternoon you didn't have a good time."

I nodded. That I'd fought with Clarence was only just starting to sink in. "Well, I guess I'm sorry I dragged you out here."

She smiled. "Oh, please don't apologize. I really dug it when you pulled me out of Clarence's room. You should have seen the look on your face. The whole scene was very romantic, like I was being fought over and kidnapped. Besides, I'd much rather go back to your place than listen to Clarence go on about the latest developments in hydroponics. Like does he actually think anyone else but him cares?" She laughed. "I don't know if you know it but he's thinking of taking the entire business indoors with hydroponics because of the grazers. Plus, when he drinks and with all that he smokes, he really doesn't have the easiest time getting it up." She paused for a beat to read my reaction. "You would like to be with me tonight, wouldn't you? But I have to tell you I'm not on the pill, so we'll have to use rubbers. I mean, if you don't we could still fool around together, but I do draw the line about how many times a day I let a guy come in my mouth."

"I always enjoy meeting a woman with standards."

We were walking across the yard toward Harmony's car, which was parked next to Clarence's old green pickup. Tumbled sideways on Harmony's back seat was a stuffed satchel, a leather tag on one handle, inside the tag's plastic window *Emily J. Fournier.*

"You don't have to worry about getting pregnant with me," I said, lifting the satchel from the seat. "I've had a vasectomy."

We walked back toward my car. "A vasectomy," Emily said, surprised. "I mean, at your age. Why?"

I stared at the faded bumper stickers on the back of Clarence's truck as I considered how I'd answer. To the right of the twin leaves of marijuana and the slogan about how man made beer and God made pot was a new sticker depicting a merrily dancing skeleton with a top hat, sunglasses, and cane.

## HAVE A GRATEFUL DAY

"Because of something I did," I said, "years ago, back in Chicago, before I came up here. Because of this girl I knew, this girl I loved, back in Chicago. I got her pregnant."

∿ ∿ ∿

Emily stayed at my place, and later in the week borrowed my car to visit the commune. I declined the invitation to go with her and let bygones be bygones, pretend that nothing all that heavy or serious had occurred. Heavy and serious things had occurred, and the things affected me, even if the karma I'd incurred through my relationship with Roxanne suggested I deserved them. When Emily returned, she brought me a pair of letters.

Clarence's letter said that since he was high his recollection of what took place was fuzzy, though he did recall something about me accidentally knocking him down and later on stumbling into him, accidentally kicking him in the ribs, which, if I cared to know, were still tender and bruised. Though in time the body heals itself, he wrote. If only the mind could imitate the body as easily. With regard to his having fallen and been kicked, he expected no apology unless I'd deliberately intended to hurt him. As for what had been said between us, he wrote, he couldn't recall the conversation.

Then he asked me to think about the financial realities of living in Clayoquot Sound, not the easiest place on God's green earth to find gainful employment, and certainly not in the amount of tax-free lucre that he paid. Unless I wanted to squat on the beaches or wallow in fish guts for the rest of my life it might be in my better financial interests to apologize to him, that is, if actually hurting him had been my intention. In the meantime, he concluded, he'd tend to his injured ribs.

His letter was in bright blue ink, splotched in places since he'd written it with fountain pen. His handwriting was large and bold, with unnecessary flourishes and swirls on the tops of capital letters and the tails of lower-case g's and y's that made me picture the waxed tips of his mustache and wonder how Sister Ascension would have graded him.

Harmony's letter was typed on heavy bond paper, off-white, with a watermark from some swank stationery store in Victoria, what appeared to be a queen's jeweled crown. She regretted the way I'd learned about her involvement with her new friend from Vancouver but since I wasn't supposed to have stopped by the commune that evening she didn't think the situation was her fault. Emily had assured her that we'd remain at my place, she wrote, and so naturally she took her friend at her word. How was she to know Emily would change her plans? Wasn't it sensible to take an old friend at her word? Not that it was Emily's fault, Harmony wrote. Fault shouldn't be the issue. Nor should blame or anger, both of which she was certain I was feeling and both of which were, in her eyes, inappropriate.

Life was far too short, Harmony concluded, for attributing blame or for feeling resentment or anger. There was no place in her life for negative vibes.

❧ ❧ ❧

Emily liked to play games. She liked acting out scenarios in which she and I would play various roles which she'd loosely sketch out before-hand and then with a snap of her fingers we'd be required to fall into, improvising our parts as we went along.

Our games were the usual variations on power: the Security Guard and the Nervous Shoplifter, the Teacher and the Student Who Needed a Good Grade, the Master of the Manor and the New French Maid, the Young Baroness and the Fiery Italian Blacksmith. We played the Pirate Ship's Captain and the Stowaway, the Lawn Boy and the Estate Owner's Lonely Daughter, the Precocious Babysitter and the Man of the House, the Paper Boy on Collection Day and the Woman Fresh from the Shower Whose Robe Would Slip Open as She Searched in Her Purse for a Tip.

At first I enjoyed the games but after a few weeks they made me weary. All too frequently I'd slip out of my assigned character and revert to my actual self. It was only after Emily left that I understood the games were preparation for her return to Vancouver, where she lived and worked.

She explained that her times in Tofino were pure vacation, her version of Mardi Gras, of Carnival, of celebration preceding the long stretch of Lent, which in her case meant going back to Vancouver to labor. The games were a type of mask; the roles, a form of costume. One nice thing about Clarence is that he understood this fully, she said. Being masked or in costume freed one to do things one wouldn't consider doing otherwise, she maintained. It was only after she'd left that I realized the games were also a way of insuring that she could keep anyone who got close to her at a distance.

I realized later that the game I really wanted to play with her was the Sassy French-Canadian Friend of the Deceitful Sister of the Town's Colorful Marijuana Dealer and the Confused Yank from Chicago Who Was Trying to Sort Things Out in His Life. There'd be no rules. We'd simply spend time together, see where things went.

❧ ❧ ❧

"That afternoon in the rainforest when we fooled around," I said to Emily one day out of the blue, "was that part of a game you were playing?"

"Well," Emily said, "let me explain. Like we saw you, I mean the four of us—Harmony, Raven, and this chick I never liked who was up here only once, River, I think she was calling herself, though I think her real name was Elaine or Marlaine—anyway, we were just standing there really still, tripping madly, listening to all the sounds the trees make when they breathe, when suddenly I spotted you coming along Clarence's path, quiet as a banana slug. I pointed you out to the others, and then Harmony whispered that you were the dude with the yarn on his plants." She smiled. "Green yarn, tied symmetrically in neat bows. I mean, Vince, really."

"You were tripping."

"That goes without saying. So, anyway, for a while we watched you tend to your plants, and I whispered to the others that I thought you were really cute, you know, working there, with that intense look you get on your face sometimes. Then Raven whispered she wanted to go over and talk to you. And then I just flashed on the two of us together and said, 'No, I saw him first, he's mine.' I asked them to leave me alone with you for fifteen minutes. I told them to fan out in three directions and make believe I was lost."

"So it wasn't a game." I wanted her to tell me it wasn't, that what had happened between us was real.

"Not one I shared with you, but in my head, Vince, yeah, of course it was a game. The rule was that I had to entice you to do me. The rule was there couldn't be any words. I was concerned I'd scare you off, that you'd run away or, worse, start talking. If you had talked to me, I mean uttered one single word, the game would have been over just like that." She snapped her fingers. "I would have ended things right then and there, and if you had tried anything more I would have screamed and slapped you." She took a breath and smiled. "But something inside of you was smart enough to sense how to play along, as if you too knew the rule that there couldn't be any talking, that what we were doing was a dumb show in which I had to make you want to do me, and that neither of us could talk. And when you first saw me and stepped toward me, believe me, you burst brilliantly into flame."

"You know," Emily began one afternoon after we'd made love, as we roused ourselves from bed and began picking up our clothes scattered on the floor, "someday we'll be older and married and we won't be able to play like this anymore." We'd just played a game where we were strangers who'd confused our hotel rooms. Apparently the keys the hotel had given us fit into both locks.

"Someday we'll be married?" I said.

"Yeah, I mean, not to each other"—she laughed—"but to other people. You know what I'm talking about. We'll grow old. We'll settle down. We'll *mature*." She said the word nearly as if she were spitting.

"I'm pretty sure I'll never be married," I said. I knew I was toxic, like one of those deadly radioactive atolls out in the Pacific where the States had tested their nuclear bombs, like the dreadful pond in Sister Ascension's story, full of polio germs.

"Well, at least I will, you know, when the time's ripe and things feel right to me." She put on her underwear and bra, a matching set, clearly expensive, light blue, with black, lacy frills. "You should see me in Vancouver, Vince, you'd hardly recognize me. Skirts just above the knee. Grays and blacks, mainly. White or off-white blouses, modest jackets. Hair pulled neatly back, just so." She pulled her hair back for a moment as she glanced around. "You never keep a mirror in here, do you?"

"Why should I? There's one in the bathroom."

"It's always bothered me that you don't have a mirror in your bedroom. There should be one here." She pointed to the wall across from the bed. "Where you have that crucifix. So you can see how you look as you dress."

"I really don't care how I look as I dress."

She rolled her eyes at me and continued dressing.

"So," I said, "I take it that back on the mainland you're a real conservative."

She nodded. "Fiscally, at least. I dress well. Very well, in fact. I have to. I work in finance, on West Hastings, in the financial district. You wouldn't trust someone with your investments who didn't look the part, would you? You'd be amazed at the size of some of the portfolios I'm asked to handle."

She seemed distant and strange, as if she were an old friend I'd spotted from across a large room at a reunion but upon nearing her discovered she was really someone else. "If I had a portfolio, I'd trust you with it however you dressed."

"No, you wouldn't." She stood in her underwear by the side of the bed, folding the clothing she'd taken off earlier, as she picked it up from the floor. I admired the way she pressed soft, careful creases into her blouse. "You wouldn't trust anyone. You're not the trusting type. You're the type who'd keep his portfolio private, stuck between his mattress and his box spring, or locked up somewhere in a safe, even if it meant that over the long term it wouldn't grow."

She walked to my closet, wearing only her bra and panties, and began sorting through my long-sleeved shirts. "You don't have any dress shirts with French cuffs?" she asked, then without waiting for an answer pulled one of my shirts from the rod where it was hanging and held it to her nose and sniffed it and then slipped it on. I was glad to see her put the hanger back in its right place, not with my work shirts but in the section with the other empty hangers, and with the hook like all the other hooks, facing the closet's back wall.

I approached her, curious, wanting to unbutton the shirt she'd so carefully buttoned. I wanted to do a second time what only half an hour or so before we'd done but this time do it cleanly, just her and me, Emily Jeannette Fournier and Vincent Anthony Sansone, minus the screwy hotel room cards and all the other trappings of mask and game.

"No," she said. "Thank you, but no." She pressed her palm against my chest and pushed me away. "I'm going to take this shirt with me, if you don't mind."

It was then, at that moment, that I understood.

She picked up her folded blouse from the bed and carried it down the hallway to her satchel, which I saw was already packed.

"I have a small closetful of shirts," she said back in the bedroom, as she pulled on her jeans. "Well, I should say that actually I have a rather large closet, but in that large closet I have a small, very select collection of shirts, six or maybe seven, that over the years I've taken from very special guys—"

"After it's over."

"Yeah," she said, tucking my shirt carefully into her jeans, "after I've decided that it's over. When the time feels right to me. Before things have started to turn. You know how a carton of milk gets when you're gone from your apartment for a week or two and you find out you forgot to put it back in the refrigerator? I leave before things turn, when things are still good, when later on I could still tingle with the memory of the sound of the guy's voice or the way he'd touch or kiss me."

I stared at a strand of lint on the rug beneath the bed, then bent and picked it up and balled it between my thumb and first finger.

She told me that she didn't want a goodbye kiss or hug and that she didn't want me to walk out with her, that she'd arranged it so that her ride back down-island would be waiting for her at the bend beyond my driveway.

What could I say other than to take care.

"Just so that he'll stop bugging me," she said, "you're going to patch things up soon with Clarence, aren't you?"

I shrugged. "I'm not very good at patching things up."

"That's just an excuse. That means you don't want to."

Again I shrugged.

"But I can dig it. That's cool. I understand. I'm that way myself, too." She took a step toward me, then stopped and stared down at her hands, as if she didn't know what to do with them. "You really do need a mirror in here," she said after gazing back at me and then around the room. "And, for God's sake, lose the crucifix."

ᔈ ᔈ ᔈ

After Emily left, my house seemed pretty miserable and empty. No music I put on the stereo was able to fill its lonely silence. I realized that not only had Emily left but Harmony and Roxanne had, too, and then I thought of all the people in my life whom I had left. It seemed to me that the very essence of life was loss and separation. Even Louis Armstrong's voice and trumpet, so solid and textured that his music nearly always lifted my soul, seemed superfluous and flat, mere sound marred by the various scratches on the LP. No sound could distract me from my sadness. No book I picked up to read could hold my eyes.

I turned back to my house and its petty, desperate order. My alphabetized record albums rested neatly in the shelf beneath the stereo. Occasional candles squatted on glass plates in precise relation to the corners of the surfaces on which they rested. In the bookcase, fiction massed with other fiction, nonfiction with nonfiction, collections of poetry with other collections of poetry. Some books stood upright like rows of matchsticks. Others lay on their sides like stacks of bricks. In the kitchen, the lonely second hand of my wall clock swung around silently while the fading faces of the '69 Cubs stared blankly at my table and chairs, at the bowl of purple olive snail shells on the windowsill, at the cabinets and drawers where knives lay inside their rack with other knives, each blade facing left. Spoons lay perfectly segregated, tea with tea and soup with soup. Forks lay atop other forks in groups of threes. Plates rested in the cupboards in so precise an order that I could close my eyes and describe the character of each pile, the symmetry with which I returned them each time I washed and dried them.

Back in the bedroom, I knew I'd have to strip the bed and wash the sheets. I didn't want to be reminded of her later on, be caught unaware, wake up the next morning or the morning after that and smell her and in a moment of half sleep and forgetfulness reach out for her, thinking she was still here. There are times I envy the married, those who sleep in bed with someone else so often that over time they take it for granted. Only those of us who sleep alone, those of us whose long progression of nights goes untouched by another, understand what I mean.

᠊ᢙ ᢙ ᢙ᠊

I drove into town after thoroughly cleaning my house. I'd go to the Maquinna and maybe shoot some pool and lay one on, carry on like a real resident of Tough City, drink until I was broke or I got into a fight or threw up all over myself or passed out. Back then I had the idea that painful things were like arrows and fish hooks: to get them out you had to push them in deeper and then all the way through your muscle and skin even though doing so heightened the pain. But after my eyes adjusted to the smoky darkness of the pub I saw Ignatius sitting at the bar, nodding to me as he stirred a minor avalanche of sugar into a mug of coffee.

He seemed pleased to see me, and as I neared him he took off his Adidas cap and ran his big hand over his hair and smiled. "So I see you made it through winter."

I sat on the stool next to him, then caught the bartender's eye and ordered a shot and a beer. Since the day the Steller sea lion had leapt into my skiff and Ignatius and I eased the terrified beast back into the sea, I'd seen Ignatius at least a half dozen times in the slashes alongside the rainforest, where we exchanged pleasantries and talked about the weather or the medicinal value of local plants or the coming mushroom-hunting season. Now that I thought of it, he seemed to always be around. Our conversations were always cordial, and since I'd be at work, tending Clarence's gardens, I always had some fabricated story about my reasons for being where I was. I remembered our continual promise to have coffee together in town and so I turned to him and nodded and said, "The next round's on me."

"I appreciate that."

We sat in silence while I waited for my shot and beer. He put his cap back on and poured more sugar into his cup. The sugar dispenser was the common kind, with ribbed glass sides and a conical aluminum lid with a tiny flap. It reminded me of all the diners on Clark Street and down on Broadway back in Chicago.

"I see your friend's started the new season's work alone."

I knocked back the shot, which burned its way magnificently down my gut, then drank half of my beer. "Which friend is that?"

"I was worried something happened to you," he continued. He poured cream into his cup from a small pitcher until his coffee was the same soft brown color as his skin.

"I survived."

He smiled and sipped his sweet coffee. "Sure. You're sitting right here." He pointed to my empty glass of beer. "Pretty early in the day for that, isn't it?"

I tried to get the bartender's attention. "So you've seen Clarence?"

"His name's Clarence, is it? I didn't know that. I've always thought of him as just the Englishman." He gestured in the air, and the bartender turned. "Would you please bring my friend here a cup of coffee?"

"Coffee?" I said, holding up my empty beer glass.

He laughed and lifted his mug as if in a toast. "This round's on me."

I pushed away my empty glass. "You call Clarence the Englishman?"

"You know," Ignatius said, turning on his stool toward me, "like some junior officer on board the *Discovery* or, say, the *Chatham*." When he saw in my eyes that the names failed to register he added, "Vancouver's ships, the ones that sailed up here after James Cook."

I thought fast, trying to follow the trajectory of his thought. "You're right, he dresses like a young British naval officer."

"No," Ignatius said, "he dresses like that old fool on the pack of rolling papers, but his attitude is like a British naval officer."

"He's deliberately anachronistic."

"There's nothing anachronistic about him. His type is always around."

"So he's working alone now, you say?"

Ignatius nodded.

I thought it best to change the subject and tried to remember what I knew of the island's history. "Vancouver and Cook," I said. "Weren't the Spanish up here, too?"

"Sure," Ignatius said. "Spain sent a man named Juan Perez, who sailed a frigate, the *Santiago*. The fellow who followed Perez was—give me a minute to get it right—Juan Francisco de la Bodega y Quadra." Ignatius rolled his eyes up and away as he remembered the name, and he smiled after he did so. "Bodega's ship was a schooner, the *Sonora*. He sailed with a man named Hezeta, who captained a frigate, the *Santiago*, but after some of the Spaniards were killed by a band of natives down on the coast of what's now Washington state Hezeta turned back and sailed down south."

"So who was Tofino?" I asked.

"Just another Spaniard who settled and died here. There's not much written about him. My guess is he died from boredom or drink."

"You must read a lot," I said after a while, after my cup of coffee arrived.

Ignatius nodded. "Wherever the Spanish went the priests were half a step behind, baptizing anything they could sprinkle water on. And as soon as they sprinkled you with one hand out came the other holding their big stick, eager to break itself over the backs of boys like me." He laughed. "The Jesuits sure got me when I was young, but in the process at least they taught me how to read. Reading's the one good, lasting thing they gave me."

I sipped my coffee, black as my mood. "With me it was the Sisters of Christian Charity and later the Christian Brothers. The brothers used a paddle they called the 'board of education.' We had to lean over, hold our ankles."

"They like it when you agree like that. When you go along with the punishment and pain. Even better, when you ask for it. Best of all, when you learn to do it to yourself."

I shook my head. I had nothing to add to that.

"Sisters of Charity, Christian Brothers, Jesuits: different names for the same thing. But reading. Now that's something. Particularly history. That opens up a person's life."

"I don't know anything about the history of this area. Or history, for that matter. All I know is what I was taught in school. You know, things like, '*Columbus sailed the ocean blue. To find this land for me and you.*'"

"Not for me," Ignatius said with a smile. "Columbus sure didn't sail here for me." He nodded, then looked toward the door. "The day's young. There's still plenty of light. Finish your coffee, and go piss out that shot and beer. There's something out on the water I want to show you."

☙ ☙ ☙

We walked out into the sunlight and down to the Fourth Street Dock, where Ignatius talked with a man in a checked blue flannel shirt and then led me to a small Zodiac. "Get in," he told me, and then he and the man went into the shack on the dock and after a while Ignatius came out with two jackets and tossed me the smaller of the two.

He was silent as we headed out, weaving his way toward Deadman's Island through channels and passages familiar to me though not at this speed. Lone Cone's majestic peak on Meares towered over us, and I gazed up at it as a bald eagle broke from the shoreline's trees. *Ki-ki-ki-ki-ki-ki-ki*, cried the eagle as it spread its dark wings and soared overhead. I sat back and relaxed. Being out on the water always changed my perception of things and made me feel calm and relaxed as well as small and powerless. It suggested to me that my steps on God's wide earth were insignificant as well as temporary, that I was the least bug scuttling about on the face of some great creation I barely knew or understood, that the truer time kept by the mountains and oceans cared little for twenty-four hour clocks and twelve-month calendars, the petty concerns of lives that lasted, at best, a mere century.

The time out on the water was far better than getting drunk, I realized as Ignatius slowed the Zodiac as he veered through the reefs and islets off Vargas Island's rugged south coast. I knew the islands were called the La Croix Group, but who was La Croix? Who was Vargas? What names did these land masses carry, I thought suddenly, before the Europeans tagged them with their own?

Then we reached the open water of Ahous Bay and Ignatius glanced back and forth at the shoreline—watching for grays, I'd realize later—and then we swung toward and around the northern edge of Blunden Island where he slowed the Zodiac to an infant's crawl. Ahead was an outcropping of noisy reefs topped with Steller's sea lions hauled out in the sun.

"I wanted you to visit your friend," Ignatius said, pointing. He eased the Zodiac into the channel between the rocks, the bottom halves of which were laced with slick seaweed and the tops of which were covered with the same pungent oatmeal that had taken me so long to scrub out of my skiff.

"You really think she's here?" I said.

"Here or down on the rocks off Lennard. But if one jumps into the boat after you, we'll know for sure."

One of the big males noticed us then and heaved his rippling bulk upward and yawned open his mouth and roared. His roar was part bark and part moan. It set off the others, a few who waddled down the rocks of the rookery and slipped quickly into the sea and others who barked back at the big male, who rolled his head back and up at the sky and bared his teeth a second time and bellowed at us mightily.

"He's laying claim," Ignatius said. "He's letting us know this rock is his."

The bull was a magnificent creature. The coarse, tawny hair on his thick neck along with his wide shoulders gave him the appearance of having a lion's mane. He pushed himself up a good eight feet in the air, towering over us as we idled in the water below. He weighed, I guessed, at least fifteen hundred pounds. His chest was darker than the rest of his body, and his eyes were impressively aware, angry, golden. He thrust his snout toward me and gave out a pair of short barks and then rolled his neck and head back, as if dreamy or drunk.

"He's telling you the females here are his, too," Ignatius added.

I laughed. "On either count, he'll get no argument from me."

"These are base creatures," Ignatius said. "For them, life's mainly a matter of seizing and holding territory. The younger ones off in the water there, they've got no ground, you see. They're just waiting for these old bulls to grow weak. That smaller male"—Ignatius pointed south, toward a smaller outcropping of rocks—"he's waiting, too. He knows he's next in line for this rock. Give him a few years and he'll be the one here claiming it. The males establish their territory, you see, and let the females come to them."

The sea was calm, with little chop. Ignatius slowed the Zodiac against the waves so that we rocked in the channel gently, sitting nearly still in the water. "That big bull makes me think of your friend,"

Ignatius said. "The Englishman. Just look at him, all riled and puffed up, certain beyond doubt that he's in the right, telling all the world that the little piece of land he sits on is his."

At first I didn't understand, but after a while it all began to make sense.

"You know, at one time the People lived on all the land, all of what's known today as Canada and the United States and Mexico." Ignatius spread his arms wide. "All of it. All of it. As far north and south as the birds could fly. As far east and west as the two great seas. For hundreds of centuries we lived on the land in balance and harmony, until the Europeans came and for a few years we lived together. But in no time the Europeans pushed us west and then further west and further west"—he drew his hands closer and closer and still closer together—"until we have the very very little that we have now, a few shit-covered rocks in the middle of nowhere, just like this creature."

I stared out at the braying sea lion.

"We've always taken from the land and water whatever we've needed or what we've wanted, and the land and water always provided."

I leapt toward the conclusion his argument was circling. "Even others' crops?"

He stared at me. "If the land belongs to everyone and no one, then isn't what grows on it everyone's and no one's, too?"

I nodded. "But what about the ones who do the work of cultivation?"

"It's only fair they get their share. But isn't their claim to total ownership just as foolish a display as this?" He gestured toward the roaring bull.

Ignatius didn't have to say any more.

The wind was picking up as the sun dropped lower in the sky. I drew the jacket Ignatius had gotten from the shack near the dock more tightly around me. We eased out and beyond the reefs. Once back on open water he gave the Zodiac full throttle.

I thought about the incredibly great expanse of land that's now called North America, then looked back at the sliver of rocky outcropping that made up the reef. I thought about the strong and powerful and what they insist is their right to do to those less powerful and strong. I thought about the country I'd left and its war in southeast Asia. I thought about what had happened to my grandfather, about his fishing boat, his troller, that was seized by the government and never returned. I thought about this second country, to which I'd come uninvited, seeking refuge. I thought about my house in Tofino, the kids who camp in my yard, who knock on my back door and ask permission if they might stay there, reinforcing the idea that the slivers of earth we stand on can somehow be owned and controlled.

"All right," I shouted. I wasn't sure Ignatius could hear me over the noise of the wind and the engine. "I agree with you. You're right. You'll get no argument from me."

# 10

# Chicago 1966

EVEN DURING THE RAW, terrible winter of the second-to-last year I lived in Chicago, Lucy wore her red-tinted sunglasses, saying that the sun reflecting off the mounds of ice and snow edging the streets and sidewalks was too bright for her eyes.

I was a junior in high school then. My taller, skinny frame was beginning to fill out. Wiry muscles now graced my arms, and when I stood before the bathroom mirror punching my chest (first with my right fist, as hard as I was able, then with my left fist, and so on, until my skin reddened and my arms turned heavy as lead) I saw a mass of thickly veined muscle, a smaller version of Charles Atlas. Each weekday afternoon while working at my father's newsstands, I hefted bundles of newspapers up and over my head. At night I threw myself down onto the floor beside my bed in the stair room and did consecutive sets of thirty push-ups, working myself into such a sweat that I'd have to towel off before I gave my fish a pinch of food and let my plastic figurine of Ernie Banks take his fourteen swings.

I was beginning to think that maybe, just maybe, my life wouldn't be a little slice of Purgatory, an appetizer preparing me for the eternity I'd spend in indescribable suffering in Hell. Perhaps my father was wrong and some small part of me was worthy and decent and good. After all, I was beginning to realize, I hadn't been born a tree. Maybe I could actually move out from under his shadow and go places. Mr. Santangelo certainly thought so, and he used two magic words:

apprentice and journeyman. Oh, how I wanted to become them! I was still dating his daughter, sweet Marie. And now, each Saturday, I was becoming friends with Ronny's girl, Lucy Sheehan.

Lucy wore a knit kelly-green scarf and a soft plaid cloth coat that anyone could tell was far too thin for winter, let alone a Chicago winter. Her coat was more suitable for a crisp September day, but it was all she had. She wore red cotton gloves that complemented her hair and sunglasses. The scarf's color picked up nicely the green in her coat's broad plaid. Every Saturday at half past five the two of us would walk from the pet shop up on Clark where she worked to her frame house on Hermitage, as the feeble imposter of a sun dipped below the limestone arch spanning the nearby entrance to Rosehill Cemetery.

The winter was so cold that the snow and ice covering the sidewalk squeaked as you stepped on it. Sometimes the ice and snow moaned and groaned. Walking outside, at once and with a sudden shock, any and all skin exposed to the air went numb and bloodless. Any moisture in the nose froze solid, into tiny balls. The cold was so harsh it pained the lungs and chest to draw in anything more than the most shallow breath.

"This weather isn't for tenderfoots," I'd say as we walked to her house from the pet store. I was referring to a short story I was assigned to read in school, Jack London's "To Build a Fire." It was a cautionary tale about an inexperienced prospector who underestimates the weather's severity and ventures out into the Alaskan wilderness against the advice of a wise old-timer. At the end of the story the tenderfoot freezes to death.

"Hardly weather for tenderfoots," Lucy would agree.

That was how things between Lucy and me started, with me, in my nervousness about being around her, making obscure references to short stories I'd studied in school, and her wanting to understand what I'd meant, doing her share to be part of a conversation that wasn't about carburetors or timing belts, dog shampoos or grooming rakes. Lucy told me she was more than happy to read a book just as long as it wasn't too awfully long and tedious. Reading expanded a person's mind, she said, as well as one's vocabulary, and she was a big believer in the power of vocabulary. There was a feature called IMPROVE YOUR WORD POWER on the comics page of one of the morning papers, and she made sure to read it every day. Plus, reading gave her something to think about while she was working in the pet shop. Soon she began borrowing my books.

I greatly admired the Jack London story, particularly for its irony, about which I'd written a long theme for my teacher, Brother Jerome. At the time I sought irony in nearly everything, even when there was none to be found. After Lucy read "To Build a Fire," we talked about it on her icy front porch steps. She said she felt no sympathy for the tenderfoot, who should have known better than to have gone out in the wilderness by himself. In the end, she said, he got exactly what he deserved.

"Do you mean," I asked, teeth chattering, "that you believe he deserved to freeze to death? Can we offer no compassion to those who are unaware and as a result of their own ignorance make tragic mistakes?"

In Brother Jerome's class this was known as "interrogating the point." You got extra credit for reflecting your own understanding of another's ideas and simultaneously advancing your own thoughts, which Brother Jerome called "proposing a thesis."

"Yes," Lucy answered confidently, as if Brother Jerome had trained her, too. "The tenderfoot deserved to die because in his stupid attempts to survive"—she paused for a moment to allow her shoulders and arms to shiver visibly—"he tried to kill his dog." (For those unfamiliar with the story, the tenderfoot is accompanied on his ill-advised hike by a dog, and toward the end tries to kill it in a futile attempt to warm his hands.) Of all the characters in the story, Lucy empathized most with the dog. (What else would you expect from a dog groomer?) She maintained that the dog was the story's true hero.

"You're probably right," I said, stomping my shoes on the porch steps to revive my numb legs, "and so the tale concludes with an ironic victory, since at the end the dog flees the brutal tenderfoot and has the good sense to go inside someplace where it's warm."

Lucy laughed and said maybe that was a moral we should heed as well. She invited me inside her house to thaw out for a few minutes before I made my long walk home. Once we were in the relative warmth of her house, she asked which story in the book would we be reading for the following week. I recommended something, anything, the first title that came to my mind, doing my best to hide my delight at the promise of being able to spend more time in her company.

☙ ☙ ☙

The next Saturday we discussed another story, Stephen Crane's "The Open Boat," sitting together in her front room. I sat on a sofa littered with old newspapers, an unwashed shirt, and a pair of socks that undoubtedly belonged to her father or one of her brothers, in front of a coffee table on which was stacked a pile of dirty dishes, assorted silverware, along with mugs filled partially with coffee and cigarette butts. She sat in an armchair beside an equally cluttered end table. Our small reading group of two would have the place to ourselves until the older of her two brothers came home from work, which, unless he stopped first at a bar, at the very earliest would be eight or eight-thirty that evening.

Lucy's father was hardly ever around, at least as far as I could tell. He and her two brothers, each older than she, held a string of jobs, mainly in factories scattered across the North and Northwest Side, operating forklifts or working at punch-presses. They were fond of small-time shakedowns—faking injuries and filing claims with insurance companies for accidents that never really happened, Lucy said— and running scams. Whatever they got from the scams they spent immediately on liquor. But shakedowns and scamming passed their time. It gave them something to plan and talk about, if not live for.

I soon understood that the frame house on Hermitage was less their home and more a sort of motel, a place where these men slept and occasionally ate, where they left behind their dirty clothes and dishes with the expectation that someone else (the girl in the family) would clean them, as they patronized the many corner taverns scattered through the neighborhood, where in dark back booths they hunched over shots and beers plotting their next move against the gullible and wealthy, anyone with money and willing to believe their lies.

After a week or two of literary conversation amidst the clutter, as soon as we entered the house I did my best to tidy things. Otherwise the mess was too distracting. I'd stack the newspapers and dishes and whatever else was lying around and carry it back to the kitchen, which was usually cluttered with even more dirty dishes, pots, pans, scraps of uneaten food. I'd throw the uneaten food and whatever else was disposable into the garbage. Alongside the sink there'd be an overflowing paper bag of garbage, its contents normally topped by crushed Pabst Blue Ribbon cans and an occasional spill of coffee grounds, the entire bag full and ripe and pleading with an ordered universe to be taken out. I'd lift the bag carefully from its bottom so its sides wouldn't rip and carry it out to the alley where I'd dump it into one of the big fifty-five gallon oil drums that stood outside the back fence and gate, always making sure to kick the side of the can first to give any rats that might be lurking inside fair warning that someone who didn't want to be given rabies was coming. After I'd taken out the garbage, Lucy would be in the kitchen lighting one of the burners on the stove with a wooden match to put on water for tea. Then she'd go into her bedroom, which was behind the kitchen, just off the hallway, to change her clothes.

We'd talk the whole time, continuing our discussion of whatever story or book we'd decided on that week. She'd leave the door of her bedroom partially open as she changed her clothes so we could hear each other better. One of the panels on the wooden door of her bedroom was badly damaged, as if it had been punched or kicked in and later repaired with scraps of plywood. I was afraid to ask about it, lest she think I was intruding on her privacy. I tried to ignore the kicked-in panel and squelched my curiosity about it by furiously cleaning whatever in the kitchen was dirty. I'd kick her brothers' soiled clothes scattered about into a tidy pile. The kitchen sink had an enormous rust spot that drooped like a rusty tear from its upper right corner down toward the drain; I'd sprinkle cleanser on the stain and scrub away at it. From her bedroom I'd hear Lucy rustling hangers and opening and closing drawers, until the boiling kettle on the stove would shriek and she'd emerge from her room free of her work clothes and their odor of dogs and sprinkling of dog hair.

Lucy would often wear some outrageously adorable little sweater—I mean the kind that could scorch a blind man's eyes—along with tight black stretch pants with stirrups on the cuffs. She always put on white ankle socks and a pair of furry pink slippers that had seen better days. After we gathered the things for tea we'd return to the front room.

She'd carry the tea things on a tray, and after several minutes lift the teapot's round lid and look inside to see if it was ready. Then she'd ask if I preferred my tea with cream. Though she had only milk, poured into a small pitcher, she always called it cream. She used actual loose tea leaves, put directly into the pot, a choice that required her to pour the tea through a strainer before we drank it. Then she'd cover the teapot with a potholder sort of thing that resembled a chicken and which she told me was called a cozy, and sit back in her overstuffed armchair with her saucer and cup and let out a contented sigh.

Once, after saying that I preferred my tea black, I changed my mind and reached out toward the tray to add a splash of milk—or should I say cream?—to my cup. She tapped the back of my hand with her spoon to stop me, saying that if one wanted cream it needed to be put into the cup prior to the tea's pouring. Why? I asked. She said she didn't know why but that was the way it was done. There was a right way and a wrong way to take tea, she said. That was the proper term, *taking tea*, she stressed. She'd read all about it in a book she'd checked out from the public library.

Part of the pleasure of taking tea was observing its etiquette, she said. Tea was to be sipped rather than slurped. One never left one's spoon in the cup or allowed it to click or touch the side of the cup. Rather than grasp the cup with one's entire hand, the index finger was to be slipped into the cup's handle up to the first knuckle, and the little finger was not to be extended but instead curled softly into the palm. One lowered one's eyes and looked into one's cup rather than at others while drinking. When not being raised to the mouth, the cup was to rest upon its saucer, which could remain on the table or the tea drinker's lap.

From then on each time she asked me if I preferred my tea with cream I always told her yes, but, please, only a spot. And even though I used my broadest British accent when I said it, she never detected my stab at irony. After a while I dropped the accent and answered only with, "Yes, please, thank you, just a spot."

You could tell someone had tried to brighten the room and that the attempts were failing. On an end table beside an ashtray normally overflowing with cigarette butts was a vase of plastic flowers, red roses and something pink, carnations or begonias, their petals and leaves finely coated with dust. On the wall above the bricked-in fireplace was a faded print of the start of a fox hunt: hounds milling excitedly in a circle, horses with one or both front hooves raised, riders in top hats and tails at the ready, a youthful English bugler raising his shining instrument to his lips.

A rusting pot of water sat atop the radiator in front of the windows facing the street, a typical practice in our neighborhood, to give the dry winter air in the house some humidity. The carpet was worn down to its backing in spots, particularly near the television set, whose imposing rabbit ears were generously wrapped with wands of crumpled aluminum foil, thick as buns used for hot dogs. Atop the headrests and arms of the sofa and matching overstuffed chairs were the expected lace doilies, though the ones in Lucy's house were stained and had yellowed with age. Those nearest the ashtrays were flecked with dark cigarette burns, which led the eye to notice the many other circular burns on the worn fabric of the sofa itself.

I found that the condition of Lucy's house embarrassed me. Not because the Sheehans didn't have much, because my family didn't have much either, but because the place looked so utterly defeated. You could tell that at one time, years ago maybe, when things were newer and perhaps more carefully maintained, the place had been inviting and maybe even handsome. I felt embarrassed for Lucy because I recognized this, and because I thought she sensed this, too. It was like seeing something about another person's life that was too sad and tragic to see. If this were my house, I thought, I'd be too embarrassed and ashamed to let others see it. I'd never invite anyone inside.

Everything in the house was worn and cheap, and I was gradually learning to despise things that were worn and cheap. I was beginning to think I was wiser than the adults who ruled my world. I'd rather buy one good thing, I thought, than a dozen cheap things. I'd rather live in an empty house with nothing but bare floors and clean, unadorned walls than in a house like this, cluttered with old dusty things, or in a house like my parents' house, where, I was beginning to note, even though the place was more tidy, everything was still worn and cheap.

But Lucy would set the tray of tea things on the scarred coffee table as if we were inside the finest mansion on upper Sheridan Road. She'd insist that I hold my saucer and cup in my left hand or on my lap, napkin draping my left knee, as we discussed the week's chosen reading. And even though the rims of the cups were chipped and the designs in the center of the saucers were barely visible, and even though my nose could smell the dust that pervaded the room, we were to look downward and sip the tea within our cups happily. We were to make do with what we had, with decorum and grace. While we took tea together we were to use our best manners as we questioned each other's reactions and theses.

∾ ∾ ∾

Saturdays with Lucy grew more complex after we read James Joyce's collection of stories, *Dubliners.* "Counterparts," a story about a frustrated man who's treated cruelly by his employer and his friends, and who comes home late one night and beats his son mercilessly for letting the fire in the kitchen grate go out, struck such a chord with me that I nearly began talking to Lucy about my father, how we failed so miserably to get along, how I must have let the fire in his grate go out again and again. Instead I said nothing, unable to put even the first sentence of my own story into words. Lucy felt equally drawn to Joyce's "Eveline," a tale about a young woman who fails to take advantage of her boyfriend's offer to run away with him from Dublin to Buenos Aires but instead chooses to stay in her family's dusty house to care for her father, as she'd once promised her mother on her deathbed.

Lucy had little problem talking about her feelings. "I'd be out of that dirty house so fast," Lucy said, "heads would spin like tops just trying to look at me."

I nodded in empathy. Empathy was another of Brother Jerome's key concepts, and something important that stories and dramas gave to the world. "Yes, and isn't it ironic that Eveline chooses to stay."

"Ironic?" Lucy asked. "I'd call it downright tragic. That girl has her whole life ahead of her. She doesn't owe her family anything. And here's her boyfriend, Frank, offering her a trip to the New World. I mean, the boat's right there waiting for her at the dock. All she has to do is walk down the ramp. But she just stands there at the end, gripping the rail, frozen. If that isn't tragedy, I don't know what is."

"Brother Jerome told us the book was about paralysis," I offered. "So I guess, like all the other characters, Eveline really doesn't have much of a choice."

"But she does have a choice," Lucy insisted. "I think that's the whole point. The problem is that the choices most of these characters make are bad ones."

"So if you were Eveline, you'd leave your home and all you've ever known?"

"In a heartbeat."

"You'd go anywhere? Even to a place you've never seen? Even South America?"

"Absolutely." She smiled. "If you can keep a secret, I'll tell you one. All Ronny would have to do is ask."

"You mean he hasn't yet? Unbelievable. You know, if it were me in his shoes. . . ."

"He's still young." She leaned forward to pat my hand, which rested on my knee along with my napkin. "He's not as mature and sensible as you are. He knows he can go out with nearly any girl he sets his eyes on. He's still out there, you know, sowing his oats."

"And that doesn't bother you," I said after a while.

"Of course it bothers me. What do you think, I'm made of stone?"

"He always says you're his *numero uno.*"

"That may well be," she said. "It's the *due, tre, quattro,* and *cinque* I worry about."

"Well, I wouldn't if I were you."

"You don't know." Her face grew sad. "You haven't seen him in action, when he turns on the charm. He could unfreeze a glacier. He's like one of those gunfighters in the Old West, always looking to put another notch on his belt."

"I thought they carved the notches on the handle of their gun."

She shook her head wanly and laughed. "What he does when he's not with me bothers me tremendously, but there's nothing I can do about it. That is, other than wait."

"You could go out with other guys," I said. "I'm sure there must be plenty who ask."

She gave me another wistful smile. "Not as many as you'd think."

"That can't be right," I said. "There must be hundreds. Thousands. I bet every guy who walks into the pet shop thinks about asking you out."

"No offense," she said and laughed, "you know, present company excluded, but have you ever really looked at what type of guy frequents a pet shop?"

"But what about when you're out on the street? You know, just walking to work. I bet every guy who sees you thinks how nice it would be to go out with you on a date."

"No, they think about how nice it would be to do what some people do *after* a date."

"But there have to be some nice guys out there somewhere."

"Yeah, maybe in another universe."

"No," I said, "in this universe, for sure."

"Maybe," she said again, "but none of them were born with tongues."

My mouth was getting way ahead of my thoughts. "Then they're just stupid," I said, "every bit as stupid as stupid paralyzed Eveline."

"And you're just sweet," she said, standing suddenly from her chair and putting down her cup and saucer and then sitting beside me on the sofa and kissing me softly on the cheek. A wisp of her red hair brushed the tip of my nose. I could feel both her lips press against my skin as she gave me the kiss. Her hand gave the shoulder nearest her a gentle squeeze. I tingled from head to foot, as if I'd brushed up against an electric fence.

"Enough for today," she said, standing and clapping her hands. "It's getting late. Let me clean up, Vince, and let you get on your way."

I was still all abuzz, with a sudden raging bulge inside my baggy blues. I didn't know how else to say it. "I don't think my standing up right now would be a very good idea."

"Paralyzed, huh?" she said, laughing. She tousled my hair as if I were just a little kid and then threw her head back and laughed. "My, my, my, how very ironic."

❧ ❧ ❧

"But you know she means well," Marie said softly into my right ear, "and you have to admit, taking the long view, what she says only makes sense. I mean, we've been going out together now for nearly three years. I really can't argue with her since everything she has to suggest sounds so logical."

"It doesn't sound logical to me," I said, leaning my head back to look at Marie's face. "To me it sounds like a way to bust us up."

We were slow dancing at a sock hop, Sunday night at Gordon Tech, open to all the kids on Chicago's North and West Side who didn't want to stay in their house with their parents and watch *The Ed Sullivan Show* and *Bonanza* on TV. The "she" to whom Marie was referring was her mother, who'd given Marie an ultimatum: either break up with me or date a series of other boys, at least a baker's dozen, they'd decided, after Marie had broken down in tears in response to the first option, so that Marie could gain sufficient experience prior to making a major decision that someday, according to the sage and all-seeing Mrs. Santangelo, Marie would regret for the rest of her ruined life.

We danced on the slickly polished wooden gymnasium floor, swaying gently together in each other's arms. "My mother says you don't buy the first cow you see."

"Oh, you're shopping for cows now?" I said. "Didn't your mother ever hear about love at first sight?"

"She doesn't believe in it. I mean, she doesn't believe we actually love each other. She says that with the first cow it's probably only infatuation. And if it is real love, she says it'll still be there after I'm through with the baker's dozen."

"You realize she's mixing her metaphors."

"No, she's not. Bakers use milk."

I shook my head.

"Vince, I'll only go out with each one of them once. Or at most twice."

That shut me up for several moments, the thought of Marie actually going out with other guys. Thirteen guys. Thirteen flesh-and-blood guys. At least one of them taking her hand in his. Another putting his arm around her. A third, dancing closely with her, holding her in his arms, as I was now. A fourth stealing a kiss on her soft cheek, and then her sweet, full lips. Somehow when they were still a baker's dozen, they seemed less threatening, a cardboard box of doughnuts, some chocolate covered, some sprinkled with powdered sugar, some jelly or cream filled.

"A penny for your thoughts," she said.

"And how is she planning on your meeting these thirteen bozos?"

"I don't find your making fun of this very helpful, do you?" Though I couldn't see her face I knew she was pouting. "You're not being helpful in the least."

"It's a serious question, Marie." We danced in silence for a while. "I mean, what are you going to do, put out a classified ad?"

"My mother already has a list of friends whose sons—"

"Excuse me," I said, leaning back so that she could see my eyes, "but the last time I checked I thought we were in America." I made a show of looking around the dance floor. "Correct me if I'm wrong. This is America, isn't it? 'See the U.S.A., in your Chevrolet.' Isn't the going-out-with-sons-of-friends thing pretty old country?"

"Vince, it's not as if she's setting me up for an arranged marriage."

"No, it's more like she's trying to prevent one." The words were out of my mouth and resonating there in the air between us before I fully realized what I'd just said.

She gave my hand a sudden squeeze. I didn't dare look in her eyes. In my arms, she felt as if she were smiling.

"You have to admit she has a valid point," she said after a while. "If I date one boy each month, I'll be through in a year—"

"A year and a month."

"Of course, a year and a month. You interrupted me. I hadn't finished my sentence. Please don't interrupt me. And then afterwards we'll both be nearly finished with school, and then we can, you know, just like you just said, announce our engagement."

I nodded as she continued, talking about the rest of my life as if she were an architect laying out plans for a building. Everything we'd do in the next ten to twenty years was there in her blueprint. How in thirteen months we could announce our engagement and go through high school graduation, after which I'd begin my apprenticeship at her father's butcher shop. We'd publish our banns in the parish bulletin. The following year we'd marry and move into one of the third-floor flats in her parents' six-flat on Farragut. By this time her father had closed the sale on the building. Marie had already picked out the flat in which we'd live, and her parents had assured her that, if all went as planned, it would be vacant when we needed it. We'd live close to her parents (the same building), but not too close (third floor versus first). It would be the best of both worlds. Marie would make sure her parents would pay for the repainting. One of the back bedrooms had great southern exposure and would make an ideal nursery. The flat was reasonably big—three bedrooms—but we'd certainly need every square foot of available space since there would be one bedroom for the boys (*the boys! plural!*) and a second for the girls (*the girls! plural again!*) though at first a single, well-decorated nursery would do. (*A well-decorated nursery!*) Twins ran in her father's side of the family, she said, so maybe at some point we'd kill two birds with one stone. (*Twins! Two birds with one stone!*) And since we'd be living so close to her parents we'd have the advantage of having a nearby babysitter, her mother, around much of the time to help (*her mother around much of the time!*) and we'd be able to have dinner with them each Wednesday night and, of course, every Sunday afternoon, an hour or two after we returned from Mass,

not to mention birthdays and holidays and other special occasions. I'd
have full use and eventual ownership of her father's '56 Chevy Bel-Air,
which was patiently waiting for me beneath the sheets and blankets
in their garage. In time we'd own the six-flat, whose rents, according
to her father's figures, even with us living there, more than paid for
its mortgage and taxes and upkeep. And, best of all—the jewel in the
crown, the *pièce de résistance*—in time I'd be offered the cash cow itself
(she intended no pun here): Santangelo's Quality Meats up on Clark
Street.

The letters EAT flashing inside MEATS on the neon sign. Then,
one by one, each of the other words on the porterhouse-shaped sign
would shine in brilliant red, and then the cycle would begin all over
again. EAT, then *my* name, then QUALITY, then MEATS, the three
words each holding their light for a two-count, then dropping back to
black, then beginning again with EAT. On and off and on again all
through the long, dark night.

SANSONE'S

QUALITY

MEATS

Forming a never-ending möbius of light flashing brilliantly
through all of eternity.

Riding the busses and walking her home that night from the
sock-hop I said little, which Marie interpreted as sadness over her
news. She squeezed my hand in comfort so often that I thought of my
fingers as udders, since I myself was now a cow, the fisherman's cow,
the one the butcher's lovely daughter couldn't buy since I was the first
in the market she'd seen. All the while she chatted merrily about possible names for the twins, the color of curtains for the two nurseries,
how quickly the days of the baker's dozen would pass.

What had my life become? I asked myself. Is this what I wanted?
This hand in mine, for richer or for poorer, for better or for worse,
for the remainder of my days? If I were a character in one of the sto-

267

ries Brother Jerome assigned his class, what plot would my life follow? Where would the moment of choice lie for me?

As if in answer to my questions, there in the front window of her first-floor flat stood the silhouette of the butcher himself, Mr. Santangelo, his strong and imposing figure backlit by a living-room lamp, raising one arm in a gesture that, as Marie quickly kissed my cheek before turning and running up the sidewalk and toward her front hallway door, I saw was a wave to me followed by a hearty thumbs-up.

❧ ❧ ❧

For another hour or two that cold Sunday evening I wandered the neighborhood streets, dazed, hands stuffed into the narrow front pockets of my stovepipes, my mind awhirl. Never before had I thought seriously about marrying Marie and what kind of life I'd have if I did. I'd never thought about nurseries or a boys' room or a girls' room. The idea of apprenticing with Mr. Santangelo was exciting and attractive, something he'd mentioned previously and something that would get me out from beneath my father's long shadow, but I didn't fully understand that it came with a price, that it was part of all of the rest. I rolled possibilities about in my mind until my brain grew as numb as my arms and legs in the cold. Not thinking of the hour, I finally headed home.

He was waiting for me in the darkness of the front room, likely having catnapped on the couch. Like a panther in the night he sprang out at me. "Son of a bitch," he announced, "do you have any idea of how late, of what time—"

The hallway floor tilted and lurched, causing me to stumble back into the recess of my stair room. Then, one by one, in the confines of that small space the pieces of my furniture betrayed me. Or perhaps they wanted me to dance and were simply teaching me the steps.

Wooly bully.

The hard, knobby front of my dresser slammed my back. Technicolor cartoon, the drawers leaping out one by one, curving like elbow macaroni so as to better punch me with their knobs. They pummeled my back and sides for a while, while three birds with blackened eyes flew in tight circles above my head. Then the edge of my bed grew jealous. It wanted to twist and shout with me, too. So it knocked me down to its level, and then the birds chirping in circles over my head scattered and flew away as an avalanche of water splashed down on me from somewhere above.

By then some part of me was well away from the scene, taking refuge somewhere up in the air, away from the fray, hanging onto the curved and blunted point of a nail beneath the bottom of the flight of ascending stairs. It seems that over the years the physics of my special place metamorphosed and now I'd learned to float. Around me as I hovered, feeling nothing, doing my best to block the sounds of whatever was happening on the floor beneath me, were jagged rows of blunted nail points.

I thought that was a pretty smart thing, that someone had done that with a hammer to the nails, smashed their tips sideways like that, softening the points, because otherwise the person whose head was being slammed back and up against them might really end up hurt.

☙ ☙ ☙

Some time later, after I'd put myself back together, I searched for my dead fish.

My guppies and neon tetras lay curled on the floor like toenail clippings, their bellies shrunken, eye sockets caved in, tiny mouths frozen open in a last, desperate attempt at breath. They reminded me of the pictures I'd seen of the victims in ancient Pompeii after the mighty volcano had exploded. I picked up the shards of shattered aquarium glass and cleaned up the spilled, puddled water and unplugged the now-useless aerator and heater. I piled the corpses of my fish atop my dresser, to be disposed of, perhaps in a blazing pyre, in the alley.

Then I set to looking for the corpse of my lone spotted catfish, the little guy who did all the work, eating the scraps that fell to the bottom and thereby keeping the tank clean. He was just like the unnamed oiler in Crane's "The Open Boat." But though I searched near and far, through all of the next week, I found no trace of him. Finally I decided that he was like Danny Velinski, the Tunnel King, the character portrayed by Charles Bronson in *The Great Escape*, the guy who did the bulk of the work despite his personal fears. I figured my lone spotted catfish had somehow managed to make his way across the border to freedom.

As for my statue of Ernie Banks, he was a bit scratched but otherwise fine, though his bat had been broken in half—sawed off by a blazing fastball, more than likely—and it did take me the longest while to locate his blue cap. But once I snapped it back on his head I had to admit that he looked pretty stupid on my bare dresser in his batting stance, wrists cocked, an empty hole between his hands.

And then, because my fish had been executed by the Nazis, and Mr. Cub wouldn't be hitting any more home runs, coming in at night before my assigned curfew seemed absolutely senseless. It would be a waste of perfectly good time, time when I could be outside in the cold of that dreadful winter walking the dark, empty streets, deliberately freezing my ass off.

Each weekend night, after I finally succumbed to the need for warmth and returned to the place where I slept, I was able to do the dance with my dresser again, until I mastered each of its steps. I mastered the open-hand dance, the closed-fist dance, even the belt-and-buckle dance. What new variations, I'd wonder each night as I walked the frozen Chicago streets that winter, would await me when I came home?

❧ ❧ ❧

I'd stand in the darkness of the gangway across the street from Marie's parents' six-flat on nights when she had dates with the baker's dozen, my teeth chattering in the frigid air, my mind hoping I couldn't be seen. After a while a lone figure would amble down the sidewalk, occasionally glancing up at the houses to check addresses, as if the chump hadn't the least care in the world. He'd turn in at the walkway leading to the six-flat's vestibule, extend a hand as if ringing a bell, then open the inside door as he was buzzed admission.

At the door of the Santangelos' I imagined warm greetings and handshakes. A shout toward Marie's bedroom to inform her that her date had arrived. Marie walking coyly up the hallway, eyes level, then at the last moment casting her big baby browns up at her new date and flashing him a knockout smile. She was always great at making entrances.

She'd slip on her winter coat, a coat not unlike the one on whose collar the body of Christ had taken a brief respite, and bid her parents good-bye, then venture out with her latest guy into the crisp cold air. As the hallway door swung shut behind them I could hear her chattering away like a pet-store parakeet who'd just been given a new spray of millet.

I'd slink back into the darkness of the gangway and then run wildly down the alley, crazy, sad, insane, flinging a few garbage can lids behind me—whatever I could grab—and knocking over some of the cans as I ran, scattering garbage and dozing rats.

I'd end up near Hollywood Avenue at Ronny's garage, where I could kill time and get out of the cold and be by myself for a while. On the weekends Ronny was either away at National Guard duty or out dating any of a long, endless string of leggy girls fond of thick eyeliner and mascara, a few of whom he'd bring by the garage, so most of the time I had the place to myself. I'd turn on the electric heater Ronny kept in a far corner during the winter and work on the speed bag as I listened to the radio. As I pummeled the speed bag with all of

my might, I'd stare at the miserable blonde on the calendar falling out
of her bikini top while straddling the deceitful, false and disappoint-
ing world. Sometimes I'd tinker with one of the cars parked there
until I grew bored. I mean, I found little romance in changing fuel fil-
ters or setting gaps on spark plugs. Most nights I'd dance by myself to
the radio, cranking up the volume whenever the DJ played anything
by The Animals—particularly "It's My Life" and "Don't Let Me Be
Misunderstood" and "We Gotta Get Out of This Place"—and then
sweep the place out with a broom, liberating the corners of spider
webs, emptying ashtrays and wastepaper cans, arranging the tools,
keeping myself busy and warm by tidying things up.

One night Ronny dropped by early after one of his dates and
caught me dusting the junk hanging on the far wall: several old ther-
mometers, whose gauges seemed stuck at forty degrees Fahrenheit,
and a wide assortment of hubcaps. Before I realized he was there I
heard his laughter. He stood behind me, arms crossed, shaking his
head, a Halloween grin on his face.

"Look at you, what a pitiful fuck," he said to me, laughing. "What
in the world are you doing hanging out here on a Saturday night?
Haven't I taught you anything? Man oh man, you're an embarrassment to the male race."

"Up yours," I said.

"I guess you'd like that. I suppose you've gone southpaw on us
now that your little girlfriend has dumped you."

He smiled, then walked toward me and slapped my shoulders
with the flat of his hands, hard enough to rattle my back teeth and
jaw. I was as tall as Ronny then, if not half an inch taller, and thicker
in the chest though I'm certain I wasn't a quarter as strong. He was
willowy and lithe, but with a chiseled chest that was all coiled muscle
and defined vein. His thick black hair was cut short, National Guard
style, but still slicked back from his forehead and face. Supremely
greaser cool. *Dreamy*, as Marie mentioned after she'd met him.

"She didn't dump me," was my lame-as-a-crutch reply.

"Worse, she dumped *on* you, you poor pussy-whipped fuck. You're not that stupid, are you?" He paused. "Face the facts. Where is she right now, and where are you?"

"We've got this arrangement," I began.

"Yeah, she goes out with other guys and you play maid in my garage."

"I mean, we've got this understanding."

He stepped back and gave me a slow, patient smile. "Oh, now I see. Now I've got the whole picture." He stared at me and nodded, then began to laugh.

"She let you screw her, didn't she?" He didn't wait to see if I'd give him a response. "I'm right," he said, "she screwed you, didn't she?" Again he laughed. "How many times was it? Once? Twice? Half a dozen? Enough to give you a little taste, huh, but not enough so you'd expect you'd be getting it regular? Tell me, am I right or am I right?"

I didn't say anything even though he was right. Marie and I had made love once, on the night of my grandfather's funeral.

"I'm right," he said. "It was once, and all of it took place so fast it's still all a blur in your mind."

He was so dead on that I didn't know what to say, so I said nothing.

"You know, that little girl's a lot smarter than I gave her credit for. She *really* has you whipped. I've seldom seen a case this bad. No wonder you're putting up with her shit."

"I'm putting up with her shit?"

"Man, just the oldest trick in the book." He put an arm around my shoulders and led me toward the space heater, and we sat down on a couple of orange crates, like we used to in old times. As he shivered and blew his warm breath into the cup of his hands I thought of the grizzled Arctic explorer and the tenderfoot in Jack London's story sitting around a warm fire before the tenderfoot sets out on his lone journey.

"A girl puts out a little bit," he said, "and the next thing you know she's got the guy in her pocket. In lay-away, you know what I mean?" His dark eyes were soft and finely lashed. "You think you've screwed her, but the truth of it is that she's screwed you. I'm referring here to your mind, and I mean royally. You follow? The little taste she's given you of sex has like totally rewired your thinking. She's got you in the bag now, man, in storage, like at the cleaners', tucked inside a plastic sack hanging in her closet. She's got you thinking you owe your entire future to her, right? You're pricing engagement rings. Meanwhile, she goes out to see if maybe she can work out a better deal."

"She's not like that," I said.

"Sure. And it'll be your lips tonight that get that good-night kiss, your hands stroking the small of her back, hoping to cup the soft cheeks of her ass."

I hung my head and said nothing.

"Don't sweat it, man. It can happen to the best of us. Just understand that while some other guy is trying to figure out a way to feel her up you're wasting your life away inside my garage dusting off my hubcap collection."

I laughed out loud. "Ronny," I said, "it's a collection?"

"What, you thought that was just junk?" His jaw dropped, as if he were surprised. "Let me tell you, some of those babies hanging on that wall are *rare*."

For a while we laughed, at each other and ourselves, like the best of old times.

"So what am I supposed to do while she dates the baker's dozen?" I asked him after a while.

"What do you think?" Ronny said, "use your head, and I don't mean the one between your legs. Fight fire with fire. She's dating a baker's dozen, so you date two bakers' dozens of your own. No, on second thought, make it three dozen. One from the North Side, one from the South, the third from the West Side and the outlying suburbs. And when you think you're through with that, after you've gone out with three dozen new girls, give yourself a higher goal, something that will take you at least a couple of years, such as nailing a girl for every letter in the alphabet. Find an Amy, a Betty, a Connie, a Donna, then go after Donna's little sister Eva. Pay attention here, bucko. I'm giving you a philosophy you can live by, something to reminisce about when you're in your thirties. Work your way through all twenty-six letters. As for me, I'm nearly done with the first go-around. All I've got left, nearly, are X and Z."

"Go on," I said. "You mean you're literally fucking your way through the alphabet?"

"Fucking A I'm fucking my way through the alphabet." He said it with an enormous, proud grin. "Actually, I'm currently working on a V, holding out for a dark-haired Veronica, like in the old *Archie* comics, you know? Wasn't she hot, I mean, for a chick in the comics? I liked her a lot more than Betty. And when I'm through with first names, believe you me, I'll start working on lasts."

I was flabbergasted. "What do you do with all these girls after you have sex with them?"

He smiled. "I check to make sure the old Trojan horse didn't break and all my soldiers are still inside. I say thank you and tell the girl again how really pretty she is. I put on my pants and check that I have my wallet and keys."

"But what about Lucy?"

"What about her?"

"I thought she was your *numero uno.*"

"San-so-ne, San-so-ne," he said, drawing out all three syllables and shaking his head, then taking my cheeks in his hands and pinching them as if he were my old Italian uncle, "every time I think you get it you say something so stupid I see that you don't. What do you think I mean when I say a girl is my *numero uno?*"

"That she's your number one girl," I said. "There can be no other interpretation."

"Close. And what makes someone your number one girl?"

275

"That you love her and want to marry her?"

"Wrong-o, you pitiful, clueless lame brain. It means she's the one you're with. At that precise moment, and only during that moment. In order to get anywhere with girls, they have to think that at that moment they're the most important thing in the world."

"You mean you're not planning on marrying Lucy?"

"Me, marry Lucy?" He laughed. "I mean, hey, don't get me wrong, she's a sweet kid and a really good time and, believe me, I like her plenty. But right now I'm looking for a dark-haired Veronica, and I haven't even started in on last names."

"But she thinks you're going to marry her," I said. Then I told Ronny all about how Lucy and I read short stories together and talk them over on Saturday afternoons.

He fell back in laughter. "You're serious? The two of you read stories? You have tea parties?"

"We talk about books," I said. "It's educational."

"You've got to be shitting me."

"No," I said, "for real."

"So what's next between the two of you?" he said, still laughing. "You going to take up embroidery or knitting? Or is she going to teach you how to give bubble baths and crew cuts to little dogs?"

I resisted rising to the bait. "We're going to work our way through the classics."

"Then I guess maybe I should set her straight about me," Ronny said after a few moments, with a sudden, sober tone in his voice. Then his eyes sparkled and he turned back into his old self. "Because I understand the alphabet's the same the world over, except in Russia and communist China, which maybe I'll get to later on after good old U.S. democracy overtakes them, but in the meantime there's a whole lot of world I've never been to." He smiled again and winked. "You ever see pictures of Brigitte Bardot and Gina Lollobrigida? Sophia Loren? Claudia Cardinale?" He shook his right hand in the air.

"Va-va-va-voom! Man oh man, I'm saving my prime years for France and Italy, know what I mean?"

෨ ෨ ෨

Lucy didn't work at the pet store the following Saturday. After listening to the latest jazz releases at Hank's and looking sadly at the fish schooling brightly in their perfectly unbroken tanks and seeing the empty grooming room, I found myself in front of Lucy's house. Just a block up was the imposing gray limestone entranceway to Rosehill Cemetery. How ironic, I thought, since this afternoon our planned reading was James Joyce's "The Dead." Appropriately, a light snow was already falling. I ascended the porch steps, rang the bell.

Lucy opened the door wordlessly, wearing a faded gray sweatshirt—FIGHTING IRISH in gold letters written across its front—along with jeans folded up at the cuffs and her miserable and sad pair of furry pink slippers. Her hair was a mess of tangles, her lips minus a trace of red lipstick, her green eyes puffy and sad.

"Lucy, what happened? Is something wrong?"

"Nothing, Vince." She opened the door wider. "Come on in. It's cold out here. Let's not waste the heat."

I wiped my shoes on the doormat and, as was my habit, slipped them off before walking inside. As I closed the door behind me and took off my jacket she said, "Oh, Vince, everything," her voice wavering on the *oh* and cracking on the second syllable of *everything*, and then she fell back against the hallway wall, fighting back her tears. I led her into the front room, where, after she took several deep breaths, we sat down together on the sofa and her story rushed out in a sad gush.

How, the night before, Ronny had told her there was nothing between them, that whatever once had been was all over now. And when she asked him if there was someone else, he said no, I just don't want to be tied down. That's it? she said, and he said, Yeah, that's it.

Not that we officially ever called what we had between us anything, but now let's call it quits. But how am I tying you down? she asked. Tell me what to do and I'll change, she said. He said it wasn't a matter of her doing or changing anything. It's just over between us. Right now, he told her, at this point in my life, I just don't want to be tied down.

I held her in my arms. She was crying pretty hard, getting tears and snot on my shirt and the cuffs of her sweatshirt, so after a while we walked back to the kitchen in search of some tissues. The room was a real mess, with beer bottles and dirty plates stacked on every available surface, including the top of the refrigerator and all four burners on the stove.

"One of my brothers had some friends over here last night," she said. She went into the bathroom, where she pulled from the roll on the wall a length of toilet paper and used it to blow her nose. "Look," she said, pointing at her bedroom door, "the animals pounded on it so hard last night they cracked the wood again. I had to push my dresser up against the door of my own bedroom."

For the first time I followed her beyond the threshold of her bedroom. The room smelled like she smelled, soft and inviting, of a mix of flowers and soap and shampoo. On her pine vanity was a wooden hairbrush, in its bristles a soft red snarl of her hair. Lying neatly beside the hairbrush were a comb, tweezers, and a hand mirror, along with various tubes and bottles and containers of cosmetics. The walls had been carefully papered, with a descending pattern of pale pink flowers and falling petals, nearly like a spring snow.

The room was spare and clean and organized: three stuffed koala bears beside her pillow, framed photographs of Ronny beside another of a woman I didn't recognize on top of her pine dresser, a poster of Frankie Avalon on the door of her closet, a plaque of the Blessed Virgin, her eyes downcast, both arms outstretched beneath her sky-blue robe, on the wall over the head of her bed.

"I never knew you liked koala bears," I said, feeling the need to say something. I didn't know what else to say. I hoped that asking her about her koala bears might change the subject and make her feel better, or maybe even smile.

"I don't necessarily," Lucy said. She sat down on her bed. "That old boyfriend I told you about, the one you sometimes remind me of, the guy who went to Saint George, like you do, he liked them. Don't ask me why. He had a thing about Australia."

"Australia," I said, not knowing what else to say.

"The land down under. He was really big on it, I think because it was so far away."

"If you don't like them why do you keep them?"

She shrugged.

"He was the guy who went to Notre Dame," I said.

"Yeah," she said, "the guy who was going places, the one with all the big ideas and plans. Who promised he'd take me with him." She reached for a box of tissues and blew her nose again. "Well, you can see how that turned out. I guess he was strike one. And I guess Ronny is strike two."

"Is this your mother?" I asked. I picked up the photograph of the woman on her dresser, a slighter, older version of Lucy, but with the same lovely red hair and full mouth and hopefully expressive eyes.

Lucy nodded. "I don't know why I'm telling you all these things."

"You're talking to me because I'm your friend," I said, "and because I told you about Marie, and because we both know how much having feelings for other people sucks."

"That's an understatement."

"Your mother's really beautiful." I shook my head and smiled. "But not nearly as beautiful as you."

"Oh, Vince," she said, coming toward me and taking the picture from my hands and returning it to its place on her dresser, after which without thinking I touched her elbow and then her sides and then drew her into my arms.

"What am I going to do with you?" she said, more to my chest than to me, as I held her, motionless at first and then with a slight, dance-like sway.

I can't say that I gave any thought to what we were about to do. I'd meant merely to give her a hug, hold her in my arms, offer her some comfort and solace and maybe get back some comfort and solace in return. Yet after several moments of finding ourselves in each other's arms Lucy turned her face up to mine and I turned my face toward hers and we kissed, at first tentatively and then more deeply and with increasing confidence and desire, and as we kissed our hands began touching and stroking each other's body through our clothes, and then after a while our fingers began to remove the other's clothing, so slowly that our kissing and holding each other and undressing lasted easily half an hour.

It was as if we had all the time in the world, or should I say that it was as if all the time in the world had been made for us, and solely for us, right then, precisely as it was occurring. It was as if the two of us were all that mattered and all that existed in the world. All was sure and without doubt, as if it had all been written down.

We pushed the foolish koala bears—their stubby arms reaching into the air—aside and onto the floor. Then we lay in each other's arms, hardly daring to breathe, atop the bed in the dying light of the winter evening.

The evening snow tapped lightly upon the panes of her bedroom window, the flakes silver and dark. After a while Lucy let out a sigh and stretched her body, soft and luxuriant, beneath the nervous tautness of mine. Outside, the snow filled the sky and fell obliquely against the streetlights, shining vainly against the falling darkness, covering the cold city streets in a momentary hush.

# 11

## Chicago 1967

During the thirteen months when Marie was dating the baker's dozen, I regularly spent late Saturday afternoons and early evenings with Lucy Sheehan. At her suggestion I'd arrive at her house about fifteen minutes after her return from the pet shop, giving her enough time to change her clothes and wash out a couple of tea cups and begin to unwind from work. I'd try not to rush or get there early, slowly walking down the sidewalk toward the cemetery, then carefully unlatching the rusting iron front gate once I came to her house, then once inside the front door, which she'd leave unlocked for me, slipping off my shoes. Lucy would come up the hallway from the back of the house with a smile and give me a hug and a kiss, and even though she was the one who had gone to work that day I'd imagine I was a tired husband returning home after a hard day at the factory. Certainly in a way it was as if we were playing house. We'd stand on the small, worn runner near the front door and hold each other in our arms for the longest time, rocking back and forth, talking and kissing.

She often laughed at the level of the excitement I'd reach. Of course I'd do my best to play it cool, but regardless of my attempts to hide or mute my desire, the visible signs of its intensity gave Lucy delight, as if my excitement were something that flattered her, a response she could take pride in, that paid her a compliment, and certainly something over which she had complete control.

As many times as not she'd ignore it. We'd walk down the hallway toward her bedroom, outside of which we'd pause to hold each other once again and kiss, and just as things would grow extraordinarily passionate she'd whisper sweetly in my ear, "The dishes in the kitchen sink are calling us. Can't you hear them? *'Vince! Lucy! We've been dirty for so long. Wash us.'*" Then we'd spend the next forty-five minutes scrubbing piles of dirty dishes and silverware and scouring pots and pans.

At other times she'd pull me inside her bedroom, patting the front of my pants and smiling. "What do you say we take the edge off this first?" Sometimes she'd play coy and ask, "Do you have a little surprise for me?" I never really knew how to answer her, though I was smart enough never to object. She'd tug open the tongue of my belt. "Oh," she'd say and laugh in mock surprise, "I see it's a *big* surprise. My oh my oh my."

Later, after we'd cleaned and organized whatever there was that required cleanliness and organization, and after we'd discussed and analyzed that week's story and drunk our cups of tea, we'd look at each other wordlessly for a while and then walk again down the hallway to her bedroom, where we'd knock the koalas to the floor and pull back the bedspread and blanket and top sheet. After a while I realized that her occasional willingness to make me come earlier was perhaps less a preference on her part that I be pleasured than a way for me to be able to make love with her later a bit more competently, with greater confidence and a reasonable amount of endurance. And in time I came to see that she desired pleasure, too. There were moments while we were making love when she seemed to be reaching a peak of pleasure, when she'd arch her hips forward beneath me, crying out, or thrash her head from side to side as if she were in some agony and I was hurting her. After she assured me that I wasn't, time would begin to slow for me then. I would have the distinct sense that I was doing something right. Gradually I became better able to pace myself and, toward the end of our thirteen months together, I gained a bit of control over when I'd come.

One afternoon, after we'd kissed for a while, I pushed her down on the sheets and dropped to my knees at the edge of the bed.

"What in the world are you doing?" she said, sitting back up.

"Hush," I said and gently pushed her back down again.

She was wearing black pedal pushers along with a pair of cotton panties. "Help me," I said. "Lift yourself up so I can take these off."

"Vince," she said, "are you sure. . . ."

Her hands grasped the waist of her pants, holding them up, but then her hands gave way and patted and covered mine. I stroked the tops of her thighs along with the tight V between her legs until I could feel her begin to relax, then pulled her pedal pushers and panties down to her ankles. She lay quietly, hands at her sides. I freed each leg from the clothing. By then she'd covered her legs with the top sheet. I put my hands beneath the sheet and stroked her legs and thighs, working my way up to her sex. Then my lips and tongue followed the trail made by my hands.

I had never seen a girl this close before so I took my time to study her, first by parting her legs and then by raising them so that her toes pointed toward the ceiling. Then I did what came naturally, slowly kissing the length of her. She exhaled a long breath and rested her legs on my shoulders, and then, as if it were the most natural act in the world, I lifted her to my mouth.

None of what I'd heard about what I was doing was true. If a woman's sex resembled anything it was a sweet piece of fruit, a halved nectarine or ripe peach.

Once, when I was at a party at the commune drifting from room to room, I walked into the kitchen where two men I'd never seen before sat at the table, with a woman in a miniskirt between them up on the edge of the table, her legs splayed casually open, a broad, trippy smile on her face. "Clean, tangy, and delightfully crisp," the first man commented, "with hints of citrus and almond." The second man nodded, licking his lips. "A tad drier than that, I think. More pecan or walnut, I'd say. And not the least bit grassy." As I neared, the woman gazed at me with lazy, heavy-lidded eyes and motioned for me to come closer. She asked if I'd like some, too. I looked for the bottle of wine she was referring to, then down at her bare legs. The men held no glasses in their hands. I said nothing as the trio broke suddenly into laughter, so shocked that it took me several moments to understand that they weren't offering me a glass of wine.

"Dear sweet God," Lucy cried out, so slowly that if it were in a book the three words would have been written on separate pages. *Dear sweet God.* The way the words issued from her throat was part growl, part hiss, part pure guttural exhalation.

Her first time. At least, she confessed to me later, the first time given to her by someone else. Something she'd always remember, she said, and certainly something that Ronny Cannon, in all his cool splendor, had never even once deigned to try.

&#126;&#42; &#126;&#42; &#126;&#42;

"You know," Lucy said to me early one evening as we lay together on her bed, as the light outside her window faded dully to gray, the color of an old T-shirt, the default shade of the late winter Chicago sky, "we can never tell anyone else about this."

"I know," I answered. We'd been together now for nearly a full year. Already I sensed that we were star-crossed lovers and it would be only a matter of time before we came to some tragic end. Brother Jerome now had our senior class reading Shakespeare. Anyone with more than six spoken lines or his name in the title came to a tragic end in Shakespeare. I sensed that freckled Lucy and I were working our way through the middle acts of some drama destined to end in tragedy, with drawn knives and swords, and plenty of blood.

"This has to be a secret," she said.

"Our secret," I said, staring deeply into Lucy's green eyes, as I nodded furiously so as to make it so.

"Besides," she said, "you're not the kind of guy who'd tell."

"Me?" I sat up and turned my head as if there were someone else behind me. "Me? A guy who'd tell?" I snorted and laughed out loud.

Clearly, I thought, my life had taught me that revealing things about myself only caused turmoil and made the furniture and walls around me dance. "Who in the world would I ever want to tell?"

"Oh, I don't know," she said as she sat up and let out a long sigh. There was a weary edge to her voice, as if she'd just returned from a long, exhausting trip or had a fatal disease she hadn't told me about. Oh sweet Virgin Mary, I suddenly wondered, did she have a secret fatal disease? "The world's a big, cold place," she continued. "You know how guys are, how they talk when they get together. The world's full of people you could tell."

"Not my world."

"Oh, don't be too sure. You could tell your friends. The guys at school." Her eyes grew big. "You could tell Ronny."

My eyes leapt from my head. "Do you think I'm insane?"

"You could brag about it, about what we've done. You could tell everyone about what I've done. You know. About me, about what we sometimes do." She hesitated. "You could tell someone about me, you know, going down on you."

I paused, staring hard at her. "Why would I want to do that?"

"Because guys do that. Because that's the way guys are."

"Not me."

She fell silent, and so I put two and two together and said, "Did Ronny—"

Her face went still, turning gradually to stone every bit as hard and sad as the winged angels topping the gravestones in the cemetery up the block from her house. "Right after the first time that I, you know, that I did it to him." She drew in a deep breath. "Anyway, later on that same week for some reason I happened to stop by the garage, and as soon as I showed up all the guys acted different. You know how they can get, suddenly being all goofy, even goofier than they normally behave, making eye contact with one another, as if they were all in on some secret joke. It was so weird, I mean, they treated me like I was a different person. I knew right away that he'd said something. I felt as if the words *blow job* were written in big black letters across my forehead."

So he'd bragged about it. L.S.M.F.T. "He's a complete and total asshole," I said.

"So it's true," she said. "I knew it."

"No, no, no," I told her. I took her hands in mine, trying to soothe her. "Don't jump to conclusions. Please. I never heard anything like that from him or any of the guys, and I'm around them all the time, so if they'd have said anything, believe me, I would have heard it." I couldn't tell if she believed me. I avoided looking into her eyes. "I was just saying, you know, that Ronny's a total asshole for making you feel that way."

"So he told everybody."

"No," I insisted. "I don't know where or even how you could possibly get that idea."

"You'd never make me feel that way."

"Of course not."

She smiled, momentarily relieved.

"Hey," I said, "the only thing I ever heard him say about you was that you were a real doll and his *numero uno.*"

She raised a hand and brushed my words away. "I mean, that first time"—she shook her head and stared off into space—"I didn't even want to. But he kept begging me." She looked back at me then. "He was making such a big deal out of it so after a while I said okay, okay, okay, but just this once. And not in my mouth. I made him promise. Then, sure enough, he pushed down on the back of my head."

She was so close to me I could feel her breath on my face. I found myself nodding. "Yeah, I think I know what that's like," I heard myself say. I don't really know why I said that, but the words came out of my mouth, nonetheless.

"You know what what's like?" she said.

I shook my head to clear the sensation and tried to laugh. Then I stood, walked a few steps away, then back toward where Lucy lay on the bed. "I mean, I can guess what that would be like, being pushed around, you know, made to do something you don't want to." I'd already told her a bit about my father, how sometimes in his anger at my countless failures he pushed me around. But what I was thinking about didn't involve my father. "Yeah, sure," I said, "I can understand how you felt."

"You don't know how really shocking it is until someone does it to you. I mean, it was like I couldn't breathe. Like I was suffocating. He just held down my head."

I didn't want to hear any more details, and I certainly didn't want to think about the darkness and uncertainty of the rat shed, of what I feared might have occurred inside it, which more than likely was only something I was now imagining, a consequence of empathizing so deeply with the details of Lucy's story. Brother Jerome had talked to us about the power of deep empathy, how some stories are capable of transforming a person's life, how empathy allows people to experience a thing so vicariously that later some even come to claim the experience as their own. He told us about nuns and priests who'd read Butler's *The Lives of the Saints* and later actually received the stigmata— bleeding wounds in their hands, head, feet, and side, corresponding to the wounds Christ received during his crucifixion—after meditating on the saints who had been blessed with the stigmata. Even the first stigmatics might trace their wounds less to miracle or divine intervention and more to a profound empathy with the suffering of Christ. While Lucy continued her description of what Ronny did to her, I shook my head and began humming to myself some insidious tune from the Top 40. "Sorry," I told Lucy after several moments, after I stopped humming. "You know how it is when a song gets in your head." The koalas on the floor lay tumbled and face-down on the carpet, and so I sat them up along the side of her bed in a nice neat row. I arranged the bears by size, in descending order, with the largest bear to my left. I picked a few pieces of lint from their ears and put the lint into my pocket. Then I positioned the bears so they all gazed out protectively in the same direction, toward her bedroom door.

"You're a sweetheart," Lucy said and beckoned me back up onto the bed. "Leave those bears alone. Sometimes I wish you were twins so I could have the one that didn't love Marie. Oh, yeah, and sometimes I wish that you were maybe four years older."

"Why four years?" There were only two years between us.

"Because someday I want to end up with, you know, an older guy, someone I can look up to."

I stretched and stood as tall as I could. "A guy doesn't have to be older for someone to look up to him. I mean, there are plenty of people older than me I don't look up to."

"You know what I mean."

"Age is completely relative."

"Yeah, right."

I nodded and sat beside her. "And since you've brought up the subject, let me go on record as saying that I'm not in love with Marie." I took Lucy's hand in mine. "I mean, come on now, she's ancient history. The last time I thought of her I laughed so hard I fell off my dinosaur."

Lucy shook her head. "You're telling me you're not in love with Marie? Give me a break. Does Dolly Parton sleep on her back? Is the mayor's name Richard Daley? You're practically married to that girl."

"I am not."

"Well, maybe you think you're not, but she sure thinks so. Believe me, I know her type. A girl like her doesn't give her cherry to the first guy in the neighborhood who comes along. Take my word, she'll end up wanting to marry you even if only to subconsciously prove to herself that what the two of you did wasn't a mistake."

That was a thesis I didn't want to interrogate. "It wasn't that big a thing," I said instead. "And anyway, my grandfather had just died. Everyone was in shock. Besides, it was over in less than a minute. I mean, if one of us had sneezed we'd have missed it."

"And all the other times?" Lucy asked.

I shook my head. "There weren't any other times."

"Well," Lucy said, sitting back on her bed, surprised, "just think of how proficient you've become over these past months. When the two of you get back together, she won't even recognize you." She laughed softly, then gave me a knowing smile. "Seriously, Vince, you're becoming a real dynamo."

I beamed.

"Admit it to me," she continued. "You're still in love with her."

"No," I said, "no, no way in the world, I just can't see it." She said nothing but still stared at me with her soft smile. "But hey," I said, "then again, maybe only if you end up marrying Ronny." I stared back at her hard. "Then maybe I'd have no other choice than to settle for second best."

"Yeah, right," she said, "as if Ronny ever—"

"Really," I said. "And he'd be incredibly lucky to end up with you."

"I can agree with that part. But it'll never happen."

"Oh yeah? I bet anything it'll happen."

"Not a chance in the world."

"A dollar?" I said.

"I know a good bet when I see one. Make it five dollars."

"Five dollars it is," I said, "and if he doesn't, well then, you know, then maybe you and me—"

She patted the back of my hand, then lifted it to her mouth and kissed it. "Okay then, sure, it's a deal then. You and me."

I let out a long sigh. "Not to change the subject," I said, wanting to change the subject, "but if you don't like doing, you know, what we were talking about before." I paused until I saw that she understood. "Then we don't have to."

"I didn't say I didn't like doing it. I said I don't like being forced." Lucy's face was beautiful at that moment. She looked strong and honest and clear. "You know what I mean? There's a definite difference."

"'I see,' said the blind man."

"As he picked up his hammer and saw." She nodded. "But let me tell you, I swear to the Mother of God"—she knelt up on the bed so that she could tower over me, framed by the picture of the Blessed Virgin on the wall behind her—"if you ever tell anyone that I said that, I'll absolutely deny it. And then I'll kill you."

"You know I would never brag about you to anyone. On my honor. I'll never tell anyone about anything that goes on between us. You have my solemn word."

"Yeah," she said, "sure." She slumped back down on her pillows. "That night when Ronny made me do it, that's what he said, too."

ঌ ঌ ঌ

Later that spring as I walked home from Lucy's I spotted a figure that looked a good deal like Marie sitting on the front porch steps of my parents' two-flat. It was early evening, not quite eight. I hadn't seen Marie in over a year. I'd long since stopped counting the number of boys she was dating. I stood at the top of the block, across the street from my house, reasonably sure the figure hadn't noticed me.

As I drew closer I saw that it was Marie. She sat on the third to the bottom step, reading a fat textbook in the light of a nearby streetlight, her stockinged legs nonchalantly displayed in front of her, crossed demurely at the ankles, as if she were posing for a picture of how to be cute. A pink button-down sweater hung around her shoulders European style, its empty sleeves dangling nearly to her waist. The sleeves fluttered each time she turned the page or paused to highlight something in her book. She clenched the cap of the highlighter between her teeth like a gambler his cigar whenever she underlined something, then carefully returned the cap to the highlighter with a click so loud and determined that its snap echoed like a shot from a rifle.

All the breath went out of me. My initial impulse was to turn and flee. What in the world was she doing there? I wondered. On my parents' front porch steps? Wearing her favorite knee-length black skirt, the one she said her father had repeatedly told her was too short? But before I could make up my mind whether to turn and run or face her she called out "Vince! Oh, Vince!" as a hot spark of something creased the air between us, like a bolt of electricity sizzling its way between opposite poles.

The textbook fell to the steps, pages fluttering, as she ran toward me, not pausing to check for traffic. Her arms opening, her black flats furiously slapping the now dark street. "Vince!" On her face was a smile as wide and full of promise as the green shore of the new world. "Vince! Oh, Vince!" she cried again as she leapt into my arms, the force of which spun us both around like a top. "Vince," she cried, after we'd stopped spinning, "last night I went out with the thirteenth guy! We can go out again, just you and me! We can get engaged now, even married! Our time of being apart"—she kissed me—"is over!"

"It is?" I heard myself reply. "Oh, joy."

So wrapped up in her own happiness, she didn't notice my confused frown.

&#x7E41; &#x7E41; &#x7E41;

After we retrieved her book and highlighter, we walked over to Farragut and then up a half block to her six-flat, where we would be alone, Marie assured me, for at least the next several hours. Her parents were attending a wedding—some distant niece of her mother's—out in one of the far northwestern suburbs. Even if they left the reception early it would take all evening for her father to drive back to the city, Marie explained. I knew that Mr. Santangelo preferred city streets over expressways, which he considered dangerous racetracks swarming with reckless hot rodders, and that no matter how long the drive he'd keep the Bel-Air at a legal and safe thirty-five miles per hour.

In the front hallway Marie threw down her book and gave me a big hug, then laughed loudly. "Remember the first time we kissed? We were standing right here." She pushed on my shoulders so that I moved back and then over a step or two "There. That's it. Your back wasn't quite touching the mailboxes. Yes, right there. Remember

291

how you pretended you were going to ring all the bells? You were such a goofball back then. Now, please kiss me the way you kissed me before."

I gave her a kiss that was brief, tentative.

"Softer lips," she said. "Try again." She smiled. "I remember it feeling as if you were breathing me in."

So I gave her a softer kiss and simultaneously inhaled.

"Close," Marie said, "close, but no cigar for you yet, big fella. Try it again but with a little less vacuum cleaner."

I held my breath. Soft lips, slow, still tentative.

"Remember?" she said, as her fingertips and then her nails brushed the back of my neck. "Wasn't it something more like this?"

The kiss that followed was part feather, part silk, the remainder satin and cream. A woman's scarf wafting gently in a mid-summer breeze, so soft and inviting that as I closed my eyes I actually saw colors, purple tinted with a glint of lavender, billowing like a mainsail on the soft, white-tipped swells of some distant sea.

"You kissed me three times," she said, her voice dropping, low and sultry, "and with the first kiss, well, then I knew it was okay to like you." She nodded in cheery agreement with her words. "With the second kiss you made me feel safe and warm, and I remember thinking about the time the Host fell on the collar of my coat, and how one time when our class was out on the playground some little kid from one of the lower grades fell down—some bigger kid pushed him—and you ran out of line to help him up. Then I knew I could always trust you." She pulled her face back from mine and smiled, the fat edges of tears glistening in her eyes. "And with the third kiss I felt—well, maybe I won't ever be able to explain it—the only word that comes to my mind is right. I felt *right*, if that makes any sense, that you as a person were right, I mean for me, you know, and that even though I hardly knew you, you and I were right together, like in all the songs they play on the radio. I knew for sure the timing of it wasn't good"—she laughed—"no, not at all, at least not back then." Her face grew wistful. "We were just kids, hardly old enough to be kissing in the first place. But I knew something then about our souls, something more than just that you were the kid who sat in front of me every year of grammar school except the year you had the lay teacher. I mean I knew your moods, how inside you could be happy but how mostly you were sad and sort of gloomy. I sensed you had it kind of rough. I knew you had secrets. There was a dark side to you. You had uncharted depths. But with that third kiss I also knew that something truly good and wonderful would connect us, forever and always. It was sort of like we were created for each other, you know?" Again she laughed. "It sounds so cornball, so crazy, so totally L-seven, but I thought that maybe if God really does create people for other people, you know, specifically, like maybe up in Heaven he actually designs and pairs them up, then God made you for me. And me for you. And at least I knew that in some way our lives would always always always be linked together."

What could I say after a speech like that? What else could I possibly do after her dreamy kisses that made me imagine a sailboat and the open sea?

We walked up the flight of stairs to her parents' flat as quietly as we could, hoping that none of the other tenants would see us. At the doorway I paused and out of habit bent and unlaced and removed my shoes. Marie looked at me strangely, then commented that in her absence someone must have taught me to be considerate. I nodded numbly.

I set my shoes on the plastic runner lining the entranceway. The runner led to a second, longer plastic runner that stretched down the length of the hallway. Unlike my own family, the Santangelos kept their rugs and sofas and armchairs nearly always covered with clear fitted plastic, removed only for special occasions and holidays. I walked into the front room, where the hard plastic on the sofa crackled stiffly as I sat down.

"Not in here, silly," Marie said.

She took my hand and led me into her parents' bedroom, a dark, immaculately kept chamber with rococo wallpaper and heavy,

Mediterranean furniture. A dozen or more framed photographs squatted atop an ornate dresser, which was backed by a round mirror edged with carved wooden pairs of fat putti whose lower parts were hidden by strategically placed leaves and clusters of grapes. Midway up the wall above the dark headboard on their big double bed was a thick mahogany crucifix featuring a crucified Christ along with a dual sheaf of palms.

I could hardly take my eyes off the figure of Christ. His wounds looked so fresh and were so startling it seemed as if he were still bleeding. Yes, he was still bleeding, I thought, and he continues to suffer and bleed every moment for our sins. The crucifix made me want to kneel and confess my countless sins.

Marie paid the bleeding Christ no mind. Instead she opened the closet door and smiled at me conspiratorially and then took out a small stepstool that leaned against the wall within the closet and climbed the stepstool and drew down from a high shelf a bag inside of which was a magnificently grained wooden box, which she placed on the foot of her parents' bed. Inside the box was a glistening set of knives.

"They're from Italy," she whispered. "My father ordered them, special, just for you. They took months and months to get here. You can't ever let him know I showed them to you. He'd be so disappointed if he knew I ruined his surprise."

Handles made of carved horn, brass ferrules and studs, glistening blades of the finest tempered steel. The Italian knives lay in their snug felt slots within the box like something magical, something medieval, something far, far beyond the narrow confines of Farragut and Glenwood, Ravenswood Avenue and Rosehill Cemetery, Ashland and Clark and the raucous tracks of the north- and southbound El, the station at Bryn Mawr pocked with hustlers and winos, pimps and pill dealers. These knives had come from another world, some myth or fairy tale, some truer, more ancient and more noble place and time. I sensed at once that they could be a sort of absolution for me. I felt that if I were to possess and use these knives my life would become different, somehow better, and with time I'd become a genuinely good, honorable person, someone like Mr. Santangelo, instead of the worthless and deceitful louse I really was.

I reached toward the knives but then pulled back my hands, afraid to touch them, for fear that I'd soil them, leave my fingerprints on them or stain them. And yet my hands ached to hold one, heft its weight. Truly, I realized, if being a butcher's apprentice meant working with tools like these, I wanted with all my heart to be a butcher's apprentice. Had there been an apprentice's contract inside the box, I would have signed it at once. I would have happily slit open a fingertip or vein and signed my name on the contract with my own blood.

Marie was telling me their names, pointing out each with obvious glee. Straight blade. Curved. Boning. Breaking. Fillet. Scimitar. She pointed out that the tang—the piece of steel that connects the blade and the handle—ran down the entire length of the handle.

"You can't ever tell him," Marie said again as we stood over the box. "He ordered them special. You should have seen him checking every day to see if they came. If he ever finds out you know ahead of time, he'll be so disappointed."

"Why are you showing them to me?" I asked.

"I know that the last three hundred and eighty days must have been hard for you." She closed the box and latched it, then slipped it into its paper bag and set it back where it had rested up high on the top closet shelf. "See, I bet you didn't think I was keeping count. I know how last winter you'd stand across the street in Mrs. Petrovich's gangway watching me on nights when one of my dates would pick me up. I'd watch you from behind the front room drapes, standing out there in the cold, looking up and down the street, shivering. Why didn't you ever wear a hat? Why didn't you go inside somewhere on the nights when it was raining? Don't you know how cold winter is, that without a hat all your body's heat goes out through your head? I mean, none of this was my idea in the first place. But now, showing you the knives, I don't want you to have any lingering doubts."

"Doubts about what?" I said. I wanted to slow things down. I wanted to spend more time looking at the knives. My eyes kept stealing glances at the bloody crucifix, at Christ's downcast eyes, which were looking right through me. He knew all that was in my soul. He knew all that I had done. I wanted to kneel there at the foot of the Santangelos' bed and ask for forgiveness. Too much was happening all at once.

Marie smiled and tapped my forehead. "Hey, maybe we'd better screw in a bulb with a little more wattage. Maybe all these months of being apart, it's made you forgetful." She brushed her fingertips across my shirt, stopping over my heart. "What do you mean, doubts about what? Doubts about you and me, you silly billy, about our future life together."

"Our future life together?" I said, as if I were the village's biggest dummy, as if I were Giufá, the simple, literal Sicilian fool.

"Here," she said, drawing me into her arms, "let's see if this makes things a bit clearer."

And she was suddenly kissing me, hard and with all too much intention. My body responded, all too obviously as she ran her hand down and then across the front of my stovepipes. Then she giggled as if I were being the naughty one. "Definitely not here, Vince. Not in their bedroom."

"No," I said. "Hey, there's no need. What's the rush? Let's wait. I mean, really—"

"Hush," she said and pulled me out of her parents' bedroom and back onto the stiff plastic runway lining the hallway. Its walls were covered with photographs of her family's many ancestors from the old country. Each stoic face staring out from its gilded frame looked like my dead grandfather. Each Sicilian stood stiff and formal, unsmiling, as if instead of facing a camera he or she were facing a firing squad.

Then she led me into her bedroom, a room with the same heavy style of furniture as her parents' room. On the wall facing the foot of her bed hung a corkboard bulletin board. Above her bed was another bloody crucifix and crossed sheaf of palms. On the corkboard were pinned snapshots of her family along with stuff from high school and photos cut out from magazines, arranged like a collage. I recognized the Beatles—FAB FOUR in big balloon letters and psychedelic colors above their heads—as well as John and Jacqueline Kennedy waving to an unseen crowd as they stood beside a black car with young Caroline and John-John. In another picture Joe DiMaggio embraced Marilyn Monroe, each looking certain that their love for each other would last forever and was true. There was Natalie Wood gazing down at Russ Tamblyn from the bars of a fire escape in *West Side Story*. There was Vivien Leigh smiling at a young Laurence Olivier. Elizabeth Taylor and Richard Burton. James Dean squinting from behind a cigarette as he leaned against the side of a car. Steve McQueen revving his motorcycle atop a hill near the end of *The Great Escape*. Twiggy in a hot-pink mini-dress. Another photo of the Beatles.

"Whoa," I said as Marie sat upon the bed and patted the space beside her.

"Don't worry," Marie said. "I know what you must be thinking. But, believe me, Vince, everything's fine. With my parents away tonight, the timing's perfect. I planned everything. Relax. They'll be gone at least another two or three hours."

On the bulletin board an open-mouthed Albert Einstein appeared to be listening to the Dave Clark Five. Or were they Herman's Hermits? Freddie and the Dreamers? The Kinks? I couldn't tell. Jan & Dean sauntered on a beach carrying a surfboard alongside a holy card depicting Saint Teresa of Avila. My eyes caught the slogan of a protest button.

## MAKE LOVE NOT WAR

"I really don't know about this," I said, realizing that just an hour or so before I'd been with Lucy. Walking home to find Marie on the front porch steps, I'd come nearly warm from Lucy's bed.

"And look," Marie was saying, "because I know you're not prepared." She drew from her dresser drawer a cellophane packet containing a condom. "You don't know what I had to do in order to get this!" she exclaimed, as if the condom were something forbidden and rare. "One of my girlfriends, I don't think you know her, her name is Suzanne, and she lives just north of Devon, anyway, she doesn't know the first thing about writing research papers and so she got a couple of these from her brother's room who right now is over in Vietnam. Oh, the Saturday afternoons I spent in the public library writing her paper for her! If I ever have to look at another three-by-five card I'll just die. But, hey, we're wasting time." She reclined on her bed and unbuttoned the top button of her blouse. "Come on, bashful. Before they get back. Show me how much you missed me."

"If you'll excuse me first." I pointed a finger toward the door.

In the bathroom I looked for something with which I might wash myself. As I loosened my pants and pulled down my shorts, the faint scent of my having just been with Lucy rose like an uppercut to my nose. I looked around the bathroom—the shelves were adorned with ceramic statuettes of fat-cheeked cherubs playing the harp and violin—as I vigorously scrubbed myself with soap.

Back in the bedroom again with Marie I worked slowly. Yes, the most accurate verb in this case is *worked*. I was so confused, so turned around, I found myself making a labor out of love. I found myself seeing not Marie's softly glowing skin but instead fragmented glimpses of the pinker, freckled Lucy, images that in my mind would bleed and segment into the soft, sweet reality before me of Marie, doing her best to disguise her obvious nervousness and excitement with laughter. The red *corno* and gold heart she always wore on chain around her neck lay bunched and to the side on the sheet. They distracted me, and so I lifted them from where they lay and placed them softly on her breastbone.

Then some other part of me felt thrilled, even joyous, and as we kissed I traced the strange, bright emotion not to the lovely young woman who lay on the bed beside me but to the glorious box of knives waiting for me on the top shelf of her father's closet.

What would I need to do to become an apprentice? I wondered. All I knew about apprentices was the little I'd been taught about medieval history. Would I be asked to sign away my freedom for seven years? Would I sleep in a corner in her father's shop? I pictured myself sleeping on a bed made of old burlap sacks in a corner of the butcher shop. I'd do so happily for seven years seven times over, I thought.

I bided my time, kissing Marie's lips and neck and the thin white skin inside her arms, then the palms of her hands, then again her neck, her lips, again the soft, graceful hollows of her neck. Then she arched her back and issued a sound I'd never before heard, some guttural drum roll, the march of a hundred-and-one colliding R's, a rolling, liquid sound that tumbled in my ears before she pushed me back playfully and said, "My oh my, Vince, my oh my oh my, have you been eating your spinach in my absence or what?"

"I yam what I yam," I said and squinted one eye at her, Popeye-style.

"Here." She handed me the rubber. "Put this on."

"Not just yet," I said and dropped beside the bed to my knees. I'd show her what I yam, I thought as I pulled her legs toward me, as my mouth began to kiss a slow trail up the inside of her thighs.

At once she tensed. Her legs flutter-kicked me away. "What are you doing?"

"What do you think I'm doing?"

"Good God, Vince," Marie said, quickly drawing up her legs and scurrying back on the bed and away from me. She leaned on one elbow and with her other arm covered herself with a pillow. "I don't know what in the world you've been reading this past year, but I don't find that very funny."

"I didn't mean it to be funny." I sat back on my heels. "I thought you'd like it."

"You thought I'd—" Her jaw dropped. She shook her head. "Just what kind of girl do you think I am?"

"Marie, I didn't know there was more than one kind."

She was angry now as well as frightened; that much I could see clearly. She sat up and covered herself with the sheet and bedspread. I should have taken that as the sign for what it was, stood, gathered and put on my clothes, agreed that we were moving much too fast given the time we'd spent apart, and acknowledged that things weren't quite right between us. I should have said I'd call her later and then walked toward the front door. I should have stopped then and told her about Lucy. But instead I remained kneeling there on her bedroom floor, dumbly, not knowing what to do or say.

"So," she said, her fingers fumbling with the edges of the sheet. "What?" she asked me. "I mean, do you think that just because we've been apart for all this time you can just try to do that? Do you think that in the last year I've become some sort of slut? That suddenly I've turned into a slut, and I would enjoy something like that? Vince"— she wagged her head at me—"that's *dirty*."

"Marie, I never thought you were a slut."

"Just because I dated those others guys? That's unbelievable. What's gotten into you? What can you be thinking?" She paused to draw in a deep breath. "That's all that went on, Vince, just innocent dating. What in the world can be inside your head? They were just dates, just stupid, meaningless dates."

"What I wanted to do wasn't dirty, Marie."

"Well, I don't know what you've been reading or who you've been talking to, but where I come from. . . ." She laughed derisively and shook her head. "Good God, the next thing I know you'll want or expect something similar from me."

"And that would be wrong?" I said. "I mean, if we kept it to ourselves? If we really loved each other?"

"Nothing would make that right, Vince."

By now I was standing, picking up my clothes from the floor where they'd fallen. I didn't want an argument, not with her, not with anyone, and in particular I didn't want to argue about love and sex. Once again my mind pictured the box of knives. All I wanted were those knives. All I wanted was to put on my clothes and leave.

Seeing that, Marie leaned forward and grabbed my hand. "Don't ruin things," she said. With her other hand she pressed the sheet against her breasts. "Don't leave. Please. Not just yet. Hey, come on back here. Please. Let's make everything just like it was before."

"Things can never be just like before," I said, and in that moment I decided to tell her about Lucy. "Listen, Marie, I need to tell you—"

But before I could finish my sentence she'd dropped the sheet and was kneeling up on the bed and kissing me, open mouthed, deep-tonguing me in the same determined way she'd kissed me earlier. As we kissed I decided I wouldn't use Lucy's name, that it would be ungentlemanly to be that specific, that I'd simply tell Marie that for the past several months I'd been involved with someone else. I'd leave it at that, I thought, with the word "involved." I'd refer to Lucy as "someone else." But each time I pulled away and started to talk Marie silenced me with another kiss, and as we kissed she pressed the packet containing the rubber she'd gotten from her girlfriend into my hand. I'd let the packet fall to the sheets, as I gave into the temptation she was offering me. Her hands would find the packet and again thrust it into mine. Quickly it turned into a contest: my dropping the rubber, her picking it up and growing more insistent. Finally I broke the seal on the packet and with one hand slipped the rubber on. Marie then wrapped her legs around me and eased beneath me, swallowing me in much the same way that our mouths were kissing. We rocked back and forth, envy of angels and archangels, powers and dominions, cherubim and seraphim.

"My oh my oh my," she sighed.

There was nothing rushed or sudden about this greeting between our bodies, this reunion after our time apart, this fitting of one self to the other self. Maybe I did love her, I thought. Maybe she was right, and she was the one and only girl for me. And then when our love-making couldn't possibly feel any better, the sensations I was experiencing ascended to an even higher level and her sex seemed suddenly to fill with every wonderful possibility in the world, as if her body and sex were made entirely of silver light.

*Mercury*, I thought, imagining the liquid beads spilling from a broken thermometer, and then all at once I surged, over the top, spilling spilling spilling spilling in a fierce roller coaster tumble of surging tsunami earth-rattling shore-embracing waves.

Tears glistened in the corners of Marie's eyes as we held each other and kissed. There were no words either of us needed or wanted to say.

After a while we realized we'd have to part, and so we slowly parted. And as I drew myself from her I immediately sensed something was wrong. The rubber we'd used, the one given to her by her girlfriend in exchange for a research paper, had broken. It lay in a useless circle around the base of my sex, like a deflated lifesaver hanging around the neck of some limp, dead beast hauled out from the open sea.

"Oh my God," Marie said. "Oh my God, oh my God, oh my God." On her face was a mix of joy and fear. "I'll bet you anything you just got me pregnant."

# 12

# Chicago 1967

BIG DANDOO RETURNED from Vietnam, gaunt and eerily aged, with a cane and a limp that hurt your heart to see in such a big man. Something in the blankness of his eyes invited you to look away from his face and stare instead at his bad leg, which was noticeably thinner than his good one. I didn't have the courage to ask him what had happened. He and Chick and Ronny straddled their orange crates playing a dispirited round of three-handed pinochle, a pretense, really, for drinking vodka from a quart bottle of Squirt.

Squirt and vodka had become the latest tradition in Ronny's garage. You began by breaking the seal on a fifth of vodka and passing it around while someone else poured about a third of the Squirt out on the ground in the alley. Then the guy with the vodka poured what was left of the fifth into the Squirt bottle and with his thumb over the open neck gave it a couple of good shakes.

When I arrived at Ronny's garage, the bottle was nearly empty. Chick was going on about the war, how if he was in charge he could bring it to an end within the year. Concern over the war was a popularly discussed topic. Everyone had an opinion and held onto it fiercely, blindly defending it against the incursion of another's logic. Chick's solution was simple and drastic: he'd bomb Hanoi.

Just like the Stars and Stripes had done with Hiroshima and Nagasaki, Chick said. And then if old Ho Chi Minh didn't put down his rice bowl and crawl out of his rat hole waving a white flag, Chick would have the Air Force turn North Vietnam into a parking lot. He'd accomplish that with an all-out barrage of carpet bombs and napalm to be followed by ten thousand cement mixers and asphalt trucks helicoptered in by the Navy. It was so simple a solution only an idiot couldn't see it. Make their country literally something they couldn't burrow down into. Do it inch by fucking inch. The VC enjoyed hiding in trees and digging in tunnels, right? So you napalm their jungles and cement shut their tunnels. Case closed. Though I suspected that the Viet Cong would be able to dig their way out of anything, having seen *The Great Escape* more times than I could count, I kept my mouth shut.

Chick had all the right jargon down. Ordnance. Defoliation. Carpet bombs. Hot and cool landing zones, which went by the abbreviation LZ. He laid down what remained of his hand on the stacked crates that served as a table—he held only trump, all face cards—and walked over to the corner by the speed bag, punching it for added emphasis. Slash and burn the land, he punched, contain it with asphalt and concrete, punch punch, then defend the expanding points of the perimeter from attack. Punch punch punch. His Adam's apple throbbed wildly in his throat as he spoke.

Since failing his physical for the draft he'd grown even more wiry, like a chicken leg left too long in the oven. His skin had a decidedly yellow cast, as if he had jaundice or he'd used one of those instant suntan lotions you saw each summer on the shelves at Walgreens. If he'd purposely messed with his body's chemistry to avoid being drafted, he looked not only like he'd done a good job at it but that the process was still continuing.

"That'll never work," Ronny, ever the realist, said. "Get back over here and count your points."

"You got a better solution?" Chick said.

"Fucking A right, I got a better solution," Ronny said. His fingers raked his short hair. If anything Ronny was even more muscular since the Guard had accepted him, and when he wasn't working on a car his appearance was impeccable. Today he wore a pair of creased black dress pants and a tight, sleeveless T-shirt, bleached blindingly white. The T showed off the muscles of his tanned arms so nicely there were moments I thought he was beautiful. "We continue to do exactly what we've been doing, even if it takes ten or twenty more years. And we do it and do it and do it and do it and do it until we win."

"That's the pussy answer," Chick said, returning to the orange crate on which the playing cards lay. Dandoo swiped the bottle away from him. "That's fighting a fight with one hand tied behind your back."

"That's doing it intelligently," Ronny said. "That's minimizing collateral damage. I've talked to people about this, people who know. That's being in it for the long haul."

"So how big is North Vietnam anyway?" Chick asked. He looked over at me as if maybe I knew. "As big as Indiana? Half of Ohio? How long would it take to bomb and pour concrete and asphalt over half of Ohio?"

"You're forgetting the whatchamacallit," Dandoo said. "You know what I mean." He held out one big hand, big as a bear's paw, and waved it. "You know. Oh, what is that fucking word?" He glanced about, then paused and plucked the word out from the air. "Oh yeah, the terrain."

"The carpet bombs would flatten the terrain," Chick maintained.

"No they wouldn't," Dandoo said. If anyone knew, he knew, since he'd just been there, I thought. I could hardly keep my eyes off his bad leg. At times he seemed nearly the same as he'd been before, and then you'd catch him zoning out in a long, vacant stare and he'd look past you or right through you as if you were a total stranger. "Bombs just tear open these big enormous holes."

"Not with the right ordnance," Chick said. "With the right ordnance you could level the land flat as a fucking pancake."

Dandoo sucked hard on the bottle and slipped back into his empty stare.

"You're way off," Ronny said. "For one thing, 'Nam is a lot bigger than both Ohio and Indiana put together. I think you'd have to add maybe Kentucky and half of Tennessee or even all of Illinois or Wisconsin or Minnesota."

"We're only going to bomb North Vietnam," Chick said.

"So for the sake of our argument here," Ronny said, "let's make it the size of both Ohio and Indiana. With plenty of mountains and dense jungles."

"Hey," Dandoo said, suddenly, "are we here to bullshit or fucking play cards?" He took another slug off the bottle of Squirt and vodka.

"Fine," Chick said, "so we just nuke it. Hell, the Air Force has got the bombs. So we just nuke the whole country. Start at the top, then work our way toward the middle."

"Drop even one nuclear bomb," Ronny said, "and you bring in the Chinese."

"So while we're at it we nuke China," Chick said. "They're Communists, too, right? What's that we're fighting? Oh, yeah, communism. So we're supposed to stop at borders? You know how it goes, in for a penny, in for a pound, right? Zip. Zap. What the fuck." His voice turned sing-song. "Turn 'em all to Peking duck."

"You just make that up?" Dandoo said.

"And meanwhile," Ronny said, "the Soviets retaliate and nuke Washington. Then they nuke New York, L.A., Chicago, this very garage."

"Oh, yeah?" said Chick. "You see me shaking?" He held out a steady hand, then gave a wild shiver and screamed, "Fa-fa-fa-fuck the Soviets!"

"There won't be anything of you left to fuck anything after they nuke Chi-town," Ronny said. Hearing the nickname, *Shy-town*, always made me think my hometown had somehow turned from big-shouldered and bold to bashful.

"Hey," Chick said, "you know, I think maybe I can live with that. At least then I wouldn't have to sweat the next payment on my car." He laughed maniacally.

I took modest sips from the bottle whenever it was passed my way while I waited for one of the guys to suggest that they deal me in and we play four-handed, partners. From where I sat I'd be Dandoo's partner. He wasn't very savvy and hardly ever gave a skip bid when he had decent meld, but being his partner would be better than just watching. But then out of nowhere the big man came back to life and started talking about what the guys always avoided talking about, the friend who hadn't returned.

"You know," Dandoo said, as if we'd asked him a question he'd been considering for the longest time, "Lenny had it all figured out. I mean, really. He had maps. Contacts. He covered all the angles. You know, he wasn't half as dumb as some people thought."

I turned toward Chick, awaiting his wisecrack. Instead he raised the bottle and said, "To Lenny."

Ronny held up a hand to stop the toast. "Let's not drink to his memory yet. The man's only MIA."

"That's what I meant," Chick said. "That's what I meant. To his being found."

There was a long silence then, broken only by the occasional thump of Dandoo's cane on the garage floor and the bumpy noise of our four hearts beating.

"He never told you guys about his plans," Dandoo said after a while. He took a thin, hand-rolled cigarette from his shirt pocket, put it in his mouth, and then gestured to Ronny for his lighter. "He never said nothing to any of you guys about St. Paul." We sat in silence, waiting for him to finish the thought as he lit the cigarette and drew in a long hit.

I'd never seen a cigarette like that before. It was as thin as a Fourth of July sparkler and it popped and crackled as big Dandoo inhaled, as he held the smoke down deep in his lungs and then waved it over the pinochle table saying, "Any of you guys want some of this?"

Chick reached for the cigarette at once. "I'll take a hit."

"The night before we went in together," Dandoo said, letting out the smoke, "Lenny and me, we got good and fucking drunk. I mean *good and fucking drunk*, and then he told me everything." He took the cigarette from Chick and offered it to Ronny, who declined. The smoke smelled seductive, sweet. I nearly reached out a hand for it. Marijuana, I would later realize. It was like nothing I'd ever smelled before.

"He told you what?" Ronny said.

"St. Paul," Dandoo said, hissing.

I couldn't figure where the story was heading. "Saint Paul, the apostle?" I said, and Chick and Ronny laughed so hard they nearly fell off their orange crates.

"Oh, Vincie, Vincie, Vincie," Chick said, "sometimes you are such a dim bulb."

"You know," Dandoo continued, ignoring their laughter and turning patiently toward me, "the town. Up in Minnesota. Right near, you know, Minneapolis." He sucked the joint down to a nub, then licked his thumb and first finger and squeezed its tip until it was out and dropped the remnant into his shirt pocket.

"Lenny wanted to go to St. Paul?" Chick said.

"Yeah," Dandoo said, hanging his head, "he was giving St. Paul some highly serious consideration." He looked up at us, his eyes suddenly steely. "Instead of allowing himself to go in and be inducted." He let out a long sigh. "Know what I'm saying here?" It wasn't so much a question as a statement of fact. It was something we either understood or we didn't. "He'd already figured out what the rest of us hadn't yet," Dandoo continued. "That over there everything is so fucked at best it's a crap shoot." He stared at Chick's cards, an ace-high spread of spades, spanning the crate. "He'd talked to a lot of guys who'd come back and sorted out the ones who'd swallowed the party line from those who spoke the truth. So he got wise and made contacts with these church groups they got up there, the ones that take American guys over the border into Canada. Seems Lenny had relatives in Toronto that he never talked about. I guess Toronto's a big Ukrainian town, and both of Lenny's parents were born in the Ukraine. Anyways, he gave it a lot of thought, not about him being caught or jailed, understand, but what his friends and family here in the States would think of him afterwards if he did that."

"Well," Chick said, "the man may have been thinking like a scared pussy then but he's one brave motherfucker now."

"Bullshit," Dandoo said. He gave Chick such a stone-cold stare that I thought he was going to reach out over the crate and kill him. "That's bull fucking shit. You don't know the least thing about it. About being brave or being a pussy or being a man or anything."

Chick laughed nervously and shook his head and rocked back on his orange crate and gave the air a little *hyaaah*.

"You don't know anything," Dandoo said again. For a moment I was certain he was going to punch him. Even in his diminished condition, I knew Dandoo would break Chick in half. "Lenny was always a square guy, top to bottom, beginning to end. From what I heard, he tore Basic up. In the field his performance was at the top of his unit. He was the model soldier. And that doesn't mean what you fuckheads might think."

With both hands he reached for the bottle and then slowly rose from his orange crate, like a huge, wounded animal in a clearing, careful not to put too much weight on his bad leg. He stood and raised the bottle to his lips, then tilted it back to the ceiling, draining it. "I mean," Dandoo said after he was finished drinking, "who the fuck's to say what is and isn't brave?" He let the question linger in the air.

"Take me," he continued. "I've got a fucking Purple Heart and a pair of Bronze Stars, and that's supposed to make me brave?" He threw the bottle into the alley where it shattered on the ground with a crash, then gave the air an angry laugh. "Lenny could be beating his meat right now in Toronto and you miserable asswipes think that would make him a coward? Let me tell you, Lenny didn't go to Toronto because he *was* a coward. You follow me? He was afraid of what everybody down here would think of him if he did that. He was this far away from going." He raised two fingers an inch apart in the air. "The night we got drunk he told me everything."

He motioned for someone to hand him his cane. "You don't know anything," he said again to Chick. "About bravery or cowardice or conscience or manhood or anything. You're so fucking blind it's as if ever since you were a baby sucking your ma's tit you've never even opened your damn eyes."

"Well," Ronny said, as he retrieved the fallen cane and handed it to Dandoo, "out of all of us here, certainly you're the one to know."

"No," Dandoo said. He gave out a mean, sad laugh. "I don't know anything either. I mean, you should hear what's going on right now inside my head." He looked down at me suddenly and then leaned out over the card table and jabbed my chest so hard with the rubber tip of his cane that he nearly knocked me off the crate I was sitting on. "Are you getting all of this, Vince? Have you been doing what you always do, paying close attention to everything we say with those big gloomy eyes of yours? Did your ears soak up all of this? Are the old lions giving the young pup a good enough education?"

Chick laughed as he swept his cards into his hand so as to count his points. His face was blotched red, as if he'd been slapped. "Yeah, over the years I'd say we've really taught Junior here a lot."

Ronny nodded.

"Because your number's next," Dandoo said, pushing the tip of his cane against my shoulder. "And the door to the National Guard"—his cane pointed to Ronny—"closed a long time ago. And you certainly don't want to end up like me or Chicken Little here."

He thumped my chest again, hard enough for it to hurt, then tapped the cane's tip repeatedly against the side of my head. "You follow what I'm saying, Vince? You've got to choose. Every kid your age has got to choose. This is your life we're talking about. The real deal. From here on out you've got to give everything you do some real serious thought."

☙ ☙ ☙

Friday night dinner—the last supper—at the Santangelos'.

In the center of their ornate dining room table, beneath a gaudy, golden cut-glass chandelier, lay a baked fish sheened over with tomato sauce, basil leaves, and paper-thin lemon slices shingled to resemble scales. Flanking the fish were two bowls of pasta covered with sauce made of sardines and anchovies, and topped with toasted bread crumbs. Mr. Santangelo presided proudly at the table's head. As the four of us made the sign of the Cross and bowed our heads in prayer, I stared at the fish's white, unblinking eye.

Since the night of the broken condom, Marie and I had hardly held hands. Her forehead now sprouted a light sprinkle of pimples. She'd bitten her fingernails down to the quick. As for me, I fell into a dismal funk. Worried about what I'd possibly done, I stopped visiting Lucy on Saturday afternoons. Given my situation with Marie, seeing Lucy and possibly being intimate with her didn't seem right. Instead I hung around Ronny's garage, half-expecting the guys to daa dum-da-dum me or crack wise about my ankle being fitted for the old ball and chain, or else I walked the neighborhood streets in a daze, not really knowing what to do next.

Of course neither Marie nor I spoke about the possibility of her being pregnant. We both knew that putting the fear into words might jinx us, nudge the possible into something actual. It was nearly as if the sperm and egg were still deciding whether or not to join forces in her womb, and our words or silence would tip the balance one way or another. Meanwhile an effusive Mr. Santangelo acted as though we were well on our way to walking down the center aisle, and even Marie's mother seemed more or less resigned to my presence.

For a while the four of us ate in silence, and then Mr. Santangelo started in about the food, about the tastiness of the fish and the beauty of its preparation, and how one would normally expect a butcher to serve meat on a Friday evening, a nice porterhouse or rib-eye, this being after the edicts and relaxations of rules of Vatican II, but out of deference to and in honor of my presence at their table he thought it best to serve the son of a fishmonger fish. He went on to tell us that you really shouldn't have to wait until Saint Joseph's Day to eat pasta with sardines and anchovies, how Saint Joseph should be honored more often than once a year, how the bread crumbs topping the sauce symbolized the sawdust that fell from the holy carpenter's saw and workbench, and what a model the saint was for men, particularly men with new wives, men with a family, how Joseph worked each day without complaint to give everything he could to Mary and Christ, how he was the family man's truest ideal, and then Marie kicked me beneath the table.

She pointed to her knife, then picked it up and cut something on her plate.

"I agree," I said to Mr. Santangelo. "What child wouldn't want a father as kind and good as Saint Joseph?"

Mr. Santangelo nodded and smiled as he helped himself to more fish.

Marie kicked me a second time.

"Everything's very delicious," I said to Mrs. Santangelo, even though I'd said it at least two or three times before.

Mrs. Santangelo sat primly, like a small bird protecting a nest, picking at bits of food with her fork, then rearranging her silverware in a flurry, placing her knife across the top half of her plate, blade in, tip precisely at eleven o'clock, and then her fork directly below and parallel with her knife. Marie rattled her fork against her knife and then knocked her knife off the table and onto the floor. Then she stood and excused herself from the table, returning a moment later with a clean utensil.

Sitting, Marie said, as if to herself, "Here, allow me to rest my knife on the side of my plate *where it belongs*," directing her last words at me as her eyes locked like a laser beam into mine. She slid her chair forward, and then I felt yet another kick to my shins. Her knife and fork were in the exact position as her mother's. Finally I looked down at my own fork and knife, which lay against each side of my plate like a rowboat's idle oars.

"And the fish," I said again, moving first my knife and then my fork across the edges of my plate, approximating the positions of Marie's and her mother's silverware, "this fish is very tasty and succulent."

"I appreciate your saying so," Mrs. Santangelo said. "Blade in."

"Blade in," I repeated, nodding, not understanding, until Marie cleared her throat, rolled her eyes angrily, and flipped over the blade of her knife several times until I flipped over the blade of my knife so that the blade's edge faced me.

"There now," Mrs. Santangelo said, wiping the sides of her mouth with her cloth napkin and sitting back in the throne of her dining room chair with a contented sigh. She seemed momentarily pleased, as if she'd just been given the solution to world peace.

"I have a surprise," Mr. Santangelo announced, pushing himself up and away from the table. "Please. Nobody move. Everybody stay in your seats."

He returned several moments later bearing the magnificent box of butcher's knives I wasn't supposed to know about. "For my new apprentice," he said, smiling broadly, the dark shadow of his beard blueing the lower half of his face.

I feigned surprise. "For me?" I said, standing. As he handed me the box I thought that when he found out what I'd done to his daughter he'd take out the sharpest knife within it and gut me. Instead I decided to play the fool. "What in the world could be in here? A pair of shoes?" I gave the box a slight shake and held it up to my ear.

"You know perfectly well he wouldn't give you a pair of shoes," Mrs. Santangelo said. Her good mood had dissipated and she was back to her old self.

"Leave the boy alone," said Mr. Santangelo. "Let him have his fun."

"Then it must not be shoes," I said, glancing at the chandelier's tear-shaped bulbs, trying to forget about what might or might not be going on inside Marie's womb. I wanted to hold on to the moment, to push all else in my mind aside. "I don't know why at a time like this I'd think of shoes." I smiled at Mr. Santangelo, then slowly undid the brass latch on box's side and lifted the box's top.

The blades of the knives shimmered magnificently in their cushioned slots, the reflections of the bulbs in the chandelier glistening on them like moons on the waves of a silver sea.

"They come from *Italia*," Mr. Santangelo said in a near whisper.

"To my father's new apprentice," Marie said, standing and raising her water glass.

All would be right, I thought. Not simple or easy, certainly not at first, but in the end she and I and our new baby could make it right. I'd work hard each day without complaint to give her and our sweet child everything they wanted or needed. Tears rushed to my eyes.

"You won't be using them yet," Mr. Santangelo was saying. "Not for a few years, not until you're a butcher full fledged. We'll give you some time, some room, to learn and grow into them."

"Here, here," Marie was saying.

"But in the meantime," Mr. Santangelo said, "here's something else maybe you can put to good use." He reached into his back pocket and took out a small box. It looked so much like a jeweler's box that for a moment I thought Mr. Santangelo was going to propose to me and offer me an engagement ring. "God knows," he was saying, "she sits alone and untouched three hundred sixty days a year, not moving her fluids, her gasoline or oil. Sometimes I worry she'll turn into a pile of rust beneath her blankets."

Indeed it was a jeweler's box, and inside its dark velvet lining were the keys to Mr. Santangelo's garage and his black-and-white '56 Chevy.

"It would be a great favor to me," he was saying, "if every now and then you could take her out for a short trip somewhere, just as long as you drive slowly and safely."

"I don't know what to say." I was doing my level best to hold back my tears.

"A simple thank you will suffice," said Mrs. Santangelo.

"Bravo," Marie was saying, clapping her hands, "bravo, bravo." And then she stopped as a sudden look of surprise and consternation spread across her face. At once she ran from the room.

"Thank you," I told Mr. Santangelo, and then without thinking I embraced him. As his arms circled me, I fell into his broad chest and wept for several moments on his shirt. "There, there," Mr. Santangelo said, patting my back with the tough meat of his hand, as if I were a baby he was burping. "It's nothing. Nothing at all. We want you and Marie, the two of you, to prosper and be happy. We know you would never do anything to hurt or harm her in any way."

"Of course not," I murmured into his broad chest.

"Marie?" Mrs. Santangelo called. "Marie, is anything the matter? Come back here. Are you all right?"

I wiped my tears with the backs of my hands as I stepped away from Mr. Santangelo and repeated the words *of course not, of course not* as I nodded. After several minutes Marie returned to the room, the backs of her hand also wiping away tears.

"What's the matter, Marie?" Mrs. Santangelo said, alarmed.

Marie shook her head, smiling, but paler than usual. "Nothing, Mamma. Nothing. It's just. . . . No, Mamma. Don't worry. It's nothing at all."

"What?" asked Mr. Santangelo. After he received no answer, he announced that it was high time we cleared the table and brought out the coffee and dessert. "Sit," he said to me as I began to gather the plates. "We'll have coffee and a little *dolci*. Not something heavy or too much, just a little something sweet."

Mrs. Santangelo carried the platter of fish and bowls of pasta into the kitchen. She called to Mr. Santangelo to help with the coffee. Marie gathered the dirty plates, then smiled at me the moment her mother's back was turned. *It's my period*, she mouthed.

Oh, joy.

"I hope you haven't eaten too much," Mr. Santangelo told me as he returned to the room. "Remember at each meal to make sure to always leave room for a little something sweet."

⚬ ⚬ ⚬

The next afternoon, Saturday, Lucy slapped the side of my face hard, as hard a slap as I've ever received in my life, after she opened the front door to me.

I wasn't really sure what I'd come to tell her. At the least I wanted to explain how worried and frightened I was that I'd gotten Marie pregnant, and how it didn't seem right for me to be with Lucy when Marie might be carrying our baby. I also wanted to tell Lucy about my good fortune, about Mr. Santangelo and the box of knives. I hardly realized back then how much I truly loved Lucy Sheehan. Looking back, I realize I always thought of her as out of my league, beyond my reach, as the girl who belonged to Ronny Cannon. The slap scattered the thoughts from my head and sent me reeling back against the hallway wall.

"You goddamn son of a bitch."

"I know," I said, righting myself. "I'm sorry. I know I should have come over sooner."

"You don't know. You don't know anything." She slapped me again. I stood still, hands at my sides, and let her continue to slap me, struggling hard to stay there in the moment with her, with her hands that were giving my face stinging slaps.

"Really," I said. "Believe me. I'm sorry."

"I could absolutely kill you, you lousy son of a bitch."

"Hey," I said, "give me a chance to explain. Things got really crazy between me and Marie."

She balled her fists and took a step toward me again. "You idiot, I'm not talking about you and Marie. You're so stupid I could spit. Screw you and Marie. The two of you can dance in Hell for all I care. Don't you understand anything? I'm talking about us. Me and you. You and me. I'm pregnant."

"What?"

She didn't answer. Instead, she turned and walked into the front room, her furry pink slippers angrily scuffing the worn carpet. "You heard me." After I'd come inside and untied and removed my shoes she turned to face me. "God damn you. Damn you, damn you, damn you. You don't know just how bad you've screwed up my life."

Then I spoke without thinking. "And you're sure it's mine?"

The ceiling spun as she slugged me. It twinkled with silver sparklers and popping firecrackers, and as she hit me again and again it opened wide with the bursts of exploding bottle rockets and spinners and cherry bombs.

"—shouldn't even have let you in my house. You selfish, arrogant son of a bitch. I'm a fool to have ever let myself get involved with you."

The blows hadn't knocked me down. I found myself still standing. "Well then," I said, "in that case we'll have to get married."

She snorted. "I wouldn't have you."

"I'm serious," I said. "Let's get married. I want to marry you."

She shook her head and gazed around the room, then back at me. "Don't you realize how this fucks up the rest of my life? I thought if anybody could understand, you would. *I wanted to get out of here!* I wanted something more, something better. You of all people understand how this place is a trap."

I didn't know what else to do but nod.

"And it isn't even this shitty house, or this neighborhood. It's something worse, a mind set." She laughed bitterly. Her long red hair was pulled back in a pony tail, tied off with a green rubber band. She looked beautiful in that moment, as tears ran freely down her face. "Yeah, I was real smart, wasn't I? Really smart. I had it all figured out. I was waiting for the right guy to come by on his white horse and fall in love with me and take me away from all of this. Or for asshole Ronny to wake up and come to his senses."

I looked down at my hand and my class ring, which on one side of its blue stone had a fire-breathing dragon, on the other Saint George on horseback, bearing his lance and shield. I thought of the guy she'd fallen in love with who'd also gone to Saint George, who'd left the neighborhood to attend Notre Dame, who'd given her the koala bears that watched us from the floor each Saturday afternoon as we made love.

"I took pride in myself for being a card-carrying optimist. I tried to look at the glass as half full. I had so many dreams. I even wore rose-colored glasses. But I never escaped my nemesis."

"Who?" I said. "Me? Ronny? The guy who went to Notre Dame?"

"Don't flatter yourself by including your name with theirs."

"Then who?"

"It's not a who, exactly. It's a what."

"I don't understand."

"Sex."

"Sex? I don't understand."

"Cocks." She walked over to the fireplace. Behind her on the fading print over the mantle, the dogs nosed the air and the horses lifted their hooves impatiently, eager for the hunt to begin.

"Cocks?"

"Please don't play dumb with me, Vince. You know what a cock is like. You've been fucked over by them, too. You said so yourself."

I could hear her angry breathing as she waited for me to respond, then the clatter of traffic outside on the street. "Tell me about it," she continued. "Or don't. What do I care anymore? It's your business. I don't care about you. Don't tell me."

"I don't know what you mean."

"Then keep your little secrets. Wallow in your shame. Pretend things didn't happen long enough and maybe they might not have, huh?" She let out a sharp laugh and spoke as if she were spitting. "Just so that you know, my oldest brother started doing me when I was thirteen. I'd hardly even gotten my period. It was a year or so after my mother died."

"So that's why your bedroom door—"

"It went on for a couple of years, twice or three times a week, until I was maybe sixteen and he told me he wanted my other brother to join us. That night I took a knife to bed with me. When they came at me I used it."

"You cut him?"

"Not deep enough. You've met him. He's still alive, isn't he? But at least they left me alone after that."

"I want to marry you," I said.

"I could never cut him deep enough."

"I love you," I said. "Lucy, I love you."

"Oh yeah? Well, you've sure got a hell of a way of expressing it."

"My not coming around here," I began. "Believe me, I'm sorry, it won't happen again. It was a mistake."

"No, you're the mistake. Wait, let me take that back. All of you, all of you with your selfish, greedy cocks, you're all the mistake."

"Let's give this time," I said. "Let's not decide anything now." I wanted to hold her in my arms but I was afraid to. "Are you even sure? How far along—"

"Far enough."

"Well, regardless, I want to marry you and help bring up our baby."

She laughed, then looked at me, amazed. "Hey, what planet do you live on? Do you think for one moment I want to keep it?"

She laughed again—the metal teeth of a bow rake screeching against the sidewalk—and told me to get out, that the mere sight of me was making her nauseous. She said I wasn't to get all Catholic on her and think I owed her anything. I owed her nothing. Nada. Zero. Zilch. And if ever I saw her out on the street, I was to nod and keep on walking. No, on second thought I shouldn't even nod. I was to ignore her completely. But chances were that I wouldn't ever see her again, not even on the street, at least not around here, since if she had any say over the matter she'd be going far, far away.

And just for the record, she added, now that I'd gotten over the initial shock, maybe the baby wasn't really mine. After all, she said, there was no way really of telling. There were six, eight, ten, maybe a dozen or more possibilities, and each and every one, she said, was better in bed than I was.

Tears ran steadily down her cheeks as she spoke, but her voice held solid and firm. She slapped my hands away each time I reached out to touch or try to comfort her.

I asked her not to make any hard and fast decisions. Let's take it one step at a time, I said, do what's right, make the best of what has happened. Sleep on it, talk again in a day or two, when we both weren't so emotional, so upset. Let's admit that we love each other and get married, for God's sake, make ourselves into a family, raise our baby. As I spoke, the idea of marrying Lucy became more possible and real and attractive in my mind.

"Get out," she said.

"I love you," I said. I sincerely meant it. It was the truest thing I'd ever said to anyone.

She brushed my words away. "You don't know what love is."

"But I do. Believe me, I've always loved you but I've been way too afraid to ever admit it."

"Get out of here, Vince. I can't take this anymore. Now. Before I scream."

"Okay," I said, "for now, sure, for today, I'll leave. But in a day or two after you've cooled down, I promise you I'll be back."

Outside on the street, a long stream of headlights was working its way beneath the arch spanning the entranceway into the cemetery. After latching the front gate, I watched the procession for a while, counting the cars as they made the turn from the street and then drove beneath the limestone arch. I can't say why but it seemed crucially important at that moment for me to count the cars turning into the cemetery for the funeral. The streetlights came on then, first flickering, then shining with all their strength. Then an old woman in a babushka walked down the street pulling a folded shopping cart. I remained in front of the gate until the normal traffic on Rosehill resumed and the funeral procession's red brake lights vanished beneath the arch up and beyond the hill inside the cemetery in the distance.

≈ ≈ ≈

The next day, Sunday, after I was certain they'd finished eating their afternoon dinner, I walked over to the Santangelos' six-flat. No sooner had the outside hallway door swung shut behind us than I told Marie that I'd gotten Lucy Sheehan pregnant.

It was as if I'd dusted her skin with flour. As if I'd cut the muscles that held together the features of her face. The fullness of her lips went white. Her eyelids fluttered. Her knees went slack for a moment, and then she fell limply against me. I had her sit for a while on the stone steps of the six-flat with her head between her knees.

"Deep breaths," I said. "That's it. Nice and steady. Breathe."

"How could you?" she said after a while, after she sat back up.

"It wasn't intentional," I said.

"But I mean, how could you be with her, when all the time, you and me. . . ."

"I don't know." I could hardly bear facing her. "I mean, a lot can happen in a year. In thirteen months. I guess what my father says about me is true. I'm no good. Think of how much better off you are now without me."

"That's not truthful." Her eyes narrowed. Some of the color returned to her face. "You are good. But you're also incredibly stupid and untrusting and careless."

I nodded. "Whatever you say."

"Untrustworthy is what I really mean. You're untrustworthy. You're also dishonest. Plus, you don't know your own heart. You're—" She looked away for a moment and stared beyond the trees on Farragut and up at the sky. It was early evening. The darkening sky looked as if at any moment it might open up. "You know, I never understood the expression before, but now I do. You're *beneath contempt*."

I nodded.

"Did you actually think I'd fall for one of those guys I went out with? Is that what you thought, watching me from Mrs. Petrovich's gangway? I told you I wouldn't fall in love with them. I told you that I loved you. Why in the world didn't you believe me?"

"I don't know what I thought. I guess I didn't think."

"Yeah, that's right, you didn't think. That's precisely the point. And now you'll spend the rest of your life paying for it."

I nodded, knowing that one way or another her words were true.

"After all that I gave you."

"I'm sorry."

Then her face grew pale again, as if what we were discussing was starting to sink in, and as she began to cry I told her I'd better ring her bell so her parents could help her get upstairs. I told her I didn't want to wait around and talk to her folks right now, particularly her father. I told her in another day or two I'd return the box of knives and the keys.

"He'll be so disappointed," she said as she began again to cry. "You can't even begin to imagine."

Oh, I could imagine. Believe me, over the years I've imagined. Over the years I've gone over these scenes in my mind and felt them hurt me again and again. Marie continued talking as she cried, further describing her disappointment with me and what would be her father's great grief and sadness, but something in me shut down and made me stop listening. Something inside me prevented me from hearing anything else she had to say.

I went into the hallway and rang their apartment's bell—three long, shrill rings, to indicate an emergency—then walked for the last time past Marie, who sat twisted, face down, head cradled in her arms, on the stone steps in front of her parents' six-flat, sobbing.

～ ～ ～

Not knowing where else to go, I walked to Ronny's garage.

He was working beneath the hood of a car as I approached, and as soon as he saw me he rushed me, wiping his hands down the sides of his dago-T and baggy blues as he ran, then jutting both palms hard against my shoulders, knocking me back against the stones and grit that surfaced the alley. I tumbled dizzily back.

I still don't know why I went to see him, other than that I didn't know where else to turn. On the walk over I realized I was certain now about what I had to do. I'd marry Lucy, and together we'd bring up our baby. *Our baby*, I thought. Lucy was carrying our baby. In a way the news comforted me since it seemed that my life now had purpose and direction—to raise my child, with a woman I loved—though the neon sign over the butcher shop on Clark Street still flashed brightly in my mind.

"What the fuck makes you think you have the right to come around here?" Ronny said. He stood over me, fists at the ready. I was certain that if I got up he'd knock me right back down.

"I came to talk to you," I said.

"The time for talking's passed." He stared hard at me for several moments, then turned back toward the garage.

"Ronny," I said, "I thought things were all over between the two of you." I stood cautiously, though I readied myself in case he rushed me again.

"So what if they were? What's your point?"

"So my point is I thought that what I did was okay."

"Sure. Who said it wasn't? It's no sweat off my balls."

"Then why are you giving me a hard time?"

"Hey, if I was giving you a hard time you wouldn't be able to get up. You wouldn't be able to talk. You'd be picking your broken teeth from out of that pothole there. When I was through with you, you could forget about even walking."

By now I stood just outside his garage. He leaned back against the driver's door of the car he'd been working on, lighting a fresh cigarette, squinting as the smoke curled around his face. The girl in the bikini straddling the world gazed out from her dark corner. The hubcaps hanging on the wall beside her stared at us like a hundred eyes.

"I mean," I said, "it wasn't like what we did had anything to do with you."

"She's nearly three months along, you know."

"She came to talk to you?"

"Yeah, a couple of days ago. She wanted to know what the fuck was up with you, why she hadn't seen you around."

"Nothing's up with me," I said. "I talked to her yesterday afternoon."

"She came to ask me for advice. You know what I mean. Explore her options. About where someone in her shoes might go to get a little help with her situation. Who else has she got to turn to? I mean, we may not still be going out but we're still friends. Which is more than I can say about you."

"You mean you and me? I'm still your friend, Ronny."

"Yeah? You think so? You think you treated me like a friend?"

"What was I supposed to do? Come ask your permission?"

He smiled. "There are things that friends do and things that friends don't. Real friends know the difference. They don't even have to think about it." He paused. "But hey, why should I waste the breath? You got a point. Maybe you're even right." His face broke into a smile as he nodded at me and then crushed his cigarette beneath his shoe. "In fact, come to think of it, when your pretty little Marie came around here a few months ago looking for you I didn't ask your permission."

"What are you talking about?"

"You mean she didn't tell you?" He smiled again. "Well, come to think of it, I can see why she wouldn't."

"She came around here? Looking for me?"

"I thought I'd mentioned it. This was two, maybe three months ago."

"And?"

"I'm pretty sure I told you, Vince."

"You didn't."

"So, what? You want a description? A play by play?"

"What are you talking about?"

"Hey, be cool. Like you say, it had nothing to do with you. She was just looking for you, that's all. This was before the two of you got back together. You weren't here, it was late, and one of those other guys she was seeing had gotten a little fresh with her, understand, which made her all upset and weepy. She said you used to bring her here sometimes. She was upset and looking for you, you know, and you weren't here."

"Go on," I said, after it seemed he wouldn't continue.

"She needed a friendly ear to tell her problems to, that's all. So we sat in the back of one of these cars and, you know, spent a little time together."

"I don't believe it."

"Don't believe me. What do I care what you believe? You can ask her yourself. She'd just gone out with some loser from Lane Tech, to the movies, the Uptown or Riviera, you know, down on Lawrence and Broadway? I guess during the second feature he turned into a regular octopus. So he dumps her right then and there on the street after she wouldn't put out. Why else do you think she ended up here? She took the Broadway bus."

"You're making all of this up."

"I don't need to make things up, Vince." He laughed. "I really like how once she relaxes and gets going she's real nice. Like caramel. You know what I mean. You get her legs wide open and she just sort of melts."

"Fuck you."

"She's not anything fancy, just real sweet. But you know what I mean. Especially after you get her going."

I said nothing.

"So how does that feel, friend?"

"I don't believe you," I said.

"What have I got to gain by lying?" His eyes held mine. "You know, I still get sort of hard"—he gave the crotch of his pants a grab—"just thinking about her. And now that you and her are over with, I really wouldn't be surprised if she comes around here again. They always do after they get a little taste of the old cannoli. You are done with her, aren't you, I mean, seeing as how you knocked up Lucy? I figure that if I'm your friend the least I can do is to ask."

"Go fuck yourself," I said.

He smiled, then drew out another cigarette from the open pack lying on the dashboard of the car he was repairing. "Well, that's original. I'll take it as a yes." He nodded and clicked open his Zippo against his pants leg and lit his cigarette and stared at me. "There's pop bottles over there against the wall if you want 'em. Otherwise, get out of here. I've got work to do."

"So what did you tell her?" I said.

He took his cigarette from his mouth and spat out a piece of tobacco at me.

"I mean Lucy."

He shrugged and bent down over the car's engine, tinkering with the wing screw on the cover over its air filter, acting as if I weren't there.

"What advice did you give her, Ronny?"

He said nothing.

"I tell you, Ronny," I said, "our getting together, it just sort of happened."

He turned from the car and nodded. "Yeah, I know how that goes. Afterwards, that night when you weren't here, that's what me and Marie figured, too."

❧ ❧ ❧

Late Sunday night. Home sweet home.

Cement-hard glass of the front door against my back, forceful and sudden. Then the side wall, and as I tried to make my escape the opposite side wall, too. Dancing for several moments with the walls. Each reaching toward me so I might be its partner.

On my head and chest, a pair of fists beating time. One two, back step. Slow slow quick quick. Tweetie bird chirpings and five-pointed stars, like in the cartoons up on the Uptown theater's wide, Technicolor screen. *I tawt I taw a puddy tat.* Hollow thuds followed by a rush of someone's breath. *Ooooof.* Another voice saying *stop it, stop it, stop it, please, stop it,* before curling into a silent ball. The fists responding, what good are you anyway, you worthless son of a bitch. You no-good piece of shit. You motherless fuck, knocking up the neighborhood slut. Her father and two brothers, coming over here, on a Sunday of all days, demanding I pay for the slut's abortion.

Drool colored red by a streak of blood, dripping from the side of my mouth. What did you say? Working my way back into the moment, trying my best to stand.

Good thing your mother and sisters weren't here. Three hundred dollars I had to give them, to pay for it. Do you have any idea how long I have to work to make three hundred dollars? You worthless excuse for a son. You'll pay me back every red cent.

You mean she had—

They said you admitted it. How could you be so stupid as to admit it?

So she had it? The abortion?

What, they wait til Christmas for a thing like that?

But on a Sunday?

What do you think, abortionists take the day off to go to church? The whore was three months ripe! They'd just brought her home from it, said she was bleeding like a stuck pig. Three hundred dollars! To some fucking South Side butcher for—what?—five, maybe ten minutes of twisting around her guts with a coat hanger.

I steadied myself against the length of my dresser. From the punches he'd landed, a dozen holes in my chest and sides simmered with flame. I imagined Lucy in bed, bleeding, possibly dying. Stuck pig. South Side butcher. Then my eyes fell on Mr. Santangelo's box of knives. I knocked open the lid, drew out the shortest and sharpest blade as I faced him.

No, I said. You're wrong.

Don't wave a knife at me. His hands swung to slap it away.

You have to say you're wrong.

Then all at once we were again dancing, the two of us dancing my father's favorite dance, wooly bully, back and forth on my bed, which creaked with resignation and then collapsed beneath our weight. Dancing beneath the stair room's crooked ceiling, where the rounded ends of nails protruded like unexplored galaxies. I stood and faced him and wanted to cut his chest open and slice out his demon heart. Straight blade, curved, boning, breaking, skinning. I wanted him to feel pain the way that I felt pain. I wanted to butcher him in the way I imagined the men in the slaughterhouses on the South Side did pigs and cattle. The way my Lucy had been butchered. Chicago. Stinking onion creek. Tool maker, stacker of wheat. Hog butcher for the world.

But his stronger hands wrapped around mine and bent back my weaker wrists. His strong arms pushed me back and down against the far wall beneath the descending stairs and seized the handle of the knife as he knelt over me on the collapsed bed. You fucking punk, don't you dare take a knife to me.

You're wrong, I said. You have to be wrong.

The blade turning in our hands toward my chest and slicing its way down, easily, cleanly through my shirt and T-shirt and into the flesh of my chest, down on an angle across my chest, over my heart, a single bright slash, just an inch or so above my sternum. The torn front of my shirt blossoming a sudden brilliant red.

The knife falling to the fallen bed. The bulk of him—everpresent smell of fish—standing, giving my side a last kick as he stepped back.

You ungrateful son of a bitch, after all I've done for you, paying them off for you, pulling a knife on me.

After I didn't move, lying there beneath the stairs atop the broken bed, after I said nothing, his voice saying get up, it's only a little cut.

Image of Lucy in bed in her pink room behind her shattered door, bleeding. Marie lying across the front steps of her parents' six-flat, sobbing. The shining display cases of meat in Mr. Santangelo's shop. Sirloins and porterhouses and long racks of ribs. Endless rings of sausages, curled like sleeping snakes. Lucy's ridiculous pink fluffy slippers. *Dubliners* and chipped cups of perfectly made tea. Yes, please and thank you, but only a spot of cream, please. The shocking carnation blooming on my chest. Kneeling, my hands grabbed the knife so I could finish what we'd started.

Cutting into my own flesh. Completing the job, or at least trying to.

Slicing the flesh of my own chest, with the intention of cutting out my own heart, holding it in my hands and offering it up to him as it took its final beats, before his fish-smell again rushed me and his stronger hands slapped the knife away and down to the floor.

༄ ༄ ༄

Then suddenly I was running.

With the certainty of my childhood game, that a nuclear bomb was about to explode behind me, destroying everything I'd ever

known, I was out the front door of my parents' red brick two-flat
on Glenwood Avenue and running, running through the dark city
streets, black and slick now with late spring rain, shining now beneath
the pools of light puddled beside each streetlight. Running through
gangways and alleys, leaping over wooden and chain-link fences, running aimlessly, until my blood-soaked shirt made me realize I needed
to find refuge and care for and bind my wound.

I knew I couldn't risk going to the emergency room. Edgewater
Hospital was nearby, up on Ashland Avenue, a half dozen or so blocks
away, but I feared that before treating me the doctors would have to
notify the police. I imagined myself in jail, my furious father coming to the station to bail me out. No, I thought, I'd sooner bleed to
death. Inside my pants pocket were the keys to both Ronny's and Mr.
Santangelo's garages. The latter seemed the safer choice.

The big door rolled up quietly and easily on well-oiled though
rarely used rollers. I couldn't risk putting on a light, so I worked with
what light was there, streaming from a pole in the alley, as I searched
for a change of clothing and for rags with which I might bind my
chest and staunch my bleeding wound.

In the semi-darkness I found a box of old clothes, likely set aside
for donation to the Catholic Charities, and beneath it some towels
along with several men's shirts and a few slightly torn but freshly
laundered butcher's aprons. In a corner next to a push mower there
was half a case of seltzer water. I tore one of the aprons into strips,
then walked out into the alley and washed my wound with a bottle of
seltzer, then bound my chest tight like a mummy and put on one of
the shirts. I stuffed my bloody clothes in a nearby garbage can.

As I started pulling down the garage door the rest of what I might
do that night, my last night in Chicago, came to me. The idea took
shape nearly whole in my mind, as clearly and suddenly as a stranger
who taps your shoulder from behind on the street.

In the dim light you turn and try to place his face. Then, with
sudden recognition, your breath catches and you say *Oh, it's you.* Then

you realize you always knew him, and that listening to him, following him seems proper, right.

∾ ∾ ∾

I folded the sheets and quilts that blanketed the car, then placed them neatly on the side table put there expressly for that purpose. Then I put several more aprons and shirts along with the bottles of seltzer on the car's back seat for later use. I slid behind the wheel and started the Bel Air, giving her gas, easing up ever so softly on the clutch, smart enough to think of not turning on the headlights, smart enough to put the car in neutral and set the emergency brake as I eased down the garage door, slowly as a teardrop making its way down a broken-hearted girl's cheek, until I heard the lock issue a satisfying click. I was smart enough to leave the headlights off until I was at the end of the alley, where I paused and did my best to situate myself, trying to figure out which set of expressways and toll roads would take me north to Wisconsin, which I'd need to cross on my way to St. Paul, Minnesota.

I felt relief and exhilaration as I drove, as the city streets began streaming behind me in the cool night air, until a second stranger tapped me my shoulder. Yes, of course, I said as he whispered his ideas in my ear. There remained two more tasks: a final i to dot, one last t to cross.

I pictured Sister Ascension's perfect Palmer-script handwriting stretching across the green blackboard. Her o's perfectly rounded, p's precisely looped and tight. I turned the car around and sped to the alley behind Ronny's garage. Luckily for me, he was no longer there. But there, by the calendar and speed bag, next to the dusty cases of motor oil, was the full gasoline canister I needed.

*A sloppy hand is a sure sign of a sloppy mind!* I thought as I drove back to my house, then tiptoed up the back steps and into my grandmother's flat, where in bed she lay sleeping, snoring softly, like a purring cat. But tonight my sloppy hand would be neat, so neat that even my father would be able to read my signature. In the darkness my sleeping nonna reminded me of my grandfather. I made the sign of the Cross and said a prayer for his eternal soul and then one for her and a third for me. I took a deep breath to fill my head a final time with her dark smell, then moved beside the bed and tucked in her blanket and kissed her gently on the forehead. She stirred, then began to sit up, asking me what was wrong.

*Niente*, I answered. I just wanted to give you a kiss. *Dormi, Nonna, dormi.*

Back in the alley, I took the gas canister I'd taken from Ronny's garage and approached the rat shed, even though the neighbor whose face I could never remember had moved from the house years before.

Regardless, place can be a tabernacle, holding memory, storing inside its walls the energy of all that has ever occurred within. I kicked open the shed's wooden door and held my breath, not so much against the piercing odor of the gasoline which I began splashing everywhere but against memory's horrible, unforgettable smell.

The Holy Mother was with me at that moment because there on a table, alongside an assortment of tools and several round wire tomato cages, beside a set of metal shelves which held a few cans of varnish and paint, was what I had failed to remember to bring along with me: a book of matches, lightly coated with dust.

I spilled the last drops of the gasoline on the wooden floorboards, softly set down the can, then stepped back as I struck a match and let its flame fall to the floor.

There, I thought.

*There.*

Running back to the waiting car, the rain now heavier as it splashed on my cheeks and forehead. Seeing the bright reflection of the flames as they played across the car's rear window, but not for a moment looking back.

No, not for anything would I turn around to look back. I'd become a character in a book or a movie, so giddy was I from all that had occurred. The rule was that if I turned around to look at the flames, I'd have to go back and face the music.

I'd already faced it, I thought. That chapter of my life was through. There would be no returning. I was like Lot's wife, destined to be turned into a pillar of salt if I gave into temptation and looked back.

As I slid behind the wheel of the Bel-Air and glanced in the rearview mirror at the flames now rising out of the shed's doorway, I thought of myself as less a character out of the Bible and more as someone like Steve McQueen, Virgil Hilts, the Cooler King, revving the stolen Nazi motorcycle in *The Great Escape*, the greatest movie ever made. Ecstatic to be free of the prison camp and out on the open road—I popped the Chevy's clutch and let its tires smoke and squeal—I headed away from my captors and out toward the border to freedom.

# 13

# The Canadian Border 1967 / Tofino 1980

I LEFT MR. SANTANGELO'S Chevy in St. Paul, Minnesota, locked safely in the parking lot behind the church whose anti-war members spirited me across the Canadian border.

When I arrived at the church the pastor and sexton asked me to talk about my conscientious objection to war in any form, then had me stand in a circle and join hands with the other church members and pray. I rode uneventfully over the border with them in the back of an old Volkswagen bus jammed with fishing and camping gear, crossing midday at International Falls, a floppy canvas hat on my head, the dopey kind worn by the deckhand Gilligan on *Gilligan's Island*. The hat was studded with a dozen fly-fishing lures. I knew that, like Gilligan, I was departing on a voyage from which there would be no return. The church members instructed me to keep my mouth shut and let the men in the front seat do all the talking. Once we passed customs, they dropped me off several miles inside the Canadian border at a gas station just off a main highway. There, we recited a few more prayers, and they retrieved the *Gilligan's Island* hat and gave me a hard hand-shake and two peanut butter and jelly sandwiches. Before I left St. Paul I sent Mr. Santangelo his keys along with a map marked with a large X where his Bel-Air could be found.

I couldn't get over how immense Canada was, how big the North American continent was, for that matter. I'd never seen or even imagined so much open space. I wondered where all the people and houses and streets and alleys had gone. I'd never seen a mountain before, let alone one topped with snow and ice. I'd never looked at a rippling field of golden wheat. A wild river, rushing and leaping with trout. I felt as if I were on some other planet.

I felt like Midas, only in reverse. I'd become Bizarro Midas, like in *Superman*, where everything is backward. Rather than gold, all I touched turned to death and ruin.

The men and women from the church also gave me forty dollars, Canadian, enough to tide me over for a few weeks. They told me my main priorities should be food, clothing, and shelter along with maintaining a healthy and honest relationship with my savior. Whenever I became depressed, they said, I should adopt an attitude of gratitude. For the remainder of my days on earth I would be obligated to do for others as they had done for me. I was to give all those whom God had destined for me to meet on the road of life what I had been given by them: a smile and a helping hand, a hot meal along with my fellowship, a safe, dry place for them to rest their weary heads.

They also gave me antiseptic ointments, bandages and gauze for the wound on my chest, which was quite tender but fortunately hadn't become infected. They didn't appreciate the fact that I came to them cut. None of them asked me how I'd received the wound, and I didn't volunteer any details, though from their demeanor I could tell they disapproved. They debated about what should be done with me, if they should take me to a doctor, who might feel it was his duty to notify the authorities that he'd treated someone involved in what was more than likely a violent fight, or leave the situation alone. I saw that they thought me the victim, rather than the perpetrator, of the violence.

Once I reached Vancouver I held a series of odd jobs, whatever I could find. Kitchen work in restaurants, scut work on construction sites, panhandling, anything that would bring me income. I drifted about Vancouver for six empty years, doing whatever would bring me money except stealing. I felt I had to draw a moral line somewhere. As the alternatives become fewer and fewer, and the possibilities in one's life narrow toward a single point, one needs to draw a line somewhere. There are greater sins than stealing and for a while, during my last year or so there, in the park and the abandoned buildings where I slept, I consented to do them with whoever would pay me. Numb, hardly caring, outside of myself, dead, absolutely hating myself as I imagined Lucy Sheehan lying in her pink bedroom clutching her abdomen and bleeding after her abortion, as I remembered Marie Santangelo collapsed like a deflated balloon on the front steps of her parents' six-flat. My actions were an expression of self loathing as well as a twisted form of penance for all the evil I had done.

❧ ❧ ❧

I lived frugally and saved every cent until one day I was able to walk into a surgeon's office and ask for a vasectomy.

The meat cutter's fingers were graceful and thin, twin lines of neatly manicured ballerinas. He brought the left line of ballerinas up to his face, where for a moment he rested their dancing feet on his cheek. The moons on his fingernails were polished, perfect. No one on earth could possibly doubt the abilities of a man with hands like his.

"A vasectomy is a serious, irreversible procedure," he told me. "Do you realize the implications of what you're asking for? You're quite young. What if in six months or a year you meet and fall in love with someone who desires a family? Why don't you take some time to think this over, give this decision a bit more thought?"

"I can pay cash."

Later, coming out of surgery's merciful fog, a fog I nearly hoped would envelop me forever, the intense pain in my groin felt good, bracing. I leaned over the side of the bed and vomited into a glistening silver pan. The pain felt so wonderful and clean it snapped me out of my funk. I decided to leave Vancouver and vowed I'd never step foot on the mainland again. I'd continue to go west, to travel as far as the road toward the sea could take me. I'd do what my grandfather had done when he first came to this continent, continue west until I reached the sea. As I slid into my clothes and walked gingerly out of the doctor's office and onto the rainy Vancouver streets, doing my level best to clear from my face any and all expression of pain, I turned into the boy from Sparta.

Looking back on all of this now, I guess the occasional women who've slept in the tents in my back yard and knocked on my back door and shared a beer and a joint with me, who later eased their way into my bed and afterwards, while we lay there listening to jazz and sipping mugs of tea, remarked on the scar on my chest and wondered aloud if I was a cutter, someone who deliberately cut the meat of his own flesh, weren't that far off from guessing the truth.

෴ ෴ ෴

After Ignatius George and I had our talk while watching the sea lions out on Plover Reefs, I went back to working for Clarence. I'd give the job another season, I thought, then take it year by year after that.

Things were all business then between Clarence and me, even after I apologized for knocking him down and hurting him. Neither of us mentioned Harmony or Emily Fournier. It was as if they no longer even existed. Clarence was preoccupied with the year's growing crop and the inevitability of taking his business indoors, growing his sinsemella clones hydroponically. But to do so, he told me the few times that we discussed it, would entail significant risks. First, he'd need a place, but that risked it being traced back to him if it were ever detected by the authorities. Indoor marijuana operations are notorious for the obvious and easily detectible odors they produce. Second, the building would require water and electricity, and that meant linking up to B.C. Hydro, which might notice the exceptionally large electric bills and highly unusual—twelve hours on, twelve hours off—

pattern of usage. And even if he solved these problems, he said, he'd need equipment: high-intensity lights, temperature and humidity controls, carbon dioxide generators, intake and exhaust fans. All because of the fucking grazers. They're nibbling me to death, he raved. There was talk in the commune that he'd purchased a shotgun.

Come mid-September until the moment of harvest, he told me, I was to sleep with the biggest garden, guarding it day and night.

"There's no other alternative," he said. We talked on the commune's wide front porch, decorated with dozens of old buoys, streaked green with algae, their paint faded by the sun, scavenged over the years from the beach. "Grab your camping gear and a couple of cans of beans. I'm putting my trust in you, man. God knows, I have to be able to trust someone." A Steller's jay took a seed from a bird feeder hanging from the corner eave, eyed me, then flew off to a nearby tree to crack it.

"And what do you expect me to do if the grazers come?"

"What do you think?" He narrowed his eyes and smacked his fist into his palm. "Put the hammer down, my friend. You're an Italian from Chicago. Live up to your heritage. Break a few heads. Pluck out their eyeballs and then chop off their thieving hands with a machete." He gave out such a scary laugh that the jay and several other birds broke from the nearby trees. "Do you have a machete? If you don't, we'll get you one."

"Oh, sure," I said. "I'm to do violence to people for a little weed."

"You surprise me. I thought this would get your blood up. Seriously, just your being there should prevent the weasels from coming anywhere near. So make yourself a little obvious while you're out there."

"If grazers come by—" I began.

"Believe me, if they see someone guarding the fields they won't come by."

"And if I see an RCMP helicopter—"

"Well, don't make yourself that obvious. But if you do, just remember"—he cleared his throat and then with his thumb and first finger twisted the ends of his waxed mustache—"even though you may have borrowed my truck now and again and hung around here while you were seeing my sister, I don't believe we've ever actually met."

☙ ☙ ☙

The time alone in the rainforest gave me ample opportunity to think.

I recalled conversations over endless cups of coffee in the Maquinna Pub with Ignatius and his friends, men and women who sat around the table discussing the Twelve Steps, how for them they were life-saving acts. They talked about unmanageable lives and powers greater than themselves, personal shortcomings and defects of character, fear-less moral inventories and the need to admit to another human being the exact nature of their wrongs. While I found all that they said fascinating—even rather familiar, given my Roman Catholic back-ground—I couldn't keep the various steps straight in my head. At the time I didn't think I had any sort of problem with drinking or drugs. At the time I didn't know that one shouldn't work the steps out of order or without the help of a sponsor. But after several days alone in the forest, doing something along these lines began to appeal to me.

A couple of the later steps, the ones about making a list of all the persons you had harmed and making amends to them whenever pos-sible, tempted me mightily. It meant that you acknowledged your past actions and got in touch with those whom you've harmed. If you hurt them, you told them you were sorry and asked for their forgiveness. If you stole from them, you offered them restitution. And so as I sat in the rainforest guarding Clarence's largest garden I decided to con-tact the people I'd abandoned a dozen years ago back in the stinking onion creek.

In all truth, maybe I only wanted to hear from the people I'd harmed and then fled from. I missed them much, much more than

I was willing to admit. I wanted desperately to let them know I was still alive. I wanted them to tell me that maybe they thought of me every now and then. Most of all I wanted them to tell me they had forgiven me.

I remembered going to confession on Saturday afternoons, kneeling in the near-empty church of my childhood performing an examination of conscience, a moral inventory of all the sins I'd committed. The priests hearing confessions each Saturday afternoon sat inside one of the church's four wooden confessionals, ornately decorated booths flanked by a pair of smaller booths in which there were kneelers facing the side walls where the priest sat. Above the confessional's doors, painted in gilded letters, were these words:

## THE LORD HEALETH THE BROKEN OF HEART AND BINDETH UP THEIR BRUISES

On the priest's lap normally lay his breviary and sometimes a rosary; above his head, a small, shaded bulb offering just enough light for him to read. There was a slot above his door where he put his name, so you could tell which priest you'd be confessing to. You whispered your confession to him through a metal grate in the side wall. Above the grate hung a large crucifix. Around you were all the smells of the church: the melting wax from the flickering tiers of votive candles, the oils used to clean and polish the marble floors and wooden pews, the incense used at funerals and high Masses. You knelt in near darkness, waiting for the priest to finish the confession he was hearing on the opposite side, to slide closed the wooden shutter covering the other metal grate and to turn to you, sliding open your wooden shutter, as your heart beat faster with trepidation over how he might judge you, and then the grate filled with soft light and you saw the priest's black cassock and the crossed arms of his colorful stole, as the raised first two fingers of his hand inscribed in the air the sign of the Cross as he said *May the Lord be with you* and you said *Bless me, Father, for*

*I have sinned.* Then you whispered the long list of your many failures and shortcomings with the utmost regret and sorrow, and you could say or ask him anything—anything at all—you could confess nearly any sin in the whole world, because he was a representative of God the Father Himself and as long as you were truly sorry for your sins you'd be forgiven. The concept of forgiveness was nearly beyond my mind's feeble grasp. There was no sin that God would not forgive (save suicide, the nuns taught you, since suicide is an act that expresses the most profound despair and since the sinner would die before he or she had a chance to confess) as long as you were sorry and repented.

To be forgiven! Does life offer us any greater grace?

Then the priest would talk to you and give you a penance—usually a set of prayers to be recited before you left the church—and then in Latin recite the absolution, *Ego te absolvo,* as you recited the Act of Contrition, *O my God, I am heartily sorry for having offended Thee.* After both of you recited these prayers he'd say *God bless you, my son* and tell you to go in peace, and you'd say *Peace to you, too, Father,* and thank him as you rose from the kneeler, and as you emerged from the dark booth into the light of the church slanting from the high clerestory windows your soul would be cleansed. You'd feel pure, clean, refreshed, relieved, *forgiven,* just as long as you knew in your heart that you sincerely meant to sin no more and to avoid the near occasions of sin.

Even though I knew the priests couldn't tell who I was, I always thought they were able to recognize me. I always thought they knew I was an altar boy and as a result expected more from me than the endless lists of miserable failings I recited to them twice each month. I was always guilty of sins against the sixth commandment, *Thou shalt not commit adultery,* and was constantly given lectures about chastity, which, I was instructed, was the successful integration of sexuality into a person's spiritual being. That meant my sexuality should be expressed only when I was accepting children lovingly from God. Chastity was a gift from God, part of the contract we'd each made with Him when we were baptized, a moral virtue, the triumph of reason over passion, the state of being that separates human beings from the lower beasts.

I never went to confession to Father O'Reilly even though he was known for saying the fastest confessions and giving out the easiest amounts of penance. Instead I sought out the parish's old monsignor, who was so hard of hearing that he often made you repeat what you'd just said and who lectured you about your repeated shortcomings, so loudly at times that everyone else in the church likely could hear him, too, and he'd tell you things about yourself and your weaknesses that blistered your soul and made your ears burn.

The old monsignor told me that each man was like the captain of his own ship, that physical urges were like beasts that emerged suddenly from the sea's darkest depths, the mightiest of whales, man-eating creatures that would rise up out of the water unexpectedly and work to upset my ship's balance, overthrow my rule, capsize me, then drag me down beneath the waves where I would drown. He told me about the ancient Christian practice of wearing a cord or cincture around one's waist in honor of a saint, and he encouraged me to wear a knotted purity cord around my hips in honor of Saint Joseph. During moments of temptation the pressure of the knots against my skin would remind me of the pain Christ endured when his head was crowned with thorns, when nails were driven into his hands and feet. At my confessor's insistence I bought one of these cords and wore it for several weeks, even while seeing Lucy each Saturday afternoon, all the while remaining pure, until the cord's knots chafed my skin and made it begin to bleed, and one afternoon the two of us cut it off just before pushing the koala bears off her pink bedspread.

I'd brought paper and pen with me to the rainforest, along with *Desolation Angels* by Jack Kerouac. I figured Kerouac's book about being alone in the woods could keep me company while I was alone in the forest, too. I took pleasure in incidental symmetries like that. Late one afternoon I sat and leaned back against a tree, with Kerouac's book propped on my legs as a sort of makeshift desk. My inappropriate actions in Chicago required a response, and so I wrote a letter of apology to Lucy. Then I wrote a letter to Marie. I still remembered their addresses, and I could all too clearly picture their houses in my mind. I didn't try to explain myself or rationalize what I'd done or hadn't done. I simply expressed my regret and sorrow for my actions and asked them for their forgiveness.

Then I wrote a letter to Mr. Santangelo. Since I'd stolen his car and some things from his garage—the case of seltzer water I'd used to wash my wound, and the box of old clothes and butcher's aprons, which I'd kept—I knew I'd have to enclose restitution, and so I made a note to include thirty dollars Canadian with the letter. I told him that if he hadn't received the map and key or had been unable to retrieve his '56 Bel Air I'd pay him back for that, too.

Then I wrote a letter to Ronny, and since I'd stolen a canister of gasoline from his garage I decided to include a few dollars in his letter.

I hesitated as I began the fifth note, which was to my parents. I really didn't want to write to them and didn't even know how to begin. "Mother and Father" seemed overly formal. "Mom and Dad" seemed silly and false. Finally I decided to send them just a blank page and in its folds include the three hundred dollars my father had paid Lucy's father and brothers for her abortion. It was then, as I remembered the dimes and quarters I'd pocketed from my apron at my father's newspaper stands—a dollar or so a day, five dollars or so a week, twenty dollars or so a month, likely two hundred and fifty dollars a year—that I heard the grazers coming up the trail toward me.

🕉 🕉 🕉

There were four men in all. Of course, as I'd expected and feared, the first to walk toward me was Ignatius.

"I was just thinking of you," I called out to Ignatius as I stood.

"We were wondering who'd be here," Ignatius said. The other men nodded to me and then proceeded up the trail. We were just

inside the tree line and the overgrown slash where Clarence had planted his biggest garden, the one that annually produced the largest yield.
It was maybe an hour before sunset. Ignatius had a blue kerchief tied
around his neck. He was carrying a knapsack and, as we talked, set
it beside a moss-covered rock on the forest floor. "I see you're doing
some writing."

"Just catching up on some long overdue correspondence."

He reached forward and we shook hands, and then he rubbed
the palms of his hands together. His hands were big and roughly calloused. They made a gentle rasping sound as he rubbed them, like
leaves brushing the ground, as the wind picked up above us and passed
through the trees. "So where are we?" he asked. "You know what I
mean, Vince, what I'm referring to. Where do we stand? Let me know.
I need to tell the others."

"I really don't know," I responded.

"Is this something we need to discuss?" Ignatius said. "Or are we
just meeting here in the forest as friends? Because I hope you know
I've accepted you as my friend, and I respect you and your work. I
don't want to have conflict with you. If you ask me to leave, I'll honor
your wishes and leave, and I'll take my friends with me, and we'll all
leave peacefully. And the next time I see you in town, no matter what
you decide here, we'll still be friends."

"I don't want to have conflict with you, either," I said. "It's just
that I don't know what to do."

"Sure, you do. You just haven't admitted it to yourself yet."

I nodded and looked down at his knapsack. "Did you bring tools?
A box of garbage bags?"

He didn't answer. He stared directly at me, a smile on his face.

"Were you planning on taking all the buds," I asked, "or only
some?"

He took off his Adidas cap and ran a hand through his hair,
straight and dark, then put the cap back on. "Why does any of that
matter?"

"I don't know. I'm just asking. I'm trying to do what's right."

"You've always done what you've thought was right, Vince. Or at least you've tried to, haven't you?"

I shrugged. "I've made my share of mistakes." I gestured toward the letters I'd written, stuck between the pages of Kerouac's book. The moment seemed suddenly to hold great importance. I'd gotten so much in my life wrong, I didn't want to get this moment wrong, too.

"I run away from things," I said as he stared at me. "I think at some point in my life I need to stand for something. I need to stop running. Stay in one place and fight."

He knew about my past, how, among other things, I'd fled the draft. "Sure," he said, "when it's right we need to stay and fight, but that really depends on the battle, doesn't it?" He sat on the ground, folding his legs gracefully beneath himself. After a few moments I sat, too. "Take the Vietnamese. Since the 1800s they resisted the French, and then they had to fight America. Before that, they fought Japan, and before that the Chinese. How long did it take the U.S. to realize that withdrawal—"

"This is about Vietnam?" I said.

"This is about defending what has been yours for centuries, about others coming to understand that they can't just come into a place and claim to rule all they can see." His eyes held mine and for a while we simply looked at each other, as we sat and breathed. "Do you remember what I told you about those two Spanish invaders, Bodega y Quadra and Hezeta, who sailed up here in the *Sonora* and the *Santiago*? After the native people in what's now Washington state fought and killed a few of the Spanish sailors on Hezeta's ship, Hezeta turned back. Can you imagine that? The man turned back. Hezeta ordered his men back onto their ship and they literally sailed south and away. I like to think that on some level he understood that invading the New World wasn't his battle. I'm guessing that he felt somewhere in his bones or his soul that it was just plain wrong. It took the French thirty years to realize that about Vietnam. Your country's just now realizing that, too."

I nodded.

"But imagine for a moment," Ignatius continued, "that in 1775 Quadra had sailed south with Hezeta. What if Spain had never laid claim to the Pacific Northwest? What if Vancouver had returned to England after he'd finished mapping the island? What if Europe had been content with seeing what they'd seen here and gone back and left us alone?"

"The world never leaves a new place alone," I answered. "Once a new place is discovered, it's ruined."

Ignatius raised his hands, palms up, and gestured toward the forest around us. "You've seen the trucks on the road between here and Nanaimo. These forests are centuries old, nearly as old as time itself. These trees are the oldest living things on this continent. How many of these trees do you think your children will ever see? Or by the time they're your age will all of this have been logged out and sent overseas to be made into chopsticks and disposable coffee cups?"

That was what was happening to much of the rainforest here. Acre by acre, it was being logged out and shipped overseas. "I don't have any children," I said.

Ignatius didn't have to add that the land on which we were sitting belonged to everyone and to no one and that his people had always taken from it what they wanted and needed and in return cared for it, living beside it and within it in balance and harmony. Again we sat looking at each other, sharing no words. I turned then and gathered my book and the pages of my letters home. Ignatius stood, too, and slung his knapsack over his shoulder.

"This is also about reminding the interlopers that they don't have the right to plant their crops anywhere they choose," Ignatius added. "You know, your fancy English friend should consider himself lucky that he's left anything at all."

Who am I to judge what's right and not right? I thought. I haven't lived Ignatius's life, and I was a newcomer, an uninvited guest, in his country. Indeed, the land on which I stood *was* his country, I realized. There wasn't even a Nuu-chah-nulth word for "wild" or "wilderness." The word the First Nations people used for the rainforest was *home*. And so I stood and packed my things, wordlessly, then looked out at the garden greening the slash. The men were carefully clipping the ripest of the colas—every other bud—and placing them in plastic garbage bags, trying to get as little resin as possible on their hands.

I'd had my time alone in the woods, and it had been good. And now I had letters home to stamp and mail. That meant going back into town and getting cash from the bank and envelopes and postage. And since I was breaking camp, that meant letting Clarence know once and for all that I was leaving his employ.

☙ ☙ ☙

It wasn't too long afterward that I received a letter from Ronny.

*How dare you write to me,* Ronny's letter began, *you fucking loser, limp dick pansy, pitiful candy ass coward, motherfucking son of a bitch with no balls, too weak to fight for your own country during its great hour of need—*

I was about to rip the letter in half when a paragraph at the bottom of the page caught my eye.

*—spent the last three months of her pregnancy at a convent on the West Side and then gave the baby up for adoption. Catholic Services. Said it was the best thing, considering everything. Told me she didn't see or hold it since they knocked her out cold and don't let the mothers see their kids though later on one of the nurses let her know that it had been a little girl.*

I fell to my knees.

*—moved north to her own place out in the suburbs. Last I heard she was finishing college, going for something in nursing or some sort of job in the medical field, said she hadn't yet decided. Plus she has a steady guy. Just the ticket, she said. Real nerd though he has a steady job and seemed stable and likeable enough and so I guess by now they're married and probably raising their own family.*

*As for Marie I thought you'd appreciate hearing that Santangelo's Meats closed down about a year after you ran off. The next month or so the new owner tore down the old sign and converted the place to a laundromat. The father also sold their six-flat. Word is they moved out somewhere in Arizona.*

*And that fire you set to cover your tracks, ha ha, due to the heavy rain that night it burned down nothing except someone's old alley shed and a nearby garage.*

*I hope you're happy now you gutless pussy. I talked to Lucy about you just after you ran off and she said she hopes you rot and burn in Hell forever. She said she didn't know what in the world she was thinking when she spent that time with you particularly after you turned gutless chicken and ran out on her and on everybody else and even your own country in their time of need.*

～ ～ ～

I thought then about pulling another Steve McQueen, returning to the prisoner-of-war camp to try to right things. In *The Great Escape*, after Hilts, the Cooler King, successfully breaks out of the camp and maps the nearby towns, he allows the Nazis to recapture him so that he can return with the information he's gained and thereby help the others plan their escapes. If there was a way that I could sacrifice myself for those I'd harmed I would have done it without a second thought. At the least I could tell them my side of the story, explain that Lucy's father and two brothers had lied to and shook down my old man. Then I realized that my letters to everyone but Ronny and my parents would likely never be delivered. Still, I could track down Lucy, and there couldn't be that many Santangelos living in Arizona, could there?

But then I thought that no one would care about my explanation, that all the harm I'd done was done and my return into their lives after all this time would be more of an intrusion than anything else. No, I concluded (and perhaps this proves Ronny's point, that indeed I am a reprehensible coward), there was no way for me to undo what I did, no way at all to explain myself.

I folded Ronny's letter and put it in my back pocket, then left my house and headed downtown to the Maquinna. As I neared the place and heard the music pulsing from inside I hesitated and walked down First Street toward the rattling sign topped by the breaching orca, toward the dock and the water's edge.

How ridiculously appropriate, I thought. Here I was, at the literal end of the road, the official western terminus of the Trans-Canada Highway. I stared out at the blue-gray water and then up at the sky. There was an hour or so before sunset. Overhead, a flock of geese scratched a noisy, ragged slash against the sky.

I felt so much despair and self loathing I decided then and there to end it all. I'd already emptied out all my savings and sent my father over eighteen hundred dollars in restitution for the money I'd taken from the newsstands, and I realized again that I'd never hear back from Lucy or from Marie. No doubt they hated me and would always hate me. No doubt more than once each of them cursed the day they first heard my name. I turned and walked uphill back to my car and drove just south of Crab Dock, where Clarence kept his skiff.

So much for my code of stealing only from family and good friends. My final act would be yet another crime, stealing the skiff. I jumped down into the skiff and headed toward Deadman's Island, toward the aerie where a pair of bald eagles perched, abjectly eyeing me as I puttered along beneath them. *Deadman's Island*, I thought and laughed at the irony of its name. Then I swung behind Stubbs and headed for Vargas, where I hugged the shoreline as usual, weaving my way like a blind man through the rocks. The tide was going out. I didn't have any trouble seeing the rocks and wasn't nearly as afraid out on the water as the other times I'd taken the skiff out by myself. After a while, when I couldn't see any other boats were around, I turned the skiff out toward the open ocean and gave it full throttle. I'll hold it steady, I thought, bouncing up and down with the rolling swells, until I find the right spot. Then I'll dive over the side.

How long would it take before the numbness began? Two minutes? Five? I was already cold and shivering from the wind. I didn't have much body fat and wasn't that strong or sure a swimmer. As long as I could resist swimming back to the skiff I knew that without a deck suit I'd go into shock and become numb relatively quickly. Certainly in less than ten minutes. I'd have to resist trying to save myself, but even then, even if I did my best to cling to the skiff's side, I'd go rapidly into shock. It might not be all that different, I thought, than walking out onto the snow and ice on a day when the weather wasn't fit for tenderfoots.

For a while I thought about the Jack London story, then about Lucy and our afternoons together drinking tea, as I worked up the courage to leap over the side of the skiff into the water. The big, blazing sun brushed the horizon line, like a ripe orange resting on the edge of an immense gray-blue table. If I hadn't felt so rotten I would have admitted the sight was beautiful. The sun blurred the horizon and then melted and began to bleed on top of the water. I throttled down and set the engine on idle, angling the outboard's arm toward starboard so that the bow pointed at an angle to the chop, one that would hold my relative position and still allow me to face the sun. Then I stood in the boat, which even though it was ebb tide the waves were already pushing back toward shore, and considered how far out toward the sun I'd be able to swim before I'd go under. I'll swim into the sun's center, I thought. Then I took a deep breath and made the sign of the Cross and kissed my thumb as I readied myself for the dive.

Then suddenly from behind me, startling me so severely that I gasped, I heard an enormous, soft *chuff* as a gray whale surfaced just beside the skiff, breathing. A cloud of moisture in the shape of two falling plumes burst out over the water. Then the immense, silent, barnacled back of the beast broke the water's surface. My heart pounded hard as I fell back into the boat. I was simultaneously terrified and filled with awe. And as I fell back the whale swung its huge and magnificent notched tail—two wide flukes, easily nine feet across, pointed at the tips, looking like some bird's splendid outstretched wings—up and high and wondrously into the air, then back down effortlessly into the sea.

For the longest while I sat in the boat, unthinking, stunned, trembling, staring at the calm oval footprint the animal's flukes had left on the water's surface. One moment the gray whale had been there before me, majestically rising to breathe at the water's surface before taking a deep dive back down to the ocean floor to feed, and then the next moment the beast was gone, as if it had never been there. The waves were already covering the footprint, doing their best to erase the whale's tracks. I stared at where the footprint had been and then up at the sky, where the incredible tail had raised itself darkly against the glow of the sun.

That was the second time I'd been close to a whale, the second time I had the feeling of absolute wonder and humility that only an encounter with a whale in the wild can bring. To be so suddenly surprised by a creature's presence, simultaneously impressed by its sleek beauty and grace and utterly overwhelmed by its awesome size and energy. To realize there are still things that remain largely hidden from us in this world, beings that are so much more grand than we are, so beyond our understanding and awareness that their mere presence, even if only for a matter of moments, is able to take us entirely out of ourselves, able to silence the petty chatter that fills our heads and distracts us from the fact that we, too, are physical things existing in the natural world that trembles and breathes all around us. I came to understand at that moment some of the power of the natural world. I came to see the true, living presence of a higher power in the natural world.

So much for my plans of going over the side, I thought as I turned the skiff around and headed back toward Vargas and then toward the twinkling lights of Tofino's harbor.

I'd faced worse moments in my life than this one, I thought as I raced the skiff back to shore. By now, tears ran freely down my cheeks, and my body shook with sobs. I cried crocodile tears for myself and for those I loved and all who ever loved me. I wept for Nonna, who by now most likely was dead. I wept for Mr. Santangelo, who'd once showed me his hands and who told me I should never want to cut the meat of my own flesh. I cried for the boy I once was, who still lived inside me, the conscientious newspaper vendor doing his best to keep up with the furious rushes at the newsstand on Canal and Adams, the goofy kid who collected pop bottles and was a true believer in the perpetually losing Chicago Cubs, the diligent server at Mass who'd once guarded the fallen body of Christ, ready to give up his life, but who was invited instead to give his handkerchief to a girl, whose life he'd later harm, as he grew into the boy who read short stories and drank tea with a second girl, whose life he'd also harm.

Then I wept for those two girls, for Lucy and Marie, as well as for the third, the infant who would never be held by her birth mother, and whom I'd never meet or know.

Ignatius tells me that as I pushed open the door to the Maquinna later that evening my timing couldn't have been better, my manner more confident, my attitude toward Wayne accented by just the right mix of indifference and confidence. The large semicircular stage at the front of Maquinna's stood black and empty. Some forgettable piece of disco music was repeating itself from the speakers overhead. At a center table in the smoky darkness of the tavern sat Ignatius George and the newcomer Wayne C. Chase, and Ignatius had just finished telling Wayne the story of how I'd rescued the Steller's sea lion from the pod of orcas and received as my reward a skiff full of shit.

The newcomer was laughing so hard that he tipped back his chair and nearly fell. He was drinking hard liquor; Ignatius, coffee with several sugars and cream. Granules of spilled sugar glistened on the table in a pattern of arcs and circles around his cup.

"Well, speak of the devil," Ignatius called as he rose and motioned for me to come over and join them.

"And this is the young savior himself?" Wayne Chase said. Red hair topped his head like a wind-blown flame. His face was as open and wide as the Saskatchewan prairie where he'd been raised. He wore a flannel shirt and a nylon outdoorsman's vest so new your eyes looked to see if it still bore its price tags. He extended a broad, pillow-soft hand.

"Wayne Chester Chase."

I nodded and countered with my three names.

Chase had the smile of the politician who'd just kissed the baby, the sideshow barker who knew how to fill every seat in the tent. By his manner and the large garnet ring on his finger I could tell that he and serious money were no strangers, that he was here in town to spend some of it and in the process receive in return even more.

"Have a seat, take a load off," Chase said, still pumping my arm. "You must tell me all about it. Every detail, so I can share the story with my backers."

I stared at him as if he were speaking a foreign language.

"That was some mighty skillful nautical maneuvering," Ignatius said, "knowing when and how to turn the boat so that the poor seal could escape into your bow."

"Sure," I said, nodding to Ignatius as I grabbed a nearby chair.

"You must be awfully familiar with the water around here," Chase said. "Now me, the only water I know is the kind I splash in my Scotch." He laughed and raised his glass. "I wouldn't know the local waters if you threw me into them. And now that's where the two of you come in. As I was just sitting here explaining to Mr. George, while I may be an outsider and new to these parts, that doesn't make me blind to its potential! No sir. Not me. Not at all. If anything, I can see what you have here with fresh eyes."

Ignatius gave out a soft chuckle and took a sip from his mug of coffee.

"It certainly is a pleasure to make your acquaintance, Mr. Sansone"—he'd dropped the third syllable, rhyming my last name with *sandstone*—"and, if you're not in a rush I hope you'll do me the pleasure of allowing me to buy you a drink. I'd like to discuss with you a little idea that just may lead the three of us into a business proposition."

❧ ❧ ❧

Mornings, before the sun burns off the fog. While the first run's customers are still in the office zipping themselves into their deck suits, and the chatter crackling over the shortwave consists of the usual greetings and word of who did what and with whom last night, you wipe down the seats on the Zodiac and then start up the engine and tap each of the gauges, as you always do, not only to double-check that they're working but also out of habit and for luck. And when the office manager radios that they're bringing down your crew your eyes catch on the sullen silver figure pinned to the wooden crucifix on the rosary that you've attached with twine to the side of your console, and for a moment you pray.

*Bless the forests and all that live on the land. Bless the water and all that live in the sea. Bless us, we who live on both and venture between.*

You touch two fingers to your lips and then touch the crucifix, then turn and count your crew, who swagger down the dock in their bulky orange deck suits like astronauts on their way to the flight pad, with the office manager leading them, like a shepherd with his flock. He introduces you by your first name. You smile and say hello and welcome and how are you this morning to everyone as you again count heads and look into each set of eyes to see if any are wary or afraid and therefore liable to become seasick or otherwise not enjoy the trip, and if you see someone who is wary or afraid you smile and reassure them, tell them to sit near the console and let you know how they're feeling during the run. No one's died on your watch, at least not yet, you joke as the manager unties the Zodiac from the dock and you adjust the volume on the radio and check your watch and smile again at your crew and tap the gauges and crucifix and touch two fingers to your lips and then you're off.

The day's first run is always the sweetest. Because each morning you don't know where the whales are, because you know only where some of them were last evening at the end of the sunset cruise, and the whales might have done any of over a score of things in the interim. The very worst is when they move offshore to feed, likely on a larvae bloom of shrimp, or at least that's the going theory of why they sometimes, inexplicably, move offshore. Fact is, no one really knows what they do offshore. If you knew, you'd be better able to predict their whereabouts, anticipate their next move, but you don't know, a truth that takes you seasons of work to realize and admit. Imagine how little a creature from the ocean would know about man based solely on what a handful of humans do in or on or near the water's surface. This lack of certainty sometimes depresses you since it's yet one more thing you can't control, and, God knows, if you've struggled with one thing during your life it's your craving for control. At the same time, as you grow older and more mellow and as the seasons pass, this very lack of certainty comes to thrill you. You come to understand it's a part of the process, this business of chasing down whales.

So this morning you forego the usual, showing your crew the nesting eagles on Deadman's Island—you'll do it on your return— and instead play a hunch, speed through the passage on the way to Ahous Bay on Vargas. There's only a light wind from the southeast, and on the sea slightly rolling swells, very little chop. Lone Cone on Meares towers to the right above you. You're hoping that today, as the fog lifts, the whales will be feeding off Vargas. Your eyes check the gauges, you listen to the sound of the engine and the chatter on the radio, and then, as has become your habit, you begin scanning the shoreline for blows.

You look down at your crew to see how they're faring, if anyone is showing signs of getting sick. They're sitting happily, all twelve of them: a pair on the starboard side snapping photographs, a father near the bow pointing out something to his daughter, a couple right in front of you laughing as they retighten the velcro straps on the wrists and ankles of their deck suits. You're the first boat out of Tofino's harbor, as you hoped you would be. You point out an eagle flying over the treeline just ahead. The majestic bird hangs in the air. On the radio someone is talking about what happened late last night at the Maquinna.

It took months for the whales to grow used to your boat, or used to you, as Ignatius suggested. At first it didn't make sense to you that whales could tell the difference between one boat and the next. After all, a boat is a boat, isn't it? It doesn't become something different overnight when it's in dock. It displaces the same amount of water each time it slices through the surface of the sea. An engine is always the same engine. Though as soon as the argument was out of your mouth you realized you were wrong. Ignatius just looked at you, as he often did, and smiled. Hearing is their most highly developed sense, he said. They can hear even passing helicopters and float planes. And they don't just *hear* sound, Ignatius told you, they *feel* sound, and they do so with the entirety of their immense, sensitive bodies. They can tell not only the difference between one boat and the next but who's behind the wheel, and even what mood the pilot is in that day. Whether you realize it or not, he said, every guide out on the water develops his or her own way of doing certain things, and these methods become the guide's signature. When you shook your head in disbelief he said you can tell the difference between my voice and someone else's, can't you? By my inflection and tone you can tell how I'm feeling each day and my mood? At the very least it's the same with the whales and how we run our engines.

They can go down for five or six minutes, Ignatius taught you, even a full twenty-five or thirty. They can get away from your boat if they want, if you're bothering or spooking them or for whatever reason they don't want you to be near. As if they overheard his words, the whales avoid you each time you draw your boat near them. And once, when out of frustration and the foolish desire to exert your puny human will you actually try to chase after them, they chuff and disappear completely from sight, leaving only their calm oval footprint on the surface of the water ahead of you.

After six weeks of the whales eluding you, you nearly decide to give up, thinking there's something inherently wrong with you, some essential flaw in your soul or your technique, something about you that exudes a sort of powerful whale repellent. Patience, Ignatius cautions. It took a good month for them to get used to me. You know for certain that he's lying. The older guides say that when Ignatius was a boy growing up on Flores he sometimes swam with the whales. Oh, they tell you, sometimes as a boy he'd be out in one of the bays playing with them and he'd get hungry and a gray would nudge aside her calf and nurse him. You know that the whales come right up alongside his boat, *The Ahousaht Spirit*, the big family boat that seats as many as thirty, and the creatures sometimes even gently nudge its side. You know the technical explanation is that the contact helps them to scrape off some of the irritating barnacles and other clinging sea life that plagues them, but there's no denying the fact that they do this only when Ignatius is at the wheel. He has the golden touch. The right vibe. He's drunk whale milk. Even on the worst of days he's a bona fide whale magnet. Tourists swear the whales stop feeding and swim out of their way to seek him out. They wave hello to him with their flippers. You know he has secrets. You hope that someday he'll tell you more of them.

For now you'll settle for being merely good, simply able, competent. You're learning the waters and what there is to do, and you're beginning to understand how, out here, there's precious little you can control. That's the biggest lesson. You're in control only of yourself. After the seventh week or so you resign yourself to it. You can't control what will occur in the next moment. All you can do is tend to this moment, do what you know, do the best you can, in the moment that is immediately before you. So you continually scan the shoreline. You look for spouts. You know where all the kelp beds are. Your eyes go over every inch. One day you stop trying so hard, and you hope that will make the whole venture of chasing down the whales a bit easier.

Getting close to the whales is a matter of common sense, you remind yourself, of knowing your limits and your boat's capabilities. Never motor in at high speed on a whale or a queue of boats. If you see a line of boats two hundred feet away, motor in a hundred and fifty feet and then idle in the remaining fifty. Now you can come onto a scene involving other boats and a breaching whale, and you know what to do. The first boat on the scene has the right to give the whales the ocean side. Subsequent boats get in line so that the first boat doesn't have to compromise its position. You know never to box a whale in between your boat and the shore. You learn how to give the whale ample room, to anticipate its dives and surfacings. You learn to hold your position by pointing your bow into the wind and running the engine at low speed. Sometimes you use one of Ignatius's favorite techniques and hold your place by stopping the boat altogether in a thick bed of kelp.

Then one day, for no apparent reason you can think of, the whales either accept you or decide to resign themselves to your presence. The resident male everyone calls Scarface, due to a crosshatch of scrapes near his blowholes and a pair of ugly scars, likely from a boat's propellers, running parallel from his head down nearly down to his keel, breaches near your Zodiac one bright afternoon, much to the delight and pleasure of your crew. It's nearly as if he came up out of the water and smiled and shook your hand and offered you membership in the club.

Soon Notch and Double Notch, whose flukes bear bite marks from killer whales, swim easily alongside your boat, as well as Barnacle Bill, Marilyn, and Casper, whose back is a pale shade of gray and who is often found in Grice Bay feeding on ghost shrimp. Then you grow familiar with everyone's favorite, Darling, a sweet, smallish female known to surface suddenly alongside kayakers, and whose calm disposition seems to invite touch. Resting on the rolling tide in a thick bed of kelp, you leaned across the collar of the Zodiac and reached down and touched Darling once. Beneath your fingers you saw her skin quiver. Her skin felt as smooth as a peeled egg.

But this morning as the sun climbs in the sky you realize again that you're the first and only boat out here, and your eyes work hard to pierce the fog. The fog hangs in gray, gauzy patches over the water, and then the radio crackles with word of a bad break. A float plane coming up from the south has spotted a pair of grays feeding off Combers. Combers Beach is back the way you came, far to the south, where all the other whale boats leaving Tofino harbor this morning will surely now be heading. So much for getting a jump on the others and playing a hunch and guessing north.

You're nearing Ahous Bay now. You cut the engine, your eyes sweeping the shoreline. You lift the radio handset and inform your office manager that you've reached Ahous Bay. He laughs and tells you what you already know, that today you gambled and guessed wrong, that it sure looks like today's big action is south, off Combers.

At the least you can swing past Blunden and take them to Plover Reefs, you think, and show your crew the tufted puffins there. With luck a few of the big bull sea lions will be hauled out on the rocks. Maybe you'll spot your favorite sea lion, the one you rescued from the orcas. You glance at your wristwatch. There's still time. Then you can speed down to Combers and wait in line, the last boat to arrive, at the end of the pack. But your time with the whales there won't be long, and there will be the distraction of all the other boats, and you'll be bound to run over schedule, which will hardly please Wayne. Your eyes scan the shoreline. Heading down to Combers will burn precious gas and eat precious time, and after all is said and done your first run today will be far less than an ideal trip.

You know that for most of the crew this is the only whale trip they'll ever take in their lives, their one and only chance to be with the whales. You know that it isn't so much seeing a whale that's special or significant since everyone on your boat knows what one looks like from countless images in movies and on TV. No, what's special is being *with and among them* out on the water, being with them intimately and uniquely, in an entirely natural setting, with the wind on your face and the many-layered sounds of the ocean echoing in your ears. It's the recognition that there exist in the world some things that are greater and far more grand and magnificent than man or anything made by man. Profound contact with the natural world is an insight that can touch and alter a human life. And now the twelve who sit before you will have to settle for a less than spectacular run down to Combers.

But then, as if on cue, deep in Ahous Bay you see the first blow.

Its mist, from the gray's dual blowholes, hangs over the water in the shape of a heart. Thirty yards over you spot a second blow. Now your crew has seen the second blow, and everyone in the boat stands and points. Someone lets out a cheer. The couple in the seat in front of you smiles and embraces. The daughter in the bow with her father jumps up and down with delight as she squeezes his hands. The morning fog visibly thins. You're the only boat out here with this pair of whales. And then beside the second blow you spot a third.

Three whales, each surfacing, there before you in the bay.

*Glory.*

# 14

# *Tofino*

# *Mid-1980s—Present*

"WHAT CAN BE DONE ABOUT the past?" I asked Ignatius George.

We were wiping down the seats on the family boat, the Boston Whaler named *The Ahousaht Spirit*. It was the end of a long day, an hour after the sunset cruise. The evening light was dying in the west. We'd just filled the *Spirit* with diesel and were readying it for the following morning's first run. Across the water from where we stood on the *Spirit*, Lone Cone on Meares and Catface receded in the falling light.

"Not too much," Ignatius said. The soft cedar hue of his skin glowed in the light of the big humming fluorescent lights hanging up and over the dock. A dozen or so insects bumped up against the lights, then flew in furious circles beneath them. "Why, what would you like to do with it?"

"Change it," I said.

Ignatius smiled as if I'd just told him some grand joke.

"Kill it," I added. "Obliterate it. Drill a hole in my head and tear any and all memory of it out by its roots. Get it somehow behind me, once and for all. Erase it forever from my mind."

"Oh, you can do that easy. Or at least try to." He pointed toward town, up toward the Maquinna that stands at the top of the hill, its neon lights shining like a lighthouse. "I tried that once for years and years."

We worked for a while in silence. "Years and years, huh?" I said after a while.

"Years and years and then some. You didn't know me then. It was before you came up here. I was a real pro."

Now it was me who was smiling.

"I used to think I was born with a hole inside me." Ignatius laid his hand on his chest. "Part of me, right in here"—he slapped his chest with the flat of his hand—"felt real empty and numb. Then one day I found myself alone in my uncle's house, you know, looking for something to do, something to eat, some trouble to get into, and way down in the bottom of a cupboard hidden inside a cardboard box I found a paper bag, and in it was a pint bottle of whiskey. I was only about nine or ten. I'd seen the men drink whiskey—the women, too—and knew how happy they all got when they drank it. So I unscrewed the cap on the bottle and took a little sip. I liked the taste and so I took another, and then another. After a while the dead part inside of me woke up and danced."

I smiled.

"Nothing I had ever experienced before gave me that feeling. It was like turning on a switch. You know, when you walk into a dark room and you can't see, and so you flip on the light switch. The feeling didn't last forever but whenever I had it, well, there was nothing else in the whole world like it. It was as if I was one with all Creation. I knew I'd do anything to get the feeling again."

"And that was the start," I said.

He nodded. "You know it's a progressive disease. After a while three sips just don't do it." He extended a hand, his thumb and first finger several inches apart. "After a while I'd need three glassfuls. Then, toward the end, three bottles. And if you'd asked me then if I wanted a drink I'd have told you no, what I wanted was a hundred drinks. A thousand. I didn't even trust people who didn't drink. Drink was so good, I suspected that the ones who said they didn't drink were lying. Of course during all of this I knew I had a bit of a problem, but I didn't think too much of it since there was always somebody around me, someone else, who had it worse."

He folded his arms over his chest, then rubbed his chin and shook his head and laughed. "You know the one about the two guys in the psycho ward? They're out in the hospital hallway, see, lying side by side on a pair of gurneys, and the one guy's held down motionless by these four huge straps. One strap lies across his arms and chest, one over his midsection, another over his thighs, the last over his lower legs. On the other gurney is a guy who's held down by only three straps. The three-strap guy looks over at the first guy and says, 'Man, are you fucked up!'"

We laughed.

"The guy with the three straps," Ignatius said, "that was me all right. Always noticing somebody else who had it a bit worse."

We worked for a while without talking. "So what changed?"

"Oh, nothing really. Everything. I just reached a point. . . ." His voice slowed and hung for a moment on the breeze. Now the sounds of the others working on or near the water came to us—the conversations of other men on the nearby docks, the clank of metal on metal, laughter, the slow and even rumble of a boat's engine. "One afternoon I came to on some stranger's sofa. Nobody I knew or could remember. It was the middle of the day, with the sunlight pouring in from the windows. The light was so bright and blinding it was like a high, steady scream. This little fellow with a dirty face and chubby cheeks wearing a T-shirt and no pants stood on the floor next to me, studying me, his face so close to mine that I could smell his sour breath. The kid couldn't have been more than four or five. He looks at me, and then after a while he gets up on the sofa and on top of me, you know, at first with his legs on either side of me, straddling my chest like I'm his horsey and he's playing some kind of game. And then he stands and lets loose on me this great, tremendous stream of pee. All over my chest, my shirt, down the hollow of my neck, some of it even splashing on my face. Then I realized that the light I could hear screaming was actually a baby in the other room, and both of these kids hadn't been fed in over a day, and I was the only adult around."

"So you got them food," I said.

"Sure," he said, "right after I took off my shirt and washed the pee off my chest and face and neck and then found a big bottle of aspirin."

The incoming tide rocked the boat gently, the waves against the dock's pilings making a series of gentle slaps.

"You have to let the past go, Vince," he said. "First, because there's no going back and changing it. And second, because for all we know everything that happens may actually be in our best interests. Even the worst things, the very things we most fear. Who are we to judge? There are plans we can't ever understand. Look at how many of my people are still troubled by the changes that have taken place over the last five hundred years, by all that's been taken away from us. I'm not saying that you accept it or that it's right—I certainly don't think any of it was right—but I understand that after the sand's run down through the glass you can't make it go back up again. All you can do is take control of yourself. So one day you stand up and face yourself, and you face all your anger and resentment and fear. You find ways to get rid of it and fill in those holes before the anger and despair kill you."

"You make me think of my father," I said, remembering his angry conversation with Nonna about their lost boat in Monterey on the day my grandfather died.

"Your father, my father, sure, all of them. What we're talking about probably holds true for all of the fathers in the world. Mothers, too." He paused for several moments. "In order for me to live, I need to think that everything that has happened to my ancestors and me was the best thing for us, and that where I am at any given moment is the best and right place for me. Now my main job is to choose, out of all the things possible, to do the next right thing. Each morning I have to say to the world, 'For all the things that have occurred in the past, thank you. To all the things that are yet to occur in my life, welcome.'"

I nodded.

"You know," Ignatius continued, "that day in the stranger's house with the two hungry babies there was a half-full bottle of whiskey standing on the counter in the kitchen not too far from the bottle of aspirin. It was even my favorite brand. But by the grace of God my hand reached for the aspirin. That's really all you can do in this life, I think. Pray that the grace of God directs your hand to choose the next right thing."

"You make it sound so easy."

He laughed. "Believe me, the only easy part is the saying it."

We worked on the Whaler for a while, and then I said, "So I'm supposed to think that all that has happened to me was the best thing?"

"I'm not telling you what you're supposed to think, Vince. You're free to hold any opinions you want and to do whatever you choose, whatever you please. All I'm telling you is what seems to have worked so far for me."

॰॰ ॰॰ ॰॰

Each dawn during the first half of the lunar cycle, from the new moon to the full moon, Ignatius bathes at the water's edge, scrubbing and then lightly beating his flesh with freshly cut strips of hemlock, about a foot long or so in length. He stands in the breaking waves and washes his entire body, beginning with his hands and arms, then moving to his chest and back and head, purifying himself in the traditional way of the Nuu-chah-nulth. He tells me the ritual is a form of meditation and he was taught it by his grandfather, who in his time was one of the men in the band permitted to hunt whales. His grandfather claimed whales could distinguish the men who scrubbed themselves with hemlock from those who did not.

There are words that Ignatius recites when he bathes, but he's never told me them and I've never asked to hear them. My guess is that his prayer is similar to the one I recite three or so times each day, each time I take a new crew out to sea. He says that he couples the beginning of his bathing cycle with a four-day fast, during which he takes mainly water and only occasionally tea or bouillon. He says that the bathing, particularly when he's fasting, is an expansion of himself, and that when he's out on the water searching for whales he needn't depend solely on his eyes to scan the surface for their blows, that an inner sense or vision knows where they are, if they're out to sea or closer inland feeding off the bottom mud, foraging for amphipods and other goodies as they filter enormous amounts of sand and mud through their baleens.

We talked about the tribe down on the Olympic Peninsula that hunted and killed a gray whale, claiming it was their cultural, ancestral right. Ignatius said he was certainly willing to grant them that right, but since they argued that whale hunting is in their tradition they probably should have carried out their hunt completely in the traditional way, by hand, with traditional tools rather than with modern steel harpoons and elephant guns.

Even the tribe's elders spoke out against the hunt, Ignatius said, and pointed out that at the same time the tribe hunted whales they'd also owned slaves. Following the younger ones' logic, did the tribe have a cultural, ancestral right to own slaves now, too?

If life teaches us anything, Ignatius says, it's a lesson of transition and change. He fingers the small cedar carving—a native mask—he wears around his neck on a leather string. Some beings undergo the process slowly, some much more quickly, but over time everything changes and is constantly in transition—everything is alive, dancing—even the greatest of mountains, rising and falling in time like waves in the sea.

∽ ∽ ∽

Clarence put the commune up for sale several years after I stopped working for him, and it was bought a season later by a syndicate representing a Hollywood director. Bulldozers drove in and knocked down everything but the great house, and then the land was cleared so that the house had a full, unblocked view of the ocean. Over the next several months the place was renovated and expanded into a California-style mansion. There was a spread about it in some swank magazine. Over the years tough little Tofino turned from a picturesque fishing and logging town accessible only by a gravel road or water or air into one of North America's top tourist destinations. Now it's a vacation spot routinely featured in *Condé Nast*.

Well over a million tourists come here each year. Filmmakers shooting in Victoria and Vancouver regularly fly their stars and starlets to Tofino for weekend stays in the posh hotels that now command the oceanfront. We try not to stare when we see the stars in town, as they slum with us at local eateries wolfing down polenta fries and fish tacos. Their float planes straddle the downtown harbor like elegant dragonflies. Now, nearly everywhere you look along the oceanfront, a new mansion or hotel or golf course is going up.

The changes have driven up the price of real estate so high that many of the older locals no longer can afford to live here. Taxes are so high that some locals were forced to sell their homes and move down-island or back to the mainland. Others found that the only way they can afford to stay in Tofino is to rent out their homes during the summer tourist season, while they live in an efficiency in Port Alberni or Nanaimo. As for me, I'm still here, like a barnacle, still holding on.

I've become friends with Jeremy Baxter, the boyfriend Harmony dumped as she began things with me, after he joined Big Ed's men's group. Through Jeremy I've learned that Clarence now lives outside Brackendale up on the mainland. Apparently he was able to successfully convert his business into hydroponics and is worth millions, particularly since marijuana use in B.C. is now virtually legal. Harmony either became a lawyer or married a lawyer—Jeremy wasn't quite sure—and lives in North Vancouver near Lonsdale Quay. She now goes by her birth name, Eleanor. As for Emily Fournier, her career in global finance has taken her to Hong Kong. And Roxanne Parker, I imagine, is somewhere back in the States working with wounded children.

Hippies still flock here each spring and summer, and now surfing is all the rage, with wetsuit shops on nearly every corner and a variety of new businesses eager to give lessons. Some kids still come to my back door, surfboards in hand, looking for a place to crash. I welcome them all and, whenever I'm at home, prepare something hearty and warm in a pot on the stove for them to eat. I offer them all a smile and a helping hand, a hot meal and my fellowship, a safe, dry place for them to rest their weary heads.

〜 〜 〜

My search for balance and change involves attendance at the men's support group held each Thursday evening in the back room of Queen of All Saints. The four or five or six of us sit with our group leader, Big Ed, and occasionally with his friend Lillian, in overstuffed chairs around a cigarette-scarred coffee table. We sip decaf and share the stories of our lives, doing our best to speak truthfully. We toss small square blue and red cards at whoever is talking, to let them know how we're hearing them. Big Ed begins each session by asking who among us would like some time. Whoever wants or needs time to sort something out talks first. The others listen, and after a while they respond. Both Big Ed and Lillian interrupt now and then to ask questions or reflect back to the speaker and the group what they hear.

And now Lillian has proposed to us that her Tuesday night group, which is made up of four or five or sometimes six women, merge with our group, or that our group merge with theirs. There's no reason for the genders to remain separate, she tells us. We men have been out in the woods painting our faces and beating our *Iron John* drums long enough. Men can learn from women, Lillian says, and women can learn from men. The sexes have important things to say to each other. Apparently she and Big Ed have been discussing the idea for a while, and Big Ed has been sitting in on the Tuesday night women's group. So that neither group thinks that it's taking over the other, Lillian and Big Ed propose that the new co-ed group split the difference and meet on Wednesdays, same time, same place.

So now, each Wednesday night, in the back room of Queen of All Saints, the eight or nine or ten of us—men and women both—gather around the scarred coffee table. I get there early so I can put on a fresh pot of coffee and straighten the chairs and clean up. We talk about our lives and share our past stories, bit by bit, memory by memory, over and over, again and again, beneath a rain of blue and occasional red cards, until the words on the tapes spinning inside our heads reflect a more truthful understanding of ourselves, as we straighten and sort out our narratives and begin to understand and adapt, and grow and change.

It gets so that it doesn't matter who's talking that night. You're nearly always able to work on your own issues and put them into perspective after listening to others go over theirs.

☙ ☙ ☙

What brought me to Big Ed's group in the first place was my meeting a young, pretty woman named Laurie.

Her last name ended in a vowel, something melodic, multisyllabic, Italian, and when she showed up on my back porch in the late '80s she proudly let me know that she was from my neck of the woods, the great American Midwest, one of the north suburbs of Chicago, to be exact. Laurie was among the many that summer who'd hitchhiked to Tofino after catching the ferry at Horseshoe Bay. She wanted time at Long Beach, a hike in the mighty rainforest, a breath of the fresh, wild air, and like all the others who arrive in Tofino with little or no money she arrived with the hope of finding a free place to crash.

This was fourteen, maybe fifteen years after Roxanne and Josh laid their sleeping bags alongside my woodpile, rearranging its tarp so that it shielded them from the night's cold and wet. Seven or eight years since I began work with Ignatius at Chase Whaling Station. Over twenty years after I'd left Chicago. This was before I remodeled my back porch to include a shower and bathroom and pine bookcases for a lending library of paperbacks, before I asked my campers to think about doing an hour or so of community service for each night they stayed. This was when I was still open at night to knocks on the back door from kids hoping to use my shower and bathroom, which I never refused anyone, though until I met Laurie I'd never discouraged any female from lingering afterward and talking with me, letting the evening lead to whatever ease or comfort they preferred, which on occasion was an hour or two or sometimes a night or a couple of nights on the clean sheets of my bed.

Laurie was absolutely lovely, a slight girl with dark reddish hair and big brown eyes, the color of milk chocolate as it just begins to melt, and lashes so surprisingly thick and lush her eyes seemed lined with kohl, though I could see immediately as she stepped out from the bathroom after her shower that she was wearing no makeup. She'd wrapped herself in a white towel that showed off her soft tan and told me how it was a real shame that now that she was clean—truly clean, she said with a grateful smile, for the first time in weeks—she'd have to put on dirty clothes, and did I have maybe a washer and dryer, and if so could she bother me even more than she already had to use them? She'd brought along her dirty clothes in a knapsack, which rested just inside the back door.

I liked that she had the honesty simply to ask. "No problem," I said, pointing to the area just off the kitchen that served as a laundry room. We walked back through the kitchen to retrieve her knapsack.

"I'm dripping all over your floor," she said, laughing as she held the towel up over the tops of her breasts.

I smiled. "Well, that's why God invented mops."

Atop the dryer was a wicker basket inside of which were my clean folded clothes: a couple of my T-shirts and a few pairs of boxer shorts. "Do you mind?" she said, reaching for a T-shirt and a pair of shorts.

She let the wet towel fall to the floor. Then she turned toward me and nonchalantly slipped the T-shirt down over her head.

Her body was even more lovely than I'd imagined. She rifled through the basket. "Oh, wow, I really like these," she said as she selected my midnight-blue boxers covered with spouting cartoon whales. They were the shorts Roxanne had given me. Laurie held them up at eye level, admiring the white, grinning whales before stepping into them and pulling them up beneath the T-shirt.

"They came with the job," I said. "Standard issue. Every time I go out on a run I'm supposed to wear them."

She laughed again. "You know, for a moment there I almost believed you."

I smiled.

"Aye, aye, captain," she said, going along with the joke. "'Thar she blows.'"

Her knapsack held barely enough clothing for one load, but nonetheless I separated the whites from the colors while she played with the Frisbee—its bright orange color now faded to a soft yellow—that was a gift from Roxanne to Josh and which rested against the wall on the laundry room shelf. She noticed the team photo of the Cubs on the wall and said she'd never been to Wrigley Field but had always wanted to go. As I started the first load she asked if she'd disturbed me when she came over, and I told her no, I was just sitting around reading. She asked me what, and I told her a book of Allen Ginsberg's poems. She'd read Ginsberg and found him dense, too full of references to things she didn't understand. She asked if I'd read Kerouac's *On the Road*.

"Yes," I said, "though to tell you the truth I'm not really partial to novels."

She asked why, and I told her that in novels things always have to come to an end. The author is forced to funnel things down an ever-narrowing hallway, dropping characters from the plot and reducing or resolving complications with each passing page, whereas in life, even when you wish it weren't the case, past characters and events simply go on reappearing and resonating. They stalk you and haunt you like ghosts. They appear out on the water, like something out of Shakespeare, rising and swelling and splashing angrily, or they walk beside you on the sidewalk in the rain, reaching inside your sou'wester and squeezing your heart so firmly you have to stop where you're standing, barely able to breathe. They make you go over in your mind everything that happened, and you think of all the things you might have done, or not done, all the words you should have said or never should have given voice to.

I didn't think she understood my point. "But that's what I like most about novels," she told me, "that you can get into them and that things you worried about in the beginning develop and change. Novels offer the promise of change. And that's what I like about people." She touched my arm. "That you can get to know them, and at first they're simple and then they're more complicated, and then you can come to want to know them even more."

We stepped out of the laundry room and sat at the kitchen table.

"A couple of years ago," she said, "back when I was in high school, I wrote a lot of poetry that I guess no one but me would ever understand, though I always imagined that somewhere out in the world there was some secret reader who'd understand every one of my images and references and know exactly what I was writing about, even though I did my best to be poetic and disguise things."

"So you think it's poetic to disguise things?"

She laughed. "Sure."

"Why not just try to say things straight?"

"Because life is so boring when things are obvious." All the while she talked her bright eyes never left mine. "And because I didn't really want anyone to understand what I was saying. But at the same time I did want to be understood, but only by a special person, someone smart enough. Know what I mean? Like they'd have to be smart enough to deserve to get to know me? Do you ever feel that way?"

I nodded and walked into the next room and slid Dexter Gordon's *Go!* onto the turntable, then returned to the kitchen and opened a couple of beers. Because she liked *On the Road* I wanted to tell her that Dexter Gordon had taken the title of his album from the title of a novel by John Clellon Holmes, the very first novel written about Kerouac and the Beats, and a book I greatly admired. But as the connection formed in my mind it sounded too old and teacherly, and so I didn't offer it. Instead I took out from the refrigerator a wedge of cheese, and I got some crackers from a box in the pantry. I put them on two plates along with a knife as Gordon's elegant tenor sax eased into the first cut's opening bars and the washer in the side room worked on the Chicago girl's first load of clothes.

"Do you have any Nine Inch Nails?" she said as I set the food on the table. "Maybe some Nirvana? Lou Reed? The Ramones? 10,000 Maniacs?" I shook my head no at each name, and she began to laugh. It became a game, an opportunity for her to more fully explore the precise depths of how musically out of touch I was. Meat Puppets. Bad Religion. The Sex Pistols. Pagan Babies. Nick Cave and Bad Seed. Minor Threat. No Empathy.

I laughed and laughed, shaking my head no, no, no.

"Not even any Talking Heads?" she asked as she began to eat. "Maybe *Remain in Light* or *Stop Making Sense*? I mean, I really, really, really like *Remain in Light*. I know it's centuries old but 'Once In a Lifetime' is still like one of my favorite songs. Ever since I've been up here I can't get it out of my head."

"No," I said again.

"So all you have is all of this old jazz?"

I thought of all the hours I spent in the record store up on Clark Street thumbing through albums, listening to the cool strains of jazz while waiting for just the right moment to go next door to the pet store to see Lucy. I remembered the sweet excitement of anticipation, the sudden rush of delight of watching Lucy turn from behind the grooming room's glass window and recognize me. I smiled and said, "Yeah, all I have is all of this old jazz."

"I'm so hungry," the Chicago girl said.

"Then you came to the right place. Here, help yourself."

She looked truly fetching in my Chase Whaling Station T-shirt, her short hair growing lighter and less red in color as it dried. She sat at the table with her legs folded beneath her, breasts jutting through the thin fabric of the T-shirt. As she ate she told me about her big Italian-American family. She, too, had been educated by nuns fond of telling frightening cautionary tales about foolish boys and girls, nuns all too eager to correct wayward students with ear pulls, slaps, and yardsticks that whistled through the classroom air. As we moved to our second beers I could imagine how the rest of our evening together would progress. As if in response to my thoughts she smiled and gave my hand a sudden squeeze. Then she told me something that stopped me cold.

While both sides of her family were southern Italian, she wasn't sure that she actually was. After I laughed and asked her what she meant by that she told me that as a baby she'd been adopted.

"I mean," the young girl said, "to look at my eyes and nose and darker features you'd think I was Italian, wouldn't you? But then what do I do with this red hair, with all these freckles? No one else in my family has this many freckles." She stretched her suntanned arms toward me and pointed to her freckles.

"I'm a big mystery," she said and laughed, and with that she tilted back her beer bottle and drained it, then plunked it on the table beside her first and leaned toward me. I couldn't move as she put one hand behind my neck.

"And you're a sweet guy," she said, her fingertips caressing my neck, as she moved her chair closer to me and tried to kiss me.

Of course the possibilities weren't lost on me. And of course I knew that the chances of her actually being my and Lucy's daughter were astronomically thin. And later that night, when I sat at the kitchen table with paper and pencil and the driver's license I'd slipped from her purse and did the math, I saw she'd been born in the wrong year. But at that moment, as her fingertips pressed the back of my neck and the full lips of her mouth drew closer to mine, I was struck by the reality that indeed Laurie was *somebody's* daughter, and that my own daughter who was just about the same age was somewhere out in the world that night as well, physically occupying a body, possibly one with her mother's red hair and freckles and my darker features and Sicilian nose, and the young girl was possibly happy, sad, alone, in trouble, possibly just now meeting a guy like me.

"Thank you," I said, turning my cheek to her kiss. "No, really, please, don't. I'm old enough to be your father."

She laughed and nuzzled her body against mine. "You are not. And even if you were it doesn't matter. To tell you the truth"—she poked my chest playfully with a fingertip—"I kind of like older guys. They're much more mature than boys my age."

"It matters to me," I heard myself say. I pushed her away and stood.

"You don't find me pretty enough?"

"Don't be ridiculous. That's not it at all."

"Hey," she laughed, "you don't have to worry about anything. I'm on the pill."

"You don't understand. Truly. This isn't anything about you."

I busied myself at the stove, putting the burner on beneath a pan and drizzling into it some olive oil. Seized by the desire to feed her, I chopped an onion and smashed a fat clove of garlic. We didn't talk much then. Everything I thought to say seemed false, moralistic, like one of the dumb cautionary stories told by the know-it-all, know-nothing nuns.

I wanted to tell the girl to be more careful, that she didn't know what kind of guy I was, that for all she knew I was the kind of guy who got off hurting girls like her, young girls who trusted friendly strangers, that I could be the kind of man who'd scar her for life.

Indeed, I wanted to tell her that I was the kind of man who'd scarred others for life.

The sound of sizzling onions filled the room along with the whirling of the washer finishing its spin cycle and Billy Higgins on the drums playing the end of "Second Balcony Jump." After the onions softened and grew clear I added the garlic and three or four fillets of anchovy, which I mashed into the olive oil with the back of a fork, along with a can of chopped tomatoes, a pinch of dried basil, a touch of oregano. I put on a pot of salted water to boil for pasta, and when the pasta was nearly done I finished it off by cooking it in the sauce along with a half-ladle or so of its water and then grated over everything some Pecorino Romano cheese. Laurie had flipped *Go!* onto its B side. The long, lovely opening notes of "Where Are You" began as I brought the bowl of pasta and sauce to the table.

Then she sat down and ate, ravenously, redirecting her appetites toward the food.

I had her sleep in my bed while I cleared the table and washed the dishes and glasses and pans and ran the second load of her wash and began folding her freshly dried clothes. At some point while folding a pair of her blue jeans a rush of hot tears seared their way from my eyes. I distracted myself by making a fist of my right hand and was about to punch my left shoulder as hard as I could but then instead of doing so I paused and let the tears fall down my cheeks and with my fingertips stroked the soft, warm fabric of the girl's jeans.

Then I sacked out on the sofa, setting Ginsberg aside and picking up John Berryman's *77 Dream Songs*, reading about weary Henry and the curious Mr. Bones.

The next day, as the morning sun burned off the fog and blued the sky, after I fed my not-quite daughter a big breakfast of fried eggs and buttered toast and jam and tea and orange juice, while she excused herself to use the bathroom, I slipped the pair of cartoon-whale boxer shorts along with the Chase Whaling Station T-shirt and all of the dollars from my wallet into her knapsack.

⚭ ⚭ ⚭

I should mention my dreams.

I'm standing in a room with my father and my grandfather, likely the front room of the upstairs flat, though the windows looking down on Glenwood Avenue stare down on Tofino's First Street Wharf. Out in the gray-blue waters of the Sound somebody calls for my help, drowning. My father paces the room, the anxious boxer moments before the bell marking the beginning of the first round. My grandfather sits in a straight-backed wooden chair as if he's a king on a throne. Both shake their heads at me, visibly disappointed. *Who do you think you are*, they say, *to talk about what goes on inside this family? Who gave you that right? Just who do you think you are to speak?*

Sometimes I try to push past them but I'm unable to move. I try to answer them, but my mouth is clotted shut. Then I'm back inside the fish plant, knife in hand, slitting salmon from vent to gills, ripping their guts out and dropping the offal into the gut grinder. Then a fish turns into my grandfather. I slit him open, and his bloody guts spill out into my hands.

*Thief*, my father says. *Draft dodger. Arsonist.*

Overhead, fighter jets drop a barrage of carpet bombs along with napalm. The bombs shriek like boiling tea kettles as they fall. My father grabs me by the neck and shakes me. Worthless son of a. Bleeding like a stuck pig. I tumble with him in bed until the staircase above us, studded with the flattened tips of nails, begins to fall.

Sometimes everything falls. The white Communion Host from the side of Marie Santangelo's tongue. The tiered wall of aquariums in the pet store up on Clark Street. The row of koalas that keep vigil on Lucy Sheehan's bed. The winter snow outside her bedroom window, that ticked so softly against the pane the first time we made love. With my gold-plated paten I try my best to catch the snow before it hits the ground, but each of the flakes hits the ground just beyond my reach. Indeed I am a tenderfoot, I think, destined to die by myself out in the cold! The blank-eyed woman straddling the world on the calendar tumbles toward me. Bappada bappada bappada. The paten in my hand becomes a knife, one from Mr. Santangelo's marvelous box of knives, the box of knives with names, and again I am gutting my grandfather. I look down and turn the knife in my hand, blade in.

There is a flutter of falling red and blue cards. *Final markets!* I shout, desperately. *Red Streak! Final markets!*

*Well, that's one of the risks of speaking,* Big Ed tells me. *To talk honestly about your parents, about your family, is to betray them.*

And so my hands turn the knife inward, toward myself, my own flesh, and I begin cutting my own body. The letter A, lacking the crossbar. Then a B, a C, a D as I work my way through the alphabet. I need to work my way through the alphabet, I think. Then usually what follows is a tumble of images. A room full of candles, with a tie-dyed sheet stretched across the ceiling, billowing like a sail, and then the room becomes Clarence's skiff as I search the waters of the Sound for whoever it is who is calling me. Someone somewhere is calling me. Lucy? Marie? My lost daughter? I watch for blows, for the dark blur of a fin or upraised hand. But I find only the tattooed woman sitting on the bed of pillows, who asks me if I need to look. *No, I* answer, *I need to show, to confess, to plead for forgiveness,* and as I unbutton my shirt my heart thuds so loudly that my ribs spread open and my chest explodes. Then I thrash awake, holding my bloody heart in my hands, a butcher in a white apron raising a piece of red meat up to a scale to be weighed.

~ ~ ~

Everything happens for a purpose, Ignatius tells me. Every single incident that takes place in our lives is part of a larger, grander design, one we can hardly recognize, let alone begin to comprehend. All of our previous moments have combined their energies to deliver us to this one, the one we hold before us, in our hands, the very moment in which we exist and draw breath. The challenge is to accept it and not fret, to choose the next right thought, the next right word, the next right deed from the infinite number of possibilities lying before us.

So you draw the next breath and tell the next round of hippies crashing in the tents in your back yard that they're free to take any of the paperbacks on the back porch as long as they replace it with another, and, please, none of that gothic horror slasher stuff. You kneel and pray before the outstretched arms of the statue of the Blessed Mother—atop her head a crown of stars—that stands above the tiers of flickering votive candles in Queen of All Saints church, then light another candle for the daughter you'll never meet or come to know. You pray that the Virgin Queen will always keep her safe. You sit around the coffee table in the back room and work on your narrative amidst the flutter of red and blue cards, trying to make your story true and straight. When you're out on the street or on the water and your heart tightens, as if a fist is squeezing it, just like in your dream, you remember to take a deep breath and breathe. You tap the gauges on the Zodiac's console and whisper a prayer. You pray for all creatures, above the water and below, for the travelers who eagerly don orange deck suits and entrust you with their lives as you skim them across the choppy surface of the sea.

You hope to show these travelers something they've never seen, something that will take them out of themselves, even if for only a moment, something greater than anything they've previously experienced. You tell them about *qwa' aak qin teechmis*, the native words for *life in the balance*, how the entire area of Clayoquot Sound has been designated by the United Nations as a biosphere reserve, dedicated to a balanced relationship between people and nature, in full acknowledgment of aboriginal titles and rights.

You show them the eagles' nest on Deadman's Island, idling the boat until they hear the fledglings in the aerie cry out to their parents for food. You take them to Plover Reefs to view the sea lions and tufted puffins. You swing past the noisy bird sanctuary on Cleland Island. Then you watch a pair of grays, Barnacle Bill and Darling, feeding near the kelp beds off Flores, and as you idle in the bay along comes gentle Darling, predictably surfacing closer and then still closer to the boat.

The chatter on the radio lets you know that a seaplane has spotted a migrating humpback, possibly two, so you glance at your watch and tell your crew to take their seats. You then race to the coordinates, heading straight into the swells so that the Zodiac jumps, skittering hard across the surface of the sea. Each time the Zodiac bounces down onto the water it raises a spray that gives everyone a good soaking, gives your crew the fast, hard, breathtaking ride the staff back in the office warned them about. Your crew buzzes with delight. When you arrive, there in the water before you are the two humpbacks, a thirty-five-foot cow and her young calf, a third of the size of its mother, swimming fast through the sea and the air.

You slow and ride the waves with the pair, matching your speed to theirs, running parallel with them as they head out into the deep open ocean, into the deep blue, blue sea stretching out before you and beyond to the point where you imagine it splashes up against the lighter blue sky. The mother whale surfaces with a loud and resonant *huff*, extending a broad pectoral that looks nearly as long as your boat, and then she rolls and playfully slaps the water's surface.

For a moment you slow the Zodiac, and then the arched back of the baby surfaces, imitating the mother's actions almost identically. You watch the mother go into a deep dive as her wide, notched flukes reach up and out and crease the light. Then the calf beside her breaches, rising up from the water and flying through the air miraculously like a bird, and everything around you stops, all sound and motion, and everyone watching grows silent and holds their breath and imagines that the moment will never come to an end, that the graceful arc through the air will continue forever and the baby will never fall.

# ACKNOWLEDGMENTS

Thanks to Dick Hazen, who not only introduced me to the Pacific Northwest but whose generous hospitality enabled me to return there again and again, and Irvin Frank, who befriended me in Tofino and took me out onto the water and patiently taught me about the whales.

Thanks as well to Anita Miller, Jordan Miller, and Cynthia Sherry for their belief in my work, and Joan Sommers, Zhanna Slor, Mary Kravenas, and Courtney Buras for their immeasurable support and assistance. I'm also grateful to the many others who helped and encouraged me: Joy Johannessen, Sulo Hovi, Amos Magliocco, Bob Bledsoe, Fred Gardaphé, Eric Rensberger, and Rowena Lankford. Finally I once again thank Diane Kondrat, my faithful first reader.